The
LOST
CHART

NEIL GUNN

D1344064

RICHARD DREW PUBLISHING
Glasgow

First published 1949 by Faber & Faber Ltd.

This edition first published 1987 by
Richard Drew Publishing Ltd.
6 Clairmont Gardens
Glasgow G3 7LW

Foreword © Dairmid Gunn 1987

British Library Cataloguing in Publication Data

Gunn, Neil M.
  The Lost Chart. — (Scottish collection)
  I. Title   II. Series
  823'.912[F]   PR6031.U64

  ISBN 0 86267 177 9

Printed and bound in Great Britain by
Blantyre Printing and Binding Co. Ltd.

FOREWORD

One of Scotland's most distinguished 20th Century writers Neil Gunn enjoyed a writing career that spanned thirty years, ending in 1956 with the publication of "The Atom of Delight". This book is described by his biographers as fictional autobiography. The epithet fictional does not mean a ploy to mislead; it means reflective philosophy, a description of incidents and moments that have direct relevance to the moulding and enriching of a life. These incidents and moments take on the form of a search for completeness and happiness, a search that appears in one form or another in all Gunn's novels. In such books as "The Lost Glen", "Second Sight" and "The Silver Bough", all published in the Scottish Collection, the search is directly or indirectly carried out by people of different backgrounds and ages. The failed student in "The Lost Glen", the thoughtful and sympathetic Englishman in "Second Sight" and the enthusiastic archaeologist in "The Silver Bough" are all on a form of quest. The locale for all three books is the Highlands of Scotland.

In "The Lost Chart", written in 1949, the quest for enlightenment is there but the environment has changed. The backdrop of the Highlands has given way to that of Scotland's commercial capital, Glasgow. The backdrop itself is not the only change as the atmosphere in which the story dramatically unfolds is pervaded by the effects of a conflict being enacted on an international scale, a conflict better known as the Cold War. In terms of the work of Le Carré and Fleming The Lost Chart can be described as a thriller, but a thriller with a difference.

The Lost Chart moves on two distinct planes — that of espionage and violence and that of what lies behind the conflict provoked by the clash of values and political ambitions that is the Cold War. Shipping Executive Dermot Cameron gets involved in a street brawl, loses a chart of the approaches to a remote Hebridean island of strategic importance and finds himself in the midst of a tussle between the Secret Service and a Communist Fifth Column. For Cameron the hunt for the lost chart is not only to find a sensitive document of military importance but also to seek a mental chart of a way of life that had been lived for hundreds of years in the Hebridean island with which he had become acquainted as a seaman in the War. For him the chart represents a power of vision in a world on the brink of disaster. Disaster is enshrined in such gloomy and frightening statements as, "There are folk who think they can make this earth a paradise — and are prepared to blow it up to prove a point", and, "I have often told you that the means not only conditions the end, but that the fellow using the means becomes like what he is using". Such statements are reminiscent of those made in Dostoywsky's "Possessed" and Conrad's "Under Western Eyes". Even such a slavonic phrase as spiritual nihilist could be applied to Dermot's principal antagonist, Basil. His views, rational, theoretical and destructive, stand out in sheer contrast to the simple life enhancing attitudes of the young islander, Christina, who evokes for Dermot the idea of a lost way of life. That Christina and Dermot's artistic friend Joe should come together and fall in love is not surprising as both possess an innocence in their attitude and approach to life that is refreshingly free from all that the sinister Basil stands for. This innocence comes over clearly when Joe, the artist, describes Christina and her Hebridean island to Dermot. "She comes from a little island in the West. And the only painter out there is God. Basil has it all wrong. There cannot be a regress when you are searching for light. . . . Even when you are searching only for a song. . . ." And Dermot as if taking up the refrain later in the story passes comment on a song. "The song — and the singing — had a whole civilization behind it, an attitude to life and to death over a long time".

The Lost Chart is certainly a thriller with a difference. At the end the reader feels compelled to set off with Dermot on a final adventure in search of what has been identified as the real lost chart.

Dairmid Gunn
Edinburgh 1987

I

"What size was it?" asked a quiet voice in his ear.

Dermot turned his face from the shop window. "Oh, it's you!" he said to the Assessor. His dark features caught an attractive smile and he glanced back again at the display of fishing tackle. "I did not weigh it then, but I know now it was just over three pounds—perhaps three pounds two ounces."

The Assessor, who had a way of standing quite still, smiled slowly, and their eyes met for a moment in a gleam of humour. "When was that?"

"Let me see," said Dermot. "No, I wasn't twelve until the following May. Eleven."

"A sea-trout?"

"In a Highland burn." Dermot's eyes were again wandering over the split-cane rods, the reels and fly-cases. In the dim street light they had had an underwater look, for the shop was closed.

"That leaves you eleven years to go still further back."

"Nostalgia, you think? I doubt if it's as easy as that."

"No?"

Dermot shook his head. "It was simply another age." He turned his back on the window and tied the top button of his overcoat. A long slim cylinder of cardboard slipped from under his arm, but he caught it deftly before it hit the pavement. He stood an easy six feet in his shoes and was thirty-two years of age.

"Been seeing Intelligence—or just an ordinary blue-print."

"It's always an ordinary blueprint."

The Assessor's breath broke in soft snorts in his nostrils. "What about a drink?"

"Well—no. I should really get home to-night."

"In that case, you have plenty of time. And there are one or two points I should like to mention about our business in the morning." The Assessor also was tall, but fair and comfortably stout and fifty. Like a pillar, he began moving away. "Another age?"

"You still think it was nostalgia? It wasn't. I suddenly saw it wasn't. That age is gone."

"You mean you couldn't go and fish and enjoy the sporting life again?"

"With luck I hope to—this coming summer. But——" He shook his head. "No. It's gone. The assurance, that opening out, the feeling of being absolutely where you want to be, beyond thought and care. Lord, it was wonderful!" he concluded in a sudden bright marvelling.

"It may come again."

"No." He shook his head. "However you go back, you must take yourself with you—and your age. Humanity never goes back."

"Doesn't it? It looks to me as if it were going back with a vengeance."

"That's different. There was no vengeance in what I was thinking of. I suddenly saw it. It was—it was a blossoming."

The Assessor turned his head slowly.

Dermot met the look with an equal humour. "All the same, that's what it was."

"All the same," said the Assessor, "your skill may yet come in very handy."

"In the new Dark Age."

6

"It's no laughing matter."

Dermot paused on the bottom step to the Dial Club. "You think not?"

"Well, the small pockets of humanity left, wouldn't they have to become hunters again?"

It was a common enough notion, but as though Dermot had now apprehended it for the first time, his eyes glistened in the light from the white globe above the door and he laughed, gripping the slim iron rail with a gloved hand. In the cloakroom he looked around for a hiding-place.

"Put it in the outside pocket of your coat and then fold your coat over—like this."

"No," said Dermot dubiously. "Oh, I'll take it with me."

There was a burst of voices and laughter, and then one voice, Basil's: "Ha! The Marine Assessor and the yachtsman. Let's put it to them."

With a murmured greeting the Assessor moved on to the small counter. "Well, Marguerite, have these fellows been drinking all the whisky?"

"Not quite," answered Marguerite, lifting a bottle.

"If that's all that's left, make them large."

Basil Black was slight and black, with a vivid fleering life in him and a slightly misshapen right shoulder. When sitting near a table, he was inclined to put his chest against it and shoot out his left hand, with fingers thin, long and active as adders.

"I thought all war talk was barred," said the Assessor, stretching his legs comfortably and feeling for his pipe.

"No holds are ever barred in the real thing," declared Basil. "However, this is not war, this is—the assessment of a speculation, which should be fair into your barrow— or boat."

Through the mirth the Assessor asked, "Well?"

7

But Basil had caught Dermot's unobtrusive pushing of the cardboard cylinder against the arm of his chair.

"Charts fascinate me," he said, waiting for Dermot's eyes.

"Who said it was a chart?"

"So it is a chart!" Basil showed he had fished the truth out of a too quick response.

"Even if it were—what of it?" Dermot was casual.

"Sailing orders?"

"You're just the sort of fellow I should tell, shouldn't I?"

"Which raises the point we were discussing," said Sandy Graeme. "Assuming civilization is atom-bombed and you have a chance of taking a few companions with you to a remote glen, who would you take?"

"You are reduced to that?" the Assessor asked.

"Assuming you were reduced to that?" insisted Sandy.

The Assessor looked from face to face thoughtfully. "I would take a cow," he said.

This childish variant of the infernal war talk, which in the last few months had become socially taboo, now opened out unlimited possibilities of mirth, and, from Helen of Troy to Donald Duck, fantasy moved its creatures, for more or less reputable purposes, into a remote glen. The mirth became extravagant as it introduced the Vipers, the very important persons, first of their own city and then of the nation, which inevitably called forth those from other nations and particularly from the enemy countries, until politics reared its old familiar head with the eye that gleamed from infra-red to ultra-blue.

"You're not saying much!" Basil suddenly challenged Dermot, who had in fact not spoken, though he had laughed enough. There was an involuntary silence, as though the noise had been cleft.

"When you said there were only five people in Scotland fit to be kept alive," replied Dermot, "I merely wondered who the other four were."

When the Assessor laughed, his head tilted up on his shaken body.

"I could tell you them, too." Basil leaned forward.

"But you won't—not the real ones," said Dermot.

"No?"

"No," replied Dermot, his smile catching an ironic concentration as he lifted the cigarette to his mouth and slowly blew forth smoke. "Excuse me," he said and politely waved the smoke away from before the piercing black eyes.

Basil's face darkened and he drew slowly back. Suddenly everyone realized that the names, even if Basil had thought of them, did not matter, but that something else mattered; everyone except Joe Duguid, the painter, who said simply, "What no one can tell me——" whereupon, as though he had pulled a switch, laughter rushed into the silence and frothed.

"Well, Joe, what can't they tell you?" asked the Assessor.

"What's going to stop it."

"O God!" groaned a member.

"You see," said Joe in a naivety beyond the realm of any sound, "I just can't see what's going to stop it. There's nothing. And if there's nothing——"

"Then it can't be stopped."

"No," said Joe.

"Christ!" said Basil, and he looked from Joe to Dermot in an inclusive assessment, and laughed, but none of the others laughed.

"So it really is important," concluded Joe.

"What is, Joe?" asked the Assessor.

"The kind of people who will be left here and there to carry on."

9

"So it was you introduced the game? That puts a different complexion on it altogether. I thought it was Basil."

"When it wouldn't have mattered?" said Basil.

"Not much," said the Assessor. "For you are merely a determinist conditioned by your ideology. But Joe is seeking the light."

"Seeking the light!"

"The sunlight, in which things grow. Joe paints it."

"I try to," said Joe, "but it is very difficult. However, what I would like to know is, can any of you tell me what can stop the war happening? I can't think of anything or anyone."

"Nothing can stop it," said Basil abruptly.

Joe nodded in the sudden silence. "That's what I think, too. There's nothing; man has made nothing to stop it."

To Dermot, Joe's forlorn words had in them the sound of a distant cry, and much of the conversation that rose in a wave again was lost on him, for he was with Joe walking through halls that were empty, asking the question which there was no one to answer.

2

As they left the club, Dermot asked, "What's the joke?" for the Assessor had come down the steps with a smile on his face.

"It was Joe. He stopped me. That notion of his is going to worry him."

"Do you think he's as simple as he seems?"

"Yes. Don't you?"

"No."

"I asked him, 'What's really worrying you, Joe?' When he smiles you would think the bones in his face melted. It's a sort of unfinished face. He said, 'I should like to think there would be someone left who would go on trying to get the light.' He meant his painting. That's all that's worrying him."

"It's a fair amount."

"And the painting, of course, would have to be his way of painting. Otherwise—there would be no light."

"What do you think of his painting?"

"I asked that of the Director the other day. They're not crabbing him. They would like to help him on. Which may be a bad sign, or just kind-hearted."

"Perhaps he hasn't it. But he has something."

"Well of course. So you'd better say your words."

"Words! Words to him are real as birds. In us they are noises that skate around." Dermot wanted to say that he had been in empty halls with Joe, that the emptiness and the silence had terrified him for a moment, not in a personal but in an everlasting way, and as he could not say this, he added, "When he gets a notion it becomes as actual to him as a palace."

"Palace," repeated the Assessor in mild wonder. "You don't think he's as simple as he seems?"

But Dermot could not get back into the mood of easy humour which characterized their friendship, making it natural and delightful. Besides, the word "simple" could run the full gamut from idiocy to sainthood. "No," he said. "I think he's all there. We were uncomfortable when he asked what's going to stop it, simply because he was all there when he asked it and we weren't."

"He brought Basil all there—slap up against it! But

11

then, I suspect Basil doesn't want anything to stop it."

"It's an appalling thought—that nothing can stop it." They walked on. "Have you really committed yourself to that thought? I've never cared to ask you direct."

"It's in the air; it's everywhere. Do you notice that people laugh now. It's often a queer sound."

"I don't want to say that nothing can stop it either. But—what is there? Where?" asked Dermot.

"Your mind goes hurrying all over the earth looking for the thing, and it's not there. Then your mind comes back to yourself and sits down—and waits."

"If nothing on earth can stop it——"

They now walked for some way in silence. "You wondered, perhaps, if anything outside the earth could stop it?" said the Assessor. "To cover all the possibilities is no more than logical."

"Wasn't there a classical scientist who said that given a long enough lever he would jack-up the earth?"

"But he didn't find it. So his modern brother got the cleverer notion of blowing it up from inside."

"Do words ever make you sick?"

"Basil has affected you. Now *there's* a lad worth the watching. I doubt if he's as forthright as he sometimes seems. However, that's not answering your question about God." They came to the corner of the street and stopped.

"I'm not asking it, so save your words to cool your porridge." Dermot smiled again. "All the same, I think Joe is the only one of that bunch I'd like to take along."

"Do you think he would enjoy watching you killing the beautiful birds and the silver trout?"

"He enjoys eating them, anyhow."

The Assessor snorted softly, looked at Dermot as he turned away, and said, "Good night."

Dermot felt more depressed than he had been for a long time; depressed, but also savage. Meanings now were not in the words you spoke, but in the air around them, in things behind. They were used as strategy: the most modern thing in ammunition. In comparison, a hand-grenade was honest—and less destructive. His imagination saw a thrown grenade blow Basil to bits. Dermot blinked and the cardboard cylinder crackled, crushed beneath his arm. As his fingers worked it into the round, he smiled bleakly. These uprushes of the destructive impulse! He saw Basil's face, the piercing eyes. There was a fundamental animosity between them, and he hated animosity, he hated destruction, he loathed it. But it had been growing on him, getting a momentary life in him, as though the air were full of its spores.

The air was! He breathed more fully, with a gleam of the normal good nature. In a straight showdown with a fellow like Basil he would deal with him all right! So the Assessor thought he was worth the watching. Did he mean—fifth column? Surely not! The fellow made no secret of his opinions; like thousands of others, everywhere. Dermot himself had always had a sympathy with what was fundamental in these opinions, economic and political. Who hadn't? That wasn't it. That wasn't it at all.

Dermot was walking automatically. He was now in a quiet street, and suddenly in the quietness his mind fished up an idea: a fifth-columnist could work very effectively on the human mind by so confusing it that it had uprushes of destruction. Spread that—and you spread disintegration and give the enemy a walk-in.

Dermot stopped. As the picture of disintegration swelled, utterly fatal in its detail, Basil smiled through from behind.

These thoughts and visions were dispelled by a real cry, a girl's scream from along the street. Dark bodies were in commotion where the houses curved away in the dim light. Dermot started running. One man had his arms round the girl's waist from behind; the other was trying to tear something from her, swore as her lifted kicking feet got him, backed, and called, "Look out!" as he saw Dermot coming. Dermot checked and swayed so suddenly in front of the ducked head and the bunched shoulders that the man missed with his left and Dermot came bodily upon him with a short-arm jab at the jaw. They were both swung off balance, and as Dermot squared up the girl was slung right across him by the powerful wrench with which the second man had at last torn her handbag from her. She had never stopped screaming, windows were up, voices were shouting, a police whistle blew. In blind wrath Dermot was running after the man with the bag, when he was tripped from behind and pitched solidly. His head hit the stone setts of the carriage-way and, though unaware of pain, he felt dizzy and unwilling to get up, knowing they had got clean away. He should have nailed one of them. A hand was on his collar, jerking him up. This was so infuriating that, as he staggered to his feet, a blood-flush blinded him.

"Come on! Come along!"

He caught at the wrist, dug his nails into it, unable to speak.

"Here—you!"

As the mist cleared, he saw the policeman and planted his feet. "You fool!" he said. "You've let them away!"

"Less of that! Come on!"

"Here, damn you, stop that!" Dermot tore himself free. "Stop it, will you?" And he stood facing the policeman, gulping, the wrath in his voice and fists very different from a bag-snatcher's wrath, the accent intolerant and sheer.

"Who are you?" demanded the policeman, hesitating.

"Is that all you can do?" The scorn was more than

14

oaths. Dermot began tugging his clothes straight and dusting them. Then he remembered the girl and looked back along the street.

"Come along and explain yourself," commanded the policeman, but he kept his hands to himself.

"I'm coming," said Dermot, "and I'll explain more than myself."

But the girl seemed to have vanished from the bend of the street, as though she had run away. However, on actually rounding the bend, he saw her farther along with a tall figure confronting her, a second policeman.

"Two of you," said Dermot, the quiver still in his voice, "and you've let them clean away!"

The policeman said nothing.

"Well?" demanded the sergeant.

"He says he's not one of them," answered the constable.

"You seem to believe him."

"If you touch me again——" said Dermot as the sergeant came very close to him.

"Yes?" said the sergeant.

Dermot was assailed by an overwhelming impulse to hit the sergeant.

"Can't you speak? Who are you?"

Fortunately for Dermot, he looked at the girl, saw her body tremble as she sniffed a sob into her throat. With bent head, she stood forlorn and piteous against the railings.

"My name is Dermot Cameron, in the shipping firm of Burns and Armstrong." He opened his coat, got into a breast pocket, and, after fumbling in a wallet, presented his card.

"Oh," said the sergeant. "And what were you doing here?"

"I was trying to do what neither of you seemed anxious to do—catch them."

The sergeant turned to the constable.

"As I came up," said the constable, "they were making off. This man tripped on the kerb and went by the head on the street. I thought it was our only chance of getting one of them, so I nabbed him."

"I was tripped," said Dermot, "by one of the two who attacked the girl. I was after the fellow with the bag."

"Do you mind, sir, coming along to the station so that we'll get this straight? It's not far."

"Certainly," said Dermot.

"You come along," said the sergeant to the girl.

But she made no move. Her bare wrist wiped her nostrils slowly, pressing into them as she sniffed.

"We want a description of them, all the details we can get to help us find your bag for you. Come on now." The sergeant's tones were sensible and friendly.

"Want to go home."

Coming into the waiting silence, her words had a curious childlike authenticity for Dermot. But they also had something more, from some place or time remote, something more particular than a Highland accent. It could not be from his childhood, because she was obviously not more than twenty-five, yet he was instantly and warmly moved.

The sergeant explained again why he wanted a description of her assailants, of her bag and its contents, in so patient a manner that Dermot was struck by the man's humanity, for he assumed the sergeant could lift the girl without more ado if only for a breach of the peace on a public street.

But she stood still, her head down. "I want to go home. . . . Don't want to be in trouble." Her head lifted, her shoulders began to heave, and she turned her face from them.

Dermot realized she was frightened to go to the police station.

"But there won't be any trouble," said the sergeant. "We're only trying to help you. So come along." His tone was firming.

"Don't worry," said Dermot to her. "I'm going, too. I'll look after you."

She slowly turned her head, then lifted her eyes and glanced at him. Though the light was dim, he could see she was dark and reasonably good-looking, without the city quickness or smartness, a girl from the country, probably a maidservant or children's help. But again there was more than that. He saw her eyes land on a small group who had paused by a near doorway. A voice called from a window above. She started away with the sergeant.

Behind them, the constable said to Dermot, "The light was bad. I mistook you."

"I understand. We'll forget it."

The constable said no more, and Dermot respected his silence, for though obviously new on the job this young countryman was clearly prepared to uphold both his own action and the dignity of the force.

She was of medium build, but walked differently from the ordinary office girl; a rhythm rather than a series of staccato jerks. But however he tried to define, tried to remember, nothing definite would come back to him.

In the police station this bafflement grew, for now he saw her face, the cheek bones, the dark eyes. When she gave her name as Christina MacNeil, he stared at her.

"Your address?"

"17 Lomond Mansions."

"Your profession? . . . What do you do?"

"I'm a servant."

"You don't belong here? . . . Where did you come from?" The station sergeant seemed suddenly interested in her voice; considered her in a friendly, thoughtful way.

She did not answer.

17

"You would rather not tell? Why not?" His eyes grew quizzical; the pen rolled slowly between his fingers. "Let me see. You come from Uist?"

Dermot felt slightly tortured, as if the girl's reluctance were in his own breast, yet he awaited her answer far more urgently than did the police official. He shifted his eyes from her face to the desk, to the walls of the hard sombre room.

Suddenly the recording officer spoke in Gaelic. The girl started, then answered in the same tongue. They spoke quietly and, as it sounded, quickly.

"Cladach, Mallaig? Very good. Now——"

But the station was startled by Dermot, whose right hand went slap across his body and under his left arm. "It's gone! I've lost it!" His wide eyes stared. "I must have dropped it. On the street. I must find it at once. It's very important." He swung round to the door.

"Here, wait a minute!"

"I'll come back. Must get it. Someone may pick it up."

"What was it?"

"It was—it was something in a cardboard cylinder, like a—chart."

"A chart? Of what?"

"It's official. I must get it."

Once outside, Dermot said "Come on!" to the constable who was detailed to go with him, and started running. It must have dropped·from under his arm when he attacked the bag-snatcher, he explained, but when they reached the exact spot they could not find it. Dermot covered the street in increasing arcs, yard by yard; dragged a foot against the kerbs; went over railings and got the constable to shine his electric lamp into every last cranny.

"It's no use," said the constable at last. "We've been over that twice already. It's been picked up."

But Dermot could not believe it, would not give in.

"Was your name on it?"

"Don't think so."

"Lost something?" asked an elderly gentleman in a quiet voice.

Dermot glanced at him. "Yes."

"What was it?" asked his fur-clad portly companion in a peremptory voice.

"Nothing much," replied Dermot, turning abruptly away.

When they reached the police station the girl was gone.

"She seemed afraid of her mistress, of being late. Besides, you've been—fifty minutes."

Dermot looked at his watch and showed his astonishment, then he shrugged. "It's been a night!"

"Let's go over it from the beginning."

By the time the police knew exactly who he was, learned of his visit to the club and his departure from it with the Assessor, they were friendly and helpful.

These assaults, not only on defenceless women but on solitary men, were mounting to a pitch they had never achieved even after the last war. It was becoming more than a headache, they assured him. Dermot showed his sympathy by trying to describe the two assailants with the utmost precision. When it came to the chart, he said frankly: "All I can tell you is that it's a sea chart with some markings on it. I cannot be more definite. It's a matter of—security."

That interested them to a questioning silence. But Dermot had definitely finished. "Well, Mr. Cameron, it's a quiet street, a good locality, and therefore a real chance it may be handed in. If it is, we'll get onto you at once. You might leave us your home—and your office— telephone numbers."

3

As he left the police station, his feet took him back to the scene of the assault, and he went all over the ground again. To have messed up the very beginnings of his special assignment; to have been proved incompetent before he actually took on the job!

He was still looking for the chart two streets away as though some runner might have miraculously dropped it. In his sitting-room in the private house where he lodged he wondered desperately whether he should ring up Grear at his home. He was so ashamed of what he would have to report that he decided it was too late, and was relieved to find that in fact it was getting on for one in the morning. He dropped into his chair.

At the words "Cladach, Mallaig" he had seen Cladday and the chart simultaneously in a flashing vision. The girl's name, MacNeil, had already keyed him up. There was no doubt at all about it now: her voice—it could not be her face—must have disturbed the hidden ocean wherein Cladday lay. But now he realized how really deceptive or tortuous the mind could be. First, there had been the interview with Intelligence in the person of Grear, the chart with the island of Cladday as its central point of interest, the circled patrol area with its special markings; then, in the club, all that talk about retreating to some "pocket" in the wilds before or after the cities were blotted out, when he had secretly pictured Cladday as the ideal hide-out and one that might in quite literal fact be his; while all the time Cladday itself, where as a young man of twenty-three he had been blown up, shot into the sea, all but drowned, held its secret—its deep secret—against the face of Basil.

Altogether it was too much for him. Restlessly he looked about the room, wondered if there was anything he could do to-night yet, if he had made the urgency clear enough to the police, wondered about the police. . . .

She was like someone. That remained. She was like someone. All at once the small patrol boat on which he had served during the war was coming into Cladday. . . . Later, the sand dunes in the deep summer twilight . . . the children playing their mysterious game on the knoll, rushing round, laughing, pushing, looking at the sky, watching the sky as for some portent or sign; then the shouts when they found it . . . the girl coming rushing straight for him and his desperate fear lest she find him lying there, spying on them, spying on their island . . . but she swerved to the old cow, whose breathing he could hear as, legs tucked away, she placidly chewed her cud; threw her arms round the old cow's neck and told what they had found, softly, with hurried endearments; and the old cow, whose ear had been tickled, flapped it in her face and went on chewing; and there she was off again, to join the other children who were dancing on the green knoll, and then their voices, receding towards the croft houses . . .

He had seen the girl a few days afterwards, in MacNeil the coastwatcher's house—his granddaughter. She would have been about fourteen or fifteen . . . during the war, the second world war . . . almost ten years ago. She would now be about twenty-five.

He grew very still, staring into the girl's face, then he got up and looked around the room, stood motionless as though hearkening to something at a great distance, took a turn round the room, crushed out his cigarette and sat down.

It could not be the same girl. The maidservant had come from Mallaig. Quite possibly a relation, the nearness in blood and west-coast upbringing producing the resemblance—a common enough experience. Besides, she had shown no personal recognition. On the contrary, she hadn't even looked at him in the police station. And he, a young man in naval uniform, must have been unusual enough on that lonely island to have been at least looked at, scrutinized, pretty closely. Lord, yes, considering all that happened, leading to the tragic death of that remarkable man, her grandfather, the coastwatcher. He had a throe, as if invisibly pierced; then got up, lit a cigarette, and clicked on the electric fire.

Through the blown smoke, from a desire to defeat all else, he deliberately looked again at the children on the knoll. He could not make out what they said, for Gaelic was their tongue, but that did not matter, or mattered just as bird notes did. Sharp cries, laughter, an interweaving gaiety and mirth; lining up again, heads against the evening blue, conning the sky . . . a sly jerk, a push, and they were off once more.

He had wondered if they were expecting a plane, perhaps hoping to see the green and the red lights in the deep dusk, a real fairy ship to them. For a few moments he had even been professionally curious. . . . Then came the outburst of discovery, the high exultant cries, but in that moment there was nothing that he could see, and certainly not a plane, though he had flattened quickly as the oldest of the children, the girl, came rushing at him and swerved like a blown flame. She had told the cow and added whispered endearments that were as clear in meaning to him as though he had understood every word.

An intimacy, a warmth, a necromancy . . . it came over

22

him again as he stood by his chair, bathing him in its liquid light, the deep half-light of a summer night in the Islands, in which everything from the black skerry to the edges of the sand dunes, from the grey face of the sea to the burning gold of the first stars, the breaking of a wave to the faraway barking of a dog or the near calling of a bird along the shore, was translated. . . . A smile invaded Dermot's face, a certain irony, because this experience of the deep twilight was something so personal that it could not be told. And when it went beyond a certain point, beyond the translated beauty, into the grey silence where breath was not drawn, then—it might not be experienced by anyone else, not *like that*.

He made to move about the room, but dropped into his chair instead, and as he did so his voice said casually, under his breath, "It's her all right."

Of course he might be wrong. He took off his shoes, found his slippers, started pulling his tie adrift. When at last he got to bed, he couldn't sleep. Everything everywhere was becoming fantastic, of course. Men were living in an expectancy less urgent than a nightmare, but more fatal. And they couldn't quite get used to it, not altogether. Honest laughter was outside their time, like the children on the knoll. The bird whistled along a shore infinitely remote, and even if you found the place it wouldn't be the same shore. Not now, not in this age . . . and his mind went back to the police station. From above it looked a dark central place now, an inner knot, from which lines radiated through the city, lines that were streets and cross-alleys, like the lines in a spider's web, along which policemen went and returned . . . along which the chart might be "handed in", the lost chart of the seaways to Cladday.

He was late in the morning, had only time to gather his papers at the office and pick up the Assessor on the way to the lawyers. As they walked along the busy street, discussing one or two points in a difficult shipping case, which it was hoped to settle by arbitration out of court, the morning sun came through in a burst of light.

The Assessor lifted his hat, glanced over his shoulder, then looked at Dermot. "Who did you lift your hat to?" he asked.

"What's that?" said Dermot.

The Assessor continued to regard him over his shoulder, for, though Dermot was smiling, a slight colour had come into his face.

"She was either a duchess or your very best girl."

"Did I lift my hat?" Dermot lifted his eyebrows over bright eyes.

"You made me lift mine, anyway. However, I'm not curious."

"It must have been to the sun."

"All right, all right," said the Assessor.

Dermot laughed. There was something solid and quiet about the Assessor, a bollard you could hitch up to, a buoy in the inner waterway. A fattish face, with a smooth moustache, rather small blue eyes, upright, the bowler hat giving a distinction to his normal air of silence, of competence, of patience.

For some time Dermot had been wondering whether he should mention his last night's experience to the Assessor, but was shy of doing so, for he was haunted by a feeling of guilt at not yet having informed Grear. He could not ask the Assessor for advice on what was his plain duty. Perhaps by the time they reached the lawyers his office would have put through a call from the police. And here they were.

"I'll tell you again," he said to the Assessor with a smile as they mounted the stone steps.

They were shown into the senior partner's room, who greeted them in a friendly humour and offered cigarettes.

"The others haven't come yet," he said, "so try and find a vacant chair."

"I left word with your girl that if a phone call comes through I'd like to take it," said Dermot.

"Surely," said the lawyer. "Expecting trouble?"

"Oh, no more than usual."

"Enemy bottoms?" The legal eyes twinkled.

"Not exactly."

"Seen the paper this morning?"

"No."

"Going to do all the sea carrying in their own bottoms now. You'll be out of a job!"

"Oh, that!"

"So you knew about it?"

"They've been jockeying for position there for a long time. It's a real threat, but the inside notion is that they're using it at the moment as a move in another game."

"What game?"

"Well——" Dermot shrugged. "Presumably it's ultimately all the one game. It helps to shake us in our shoes meantime."

"Shiver us in our timbers, you mean," said the lawyer, stopping short of the sharp laugh now so usual. "Probably they simply haven't enough ships."

"Certain, I should say," Dermot replied. "If they had, they wouldn't make their move in this way."

"No?"

"No," answered Dermot. "Now that they've made that move, we'll have to study the whole board over again. At least, those in the top flight will. But we'll have to do our own particular studying, too, over the sea moves. For of course we know they've been building hard."

"But how *do* we get facts—I *mean* facts—about their shipbuilding?"

"Many ways—including a whole vast game of inference.

For example, steel allocations, and here you have got to take into account not only the main economy but also the satellite economies, and in one or two of the satellites we have, I fancy, a pretty accurate notion of what's doing. If a satellite is starved of certain steel——"

"But ultimately would the satellite matter a docken blade?"

"Strategically, yes," answered Dermot.

Eyes lived their own gleaming lives for a moment, then the lawyer laughed. "My God," he said, "one never seems to get anywhere!"

"One always seems to get nearer home," said Dermot in the same amused voice. The Assessor looked at him.

"Nearer home?" repeated the lawyer, and his mouth remained open in a round hole bounded by crinkled grey skin.

His desk telephone rang. He listened, said "Right", and the instrument gave a fairy tinkle as his hand withdrew. "They've arrived; been shown into the board room. There are two points I want to make quickly——"

Dermot was late going out to lunch. No message had come from the police and he had not rung up Intelligence.

"I kept it for you," said the waitress.

"That was good of you. How did you know?"

"Because you always take steak and kidney when it's on."

"If it weren't for your looks, I'd say you were tired. Had a rush to-day?"

"Well, a bit, rather." She was thin and forty, and he suddenly thought that paint and powder gave her a scarecrow appearance. Her scarecrow game of keeping it hot for a husband. He looked at her legs as she walked away and was dumbly moved. It was an awful thing to have legs not doing their natural job. He was comforted by her thought of him. Keep a portion of steak and kidney for a regular. The whole morning had gone very well. Wonderful how a common fear, preferably underground, helped arbitration! But he had spoken well, had felt not the power but the lucidity. His private worries should have rattled him, but they hadn't at all. Quite the contrary. That was remarkable. And his fairness had been so fair that when Budge from the other side started the usual too-high pitching of his claim it had sounded silly. Only for one instant had the lava rumbled—when Budge, feeling the very air against him, had become outrageous; but the air was enough, and Budge stuttered to an end all the more lame because he couldn't find some report in his swollen brief-case. Extraordinary, that unspoken moment of understanding all round the table while Budge searched for what didn't matter.

What he could do was go and see Grear at the same hour as he had seen him yesterday. He could say that he had felt reluctant to use the telephone because—well, for security reasons. It might sound lame. . . .

"Brown study?"

He glanced with surprise at the waitress who had now placed the bill by his cup of coffee. He smiled. "Merely the worries that afflict the just."

"You've said it. . . . Thank you, sir."

"And thank you for the steak and kidney. That was a friendly thought."

"The only kind that does the heart good."

"And now *you've* said it."

She smiled, but reluctantly, as if she didn't quite hold with smiling. But he could see she was pleased. As he left the restaurant, his eyes glimmered in an irony that was helpful. He saw that it was reasonable to wait for a police report before approaching Grear. He would ring up the police station just before going round. A report to date could then be made—to be followed by an appreciation. The proper jargon, anyway.

He bought some cigarettes, dictated three letters, and suddenly asked for the city directory. "No thanks, I'll find it myself." When his intelligent secretary had gone out, he turned up 17 Lomond Mansions without a moment's questioning of his memory. Mrs. H. B. Spicer. The name seemed vaguely familiar. Probably welfare committee. She would be out drinking tea or at a meeting. Anyway, Christina MacNeil would come to the door. He tapped the open page with a thoughtful finger, looked at his watch, told his secretary through the phone when he would be back, and left the office.

But it was Mrs. H. B. Spicer herself who came to the door. "Miss Christina MacNeil? No, she's gone. She packed up. Ha-ha! *Miss* Christina MacNeil has vanished. I don't even know where to! Ha-ha-ha!"

"Really! But I thought—she was——"

"She was—until this morning! But now that charming young woman with her soft manners—ha-ha!—has gone. She left me. Whether the police could stop her leaving or not, I don't know. Who are you?"

"Dermot Cameron. Burns and Armstrong, shipping firm."

"Oh, but I know Mr. Armstrong. Come in. Excuse me keeping you on the doorstep. Not at all. You must. I knew his sister very well. We did time together. It's not even dusted," she said of the room they now entered. "Do sit down. I'm so glad to see someone about her. Do tell me."

The old story flashed back upon him. She and Miss Armstrong had beaten up a policeman with their umbrellas. Fortunately the policeman had not lost an eye, though for a day or two it was touch and go. One of the ladies, he alleged, had poked him in the said eye with an umbrella point, which point, in evidence, was shown to be sheathed in brass. Neither denied that this might well have happened, for on their part they alleged that they were acting purely in self-defence against a wanton and brutal male attack on the liberty of the female subject. Each, indeed, under cross-examination, was inclined with a fine selflessness to claim the distinction of having done the poking. The legal action on both sides had searched out so closely and with such solemn wit matters affecting the freedom of the female subject and the powers of the state that political circles farther south had felt driven to give the movement for woman's suffrage an almost adult attention.

Belligerent sinews still whipped in her neck and lank grey hair showed unruly tendencies, but her nervous laughter and blue eyes held an aged pathos. Her lips, however, pursed as with hands on lap she regarded him with a prim cock of her head.

Dermot said, "I merely wanted to see her. It's—personal, nothing really important." Her husband, Herbert Spicer, had been a naval commander, killed in action in the first world war, he remembered.

"You don't mean she's a friend of yours?"

"Not really. I met her last night as it happened, and—well—I wanted to see her for a moment."

"Last night! Do you mean you were with her? She wouldn't tell me a thing and it was nearly midnight before she came in—nearly midnight—and she looked as though she had been through a mangle. I just felt this couldn't go on. The way girls throw themselves at men nowadays—painted, powdered and utterly inefficient—it's dreadful when I think of how we strove to win some dignity for our sex. Don't you think so? Or do you not?"

"I know what you mean. But—was she like that?"

"You should know. You said you were with her. I am merely asking your opinion. You are an educated man. How on earth—if we are not——"

"I wasn't the mangle," said Dermot.

She goggled at him, then emitted the quick cackle. He could see she had her own real sense of humour; it came bursting through as tears or anger might.

"Weren't you? Then who was?"

"It's rather an involved story. Did she say she had lost anything?"

"Lost anything?"

"Do you know where she's gone?" asked Dermot.

"I do not. This morning she was up early—early for her. But my tea was never coming. No sign of it, and by now it was almost ten minutes *past* eight. I rang. No answer. I threw a wrap round me and went to the door. 'Christina!' I called. No answer. Then suddenly there she was all dressed up, with the tea-tray. All dressed up! I asked her what on earth this meant. In her meek voice she said, 'I'm going.' 'Going? Who told you to go?' 'You did,' she answered. I hadn't told her anything of the sort. I had told her—after waiting up for *two hours*—I had told her when she came in that this was getting beyond my endurance, that if she didn't know how to behave herself like a decent woman, who had contracted to perform certain duties . . . but I hadn't told her to go. I was angry—but surely with cause. For her own sake I did not want to have to deal with—with what might happen to her. . . ." She was now in full sail, having accepted him as she would a public meeting. Apparently a slight inaccuracy in gesture on her part before the bedroom door had sent the tray and its contents to wet ruin on the floor. Thereafter a scuffle, if not exactly a struggle, had ensued over Christina's suit case, all strapped and ready—so deceitfully, but the tug-of-war had ended in Christina's favour and she had—well, she had just gone. She had cleared out. Away. Ha-ha! She didn't know what young women were coming to. She wiped her eyes. And it wasn't as if she hadn't been good to her, nights off, in every way. And done some educating, much needed. "But they're so deceitful, these soft ones from the West, that you wouldn't think butter would melt on their tongues. Deceitful, yes, and sly. And the way she took to bathing herself, yes, and using my bath salts—ha-ha!—and never able to do a thing unless she was first told. No more initiative than in that—that table. I got on to my solicitors. Not that I didn't like her."

It was a performance full of life and vexation, of wrath and public ethics, a disappointment barely this side of tears. For all her tremendous weather, she was, he could see, sadly dismasted. His eye caught a definite strain of the ship in her. With a breeze on her quarter she must have taken some overhauling. She still would.

Out of it all came a picture of a girl moving quietly about the house, remembering to do what she had been told to do, but seeming to have no initiative for a new situation, a new need, always requiring to be told, clean enough, yet careless, inclined at first to push things into corners, out of sight—the old lady laughed heartily over "a missing receptacle" pushed under the bed—but reliable and at times quite unexpectedly thoughtful and kind, especially if one was unwell.

Christina had been with her over three years and Dermot could see that Mrs. Spicer had not only got used to her but was now suffering from a profound sense of shock at having been bereft of a possession which had touched her more deeply, more warmly, than she had been aware. He found this affecting himself, rousing his own interest, and he led the old lady on. When he asked her what she meant by Christina's coming from somewhere *near* Mallaig, she answered that obviously it was a fisherman's home or croft near Mallaig. Christina's father had been lost in a convoy to Russia. A brother had emigrated to Canada and a sister of fifteen was still at home . . .

Concerning Christina's friends in the city, Dermot gathered that she knew "a lot of her own kind", Gaelic-speaking, also from the West. But as this was a known feature of the city's life, Mrs. Spicer had simply accepted it as she had the croft house near Mallaig.

"If you can send her back, I'll take her. The domestic problem is very difficult. So—try. And thank you for calling." Her handshake threw his hand up, with the fine negligence of a vessel rising to another sea; her head dipped, and the door closed.

He looked about the street for evidence of the normal world and saw a man on the opposite pavement who seemed to be waiting for someone or for a taxi. Before leaving Lomond Mansions Dermot glanced over his shoulder and saw the man sauntering along the off pavement. Why on earth should he think the fellow was a detective?

There was no message from the police. Overcoming a strong reluctance, he asked the telephone girl to get him the police station. He had to explain who he was and what he wanted at uncomfortable length, then had to hang on until the negative answer arrived. But when he had fixed up an immediate appointment with Intelligence he felt better. Grear's cool voice over the wire, incurious as to his business, braced him for the worst.

He had a fair face of regular features, a bright clean shaven face, so fresh that it looked newly washed and shining, and fair hair trimmed and neatly parted. He was probably getting on for forty, but looked if anything younger than Dermot. Greenish-blue eyes, intelligent, and with no implications of depths. He was at once sociable and cool; in mind and body as tidy as his desk. When he learned of the loss of the chart, his eyes remained on Dermot's face, not penetratingly, but very clear.

"I thought of ringing you up last night, but it was too late. Besides, I felt sure the police would find out about it to-day, and so I would have a full report. It's been worrying me, I confess."

"It would have been better to have let me know. The time element can be so supremely important that it's as well to make a habit of remembering."

"I understand," Dermot said calmly, but warm in the face. "The only other thing: I had a feeling against talking about it on the phone."

"The answer is," said Grear, as if they were playing a friendly game of chess, "that it was still up to you to make contact. That's the sort of answer they'll make to me. We've got to get it clearly into our minds that from now on it's pretty much like being at action stations."

"Very good," said Dermot.

"By the way, did I mention that the subject of your appointment was well received? In fact if you had had a commission in the last show—however, your knowledge of that particular Approach, not to mention more personal capacities, is such that if you care to see your job in its wider framework that might be useful to you—later."

This suggestion of future promotion, coming on top of a reprimand, made Dermot warmer still. "I can only do my best," he murmured, "but I'll do that—such as it may be."

Grear's clear laugh was like an amplified giggle. "We know that. Now tell me exactly what happened last night. Have a cigarette."

Dermot related how he had met the Assessor and gone to the club, though he had wanted to go home to think out the implications of the markings on the chart. He told how Basil had spotted the chart and the kind of talk there had been, then described the street attack, the police station, the subsequent hunt for the chart, and the final talk with the police, for he was determined now to make clear in how far he might have given away what had been entrusted to him.

"Very interesting," Grear said. "Very. Now I want to be frank with you—which means confidential. Basically, as you know, my job is Intelligence on the naval side. It is a special creation, for the civil population has come into the picture as never before. It means, for one thing, a very sensitive link-up with the police. I am particularly concerned with vetting personnel in these new fifth-column days. In a word, the enemy is potentially everywhere. You get my drift?"

"I think so."

"Let me illustrate. Assuming this loss of the chart— and the manner of its loss, of course, completely exonerates you—assuming this loss were to affect the security of your Approach, through the chart getting into the wrong hands, then we should have to reconsider all we have already discussed and tentatively planned."

Dermot nodded.

"About this fellow Basil." Grear blew a fine stream of smoke. "Do you think there's anything to him?"

"I have thought of that. Frankly, I doubt it. I think he is one of many of the same kind."

Grear looked at his face and remained silent.

"Yet——" muttered Dermot.

"Yes?"

"It was something the Assessor said. He said he might be worth the watching. But—I doubt it."

"Talking of one's friends makes one feel like a totalitarian. I know."

"Mere fighting is easy," said Dermot, the smile clouding his face.

"That's about it," Grear agreed. "However, I am glad to have your opinion. You think he's *mostly* mouth?"

"Yes." Dermot crushed out his cigarette. "Perhaps that sort of mouth may have a disintegrating effect. I don't know. It may have the opposite. But I don't think it's deliberate."

"No? All right. Now about this girl. You have made me feel there's something about her that touches us somewhere. Or am I wrong?"

"Not altogether, perhaps." Dermot took out his cigarette-case. "In a way, it's rather an extraordinary thing, and I'm not sure about it. I'm not sure whether I know her or not. It all hinges on the Cladday episode, the sinking of the submarine. You know the story."

"The official story, yes."

"You have also questioned me about the inhabitants— to do yourself justice."

"But you didn't tell me everything?"

Dermot smiled also. "Everything that mattered. I rather think this girl is the granddaughter of Iain MacNeil, the coastwatcher who got his medal posthumously. But I'm not sure."

"What makes you think so?"

"It was in an early reconnaissance of the island. Do you really want the detail?"

"In this case, even the smallest."

Dermot glanced at him. "Very well." He described briefly how their fast patrol boat came in through a white mist, a new warmth in the weather, feeling their way for the west bay in Cladday. The sun came through, there was the island, and, close at hand on the beach, beside two drawn-up fishing boats, an old fisherman lifting his "cheese-cutter". That was the introduction to an island literally coming out of the blue. But now Dermot paused. "That evening," he went on, "I pulled away in our cockle-shell of a dinghy with a handline. I had always liked fishing and I kept our small outfit supplied. There was sand on that west side, which to me meant flat fish. But actually I was taken, in a way difficult to describe, first with the talk the skipper had had with the old man by the boats and then by the island itself. It's easy to be romantic about islands. It's not that. I've known too many of them. Though of course there is an attraction in coming to any place that is different from what one is used to." He paused again. "This is taking too long," he said, a touch of self-consciousness invading features which for a moment had assumed an expression of memoried ease. "Anyway, I landed on the island. That was the beginning of it." He paused a third time, as though some obscure element present was all the time hindering the very process of his thought.

"Beginning of what?" asked Grear.

"The beginning of a feeling we gave to these island folk that they were being spied on. It was a pity. However, there it was. And there could not have been any one more—-understanding, more humane, than our skipper. We would, of course, have gone anywhere with him, into anything."

"You did."

"Anyway, I landed." And now without any further stop Dermot went on to describe the exciting game the children played on the green knoll. "I just could not understand what they were looking for, and because we knew of the submarine in the neighbourhood, I frankly admit I wondered if an enemy plane, under cover of the summer night, was spotting for it. Then there was a shout, when they found what they were looking for, and the oldest of the children—they must have ranged from six upwards—came rushing towards me. It was an awkward moment. I didn't like it at all. But she was merely bringing the news to an old cow—the cows are left out through the summer nights—to a little dun cow, with her forelegs knuckled under her, chewing her cud." Dermot smiled as he gave Grear a glance; tapped the ash off his cigarette. "I saw her again, in the coastwatcher's house. Don't take this as evidence at all. I probably shouldn't have mentioned it. But I have been haunted by the feeling that it may be the same girl." He crushed his cigarette in the bronze ash-tray, obviously restraining his features from showing that he wished he had never mentioned anything so unsubstantial.

"Did you find out what they were looking for in the sky?"

"Yes," answered Dermot. "It was the new moon."

Grear took a moment or two before letting the short ripple of laughter loose. "As primitive as that!"

"Well—I suppose so."

"You're quite sure? You said you couldn't understand their Gaelic. I mean you're quite sure it was the new moon—you saw it?"

"There was a new moon, at least one not more than a day or two old, but the weather had been thick for a few days. . . ."

"Yes?"

"Well——" But whatever Dermot had thought of adding he dismissed. "It's simply quite certain. And I am probably just wasting your time, because the girl told the police that she originally came from Mallaig, from Cladach, Mallaig, to be precise."

"That's part of the trouble," said Grear in his usual voice. "The police here have been in touch with Mallaig and there they know neither the address nor the MacNeils."

The bone came clear in Dermot's face and the dark eyes were very direct. He looked at Grear, but he did not speak.

"So actually we would like to know all we can about this girl," Grear continued. "That's why your story is so interesting."

Dermot gave a thoughtful nod into space. "I see."

"And why I want to know as much of it as possible. Even an attitude to the moon may explain something!"

"So it was a detective," said Dermot quietly.

Grear waited, his eyes on Dermot's face.

Dermot met the look. "Have they a detective watching the house she works in?" he asked.

"What makes you think so?"

"I was there—just before coming on here."

"You mean you've just seen her?"

"No. She's gone."

"Gone! Where?"

"Her mistress doesn't know. She simply walked out early this morning."

"You're quite sure of that?"

"Her mistress is rather distressed."

"Mrs. Spicer?"

"Yes."

Grear removed his eyes and sat quite still for a moment, his face showing no more than its usual cheerful clarity. "One minute," he said and left the room.

He's gone to phone the police, Dermot thought; and as if something had been released in him, he began breathing heavily. The hand that took out his cigarette-case quivered slightly. Grear is quite right, he said to himself; the thing has got to be done. No good thinking about it. The smoke tasted raw and harsh. And the one thing he couldn't do *now* was show a disinclination to be implicated. Keep calm before Grear—and helpful. He switched his mind to Cladach . . . Cladday. . . .

"Well, now," said Grear as he sat down again, "I'm sure you must be wondering why the fuss over a mere handbag?"

"Actually I was. Because even this matter of the address—isn't it possible that the postal address by saying Mallaig means *by* or *via* Mallaig? In the way that a fellow in the Forces would say he came from Stornoway, when actually his native place might be a small township miles from it. To save explaining where the little place is, he simply says Stornoway, or near Stornoway. It was—it still is—a common occurrence."

"Yes," said Grear. "I know. But why Cladach and not Cladday?"

"Her native spot might be Cladach in Cladday—or in some other island—and she, in her confusion—for she was terribly upset—might omit——"

"That's a point, definitely. The kind of omission that should interest the police psychiatrist. Good. A few more points like that and we may get places! Do you know Mrs. Spicer?"

"No. It was the first time I actually met her." Dermot now felt strangely relieved, as if a shadow had lifted. Why the fuss over a handbag indeed? And he had himself explained the address. So he opened out on his interview with Mrs. Spicer, evoked some of her attitudes with an engaging humour. His insight into the old cruiser's dismay had Grear laughing. "And she's not on the hulks yet. She'll rig up something, that same lady. But I don't think she'll get Christina back."

"You think Christina left because of the row?"

"Plus what went before. Think of how she must have been 'instructed' by Mrs. Spicer."

Grear smiled in appreciation.

"And about the psychiatrist. I have never actually seen one at work, but—I doubt if the *omission* really signifies much."

"You mean?"

"Well," said Dermot, "there's no policeman on Clad-day. Actually crime is unknown on a place like that. It's the old dispensation there still. Queer as it may sound to us, crime was so very rare a thing in these old remote Highland communities that if a real crime did happen it was remembered for generations. I know, because as a boy I spent a lot of time in a certain Highland place. I am quite sure of that."

"And the psychiatrist?"

"There is consequently a deep fear of having anything to do with the police. Most of us know that fear. But with them—well, it goes deeper. It's difficult to explain, to—to get the *feel* of it. However, it's there. And the omission, unconscious or not, certainly expresses, I should say, this fear not to get mixed up with the police—and——"

"Yes?"

"Somehow not merely for her own sake. She would

40

not want to be the means of bringing the *shame* of the police on her own people, her island. I may not be making this clear——"

"You are. You are making it so clear that I want to tell you something. For it's also clear to me that if the girl is the same girl—the Cladday girl—then you could help us even more than the psychiatrist. I realize she may not be the same girl, but you are the only one here who could definitely establish that. Perhaps what was lost on the chart may be made up on the handbag! *But*—it's absolutely confidential. You understand that?"

"Yes," said Dermot.

"In her handbag the police found a list of names, a few names, but two of them of rather important people in this city. There is sufficient reason for connecting one or two of the names with a certain, shall we say, political activity, though just in how far the two principal names may be active now or are scheduled for activity at the critical moment, when the buttons are pressed, is a matter —for the appropriate kind of investigation. For reasons which you may appreciate, I cannot say more."

"But——"

"It's advisable never to be astonished too much. She may be a stooge. It may have been planted on her. That's the kind of thing you have got to find out."

"Me? How?"

Grear looked at his gold wrist-watch. "I'm going to be five minutes late if I don't step on it. When I find out where the girl is I'll give you a ring. We'll then discuss it further. Meantime—keep thinking it over. If I may say so, you've done some excellent thinking already, and not only over Mrs. Spicer!" He got up.

After eating alone, Dermot could not go to his rooms, avoided the club, did not want to meet anyone he knew. He felt profoundly depressed. The truth was, he could not get used to Grear, he thought; he had never quite cottoned on to the fellow. There was something about him that made you feel he had come up, all clean and fresh, out of cold water. Never a point of real human contact; no warmth. And this was not intentional on his part; he was just like that. An excellent fellow, first-class at his job, with a brain like a mathematician's and utterly trustworthy. He had probably been aware all along of the surprising passage of time to a minute. And—he had said no more about the chart. The reprimand had been conveyed as nicely as it could from, so to speak, one colleague to another—and left there. No further discussion of it, of the implications of the loss, no expression of hope that it might turn up, nothing. Just left there.

In his unconscious flight, Dermot was getting into quieter streets, down into the poorer part of the city, away from his own kind. It was the way Christina would have taken and he involuntarily had his image of her. This image was going to bother him; he could see that. He had wakened from a dream of it so vivid that for half a minute he had felt her presence in the bedroom, an exact spot in the bedroom which he had stared at, waiting for the body to form in the darkness: the body in dark clothes, half turned away from the police and himself, with bent head, weeping, the iron railing behind her, in that street where she had been robbed.

Hardly the kind of figure for a fifth-column exercise! Or was it, in fact, the most appropriate figure? His head lifted and the city became to his vision an entanglement of streets, a vast dim maze. There was now a faint smell, like the smell of gas. A man shuffled past him. *When the buttons are pressed.* It used to be, thought Dermot, *when the balloon goes up.* The irony had a savage tonic quality. Thousands of miles away fingers pressed the buttons and this city became a ruin, the maze of streets fallen in, life crushed and slowly writhing to stillness.

She may have been a stooge. It may have been planted on her. Trust Grear to be nearer to reality, to the practical possibility! Less melodrama and more likelihood. And then Dermot realized that Grear would never have said even that without some positive reason. All at once he stopped dead. How could the police have recovered the bag so quickly? The robbers had made a complete getaway. How could the police . . . *unless they knew where the bag was*? Good lord, had the thing been a plant by the police? Had they known there was something in the bag, but, for their own reasons, had not wished to become directly involved? Had the two robbers been plainclothes men? . . . Pale faces under caps turned to stare at him. As he walked on, he saw a policeman leave a dark entry across the street.

The police state! Hell, is this what it's like? The entanglement, invisible threads, tough as wire, knotting on this dark lump in the human breast. Waiting for the thing to happen. The news, the newspapers. And all the time, in every corner of the city, *this* business of watching eyes.

He came into a populous street; a smell of fish and chips, an elderly woman's shrill laughter from the group by the pub at the corner, a raking bawdy laughter, a warmth, two girls in dance-hall finery, cat-calls; a sudden queer apprehension of human flesh, choking him slightly, from one of Basil's more provocative sayings that all human beings were lice. A lot of them now, jostling him, outside a building—a political meeting.

Here was the dance-hall. The saxophones were sobbing. A couple of girls were watching him. At last he came to the river, and the river stopped him.

The police would find her among all this all right. Unless—she had gone back home. A voice began to sing and his eye at once sought a lighted window in the shabby tenement opposite. Gaelic folk songs always affected him in an atavistic way, like some sort of drug.

He crossed the street and stood on the kerb beneath the window, a fine excitement already in his breast. Yes, it was Ellen MacArthur singing over the air. He had forgotten about her broadcast. No one could see him standing here; yet he glanced about as if he might be caught, listening to Ellen. But he could even think about her if he liked, for no one was drawing near. The movement forward of her body, the impulsive kindness, the grace. Her soft warm mouth. He let her singing get the better of him; he gave way in an indulgence that her song lifted and thinned out on the air, bringing a shiver to the flesh.

He had lately been avoiding Ellen and was aware of a dumb question in her face, beyond the singing, in the quiet moment when she stood and looked at him, wondering.

Oh, he knew, he knew. But, dammit, he couldn't. The game they played was enough, the game of apparent frankness, outrageous frankness, was enough. One couldn't break through the game to-day. One couldn't, because

44

beyond it . . . the black smear, crawling like a river . . .
seeping into the underground corridors and vaults where
men were tortured and done in . . . and war . . . war . . .

His humour caught a fine edge. Don't get sunk before
the fight starts. Above all, don't have your arms tied.
Besides, was it Ellen, really Ellen, or only her song? . . .
But he was given to the song as to the heightening effect
of a drug. When it was over he at once moved on before
Ellen could start again.

He even smiled with a certain critical irony, for he was
skilled in the art of lessening the effect, of gradually shed-
ding it. The way her voice died beyond its own last echo, he
thought, was exactly like the way a sea-wave dies out distantly on a western strand. Exactly like that, he thought,
drawing away from the sound and the picture, lingeringly,
with the exquisite appreciation that gave his mind to
itself again; but not abruptly, lifting away through
associations rather, every kind of association. . . . Cladday
. . . and suddenly he knew, as his mind came completely
to itself, that Christina had not gone home to Cladday.
No, she wouldn't have gone back there; she couldn't. As
he slowed to a standstill, he had a vision of her in some
dingy room in one of the condemned tenements made
temporarily habitable, listening to that Gaelic voice.

Through a bay in the embankment he saw the river,
broad and black, rolling soundlessly on. He paused to
stare at it, but before its sombre volume could get hold
of him his eyes lifted to the sky and he saw with an effect
of unimaginable surprise the sickle of a very young moon.
A virginal freshness, an elfin-green silver. Youthful feet,
wind in the face, an eager immortal crying. His heart
lifted and he smiled in friendliness, in ancient greeting,
before the expression stilled, like his body, and he remembered old Anna and her black river of death.

That was one of the things he had been going to tell

Grear, when something stopped him. For after the girl had whispered her secret into the cow's ear and run back to the green knoll he had at once slipped round the sand dune, and it was only when he was pulling back to the patrol boat that he himself had actually seen the young moon. As he could hardly let himself believe that this was what they had been looking for—children's games have mysterious origins—he kept thinking about it, but without mentioning it to any of the crew. Then on a morning hunt for fresh fish he landed with the telescope.

A rather broad squat woman appeared with her cow on a rope. The telescope brought her so near that as she hammered the stake of the tether into the ground he fancied he heard her grunt. Then she straightened herself, drew the back of her hand across her nose and looked around. There was a solemn earthy expression on her face as if the exercise had troubled her. But as she gazed heavenward her expression changed, slowly, into a melting look as though she were welcoming a loved one, long a stranger. Her lips began to move in speech, and then with a grace he would never have credited had he not seen it, she curtsied. The telescope wobbled and she passed out of its field. At once his naked eye saw Iain MacNeil gazing across at him from the end of his cottage.

It was a nasty moment. The feeling of bad manners mounted to guilt. He did not know what on earth to do; then decided to salute the man, to wave, as though it were all perfectly natural—he could be studying bird life —when MacNeil simply withdrew. Down on the beach, while gazing disconsolately about him, he saw the ghostly feather of the young moon in the sky.

Dermot turned away from the river. He knew the kind of men who came arguing out of a pub and he kept his face in front. He liked their voices. Warm-hearted, grand with their hands, and a fight did no harm. Their oaths were spindrift. Ships sailed out of their blood. As he walked up the side street he had a nostalgia for their humour and their noise, a desire to mix in and shout aloud with the best, to let it rip and be damned. To speak his mind to the inevitable political fellow amongst them, who would argue like a Grear, knowing what was what, knowing how to work on the human batter, add the subtle yeast, contain and mould it. To speak his mind in a forthright bloody spate, drowning the fellow in his own jargon. God, these fellows, he thought, everywhere, everywhere: the club, Intelligence, the yard, the pub. That kind of mind. For it was the same kind of mind, the same kind of intelligence, whatever the angle from which it operated, wherever the place. The mind for operating a theory, pro or anti. The mind that made use of violence, as a conductor his first fiddle.

Here, I'll have to watch this, Dermot muttered, and went along the street, smiling at himself, walking strongly.

At last opposite the railing where Christina had stood weeping, he paused. There was no one about. Deliberately he went up and caught the iron railing in his hand, as if by walking through the apparition he might destroy it. But immediately he turned away it was as though he hadn't done it. She was there in his mind; he saw her clearly, like a figure in a myth, the myth of the sorrowing woman. A fine coldness touched his skin and Anna's words to the moon came back to him like a weird prophecy.

He heard them in old Seumas's voice, saw the look on the bearded face that was eighty years old, the smile in the eyes as they looked down the arable lands of Cladday.

"Ah," Seumas said, "a man may not always know what moves in a woman's heart. And the moon is near to a woman as the sun to a man. But Anna is getting up in years and maybe what she said to the new moon was: *Many a one has crossed over the black river of death since you came here before.*"

7

"That's her address," said Grear; "5 St. Patrick's Close. It was a condemned tenement, reconditioned in the housing shortage. At least it's alleged that the rat-holes were stopped up. They're an elderly couple. He's a riveter, with nothing against him; she came originally from Harris and there may be some relationship to Christina; anyway, Mrs. Mure and Christina have been in the habit of going to Gaelic concerts together, clan or county association—you know the sort of thing."

Dermot put his small diary, in which he had written the address, back in his pocket. "But she'll be after a new job, won't she?"

"You think there may be difficulty about the dole, seeing she walked out?"

"Well, I was just thinking she would want to work."

"Quite. But the work will come through the Labour Exchange. So whether it's the dole or a new job, there is the official channel. You needn't worry about our losing sight of her."

"I—understand."

Grear smiled. "Have you thought of how you'll make contact?"

"It will have to be accidental. I cannot know her address. I could say, of course, that there had been something familiar about her face—had remembered Cladday

—had gone to the police to see if she was all right and had got her address, but——"

"But you don't want to mention the police. Quite right."

"I'll do a preliminary reconnaissance and think it over."

"We'll leave it there for the moment. Now about that chart. I've been thinking about it. It's a bit of a nuisance. For even if we recovered it to-night we could not now be certain that it had not been copied or photographed, no matter how innocent its retention by someone, even children, might appear."

"I've thought of that. For if they *had* copied it, they might want to plant it back on us in such natural circumstances that we should feel they hadn't."

"Exactly. We may have you in Intelligence yet!"

"I think I'd rather fight, with a real sea under me," replied Dermot, "if you don't mind."

"It's perhaps a more solid sea," Grear agreed. "However, we've got to make use of everything, even a loss. Have you been to the Dial Club since I've seen you?"

"No."

"What I have been thinking is that you might drop in there to-night and tell the story of how you lost it, and in particular keep your invisible eye on a fellow like Basil. It's a good story. As for the chart, it will be merely an old chart you had hunted out, with old landfalls, spots where you had landed marked on it. Even bird haunts, if you like. A yachtsman's longing for the sea. Your yacht-racing reputation is known. It struck me that you might make it sound very natural."

Dermot was thoughtful. "When was the chart printed?"

"Actually one of the same printing as you used in the war."

Dermot took a moment. "That could be done."

"Good. I don't think there's anything else just now."

49

Grear blew a cigarette fleck from a lapel and squared up his blotting-pad.

"Tell me," said Dermot. "Does the loss of the chart mean that we cannot now make use of the marked places——"

"A decision remains to be made." Grear got up. "It's a pretty hopeless position that cannot be retrieved—if a fellow makes up his mind to it. One thing at a time."

"Very good."

Dermot went along the street thoughtfully. It was being put up to him. That's what Grear had meant. If he bungled the business of Christina. . . .

"Why don't you buy the whole shop?" asked a voice in his ear.

Dermot, who had hardly been aware of staring at the fishing tackle, smiled to the Assessor, his expression like a boy's. "It's beginning to look like an obsession, isn't it?"

"Is it?"

"I think so. It's like something——" Dermot paused.

"That can't happen again?"

"Do you think the whole world is going slowly, but certainly, mad?"

"You mustn't use a word like 'mad'. In this tendency to destruction there may be a world or mass psychosis. But when a condition is universal, who is to judge it, and from what angle? Would you arrogate to yourself the capacity to judge it from your contemplation of a fishing-tackle window? From the standpoint of the universal, so singular a judgment might itself more reasonably be considered to proceed from a psychotic condition. In short, it's you that's mad."

Dermot laughed, feeling lifted up, and the rather elaborate irony was continued agreeably until they reached the club. The Assessor seemed in good form, his quiet voice playful and amused. Dermot felt grateful for the absence of anything directly personal.

"Still at it?" The Assessor sat down carefully, his drink in his hand.

"It's Joe," said Sandy Graeme.

"Health, Joe!" said the Assessor.

Joe returned the nod and the salutation with courtesy. "I'm glad you're here," he said. "They don't seem to understand that it's real, that it's going to happen. They don't know where they're going."

"Don't we!" In the laughter, the door opened and Basil appeared. "Here, Basil, Joe says we don't know where we're going," cried Monson.

"That's an easy one," said Basil. "You're all going to hell."

When Basil was seated, Joe asked him, "Do you believe in hell?"

"Why, don't you?"

"I think I'm beginning to believe in it," said Joe with the preoccupied air of one carrying on a profound inner argument.

"We couldn't do without you, Joe," said the long sleek Monson, whose hair glistened as he twisted with pleasure in his chair, "and that's a fact."

"Do you believe in God?" Basil asked Joe.

Joe looked steadily back at Basil and four men looked at them both.

"I don't know," said Joe at last. "I just don't know." His voice held a touch of distress.

"I can see what's going to happen."

"What?" asked Joe.

"There's a church waiting for you," said Basil, and he leaned back and drank.

"Everyone has his church," said the Assessor, "and his God."

"Come off it!" said Basil. "Generalizations of that sort at this hour! The sheer unintelligence of the thing! It beats me how you can go on with it."

"It may beat you," said the Assessor mildly, "but that doesn't dispose of it."

"No?" Basil's features caught their characteristic piercing irony. "I have long suspected that you have 'found God'. You sometimes emanate the superior assurance that is like a——"

"Don't hesitate."

"Mild idiocy," concluded Basil, and his smile flashed.

"And you're not really being personal. I follow," said the Assessor with an appreciative humour.

Basil's smile vanished as if an invisible criticism had pierced him; then the smile came back, but watchful and challenging, knowingly triumphant. "God the Father."

"Is that what you base it on?"

"Don't you?"

"I wouldn't say that. No," said the Assessor. "Though it's plausible." He laughed, shaken with his soft chuckles, and pressed down the ash in his pipe. "The way you lap up that kind of stuff from psychologists who pore over other fellows' anthropological stories——" He paused to look at Basil. "Do you never question anything?"

"I'm questioning you," retorted Basil. "I'm trying to hunt you out of your wool."

"But if there is a God surely he is the Father?" said Joe.

"You've said it!" declared Basil in malicious triumph over the Assessor. "That—and nothing else."

"He means, Joe, I take it," said the Assessor, "that we have created God from a childhood notion of our own fathers. When we no longer had an earthly father to rely on and comfort us we created a heavenly one to take his place. You're merely a child hunting for your father."

"That can hardly be," answered Joe, "because I don't remember my father."

The spontaneous laughter stopped upon itself. The Assessor gave a small courteous nod.

"That makes no difference," Basil said.

"How do you know?" asked Joe.

"In the same way as you would know, if you read the appropriate literature." Basil made an impatient gesture. "Man made God in his own image in order to satisfy certain needs and cravings left over from infancy. And you can check up on that by comparing the infancy of the race. It's primitive."

"There's much in the primitive that I find very interesting," said Joe. "Some of our best modern painting, the painting that has given art life again, and wonder, finds its inspiration in the primitive."

"I'm not doubting you," said Basil.

"In that case," answered Joe, upon whom Basil's irony seemed lost, "how can you think it doesn't matter? Do life and wonder no longer matter?"

"That's the stuff, Joe!" said Sandy.

But Basil gave Joe up. "I would have to begin at the beginning with you."

"I sometimes think," said Joe, "that you have forgotten how to get to the beginning. I sometimes think you are a child who has lost his way."

Amid the general appreciation, Sandy thought Joe's remark "so profound that it may not even flatter him".

Then Basil let out a great flow of talk, fingers writhing, in which he got worked up. It was not that he minded the childish myth of God; it was the danger of the thing, to-day a deliberately designed danger, to prevent the creation of a rational world. "God is a weapon in the hands of politically astute men—but that you should be taken in by it!" He leaned back. "The old Machiavellian stiletto—still functioning!"

There was always laughter for excess of talk, but Joe was troubled. "I think you're exaggerating," he said, and that simple statement shook laughter out of them all.

"You'll see I'm not," said Basil. "You're too simple for this world, Joe. You should sail away—with this silent fellow here."

"Where to?" asked Dermot, speaking for the first time.

"To *Tir nan Og*, that Gaelic paradise set in the Western Sea," and Basil mouthed the words in sarcastic mimicry of the Highland voice.

"He can't," said Dermot.

"Why not?" asked Basil.

"Because I have lost the chart," replied Dermot with a simplicity that Joe could not have exceeded.

While the remark was being enjoyed, Basil's eyes lingered for a second on Dermot's face, then his deformed shoulder gave its lift.

"But it's quite true," said Dermot. "I lost the chart the other night."

The Assessor now looked at him. "Do you mean—the chart you had here?"

"Yes. I got into a fight on the way home—after I left you—and lost the chart."

"A fight!" said Sandy. "You're pulling our legs."

"No. It really happened." Then he went on to tell the story, which so astonished them that questions were asked right and left by everyone except Basil.

"You mean the police haven't found it yet?" asked the Assessor.

"No."

"But that's extraordinary," said Sandy. "Who could have—where the blazes could it have gone?"

"Someone must have picked it up, I suppose."

"Seems odd that the police collared you, doesn't it?" said Basil.

"Not really. At first, I admit, I was angry when the policeman gripped me. But it was all natural enough. I was chasing the fellow with the handbag. The second fellow, coming behind, tripped me up. But to the police we were merely three toughs running away."

"And who was the girl?" asked Monson.

"The girl? She was a servant girl," said Dermot. "But quite neatly dressed. She had three pounds in her bag."

"It's a bloody shame," said Sandy. "They not only skinned a fellow down the Great Eastern Road the other night, they not only took the actual boots off him, they took his false teeth."

Monson started laughing and couldn't stop.

"And our wonderful police found neither chart nor bag," commented Basil.

"I don't know about the bag," said Dermot. "I haven't seen them since. But I phoned up to-night about the chart. They certainly haven't got that."

"How do you know?"

"Because they said so." Dermot looked with astonishment at Basil.

Basil merely smiled. "Before I would subscribe to that I'd need to know what was on your precious chart."

"It was merely a private chart, which I have had for a long time."

"Just a plain chart?"

"Yes. There were some markings on it—anchorages— places where we had landed. The usual yachtsman's crosses and what not. With some bird markings, perhaps. Why?"

Basil shrugged. "They might think it an odd thing for you to be carrying around. However, it would be a pity to destroy your naive beliefs and it has nothing to do with me."

"But that's absurd," said Dermot. "You have merely an

55

exaggerated prejudice against the police. I have scores of charts. Every yachtsman has—though I admit now they're difficult to get, so a fellow doesn't exactly give them away."

"Tell me, Sandy," said Monson in an aside, "did they take the false teeth out of his mouth?"

"Where the hell else would they take them out of, his——?"

But Monson was off into laughter.

"It wouldn't be, I suppose," said Joe, with a momentary divine glimmer, "a real chart to *Tir nan Og*?"

"As near it, Joe," answered Dermot, "as we are ever likely to find." Smiling, he kept his eyes for a moment on Joe's. "I should like to take you there some day. Perhaps I shall."

"The sea is difficult."

"Aren't you a good sailor, Joe?" asked Sandy.

"When a great ninth wave curls over on a western strand, you might find form," suggested Dermot.

But Joe continued to look troubled.

Then Dermot suddenly said, "Joe, I forgot. Heavens! It's the land of light; it's the place where you see light being made." He laughed. "Literally—you can watch God painting out there."

"Can you?" said Joe and his spirit broke on his face.

Dermot felt quite certain it was Christina, though he hadn't yet seen her full face. She was sitting five seats in front of him and over to the left on one of the hard chairs which filled the floor of the hall. He knew her by her stillness, and it did not occur to him that everyone else was quite as still, listening to the man who was singing the sea-surging song of Clanranald's galley. He must have missed her coming in, though he had stood on the opposite pavement watching. As the song lifted him, he saw her dark shoulders like a boulder on the edge of the tide. A withdrawn intimacy so came about his heart that he smiled, looked at the singer critically, at his large generous mouth, and with a feeling of irresistible exhilaration saw the bow of a boat lift and smash on a short sea.

Amid the applause that followed the song, a young man sitting immediately behind the girl leaned forward and spoke to her. Her face half-turned with a smile. Yes, it was Christina.

The young man, who was about Christina's own age, spoke to the fellow beside him and they laughed, moving restlessly on their chairs; then he turned round and gave a salute to someone behind. Dermot knew he had seen his face before, but could not recollect where, and found his mind questing among yachts' crews. It was so obvious that the sea-song with its bounding gaiety had made the man want to talk, to stir up his friends; the spindrift had come in laughter on his face. He leaned forward and whispered to Christina again. This time she did not turn round; she spoke to the small stout elderly woman on her left. That would be Mrs. Mure.

Dermot watched the by-play, which followed each item on the programme, with critical care, but when Ellen appeared on the platform everything else went out of his mind. She walked slowly, a faint smile for the applause, then stood still. She was dark, quite good-looking, really personable, but there was also something of distinction which he almost feared, which affected him like a kind of sadness, and when the piano began its tinkling introduction to *Caol Muile* he felt: O God, now I'm for it!

Even if she sang that song every night of the week to him, the effect upon him would merely grow. That was where it was different from an ordinary drug. Nor was it any help saying that the effect was extra-musical. For what did that mean—except that the song and the voice evoked something beyond them. It was a whole country, a lost world. And the quality in her voice—it went wandering through that world, it was a remembering of it, and the only word that for him could describe it was *innocence*. It was a primordial innocence.

He had thought all this out before, had argued it out with musicians to its folk roots, had agreed that musically it was simple enough, yet even in the very argument had found himself using it as a secret criterion of the cultured musician's real depth, much as a seaman used the lead to get the depth of the sea. And even should he agree, for a genuinely honest rather than perverse reason, that all this merely showed his own lack of true musical understanding, it made no difference when he heard Ellen again. There was the voice, and there, living and cool and ten thousand years old, note by note, each rounded like a pearl, clear in shape, opaque in colour, lovely and innocent, they came upon him. At the end he had to make a real physical effort to lift his hands and clap.

When he got outside he stood on the edge of the pavement facing the street, lit a cigarette and buttoned his coat. The night was cold and, with a seaman's look for weather, he saw the moon. As they came down the three steps he slowly turned, lowering his face to put up his collar. The manner of his approach to Christina was to depend on her recognition; he had merely to make the meeting as inevitable as possible. They were coming straight towards him, but as he lifted his face into the clear light from the globe over the door they stopped. Christina's glance was arrested for a moment and he was just going to step forward in surprise and greeting, when she turned her back. He knew that she had recognized him, and something instinctive rather than deliberate in her action made him hesitate. Hang it, he thought, this is going to make it difficult and he felt hot. There were six of them, with the cheerful fellow talking nearly as loudly as a blonde young woman with a loose mouth and a free manner. They were clearly waiting for one of the singers.

Ellen appeared, accompanied by the man who had given "violin selections". He timed it so that he came face to face with Ellen by the group and the cheerful young man was actually shaking her hand when, over his shoulder, she cried, "Dermot!"

"Couldn't resist you," Dermot admitted, feeling the quick response of her fingers.

"How are you, sir? Thought I recognized you."

Dermot looked at him. "Was it you I saw easing the sheet to give Clanranald's galley a run for it?"

The cheerful lad laughed delightedly. "I was on *Foamcrest* when you beat us by four minutes."

"It was four and a half, but we'll shake hands on it."

It was the affable mood which in that company meant introductions all round—Mrs. Mure, Miss Donaldson, Miss MacNeil.

"I *think*," said Dermot, hesitating, "I must have met you before——"

"And Mr. Deas," said Alex Macrae, the cheerful sailor.

"How do you do, Mr. Deas?"

"And this is Mr. Ganson," said Ellen, introducing the violinist. "Did you enjoy the concert?"

"Very much—though there was a lot of it."

"Oh?"

"Yes." He held her challenge a moment. "It's no good

looking like that when you know how you put the heart across simple people." His matter-of-fact tones suited Alex Macrae's exuberant mood.

"If she had any heart at all she wouldn't do it," Alex agreed solemnly.

"I think," said Dermot, "you have now said the last word."

But Alex hadn't, for presently, worked upon, he said, "Ach, Ellen, what about giving us a wee lilt before we part?"

"Alex Macrae, have you taken leave of your senses?"

"I have," said Alex. "Just one verse of *Ailean Duinn*. Come on now, Ellen; everybody's gone."

"Are you coming our way?" Ellen asked Dermot, pulling her gloves on tight.

"*Your* way, I might—if you gave us even one line."

"But I can't—on the public street. Are you quite daft?"

"Now, Ellen!" said Alex quietly. "Up with it!"

Dermot did not want her to sing. He saw Deas look around. Mrs. Mure was smiling, with the patience that could wait for ever, a small strong woman, with tender lines on her face, like the striations on a solitary rock on the old shores of her native Harris. He did not look at Christina. Ellen began to sing. It was the quiet singing, the remembering within oneself, which Dermot found most difficult of all to bear. The louder the seas, the higher the rumble and roar of the traffic rose, the purer grew the singing, the more surely it wandered in its own country, the country where small wild flowers grew and the light was clear. The ear leaned towards it and the eye was miraculously cleansed.

When Dermot had gone a few steps with Ellen and Ganson the violinist, he said, "One moment!" turned and, calling, "Miss MacNeil!" went towards the others, who paused, but drifted on when it was clear that Dermot wanted a word with Christina.

60

"I didn't want to talk to you before them all, but there's something very particular I must tell you. Could you meet me here to-morrow night, at seven? We'll go and have something to eat somewhere."

She hesitated.

"Tell your friends I suddenly remembered meeting you out West. Do come. It's important—and I should love a talk anyway."

Then she looked at him, her dark eyes full on his face. "All right," she said.

"Thank you." His voice lifted in a cheerful "Good night!" as he turned away.

Ellen and Ganson were waiting for him. In the gayest spirits he said to Ellen, "Haven't seen you for a long time. Where have you been?"

She considered him in an ironic silence that contained much. "You know Christina MacNeil?"

"I rather think so. But not on my own account, may I say. I'm always doing good turns for people. You ought to know that."

But for once Ellen could not rise to the usual nonsense. As she was never the one to sustain dumb grudges, always loving the good moment for itself however it came, he suspected that the presence of Ganson was the obscure trouble. The fellow was rather colourless, reticent, perhaps jealous. He might be hanging his hat! The thought lifted Dermot into irresponsibility, into the laughing question with the ambiguous meaning, and Ellen could not respond as if she had lost her wits for once under a dumb burden. Ganson stopped and said, "There's our tram," and when Dermot found out they were going on to a ceilidh in a private house he was beset by a wild desire to abduct Ellen. Ellen saw the look in his face and then she smiled. It was the old smile, mocking him. "Good night," she said and looked as if she might blow him a kiss, with mockery and something more in it. He was so moved that he stood at the tram-stop until she had disappeared. Ellen had this way of touching him with delight at times. He suddenly felt completely freed, and in a little while, with the gaiety of the meeting still upon him, he was thinking of Christina.

He was ten minutes before time the following evening and was wondering if she had changed her mind, when suddenly she was there at his elbow.

"Thank goodness!" he said. "I thought something might have happened to you."

She smiled.

"Now where will we go?" he asked, but he had made up his mind and they had dinner in an expensive hotel with a large lounge where talk could be reasonably confidential.

"I don't know what it is about Ellen's singing, but it certainly gets me. When I was a boy I used to spend every summer away up in a little place in the north-west called Tomluachrach. My mother's people came from there. I just wouldn't go anywhere else. Between flounders in the bay and trout in two hill lochs—one with a boat—not to mention sea-trout in the burn when it was in spate—and when it wasn't—we had great times."

She was shy, but not uncertain.

"Anything to drink, sir?"

"Yes. Let me see—what do you like?"

"No, thank you," she said.

As he presently poured some Barsac absentmindedly into her glass, his talk went on, "He was a little man, but his voice was the purest tenor I have ever heard; small, but extraordinarily clear, and he never forced it. But what got us as boys were his bird-songs, where the Gaelic sounds imitated the birds to the life. They were so—so exquisitely finished, that we always laughed. It was like a miracle. And then he would smile in his droll way, cocking his head to one side at us." He raised his glass and smiled to her, then glanced at her glass. "Do. It's a very light wine."

She looked at her glass, then lifted it a little awkwardly.

The cheek bones were distinct, rather high, so that her face seemed to narrow to the chin, yet her mouth, full and wide, was somehow not out of proportion. In the police station, she had looked dull and scared, a little stupid, holding on dourly to something inside; even her black hair had been lank and rather pitiful. Now he saw that the set of the face was old, not lively and modern, but rather like a mask, an archaic mask, shaped by the bone. He had met faces like it many a time in the north and west. But not so often eyes like these dark eyes. As she drank, the lashes lowered. It was a pity that she was so silent, so uninteresting, that she wasn't aware of her eyes. He had known Highland maids with far more liveliness and grace than the women they served. But Christina—he just knew she wouldn't have the wit to use Mrs. Spicer's bath salts. Pity. It was going to make it more difficult. He kept on talking.

When they were seated in a corner of the lounge on comfortable chairs, he asked as he lifted his coffee cup, "Have you been wondering all this time what I wanted to speak about?"

"No," she said. "Unless you want to."

He just could not find a word for a moment, as though countered by a witty woman. Suppressing an impulse to laugh, "I do want to," he said, restless in his chair. "The fact is—well, you brought something back to me, a past bit of my life. It's a part of my life that I'll never forget. It happened about ten years ago. I was on a naval patrol boat." He leaned forward and as he tapped his cigarette above the ash-tray looked at her over his shoulder with a friendly smile: "Don't you remember me?"

Her eyes returned to her cup.

"Your grandfather was the coastwatcher—Iain Mac-Neil."

She kept her eyes on her cup, silent.

"After I left you at the police station the other night, I could not get you out of my head. You see, what happened out at Cladday affected me—very much. If there was anything I could do for anyone from Cladday, it would give me great pleasure to do it. All the kindness came from your side, from your folk. All we did for a long time was make you feel suspicious, as though we were spying on you. Often I have felt: if only someone came from Cladday what a pleasure it would be to show them around, to take them out to dinner."

He drank his coffee. She put out her hand to her cup, turned it slightly in the saucer; then as though in a life of its own her hand returned to her lap. She looked across the wide lounge.

"Will I tell you how I met you first—at least how I saw you?" He was delighted at having discovered her. He had been right! At that moment there was nothing he wouldn't have done for her, wouldn't have given her.

As she glanced at him, something shone for a moment, like curiosity watching from its shell.

He told her about the sand dunes, the children on the knoll, how he lay hidden, wondering, "and then a girl broke away and came rushing straight for me. But it wasn't for me. There was a cow lying down, quite close. She put her arms round the cow's neck and told her a few things. Perhaps it was old Anna's cow?"

Her eyes left his face and a slow smile darkened her features, attractive in its shy discomfort. "No," she said in a low but quite clear voice, "it was our own cow."

"Was it?" He laughed now, not loudly, but with spontaneous pleasure. "What a wonderful game it was!

64

Children to-day are given atom bombs in their toy aeroplanes. I would rather have the new moon myself. Only I didn't know it was the new moon at that moment. It was only afterwards, in the morning, when I had my telescope with me and saw Anna leading her cow away on the tether, that I found out. It was then your grandfather saw me spying. I was sorry about that. Tell me, what did he really think?"

"He was hurt."

"I know. Our skipper felt it very much."

"He would be speaking about it over the fire at night. He felt you didn't trust him. And he was on the minesweepers in the first war; two boats he was on were blown up under him."

"I know. It was pretty dreadful."

"He could not get over it. He used to be saying, 'Here am I and I have been drawing my retainers from the R.N.R. the most of my life. What do they take me for at all?' Many a time he said it." She spoke quietly, but he saw that she was upholding her own folk, that it was the one thing that could readily have moved her.

"And then—when we dug up the buried sailor in the night——" He stirred restlessly.

"Yes," she said. "That was the worst."

"Shocking. Tell me this: did we ever really convince him that we meant nothing?"

"No. The end came—before he was convinced."

He nodded. "I knew that. Our skipper tried to make himself believe that he had convinced him. But I knew he hadn't. I'll never forget that last morning. I was pretty far through myself and I thought the skipper was away with it altogether. We were flat out on the sand and I lifted my head, for it was the grey of the morning and I knew it wasn't half tide and I wondered if we would be trapped. That would have been a pretty miserable end, after what we had come through. I saw bits of old tangle at the cliff-foot and knew then that the sea would come right in. The wind was blowing almost straight in, too, a half-gale, so there didn't seem much hope. It's a horse-shoe, as you know, with no escape. It must have been a few minutes after that. The rising sun came sheer through the cloud and I felt it on my face. I looked round about again and suddenly saw your grandfather on the eastern horn of the cliff. He lifted his hat as he leaned forward against the wind, staring far out to sea. He had not seen us. He would not be looking for only two of us there on the sand! At the distance he seemed small against the sky. It was a wild flying morning. I'll never forget it."

"I remember," she said, "being wakened by the knocking and the voices. I was up before my mother came back from the door. I knew something awful had happened. 'Run you,' said she, 'as fast as your feet can carry you to Lachlan Mor's and tell him to come to the cladach—the shore—this minute to man the boat.' "

"And I bet you ran."

"Yes," she said. "I could hardly speak at his door."

"I had never thought of that, of how they got the boat out. There would be more than the crew there?"

"Yes, there was the whole of us. I will always remember how they waited, when they saw old Seumas coming. My grandfather said quietly, 'We'll wait for him,' and no one spoke after that."

He felt himself being moved, exactly as one of the old songs moved him, but now with a more particular poignancy as though he were at the heart of the moment when the song was being born. It had often struck him as remarkable how, in the most moving passages of a song, the singer never showed any extra emotion, any emotion at all, but sang on, as though the song and what it told were coming through glass.

"So you waited?"

"Yes."

"Old Seumas would bless them and the boat."

"He did."

He could not ask her what old Seumas had said, though the urge to know the actual words was suddenly like a craving.

He looked at her. "You would follow—did you follow the boat?"

"Yes—as well as we could. It was not always easy, because it's high and broken on the west side yonder. But the boat had a little shelter, they said after, when they kept close in because the wind was a point or two in the east. But when you saw them and the seas that were running, it didn't look like much shelter."

"No, it wouldn't be much," he said, thoughtfully staring in front of him.

Without movement of her head, her eyes lifted to his face. From its strange, stormy expression it was obvious that he had forgotten her.

"You would see them when they came clear, out by the spit?" he asked, looking at her again.

"Yes, we saw them then." She was silent. "We saw them—but sometimes we didn't." A curious embarrassed smile came to her face. It was as if she didn't know quite where to look. He watched her, fascinated.

"What happened?"

"It was once," she said. "We thought they were gone. Iain Og's mother cried out."

He waited.

"Then we saw them again. But—they didn't seem to be making any way. The seas were breaking white on the skerry, spouting in great bursts. Iain Og's mother cried, 'They'll never do it!' Old Seumas said in a stern voice, 'Be quiet, woman!'" She glanced at him and away.

Dermot's expression merely grew grimmer. He nodded. "Iain Og was the lad in the boat."

"Yes. It was his sixteenth birthday."

"Was it?" His eyes travelled over her face as though they hadn't seen it properly before.

"It was," she said quietly.

Slowly he put his hand in a pocket and took out his cigarette-case. Christina didn't smoke.

"Iain MacNeil, Lachlan Mor, Kennie—what was his surname again?"

"Kennie Macrury."

He nodded. "And Iain Og. Iain looked very young against the old men." He stared at the cigarette as he smoothed it between his finger-tips, then his eyes lifted to the room. "I don't blame Iain Og's mother. I remember when I first saw them myself. They had held well out to clear the spit, and they were getting the full sea. I was on my feet now, not very strongly. I had been in the water all night. The skipper looked dead, lying there on the sand. But often during the night he hadn't answered me. When the shell hit us, something had got him in the chest. She was a small boat and sank almost at once. But I had got a lifebuoy lashed to him. It was just coming on dark, and, though we had seen it was going to be a dirty night, the wind hadn't actually got up then. Sort of dark, oily, heaving sea, but nothing breaking." He paused, then his expression softened in a smiling humour. "I suppose I am trying to make it easy for myself. But it took them a long time to work across the spit, for they had to keep her nose to the weather. When next she showed, she was always a little more clear of the point, more to the east'ard. Then I saw that she was actually coming nearer, that she was coming in on the weather and tide, stern first. There was something about it—it was so well done —it was—it was—I don't know. I don't think I was thinking of myself at all. I was weak and light-headed, of course. I felt elevated. The tears were running down my face. I can still remember a sort of wild surprise. They were grand fellows." He lit his cigarette and blew a great breath of smoke. "I have often wondered what happened to them—I mean Lachlan Mor and Kennie and Iain Og."

"Lachlan Mor and Kennie are still at home," she said.

"And Iain Og?"

"He went to Australia."

"Did he?" The question came from him in little more than a whisper as his expression concentrated on her.

She nodded, watching her hand, which had gone out to the edge of the small table; the fingers began plucking at the edge for a moment.

The whole scene came alive before him, its roar, the pounding smash and recession, the spindrift. It was only in a final automatic blindness of the will that he himself—staggering, swept away, on hands and knees again, head clear of the swirl and crawling, swept on and up, digging in, clawing the sand against the suction—had finally drawn clear and fallen in a dim consciousness by the skipper, hardly a consciousness at all, only a something that still went on fighting its own fight with the sea.

But these men knew the wind in its every point, the temper of the sea and the endurance of the rock, knew what could be done or couldn't, what might be done or just might not; and their decisions were clear. They could not beach her on the strand or the surf would swamp them. They were working over towards the east side of the little bay, for, as Christina must have heard them say later by the fire, the wind was a point or two in the east. The cliff wall was not all sheer and smooth there, but broken, with streaming ledges and a cleft that choked noisily. He saw the spot they were making for, the outjut of flat black rock they were going to come in behind; now they were feeling the drive shorewards of the tripped waves, they were holding on, pulling now, pulling away, but coming nearer the rock, slowly falling towards it, faces watching, getting ready. . . . It was Iain Og who missed his oar and fouled Kennie's when the big wave lifted them; she was round on them; Iain MacNeil jumped to fend her off, jumped onto the rock; he had her for a moment; then he slid, his feet went from him, and as she rose to fall against the rock his body acted as a fender. . . . He died calmly a little later, stretched out on the sand.

Iain Og had gone to Australia.

He could not speak to Christina.

He could not speak to Christina, because something vast and significant swept his mind, swept it clean of all reason for his being there. His brows gathered. But he could not dismiss Iain Og's departure for Australia; he could not leave it alone.

"When did he go?"

"Two years after the war was over. He was in Glasgow first. He was working at the docks. Then his mother got a letter. He was on the sea by that time; he must have posted it when he was leaving."

"I remember Lachlan Mor himself telling me how great an oar Iain Og pulled on that day. Many a grown man, he said, would have been shamed by the boy."

"Yes, they said he pulled a great oar. They were—they were extra kind to him."

He nearly groaned aloud. He had seen it, a kindly thoughtfulness for the boy, a quiet way of taking him now as a man among themselves. And he had fancied he had understood it all!

"They wouldn't be wanting him to go," he said as calmly as he could.

"No. Kennie and himself would often be away along the cliff heads having a talk at night. He was fond of Kennie."

"Did he ever talk to you—or anyone—about why he went?"

"No," she said—and paused. "He just said he would like to see the world."

Emotion had touched her voice at last. He did not look at her. Iain Og would have been about a year older than Christina. A whole drama went on behind the words. Dermot saw the scenes, the colours on the arable plots, the croft house here and there with its blue peat smoke, the two open boats drawn up below the sand dunes, the cliff-heads . . .where Kennie and Iain Og took a stroll in the darkening, away from the too familiar places . . . Kennie's easy friendly voice, the indirect talk . . . and, behind it all, an inexorable decision taken by a boy, because he had missed his oar.

It was like fate. It was, thought Dermot, the sort of thing that had appealed to the Greek dramatists, and his mouth caught an ironic twist as it blew the cigarette smoke across the table. Without the kings and the queens, without the great ones, without the gods. His eyes wandered among the small groups in the wide lounge, sleek and comfortable and well-dressed. At one table of five the three women laughed with a thin suppressed laughter, nervous with the delight of being able to laugh, of enjoying a male story. Then the five heads were lowered again, listening, and the lounge was decorous and hushed.

"Look," said Dermot in a brisk sensible way as he tapped ash into the small bronze bowl, "I was going to ask you about yourself. Did you get your handbag?"

"No."

"Didn't you? There's an awful lot of that sort of thing going on. You haven't heard from the police at all?"

"No."

"Where did you say you were working again?"

"In Lomond Mansions, but—I have left there."

"Have you?"

"Yes. I'm staying with Mrs. Mure just now."

"Look here," he asked, "did you tell the police—did you give them your new address?"

"No."

"Well! How would they know where to find you?"

She did not answer; she was withdrawing into herself again.

"Now listen to me. I know fine how you feel about the police. You wouldn't want anything like that to appear in a newspaper. But I don't mind the police a bit. They haven't found my chart for me yet. I'll be looking in there to-morrow. I could ask them about your bag if you like."

He saw that she was hesitating.

"I owe—your folk—a lot," he said quietly. "I hope you would trust me to help you, if I could. At least, I could ask about your bag, surely?"

"All right," she said in a low voice.

"Tell me," and he was now regarding her as though a sudden thought had struck him, "there wasn't anything —very private in the bag, that you wouldn't want them to see?"

She looked up at him. "What makes you think that?"

He smiled. "We all have private belongings that we

would hate anyone to see, much less the police. Heavens, don't let that worry you!" He leaned back, the smile deepening.

"It was not my own. I can't tell you. Something happened."

He leaned forward and under cover of the table put out his hand, caught one of hers, pressed it, patted it, and drew his hand away.

"I'm not asking you, Christina. Don't tell me if you don't want to. Only, I know the police. I know how they work. If I could help you, I would."

She did not show much, but he knew she was distressed now.

"If only you could give me an inkling of what it was," he said, "then I would know better how to handle them. That's all."

"I don't know what it was——" She stopped.

"All right, all right," he said, and the quick pressure of his hand was once more friendly and reassuring. "You have told me nothing. Queer things happen these days. That's fine. Look, I'll give you my address. And if ever you're in any difficulty——" He took his card from a pocket-book. "A new bag?" He smiled.

"It's not my own," she murmured, putting his card into it.

"And you lost three pounds. Now please don't think me rude, but—if I could loan you the money or anything——?"

"No thank you. . . . That worried me, too. It was a money order for three pounds, not the three pounds themselves, and I don't know if I told that properly. I bought it that day for sending away."

"But it's the same thing. Only better for you—because, if the order was filled in, then no one can cash it, but—was it to your mother?"

"Yes."

"Good. I'll find out from the postal authorities exactly what should be done in a case like that. Then I'll see you about it and we'll fill in all forms. Everything is forms nowadays!"

Under his cool friendly talk he had seen her distress tremor dangerously for a moment and then begin to ebb.

"I wonder what they are thinking of the world situation on Cladday just now?" he asked.

Her smile came through. There was something very distinctive, very individual, in the slow way it broke upon, almost transformed, her face. After all, this girl *had* thrown her arms round the cow's neck.

"Tell me, is old Seumas still alive?"

"Yes."

"He must be ninety?"

"I think so. He should be that whatever."

Now she was finding it easier to speak. He could see relief in her face, in the brightness of the dark, really beautiful eyes.

"He was a remarkable man. He impressed our skipper no end," he said.

"How is Captain Laird?"

"Not too bad. He goes about, but he has got to be careful. He never completely recovered. The broken ribs did some sort of permanent damage. I see him occasionally."

"Seumas came to think a lot of him."

"But nothing, I should say, to what he thinks of Seumas." He considered her with a speculative humour. "Old Seumas gave him something that he will never lose. An attitude to life—a way of living—something like that."

"He would," she said quite naturally.

74

"He came into the office about a week ago." Dermot's cheerful humour was mounting. "He told me he would like to make the trip to Cladday just once more. I said to him—knowing it would draw something—I said to him: 'I thought you would have had enough of that region.' He looked at me, smiling, with something behind his eyes, and said: 'Perhaps it was worth it.' "

"Seumas gets his box from him every New Year."

"Does he though? I didn't know that."

"Yes. It's an event."

"Is it? What a pity he won't be able to include a drop of whisky, times being what they are."

"He does."

Dermot laughed. "He'll never forget the kindness shown to him in Seumas's house after we carried him there." He hesitated. "You won't mind if I ask you something?"

She glanced at him.

"It's merely about the moon," he said.

Her smile held embarrassment only.

"The skipper—Captain Laird—he got very interested in some of your old customs. So did I, for that matter. I told him about how I had seen Anna making her bow to the new moon. I had to tell him—because—well, that's what first brought suspicion into your grandfather's mind—the way he found me spying, I mean. Anyway, the skipper asked Seumas about it, asked what Anna had said to the new moon. They were friendly by that time, and Seumas had been R.N.R. in his day. But what I can't remember is what Seumas himself said about the moon. You won't remember?"

"There were many old sayings."

But he was not going to be put off now. For he knew the native reluctance to speak of such things, the instinctive secrecy with which they hid them from the stranger.

"The way he explained it," said Dermot, "was something like this: 'The moon for us, she is our lamp at night. We see her travelling on her course and steering the full tides. Many a time when we would be running for Cladday at night in a dirty sea, wondering sometimes if we would make the shore, would we be saying a verse to Himself in praise of His help and for the guidance of His white moon.' " Dermot paused.

Christina sat quite still, her head lowered.

"What I can't remember *exactly*," said Dermot, "is the verse."

"It would be in Gaelic," she said.

He knew she was still putting him off. The middle finger of her right hand was drawing a short line, over and over, on her knee-cap.

"I know. But they must have put English on it, for of course it was in English the skipper had it." Then he regarded her curiously, for a memory came back to him. "You didn't help with it, did you?"

"Sometimes I would be helping with writing down what we wanted from the Main Island. My grandfather and Seumas didn't bother with writing themselves; and Iain Og was nearly as bad."

He laughed. "And the little school was closed at the time. I remember. It was the summer holidays."

"Yes." She lifted her head and looked across the lounge. "It will be getting late. It's time I was going."

"Very well. If you won't tell me, you won't. It was only something about the moon being the lamp of the ocean."

A faint colour came to her face. Her eyes glistened. "I have been trying to remember."

He waited.

Then sitting there, looking across the lounge, in a low clear voice she said:

"Glory to Thyself, O God of life,
For Thy lamp of the Ocean,
Thine own hand at the tiller,
And Thy love behind the wave."

Grear's hands never fiddled with things on his tidy desk. Now, from an ink stain which they had been examining with a mild sceptical humour, his eyes lifted quickly to Dermot's face. "You're quite sure?"

"Absolutely certain," Dermot replied. There were moments when Grear irritated him. "If Christina was not dead genuine, then you'd better wash me out. I just wouldn't be safe talking to her."

"That seems clear enough."

"She—well, she was moved. To suggest that she could have acted all that, from being the maidservant out for the evening in an expensive hotel to . . . ! There's a limit. For a time I even forgot what I was there for. We had certain experiences in common. I was positively moved."

Having considered his ink spot again, Grear leaned back. "Let me put it to you like this. Supposing Christina is questioned about you: will she say that you were dead genuine?"

"I should hope so. Certainly."

Grear's eyelids flickered.

Dermot's neck suddenly got hot. "But I *was* genuine."

"Even when you made it clear to her that you didn't

know that the police had found her handbag? At least *you* may take the credit of having acted very well—whatever Christina did."

"Yes, but . . ." The heat went into Dermot's face. He tried to smile. "Very well. You'd better wash me out. It's not my kind of business, anyway."

"From my point of view a girl can act *at least* as well as a man. That's all I mean—and I mustn't forget it. Now tell me this: why didn't you press Christina to tell you how these names were put in her bag?"

"I—didn't want to make her suspicious. I had got from her that it *was* put in her bag and that she didn't know what it was. I felt that was the important thing."

"Because you also knew that I, through the police, should know how actually it happened?"

"Well—perhaps."

"Your instinct was right, and now Christina may trust you. Let me tell you how it happened. There was a raid on a small dance hall. Ostensibly the police were after two suspects in that recent hold-up where the girl in the country post office was shot. They were very nice about it: merely a matter of establishing personal identities. Christina, as it happened, was in the ladies' cloak-room when the police entered and told everyone to stay put. A certain blonde slid into the cloak-room. She had only a five seconds' lead of the policewoman, so she was pretty slick in dealing with Christina's bag. The one thing you have definitely helped to clear up is Christina's ignorance of what was put in her bag. We suspected that she was ignorant. Now I know."

"Thanks—even for small mercies! Could you tell me who the blonde was?"

Grear considered him. "Why do you ask?"

"It wasn't, by any chance, a Miss Donaldson?"

"It was."

Dermot held Grear's eyes. "You—the police were also interested in a fellow named Deas, Ben Deas?"

"Right again."

"I happened to meet them for a moment outside the concert hall. That's all. I know nothing about them."

"Purely intuitive? Pretty good."

"I wouldn't say that. Merely accidental."

"Why then mention Deas—and not Ganson the violinist or Ellen the singer?"

As Dermot had not mentioned the meeting outside the concert hall, he now realized that it had been observed.

"So you knew," was all he could say.

Grear was thoughtful. "Also, you didn't mention the fellow Macrae."

"He's—he's a seaman. He should be all right."

Grear didn't even smile. "I'm not making suggestions. But if you could use a fellow like Macrae to get a slant on Deas—that might be useful. Only, of course, you know nothing. Your interest is entirely in Christina MacNeil. I'm not trying to prejudice you in any way. It's the freshness of your approach that—uh—could be effective."

"I see."

"Let me tell you one thing more. I can see that, in a way, you resent, let us say, what appears to be a suspicion of Christina. Now you are a very intelligent fellow, Cameron, and, if you thought for a moment, you would understand that we simply could not afford to waste time on vague suspicions, for time is the very essence of our situation—to a degree that might surprise you, if you knew more. And please don't imagine I know everything. I am told from above no more than is supposed to be good for me on the plane on which I work. Let me put it like this. When someone somewhere presses the buttons, you'll find yourself skipper of a small craft. But, in that position, you will not expect to be informed of the private

79

decisions, the over-all strategy, of the admiral in charge of the north-western approaches. Will you?"

"I get your point."

"I have to be careful—apart from security reasons, and on my own level I have certain powers of discretion—I have got to be careful *not* to tell you anything that might be a nuisance to you in a tight corner. It's always easy to deny, with conviction, what you don't know."

Dermot nodded.

"Now about Christina—for at least she is on the fringe of something that is within my province. There was one affair that troubled us a bit. It actually got into the press. We did our best to trace the source of the leakage. Often it is difficult to be definite, but a real suspicion has to be followed up. It actually concerned your friend Mrs. Spicer. Perhaps you observed that she liked talking?"

"She goes on addressing imaginary meetings, yes."

"Not so imaginary at times. Her husband was a commander who would have gone further. There are certain old dames like herself, all naval through family or marriage, who gather for an orgy of tea and gossip occasionally. Now they would never give anything away. The very opposite. They are tough dames, full of the honour of the Senior Service. It would take too long to go into all this, but the timing was such that our attention was drawn to Mrs. Spicer's house. One of the women, whose husband is still active and knew the facts—well, had she got something from her husband and blabbed? It was devilish awkward, because he is of course utterly reliable. However, the only point for the moment is—our attention was drawn to Mrs. Spicer's, *and* the only other person in her house was the maid, Christina MacNeil."

Dermot was conscious of holding himself under observation. "But if they were capable of blabbing there, mightn't they be elsewhere?"

"They might."

Dermot lit a cigarette, his features non-committal, rather stern. He seemed thoughtful. "You mentioned the press. Wouldn't the press be more likely to get such a thing from gossip than from a secret agent?"

"Depends on the thing. In this case it was of no practical value to the enemy, no secret value. But it had propaganda value as a disintegrating factor. It was designed to make the public wonder vaguely, uncomfortably, about those in command."

"Devilish, isn't it?" said Dermot.

"Just a bit of smart work."

"May I ask if the police questioned Christina?"

"Not so far as we know. Though even there it isn't always possible to be quite certain."

"How do you mean?"

"They got orders not to question her directly. And they say they didn't. But there is always the chance that a smart policeman, wanting to pull it off, does something on his own. If nothing came of it, he might omit to mention it. On the whole, I would say that there is a chance that she may have felt, once or twice, say, that she was being watched. Why do you ask?"

"Why didn't the police question her directly?"

"Well, the whole affair may have been a trifle tenuous, shall we say? Besides, it's never so much what has been done that matters as—what may be done next."

"I see."

"Why do you ask?"

"Nothing much. I rather had the feeling that Christina was suspicious of me."

"Of you personally—or just a general air of suspicion?"

"That's difficult," answered Dermot. "It's complicated, too, because when first she knew me I was under suspicion."

81

"But that was all cleared up?"

"Yes. They realized we were not spying on them."

"Only on the moon." Grear was thoughtful. "Pity we couldn't find another moon." He sat quite still for a few moments, then got up. "This has been interesting—and helpful. When did you say you were meeting Christina again?"

"Saturday night."

"Good. It's over to you."

As Dermot walked home that night, he thought: You can't help it; the thing wants to break through and make one hell of a mess. He glanced about the quiet street. The invisible was in hiding. The streets were more than ever the alleyways in a maze. Strands that gathered together, closing in—like a drag-net about a fish. This is going a bit too far, he thought, when he visioned the gleaming salmon; what he needed was exercise. All at once he was running. For a few moments he ran strongly and purposefully, with a mounting feeling of elation and laughter. Then he stopped abruptly, hearkening, the laugh arrested on his face, his chest heaving, hoping no one had observed that particular piece of irrational conduct. When he heard footsteps running on the pavement some way behind him, he at once walked on, knowing he had been detected in his folly. This was too excruciating. What on earth could he say? But his ear had already assured him that the footsteps had stopped as abruptly as his own. He kept walking without seeming to walk too fast. He was getting away, he was getting free. He would escape yet. His footsteps slowed, his brows gathered, as the question came fully upon him: My God, am I being followed?

Anger mounted. A savage desire to waylay the pursuer and deal with him, verbally and physically, took possession.

It was a quiet street. Here were some persons coming towards him: an elderly couple and their daughter going home. When they had passed, he went on for a few yards, drew into the railing by the entrance to a house, and stopped. Light streamed out for a moment from a doorway where the three entered, then the door closed. There was now no one on the street. He had just made up his mind to walk back quietly, searching every corner with his eyes, when he realized there was someone approaching, a man, with a slow even stride. He waited. The man looked at him in passing, then paused. It was Joe.

"Is it you?" said Joe, who had a habit at times of peering with a naive searching astonishment.

"Yes. You didn't see anyone running back there just now?"

"Running?" repeated Joe, looking back. "No. Why?"

"Nothing. I just heard someone running and wondered. Been to the club?" Dermot began walking on with Joe.

"I looked in," said Joe. "The Assessor and myself have been standing at the corner of the street for a long time. We were talking about you."

"Nothing bad, I hope." He must get rid of Joe, must not invite him in. The fellow would want to talk about God or light.

"No," said Joe. "It was something that was said in the club that I didn't think was true. The Assessor agrees with me. He has a very clear mind. I think—it is very clear. It is so clear——"

"You would like to paint it?"

"Yes," said Joe, with surprise.

"That would be a bit difficult, wouldn't it?"

"The queer thing is—no," answered Joe. "But when you saw it painted, you mightn't know it was a mind."

"Folk might wonder what the devil it was."

"Yes," said Joe. "They do not understand that you can see a thing only in terms of light. Now the mind is just as real a thing as anything else."

"Quite," said Dermot before Joe could go on. "But pictures always have titles. Why not paint it and give it the title: The Assessor's Mind. You know how as children we wrote under the drawing: This is a cow."

"I don't think we did, did we?"

"I'm sure I did."

"Did you?" said Joe thoughtfully. "Are you sure you didn't show it to some grown-up persons and hoped they would see it *was* a cow?"

"Perhaps I did," said Dermot with a short laugh. "Only you mustn't expect us to see a mind, particularly when it's as real as a cow. A cow is easy."

"It's not so easy," replied Joe. "Not real cow."

"Perhaps not. And what was all the argument about to-night?" They would soon be at the lamp-post where he could bid Joe farewell.

"It was about finding a place to go to when the buttons go up," replied Joe, for whom mechanical gadgets retained their devilish mystery.

"Still at that!"

"It's very important. I know nothing more important just now. Do you?"

"It's more important, surely, that a war should not happen at all." He was quite satisfied now that he had

84

been shadowed, was probably still being shadowed. He would have to talk to Grear about it. His visits to Grear were being watched. They might have to arrange to meet elsewhere. The harshness in his voice had silenced Joe. "Don't you think so?" he added.

"Yes. Do you believe," asked Joe, "that it mightn't happen?"

The wondering note in Joe's voice was too much for Dermot. "Your belief is as good as mine. But we don't want to hypnotize ourselves into believing it *will* happen, do we?"

Joe did not answer. He had become sensitive to Dermot's harsh mood. Dermot did not mind this; he could not be bothered with Joe, not at the moment. "You haven't told me yet where I came into the argument." His voice was cheerful as he stopped. "Let's hear it; it will be a nice parting thought."

"It was just about the sort of place to go to when the buttons go off," said Joe. "Basil said that it was all just escape, escapism."

"How original of him! Though I seem to remember that we had agreed not to maul that word any more." He was looking back along the street. Why hadn't he turned and taken Joe the other way to look for the runner?

"Yes," said Joe, troubled. "But he went further this time, for the Assessor challenged him. It was over your chart."

"What about my chart?"

"They were wondering if you had got your chart—that's what started it. Basil said that your chart was a perfect instance of escapism because it explained it."

"In what way?" Dermot was watching Joe's face, upon which the light from the street lamp fell directly.

"Because, he said, you were escaping back into a more primitive order of society. You were not merely running away: you were running back. He said that your interest in old Gaelic songs——"

"One minute, Joe. Did Basil introduce my liking for old Gaelic songs? Did he mention it first."

"Yes, because I remember being struck by it as something new."

"You never actually heard me talking about it in the club?"

"No."

"All right, go on."

"I didn't agree with him," said Joe. "And the Assessor said that an explorer has often to go back to find the way he's missed. But Basil wouldn't agree with that. He said it was a throw-back, a sheer piece of atavism. He got worked up. He said you were looking for your childhood. He used the word primitive a lot. I questioned him about that, but he merely answered that I was a child."

"And then?" For Dermot could see that Joe was troubled, could see the troubled soul in his face, and he wanted to savage it a little. This was something so unusual in the way of a reaction that he was conscious of enjoying it, of appreciating its tonic quality.

"Then," said Joe, "he finished by saying that you would end up in the womb."

Dermot laughed.

Joe looked uncertain, a little lost, as though suddenly one whom he thought he knew well turned out to be another kind of person. The skin below his eyes puckered upwards, and the fine creases were like an ambush holding the hurt eyes. And he tried to smile.

"He's quite right," Dermot declared. "Basil has a very considerable analytical power—when it comes to things touching the mind. He's got a certain watching cuteness. He's like a weasel. He knows the holes in the dyke."

"Yes," said Joe. His lips, which had a habit of pressing

tightly together, relaxed, and the tip of his tongue wet them. "Yes."

"And he has teeth. Have you ever seen a weasel hanging on to a rabbit? It gets its teeth into the rabbit's neck. I once saw a rabbit run away. But the weasel hung on. It floated against the rabbit like a brown ribbon. The rabbit didn't run far. It was squealing."

Joe stared in bewilderment, wet his lips again, and shifted uneasily, obscurely excited.

Dermot saw that he was feeding Joe pictures. But back in his mind he was trying to estimate the exact significance of Basil's reference to Gaelic songs. One thing, however, did look fairly clear: Basil seemed to be accepting the chart as a personal escapist affair. In that case, he had put it over on Basil all right. He glanced back along the street again.

"But you don't really think he's right?" Joe asked.

Dermot looked at him. "I do. I think he's exactly right, precisely."

Joe's lips went adrift as he stared at Dermot, lost.

"Oh, come on up, Joe, and have a drink," said Dermot. "I think there's a drop left in the bottle."

It's extraordinary, Dermot was thinking as he strode along, how this business gets a grip of you. More extraordinary how it acts on you like a chemical, so that the very juices in your mouth have a different taste. He glanced about him, very much alive, a grin on his face. The more the strands got a grip on you the more you wanted to burst through them, to tear through in a bloody good fight. There were a few things that could do with destroying all right.

As he passed the spot where Christina had stood against the railing, with bent head, weeping, his expression merely caught an extra sardonic quality. The myth was already losing hold. A maid servant and her handbag didn't amount to much—once the mind ceased being sentimental about the individual. Right enough, it didn't amount to much; to next to nothing; to damn all!

And that was a very odd picture of Grear that had come from—where? He had suddenly seen it inside his mind, all complete and finished. Undoubtedly, though, it had come from, had its genesis in, the Indian statuette he had seen as a boy when his father had first taken him to call upon old Mr. Armstrong, who had had a white beard with two points, slow movements and a Chinese grace. He had never found out—never asked—whether it had been a god or a devil. The elbows stuck out, the hands were up, the knees were thrust apart sideways, as if the god or devil had sprung up, or was about to spring, and its expression was one of piercing surprise, of a devilish penetration. For some mysterious reason, he had never thought of it purely as the figure of a devil, but rather as the figure of a god with the power of a devil.

To apply this to Grear was absurd. Yet into his mind, fully born, Grear had come in this guise. A statuette about a foot high, with Grear's excessively clean face, elbows and knees stuck out—as though a cord coming down through the fundamental orifice had been tugged.

First Christina—and now Grear! But Christina weeping against the railing was a dim figure and her clothes were dark, whereas the statuette of Grear was in clear light, with a shine on the transparent varnish that brought out the bright flesh tints.

He would find out about Christina. He would pump her. By taking her to the same hotel to-night he would defeat her first strangeness. She would feel more comfortable now. And, being a girl, she would enjoy it. Women liked being taken to a much more expensive place than they were used to. They loved it. It always made their eyes shine.

He swung into a tramcar. Strap-hanging, he lay over, hit knees, to let the conductress pass. Did the non-humanist like, or dislike, humanity's smell? Probably liked it, snuffled it: smell's perversion. The collective smell. He suddenly saw quite clearly that Mrs. Spicer could never invent the story about Christina's using her bath salts. One up for Christina! What the blazes was Mrs. Spicer, wrinkled as an elephant, wanting with bath salts, anyhow? He tried to turn his face away, to contort himself, so that the laughter would stay in his belly. He began to feel happy. For there had been a tendency in him, a slight tendency, to sentimentalize Christina. He stooped a little and looked through the glass, but realized that no one could tell from such a position, in such an urban milieu, if there was moonlight about, and the moon must be up. Anyhow, it would be presently!

Where he got off the tram, the queue helped to congest the street, and he suddenly saw Deas pushing his way along. He was talking to a fellow whose pale face and hat suggested a superior office job. At once Dermot turned his face away, making up his mind that he would not recognize Deas. He had the perfectly simple excuse that he had met him only for a moment at night during hurried introductions. He followed them at a little distance until they turned down a quiet street. When he had passed the opening he stopped and looked at his watch. He had about ten minutes to spare. Would he go after them or not? He decided against it, for Deas would almost certainly recognize him and there was no good putting notions in his head. Dermot's position was simple so long as he was openly interested in Christina only.

When he came to the close leading to the door of the tenement house in which Christina stayed, he paused, went on, turned back, and looked at his watch when a couple of girls inspected him. They went off with a giggle. With his black felt hat, thick black overcoat, muffler and leather gloves, he would be noticeably clad in this dim region of decaying slum. Yes, he was being noticed, but clearly by no more than the curious passing gaze. Why not call for Christina? It was the proper thing to do, anyway. He strolled into the close, stepped up and into the stone-flagged tenement entrance. But now he paused again. He had said he would meet Christina outside, at the spot where they had parted. It might embarrass these people if he went in, and it would certainly hold him up, with little enough time as it was for a table at dinner. As he stood no more than three paces from the entrance, he heard steps coming into the close and involuntarily backed flat against the wall, so that anyone entering would have room to pass, while with lifted head he gazed up the stairs expectantly, thus shielding his face.

But the footsteps stopped and an anxious low-pitched voice said, "No, I don't think I'll come up."

"But why not? There will only be the three of us."

Dermot could hardly believe he was not being seen.

"No. I must think more about it. Hell, I must think more about it.'"

"'But we have gone over everything. You must meet him and he doesn't want to be seen with you."

"No, Deas. Give me time. You have no idea how the

place is watched. As I say, we'll be working late next Friday night. I'll make myself the last to leave. I'll go to the strong room. I could study what I'd have to do—time it."

Slowly Dermot lowered his head, pushing it back to the wall, and slowly switched his eyes to the entrance.

"Another rehearsal!" said Deas. Dermot could see the back of his coat as it swayed into sight and out again. Their voices were little above an intense whisper, but just audible to his breathless listening. Before his companion had stopped him, Deas must have seen most of the dimly-lit passageway and felt sure there was no one there.

"You don't understand," said the other voice desperately. "When you take the keys off him, there will be a hell of a row and extra precautions; Christ, you don't——"

"But we won't take the keys off him. I've told you that. It will be a plain case of his money, his pocket-book. They'll only take an impression of the keys. See here, Mackie, I know how you feel. But what you have to do is dead simple. You'll be given a complete set of his keys. You'll open the strong-room door—take the doings—shut the door—get your coat on—have your usual word for the watchman and the fellow outside—then the following night——"

"But supposing——"

"Listen, Mackie: there's no drawing back now. You know that. We're going up here——"

High up a door slammed. Descending footsteps rang on the stone stairs.

"God, there's someone coming," said Mackie desperately. "Let's have a drink, just one. I want to have a——"

"All right."

Dermot's body leaned solidly against the wall and

strength oozed out of him, for he had been excessively strung up to cope with the entrance of the two men. He listened to the descending feet, a woman's shoes clicking on stone steps, walking along a short landing, clicking again down the hollow well, coming steadily rather than gaily, but coming. . . . There they were, neat ankles, neat legs, really attractive legs. . . . He left the wall and walked slowly to meet her, smiling, his hat in his hand.

"I'm glad you were able to come." He shook hands. "And how are you?"

"Fine, thank you."

"As a matter of fact, I was standing here wondering if I should go up. Would Mrs. Mure have minded?"

"I'm sure she would be very pleased."

"You think so? I liked her voice. But I thought perhaps there was someone in?"

"There's often people in at night."

He glanced up the stairs, amused and interested, as if he might still go up, for he wanted to give Deas and Mackie time to reach their pub.

"Some time I would like to go up, if you wouldn't mind. But not without letting you know."

"Mrs. Mure would be very pleased, I'm sure."

"Do you know whom she reminded me of?" And after he had made up a fantastic story he wondered aloud what he was standing there for, laughed with good humour and led Christina forth. They got into their tram on the main street without a sight of Deas and his friend, and as they clattered along he found himself in an extraordinary good humour. He hadn't felt so light-hearted for months. It was so genuine a feeling that it astonished him, brightened his wit, and in a wild contrast, which included Anna and her cow, made Christina's smile break into a short laugh.

"That's better," he said. "I was wondering if you had forgotten how to laugh. Tell me, do you never have a wild longing to get back to Cladday, just to see the sea and look far off without things getting in your way?"

"Sometimes."

And over dinner he asked, "Do you mind if I tell you how first we met your grandfather, Iain MacNeil?"

"No."

"You're sure? Because I wouldn't like you to think I would ever——" He paused. "I'll tell you something." His eyes gleamed. "I have a friend, a quiet solid man, with real fun in him. He's the sort who understands the words that are not said. He knows all about ships and what they're worth. We call him the Assessor. Well, a few mornings ago the two of us were going to a conference at a lawyer's office. As we were walking along the street, *the sun* suddenly burst through. 'Who was that you lifted your hat to?' asked the Assessor, for he had lifted his hat politely also, of course, but on looking round he couldn't see the lady."

Christina regarded him with a curious, almost blank surprise for a moment, as if she couldn't understand what he was talking about, then he saw understanding warm her face as she took up her knife and fork again.

"Odd thing was, I must have lifted my hat that time almost without thinking. I like doing it. It's the sort of secret that gives me the greatest pleasure. But for heaven's sake don't tell anyone!"

She was quiet, she had little to say, but to-night she seemed softer. The occasion was still a little too much for her, but she was not overcoming it by merely being self-confident, or playing up familiarly. She remained herself. She would always take a little time to find her bearings. There might not be much subtlety in Christina, but there was a curious authenticity, like some of those jade ornaments with a life of their own that yet in some withdrawn way seemed veiled to the stranger's eye. He was talking so much that normally the sound of his own voice would have wearied him, but now somehow it did not matter.

"That kind of morning with the mist just lifting. You feel your skin soft and you taste your lips. You could see the white growing whiter, ballooning out—then the sun was through. And there was your grandfather by the two boats, raising his hard-peaked hat. The skipper saluted as we ran upon the sand. We did not know who the man was. We did not know he was the coastwatcher. I don't suppose he got much for it?"

"He got five pounds in the year," said Christina.

"As much as that!" Dermot laughed. He wanted to go on laughing quietly. "It would be an ancient appointment," he said. There seemed to be centuries of history in these five pounds. "Perhaps for the Spanish Armada." He cut a piece of meat. "You do my heart good," he added with an impersonal frankness that was part of the fun and the memory. "I can still hear his 'Good morning, Captain', in reply to the skipper, and then this conversation took place:

SKIPPER: At least I have brought a fine morning with me.
MACNEIL: Indeed you have, and there was need for it.
SKIPPER: Yes, a bit rough last night. I thought I had better make contact before turning in. We're patrolling here and I should like a word with the coastwatcher.
MACNEIL: Very good, sir.
SKIPPER: Perhaps you'd be kind enough to tell him that I'll come ashore in the afternoon.
MACNEIL: The afternoon will be very suitable, sir.
SKIPPER: His name is—Iain MacNeil.
MACNEIL: I am that one."

"Oh, that's like it!" said Christina and her face lit up as if she had been handed a present.

"But the next bit of conversation was really good," said Dermot. "The skipper said something about wreck and it's not that Iain MacNeil showed anything—or didn't. Talk about the veiled manners of high diplomacy! 'Och,' he said, 'there will be some bits of timber in on the rocks on the east side, but it's not easy always to be getting at it.' "

Christina smiled back. "That was a trouble."

"Yes?"

"He had always to report what came ashore. And it was not always easy for him—because of Kennie—and Iain Og, who was worse."

Dermot laughed. "I liked Kennie."

"Ach, he was lovely," said Christina impulsively.

He remembered Kennie as a very small man, with a deeply lined face, like the face of a leprechaun, an ugly face with something in it that attracted like a magnet, so still it remained in its own field. He had a big pipe and spoke to a stranger with a solemn remoteness.

"I suppose they would sometimes be playing tricks on your grandfather?"

"They would. Kennie might come in about and *happen* to see Grandfather, and after a time he would say, 'The boy and myself was half thinking we might take a turn out round to the east side to see if any fish have come on the ground. The weather is taking off and it is going to be a good night.' And Grandfather would say, 'You'll be wanting me with you.' And Kennie would say, 'Not if you have anything better to do, for it's only a trial we were thinking of giving it. Don't you be bothering now. Indeed we may not be going at all. But the boat's nearly afloat. We'll see.' And he would say something to me, and he would smoke his pipe, and then he would be walking away."

Christina's emergence excited Dermot. He knew that for these moments it was almost as if she had been talking to Iain Og. For, of course, to Kennie or Iain Og she would talk. She would not be dumb. He was afraid to look at her.

"They would have seen something floating in." He nodded in understanding, a humoured wonder in his face. "And I can imagine Kennie saying to Iain Og, 'Wouldn't it be the greaty pity to trouble him, and him with his official position?' "

"How did you know?" asked Christina, her eyes bright.

"But what happened if they got something? I mean they would want to share out, and your grandfather——?"

"It's not much they ever got, and if it was real wreck Grandfather always reported it. But sometimes—there was great fun. It was like a play. I would get the whole thing out of Iain Og beforehand."

"Tell me something. You're making me smell the sea."

"I remember some tins of tobacco once; it was good tobacco, but Kennie said he wasn't after enjoying it at all because himself wasn't having a smoke of it. So one day in the passing he gave Grandfather a whiff, for it had a lovely smell. 'What's that you're smoking?' Grandfather asked. 'Indeed, is it asking me you are?' said Kennie. 'How should I know, though on the Main Island they were saying yesterday that it's the very best American cut plug. But try it yourself and see.' 'But surely,' said Grandfather, 'you know where it came from?' 'That's just what I don't know. And I can at least say for Iain Og and myself that we hadn't the bad manners to ask.' "

"That's a beauty!" said Dermot.

"I nearly gave it away," said Christina, "because when Grandfather had his head down filling his pipe with the tobacco Kennie winked."

Dermot laughed, pushing his plate away. "I can see

now why Iain MacNeil became remote when our skipper mentioned wreck."

"Cheese, sir?" asked the waiter. But they elected to have coffee in the lounge.

"And how are things getting on with you?" asked Dermot as he lit a cigarette. They had actually found the same two chairs in the lounge as on their first visit and Dermot had said, "This is luck."

"All right," answered Christina politely rather than with assurance.

"I have brought a form from the post office about your lost money order. You'll sign it before we go. No hurry."

"That's very kind of you."

"For the order is lost, I'm afraid. I went to the police station. They have got your bag."

"Have they?" She glanced quickly at him.

"Yes. But the money order was gone."

"Was—was anything in it?"

"No. Just the usual business: the thieves take everything out of the bag and then chuck it away. It's safer for them that way."

She did not say anything.

"They wouldn't give it to me, of course. You'll have to identify it and sign for it."

She was looking faintly distressed, beginning to withdraw.

"There's nothing to be afraid of," he said lightly. "And you must go to the police station. Otherwise—they might wonder." As she remained silent, he added with a smile, "Why should you be afraid of the police?"

"I don't know," she murmured, with an obduracy that anyone might have mistaken for stupidity, for a mere unintelligent shrinking. As he sucked his cigarette and looked at her from narrowed eyes, he thought: Either this is man's instinctive fear of the police state or—something more. He tried to estimate coolly just how much there might be in Grear's suggestion of her acting and he realized that the most perfect acting of all would be not the assumption of another personality but the apparent native display of one's own.

"The police have merely got to do their job. Most of them are very decent fellows, as in any other business. But —with things as they are—they have got to be on the alert. And they can't help being suspicious—they must be—if they find you or me in what they think is suspicious company. For example, that night when you were attacked I ran after the fellow who had pinched your bag. The other fellow tripped me up and I fell with a crack on my head. I was all but knocked out. Yet the policeman, thinking I was one of them seeing I had been running away, caught me by the neck to drag me to my feet and nearly choked me. I was very angry. But now I don't blame him. You understand?"

She lifted her face and looked across the lounge. Her expression was reserved, almost stolid. He wondered if she had really listened to what he had been saying.

"I'm only trying to help you. And don't tell me anything you don't want to. But—what you said about someone putting something in your bag—that's worried me a bit. Was the person who did it—what was she afraid of? You see what I mean?"

Christina was looking at the near edge of the table.

"I hope it hasn't worried you that you told me even that?" he asked.

Her fingers were gripping the edge of the table. It plainly had worried her.

"I'll never mention it, so you may keep your mind easy."

"It did worry me a bit," she admitted. "But I didn't say I had told you."

Her words were revelation.

"I hope," he said, "some of your friends haven't been warning you against me." He made it sound like a joke.

"No," she replied. "Why should you think so?"

As he attended to his cigarette, leaning towards the ash-tray, he gave her an amused sidelong glance, then drew smoke and let his eyes wander over the lounge. Poor Christina couldn't act. She just couldn't act for toffee. Her face had gone quite warm. And it needn't have done, for her "No" had been reasonable enough. But—she would be here to find out what she could. Hence the self-conscious warmth. At the very lowest, Miss Donaldson would be anxious for news. Good God, he suddenly thought, they're not beginning to use Christina as the natural simpleton, the ignorant go-between? He remembered again—it had hardly left his mind—Deas's plan for a robbery. He had involuntarily visualized an establishment like his own firm. For at least one night in the week there was a fair amount of cash in the safe. But it would more probably be a financial concern, perhaps even a bank. Sub-branch post offices were proving hardly worth while. And the leader of that little gang had been upstairs, perhaps in Mrs. Mure's. Christina had hedged when he had asked her, at the moment of meeting, if there was anyone in. She had done it quite well, too.

99

"I don't really think so," he answered. "But the world has gone a bit queer. It's getting to that point where you hardly know whom to trust." He stared in front of him and knew that Christina was looking at his face. "I detest it myself. But there it is. There are folk who think they can make this earth a paradise—and are prepared to blow it up to prove their point. I wonder what old Seumas would think of it—and of them!"

"I don't know," she murmured.

He waited, feeling she wanted to say something, but she remained silent.

"Ah well," he said, smiling, "why should we worry now? Tell me about some of the people you know. I liked that crowd I met the other night. I know Ellen the singer very well. You like Mrs. Mure?"

"Yes. She's very nice. She comes from Harris. She's been very good to me. She's kind."

Miss Donaldson worked in a women's drapery establishment. Deas was a foreman of some kind. Macrae seemed to work in small repair yards down the river. Mrs. Mure liked having folk in for a sing-song, a ceilidh. Others came as well. It was very nice.

But he asked few questions and none at all that might make Christina suspicious.

"You'll be able to give Mrs. Mure a hand. Any family or anyone staying with her?"

"No. She has two of a family, but they're not at home."

"Well, that suits you fine. Now, look, I don't want to hurry you, but I think it's time we went along to the police station."

She stared at him.

He smiled, suddenly put out his hand under cover of the table and pressed one of hers. "You're not going to lose a good bag! I'll do all the talking and look after you. You said, remember, that it was a black bag and that you had marked your initials, C.M., under the flap. You may have to describe it again. Come along."

She looked at him in dumb appeal, then he saw that it was not appeal but a glisten of something else, like trust or gratitude, and he felt it go straight to his heart.

When Joe got lost before a picture, Dermot had time for a glance at those coming in. A Principal of a university and a Lord Provost. Art was looking up! These one-man shows of distinguished foreign artists were becoming more fashionable than any Academy pre-view. And as for the populace, there would be queues to-morrow. What was a sensation in London yesterday—but here came old John Barclay of Moral Philosophy. The trumpets that blew down the walls of Jericho! He'll start revolving in a minute, thought Dermot; he'll go round and round; he'll go giddy; he'll drop. Dermot turned to the picture in an endeavour to control his features. There was something wildly exhilarating in the show, bright and mad, sinister and naive, splendidly synthetic and explosively atomic. Man's features were scattered about the walls in a riot of arrested violence, in a static threat waiting to be triggered off. "What do you think of it, Joe?"

"What?" said Joe, coming out of his private dwaum. The skin of his face had caught a greyness.

"That," said Dermot, nodding to the picture.

Joe looked back at it. His shoulders moved, but he made no sound. He was plainly overcome. There was indeed about him a profound atmosphere of despair.

Poor old Joe! Dermot thought. It must be a terrible moment when you come face to face with the master and realize that you have done, that you can do, nothing.

"I suppose it's pretty good?"

"Wonderful painting," muttered Joe.

Dermot thought he was going to cry. He got a piercing intuition of an artist's intensity, of how he could suffer. He regarded the picture with a detached wonder and had a sudden feeling that the picture was regarding him with a detached animosity. *You can think what you like*, it said, *but I know people like you. You can't get away from me*. And he knew that in its brightness, its glaring stare, it might very easily pursue him into his dreams or nightmares.

But distinguished citizens of the city, and of other cities, were now appearing in an almost steady trickle, and he moved Joe on. Joe was strangely biddable. Indeed Dermot had the impression that if he suggested they should clear out Joe would go with him. This made him uncomfortable. He hadn't thought Joe would have taken it so badly, not quite; though it was natural enough, heaven knew. Perhaps Joe had never grown up, as Basil had once put it. The child's ego was overcome by its own impotence in face of the finality of the master's accomplishment.

Dermot looked away, and saw Basil coming in. He at once returned to the picture. An elbow stuck out of it, as though shielding a face, for over its sharp angle stared two baleful cat's eyes. If they were cat's eyes. And if that sharp angle wasn't a harpoon.

"It's got power, Joe."

"Dynamic," muttered Joe, gravely miserable now, as though elevated in some austere way into the nothingness that mattered no more.

Basil had been attracted by "Helen's Apple" on the wall to the left of the entrance. He looked noticeably slight standing beside the well-proportioned figure of a man in dark grey. There were several people whom Dermot knew, including one or two sharply audible ladies. He put a hand round Joe's elbow and moved him on. Joe went automatically. Dermot skipped some pictures, giving them no more than a passing stare. Joe also stared, but like a traveller out of the window of a train as strange and fatal landscapes go by.

Two men were standing in front of a picture ahead, one of whom Dermot had met in the Parthenon Club. He was a consultant psychiatrist for whom even the most elderly and conservative medical practitioners had some respect. At once Dermot's interest was quickened and he brought Joe to an anchorage beside them. The subject of the picture was sex. Dead right! thought Dermot, thinking of the psychiatrist, whose name was Sim, and taking care to keep a few inches to his rear.

Sim's companion said, " 'Possession'," as he lowered his programme. "Well, that's clear enough!"

"No," said Sim in that curious neutral voice of his, "it should be 'Self-possession'." There was no manifest suggestion of a witticism, but then there wouldn't be.

"But—the male figure—for it is meant to be a man, obviously—I would say he's anything but self-possessed —rampant, in fact. The thing is obscene. The Director may find he's gone a bit too far in showing this."

"No," said Sim. "That's one of the beauties of this kind of painting: it's non-representational. If you are what is called a decent person you needn't know what it represents. It's a brilliant pattern of form and colour— with profound implication. Implication is debatable, susceptible of multiple interpretation."

"Multiple my eye! You can see only the outline of the

woman. He's taking such possession of her, she's so passive, that she's hardly there."

"Exactly."

"Exactly what?"

"He's not possessing her: he's possessing himself."

The man looked into .Sim's face, then back at the picture. There was a short silence. "God!" he said.

Dermot turned his face away, for he did not want Sim to recognize him yet, did not want to interrupt the conversation. The gallery was filling, but, as a small group moved from the centre of the floor towards a wall, he caught sight of Basil's back. He was still interested in "Helen's Apple" and near him stood—yes, the same well-built figure in the dark-grey suit. Suddenly Basil's elbow gave the dark-grey figure a nudge. Basil himself continued to look at the picture, but the dark-grey figure turned his head very slightly. Two elderly men were entering, one of whom Dermot thought he should know but for the moment could not remember. His interest, in any case, was taken up with Basil, who now drifted away to the next canvas as if the man beside him were a stranger. The man turned and strolled slowly after the two who had just entered, and Dermot saw his face. He did not know him. A fellow of about his own age and as nondescript as any respectable detective or junior partner: the kind of fellow, all the same, who often surprised one by having a flair for some branch of the arts. Dermot was so taken up by a half-amused, half-wondering curiosity at this by-play that he forgot to listen to Sim. The dark-grey figure was now interested in a picture before which the two elderly gentlemen had come to an astonished standstill, but after a moment or two he moved on alone to the next picture. Basil was going round the gallery the opposite way; though it was difficult to follow anyone more than a pace or two at a time. But in one of these momently opening vistas he glimpsed, before it closed, the figure of John Barclay, moral philosopher, before "Archangel and Trumpet". A silent humour invaded his features and he turned his face to find that Sim and his friend had moved away. Joe was fixed as a post; his head had drooped, his chin was on his tie, but his eyes were on "Possession".

"What were they saying, Joe?"

The blue eyes like hazed glass came upon his face.

"Didn't you hear what they were saying?" Dermot asked again quietly.

"Who?"

"The two fellows who were talking. Never mind. What do you think of that one?"

Joe looked at the picture again, but said nothing.

Dermot took his elbow and moved him on. He would have enjoyed a talk with Sim, but did not want to get entangled. Besides, it was getting less easy to talk without being overheard by many. Remarkable how people liked to listen surreptitiously at such a show. Sim was again regarding a picture with that neutral expression, but silently now. His was not a face of any outstanding character or strength. In fact it looked a trifle weary. Dermot suddenly wondered if that neutral face would inspire patients to forget it and so go on talking and talking about themselves. Whenever Sim spoke, however, you listened to him.

Just as Dermot was beginning to feel it was high time he got Joe away, he spotted Basil quite close. Basil must have seen him, for he turned quickly to look at a picture as he passed. At that moment a voice said, "How do you do?" It was Mrs. Spicer. "I've been so hoping to see you again to hear if you had any word of my dear Christina." The voice that started on an intense whisper cracked and shot up to a squeak. She was smiling. "I so hoped I should meet you, ha-ha!"

"No," said Dermot, "I'm afraid I don't know what's happened to her."

Basil had stopped.

"That's too bad. After you called I had great confidence that you would find her for me. You know about missing the well when the water runs dry, or is it the other way round, ha-ha! And," she lowered her voice to a conspiratorial breeze that whistled through her dentures, "the police called." She nodded. "They searched her room." She stood aback to regard the effect upon him. Her lips were close-hauled with satisfaction and grim humour. "I do wish you would get her for me. Good-bye." And she flashed him an amused and engaging smile as the wind took her sails and she fell away, her bows lifting to a cross sea.

Joe was as he had left him, staring at the paint now from a distance. Basil had moved on and was plainly making for the entrance by unobtrusive stages. The grey-clad man, as Basil passed him, appeared to nod, but without any real expression or recognition in his face. Dermot decided to keep the tail of an eye on him just to see what happened. But the man showed a normal solitary interest in the show, and presently left the gallery. Nothing had happened. It was all almost as mysterious as the something in the paint!

"Well, Joe, have you had enough?"

Joe looked at him, the grey more marked in the skin of his face, but he was growing restless now; his head was inclined to jerk about.

"Come on," said Dermot.

They emerged from that room of brilliant colour to the grey-dark drab tones of street and building, their normal milieu, their lives.

"Well, Joe, that's one thing I'll admit he has got: he's got light."

Joe stood quite still for some seconds on the pavement looking into a distance clearly non-physical. "That's not it," he said, almost mournfully and yet with a curious firming of his voice, a final combative hopelessness.

"Not what?"

"He uses the light for darkness," said Joe in the voice that speaks beyond the broken heart.

Dermot was staring at him.

"The betrayal of the light," said Joe, speaking only to himself. Then he walked away out onto the street. Dermot saw the lorry coming. Without knowing it, he screamed, "Joe! God, Joe, look out!" There was a screeching of brakes, a wild swerve, and a mudguard. . . . When the lorry had passed, grinding its way to a standstill, Dermot saw Joe continuing across the street at the same pace, for the mudguard had only flicked his coat.

15

When Dermot found himself staring into the tackle-shop window, he turned away, for he did not want to meet the Assessor, did not want to go to the Dial with its suffocating talk, and as he walked on he told himself with the desperate reiteration that churns the mind to mud that he didn't know what the hell to do. If he went and informed the police about the projected robbery he would have to tell them everything, exactly how and where he had overheard the talk, mentioning the names of Deas and

Mackie; and that, somehow and somewhere, was bound to involve Christina. Moreover, unless the police caught the robbers red-handed, had an absolutely fool-proof case, he himself might be called to the witness-box. To Christina and the Mure household he would not only be proved a spy, but a police spy, and that particularly stuck in his gizzard. And God alone knew what simple but incriminating part they might have for Christina in the actual robbery itself. Hadn't they already used her handbag? Her very innocence of what she was doing would be her strong suit for them. She was the most perfect decoy that any bunch of toughs could use.

Yet he couldn't tell Christina, couldn't even abduct her! Though he had appeared merely to be polite when asking about her friends, he had listened to the tone of her responses with extreme care, and it had been quite clear that she liked Deas and had a respect for him as an able man. His own impression of Deas had been that of a self-contained, capable, even sincere fellow. If he hadn't taken to him greatly it was for no other reason than that he never cared much for the eye which at a first meeting seemed to observe and sum-up.

Deas was no ordinary tough; more like one of those submerged politicals who would rob to get funds for the cause and consider the act gloriously justified. Yet—who could say? There had been famous murderers who looked like saints.

He had thought it out in every way and it boiled down to this: all he could say to Christina was, "Deas is arranging a big robbery; tell him to stop it or I'll tell the police."

History had shown the Highlander to possess one simple attribute, loyalty. Wrong-headed on occasion, stupid at times, but still, loyalty. Christina would hold by her friends as inevitably as the tide flows. She was the old loyal kind—like her grandfather Iain MacNeil, who had so finely proved it. And when she told Deas, what would that astute mind answer? Nothing in a hurry; then at least something as obvious as: "So your friend fell into our little trap. He *is* a police spy. We had to find out, Christina."

And he, Dermot, would have accomplished nothing in the sense that the gang would remain intact, but more wary. He would merely have made himself a marked man to . . . perhaps . . . the enemy?

It was irritating, tied the will in knots. As his eyes quested restlessly they saw the dignified entrance to the Parthenon Club and at once a longing came over him for its ordered life, its cool seclusion, its quiet rational voices. Old Mr. Armstrong had put him up for the club when he first entered the firm, and though he very seldom went there, wouldn't it be refreshing—medieval—to hear men like Sim and Barclay on "Possession" or "Archangel and Trumpet"! Just to sit and listen; not shout and laugh as they did in the Dial: just sit and listen. He went up the steps.

At once the quietude had him, the solid mahogany, the lighting that seemed dim, the commissionaire who said, "Good evening, sir; it's cold to-night again," the quiet words, the soothing ease, the non-intrusive, the impersonal forecourt to the chambers of retreat. Within a dim recess of the cloak-room an elderly gentleman removed his goloshes and hung his coat and hat on a peg before completing the ancient rites by washing his hands and observing his last mortal coils in the mirror that reflected with precision and perfect silence. Here the urbanities fulfil themselves, thought Dermot; and city life is justified in its civilization. Here the noise falls away and the bloody strife. How remote from the flower of fulfilment were those ribald spirits who called the Parthenon the Freeze.

And if the moral philosopher wasn't in the club, Sim the psychiatrist, by an odd chance, was. The dark leather, the padded leather, the fire. Cigar smoke. There is a moment, beyond all moments, when a man brings his yacht through Hebridean seas to a quiet anchorage in a Highland sea loch. Dermot sat down, accepting and returning the courtesies of recognition.

"I am not sure that I quite follow you." Sim continued: "These pictures represent in a way the price man pays for an industrial or city civilization. They are like a script you can read; and as a script they are more fundamental— purely esthetic considerations apart—than any kind of metaphysical or philosophical description of man's condition *in words*."

"Really? Why?" asked Leslie Morton, with the face of a schoolman long bred to exactitude.

"Because man can still understand things only in pictures. He never understands what anything is unless he can make a picture of it. A mathematical equation does not, I gather, convey the essential nature of that which it stands for. A definition of mysticism, in the same way, does not convey the intrinsic nature of the mystical experience. Or do you think otherwise?"

"We can come back to that. I am more interested at the moment in what *you* mean when you talk of the price man pays for a city civilization. Surely without the city there would have been no civilization at all. There wouldn't even have been a show of these pictures for us to discuss. And in so far as we may flatter ourselves that we are capable of a cultured discussion, there again, it seems to me, we must recognize culture as a city product."

"About the pictures," said Sim with a faint glimmer in his eye, "I seem to remember that paleolithic man executed drawings of high esthetic attainment on the walls of his caves. However, that's not perhaps the simple point I wanted to make when I mentioned *price*. If men went on living for half a million years in contact with nature, not to mention the millions and millions of years before that when life itself, so to speak, *was* nature—then you can't suddenly divorce men from their immemorial contacts and shut them up in cities without doing them some kind of violence. Industrial work, with its repetitive techniques, which the city civilization is built on, intensifies this divorcement. We know enough about biology and inheritance, and we are beginning to know enough about psychology, to have some notion not only of the extent and nature of the violence done to man in this way, but of the many ways in which this dammed-up violence expresses itself. I am not concerned with condemning anything. I am merely trying to understand just why pictures of that sort emerge now—and draw you and me and the others to look at them."

"By the way—and I do not wish to interrupt your elegant discussion—did any of you happen to observe John Barclay when he made contact with the canvas 'Archangel and Trumpet'?" John Ross brought fingertips in touch, while the back of his head retained its contact with the back of his chair and his lean legal face assumed the expression of a bland hatchet.

"No, did you?" asked Morton.

"As it so happened, yes. He has a peculiar upper lip. It's as flat as a spade. Remarkably trenchant. The eye-brows jut. The nose is lean. Perhaps you can explain it, Sim, but I got a boyhood vision of Indian brave with tomahawk."

"Did he use it?" asked Morton.

The door opened.

"Talk of his Excellency," murmured Ross.

Professor Barclay entered with a slight stoop and glanced about the floor as if he had lost his slippers. Dermot saw the faces near him draw smoothness over a repressed mirth. Suddenly the eyes were not the eyes of old fellows at all, but the eyes of boys.

Ross cleared his throat. "Cold to-night, Barclay."

Dermot got up, and before the professor could decline his chair went and fetched another for himself.

"Thank you, my boy. Hm. Courtesy is becoming rare enough for one to have to remark on it."

"Morton and Sim," said Ross, "were attempting an analysis of the wonderful picture show. Sim has the peculiar notion that the pictures are like a script, like a— how did you put it, Sim?"

Sim merely smiled.

"I congratulate Mr. Sim," said Professor Barclay. "For they are indeed—the writing on the wall." He took out his pipe. They waited for him with the greater pleasure because he looked more than usually grim. His eyes shot a glance at Ross from under the jutting eyebrows. "Have you heard about Douglas?"

"No."

"He was struck down last night and robbed."

"You mean Walter Douglas of the Home Office—at least——"

"Yes."

"When—where?"

"Last night, after leaving this club."

"Good heavens! I was talking to him before he left! What happened?"

"He was attacked by either four or five men. His doctor says he was struck under the right ear by a rubber truncheon. He was unconscious for a considerable time."

"Have you seen him?"

"Yes. I called. He says he feels fairly well, only somewhat shaky. The doctor is making him rest in order to palliate any possible after-effects from shock."

"Did the police get the fellows?"

"No. They all got away. A stranger who was passing by had the temerity to interfere and was himself assaulted.

He was able to verify the use of a rubber truncheon because he was hit by it, but only in the mouth." The upper lip went flat as a spade's blade.

Feelings of horror and anger were expressed. . . . It might happen to any one of them that night . . . And all for just under seven pounds sterling; for Mr. Douglas knew that he had exactly six single notes in his wallet and some loose change in his pockets. It was getting beyond a joke. It was getting serious.

"It's your writing on the wall," said Professor Barclay. "Loosen the moral cement and the whole edifice collapses."

Dermot looked at his watch, listened while Professor Barclay elaborated his thesis, and then, as if his appointment must now be fulfilled, withdrew. In the cloak-room he turned on a tap, leaned on the porcelain basin, turned the tap off. He stood quite still, then went to the telephone-box.

"Is that Mr. Grear? . . . Cameron, yes. I should like to see you to-night, if you're doing nothing in particular. . . . Right. I'll get a taxi."

The room—clearly his private study—was bright, and Grear himself equally bright and hospitable. The cut crystal tumbler was heavy. "Glad to see you!" Grear raised his glass in salutation.

"I happened to be in the Parthenon when Professor Barclay came in," said Dermot, as they settled down. "He told us about the attack on Mr. Douglas, who was in the Home Office, I know, but now——?"

Grear nodded as Dermot paused. "Let us say in X Department, for the rearrangement of offices has been tending, in consonance with our age, towards a mathematical nomenclature."

Dermot appreciated the elaborate humour. "Are you satisfied", he asked, "that it was a simple case of robbery?"

"So far as I know, yes. Wasn't Professor Barclay?"

"Oh yes. They all were. Can you tell me this: is there a clerk, named Mackie, in Mr. Douglas's department?"

"Mackie?" repeated Grear thoughtfully, looking at Dermot. "I rather think so." He got up as though to consult a file, realized he was not in his office and sat down again. "I rather think so," he repeated, "and I could very simply find out."

Dermot seemed to hesitate.

"Would you like me to?" asked Grear.

"Perhaps not—until you hear——" Dermot's expression grew worried. "The trouble is that it involves friends of mine, and I don't know for certain——"

"You would like me to take what you are going to say as personal or confidential—in the first place?"

"Yes." Dermot looked straight at him.

"I'll be perfectly straightforward. If it has no bearing on anything within my sphere, then I'll respect your confidence absolutely, whatever it may be."

"Thank you." Dermot thereupon gave a clear account of the talk he had overheard between Deas and Mackie.

"When was that?"

"Last Saturday night."

Grear remained very thoughtful, then his eyes turned on Dermot. "You didn't tell anyone?"

114

"No. I suppose I should have reported it to the police. I'll tell you quite frankly why I didn't." And he gave a succinct but genuine résumé of his internal arguments.

"You would rather they got off with the robbery than involve your friend Christina?"

Dermot considered the question deliberately. "Yes," he answered.

Grear looked away, as though this was perhaps a trifle beyond him.

"Also," said Dermot, "if it came to a showdown, I did not want to appear in the role of a police spy. I very definitely shall not play in that role."

"I see," said Grear. "Perhaps—you may be wise. Yes, I should say definitely." He remained quite still for several seconds. "So you did absolutely nothing about it?"

"I thought about it." Dermot also took a few moments. His manner was firm, even hard. "I did spend an evening down in that quarter with a friend of mine, but we saw nothing, no one."

"So you *have* told someone?"

"No. I didn't tell him. He's a painter, a simple man, interested in light, so I thought I would show him darkness."

Grear looked at him. "That, I think, was very clever."

"How do you mean?" But a touch of warmth invaded Dermot's face.

Grear was obviously cheered by a subtlety that appealed to him. "And you came here lest the projected robbery should apply not to simple cash but to X Department, to national security. That got you moving at once." He smiled, but his eyes had already a reserved light and Dermot knew that his brain was working away like a nicely complicated calculating machine, which in a few moments would present him with the correct action sequence. Grear looked at his watch. "His deputy, Mr.

Douglas's deputy, is acting for him. He has the keys, which, by the way, were firmly attached by their chain and tab to Mr. Douglas's trousers button. It will be a simple matter to have them microscopically examined at once. I don't want to hurry you, but—there's nothing else?"

"Yes."

The calculating mechanism stopped dead.

"It happened in that new art show," said Dermot. "I saw Mr. Douglas there, but could not remember who he was. I don't know him personally, but once at a Parthenon function—you know how you get introduced or have someone pointed out? Well, in the art exhibition I saw a little bit of by-play. A certain man, rather a friend of mine, whom I'd prefer not to name, was there also. He had a fellow with him, whom I don't know at all. But to this fellow my friend pointed out Mr. Douglas in an oddly surreptitious way. As I say, I did not recognize Mr. Douglas, and, beyond being slightly puzzled, did not see any significance in it. But when Professor Barclay a little while ago told his story of the attack, and when Mr. Douglas was mentioned as a club member, then suddenly several things seemed to join up, and I came straight here."

Grear's bright face caught a real resemblance to that of the statuette. "This," he said, "is a matter of first importance; it may involve top-level security. It's not money they hold in the strong room of X Department. I appreciate your loyalty to your friends. But——" He stopped and regarded Dermot with a curious, almost new interest. "What do you propose doing about your friend?"

"Nothing," answered Dermot, "beyond keeping an occasional eye on him."

"I am beginning to think," said Grear slowly, "that

116

your motives may not always be so simple as they seem." When his smile broke, it was clear that he thought he had proffered an almost embarrassing compliment. "If your information is as valuable as I think it is, it may well be considered one of the smartest pieces of work brought off by any of us in a long while. We can deal fairly confidently with outside sources. It's the internal hemorrhage, the leakage from *inside*, that's the deadly difficulty. *How* the enemy gets to know that a certain thing is in a certain place at a certain time. The bribery or intimidation of a Mackie, that can be investigated. But who may be behind Mackie, on the inside, Mackie himself won't know. To-day, when the hemorrhage is at a high level, money is rarely or never involved."

"There's just one more point," said Dermot.

Grear almost stared at him.

"I rather fancied the other night that I was being followed, shadowed. As it happened, I could not make certain. But it occurred to me—to mention it to you."

"Is that all?"

Dermot smiled. "I think that's everything."

Grear got up. "It's the kind of point that even I may not have overlooked. Now I'm going to ring for a taxi. I'll be able to take you part of your way home. You're going home?"

"I—think so."

"I think you'd better, if you don't mind, in case you may be needed. Have you a telephone in your bedroom?"

"No. But by leaving my sitting-room door open I'd hear it all right."

"The casual non-committal way you spoke over the phone from your club I now appreciate very much. Will you please help yourself to a drink while I get ready."

17

Joe brought them back to God, and Dermot, who often remained silent in these sporadic discussions, was letting Basil off with nothing. It was Friday night and the time nine-twenty; indeed his mind had translated the casual glance at his wrist watch into "twenty-one twenty hours", for any minute now, unless Mackie's nerve had failed him, might be one of action in a silent room in X Department. Exactly what kind of action, he had, of course, no idea, though the obvious one was to collar Mackie red-handed and then pump him. Under the right kind of inducement, Mackie, who was possibly a weak and certainly a troubled character, might incriminate others than himself. The process might well take all night, but it was this night, and Basil was here.

And Basil's intolerance had just that underlying nervous excitement which Dermot appreciated because he felt the same kind of excitement in himself. There was a certain gaiety in it, a curious enlivening sense of concealed triumph. And it did not occur to him to think that he was reading his own state of mind into Basil because the total effect had the illusion of clairvoyance.

"When I think of God," said Joe, "I don't see him as a father, as 'a bearded prophet'." He looked worried and sounded mournful.

"What do you see him as?" asked Basil, leaning forward, his dark eyes gleaming with irony.

"I—I don't know," said Joe. "But——"

"Blake saw him like that, didn't he?" probed Basil. "Blake gave him a magnificent beard, didn't he?"

"Yes," said Joe. "But—that's not it—that's not what it's *about*."

"About! I can judge only by what painters paint. And Blake painted God as a magnificent old fellow with a magnificent beard. And you don't need to look up Freud to know why. The trouble is, Joe, that none of you fellows have the courage to recognize the facts. I'm not using a word like 'truth', just 'facts'."

"You've merely got a cock-sure theory," said Dermot, "and you twist what you call your facts to suit it."

"Supposing you tell us where the experts are wrong," suggested Basil, his open hands pressing the arms of his chair.

Dermot admitted that Freud and the anthropologists had done splendid work for our enlightenment. "The effect of the father on the child—certainly. The further concept of the old father as the old man of the tribe, full of that overlording power of which the young men, growing up, are jealous—excellent again. I have seen it in a herd of stags, where the powerful stag in charge of his harem of hinds chases off the young stags whenever they come sniffing around. So one fine day the old man of the tribe is killed by the young men of the tribe because they can't stand any longer not having some of the power— and some of the harem. And that act of killing the old man is the beginning of the lovely theory, for now the sons are obsessed with a feeling of guilt. Why? Because they have lost the old security and order. This works on them—and in due course the notion of killing the old man grows into the religious notion of killing God. And so on and so forth. Wonderful stuff. But all really a made-up story; an effort at creating a myth in order to destroy one."

"You mean you know better?"

"Be rational," said Dermot. "You know that in important things psychologists differ, and anthropologists, too. For this theory of the origin of God and sin, I'm prepared to offer another which uses the facts better."

"And you're not cock-sure?"

"Half and half," answered Dermot, giving Basil's eyes a slow, deliberate, amused scrutiny.

Without movement of his head, the Assessor looked from one face to the other, but Joe stirred restlessly, staring now at Dermot.

"What?" asked Joe.

"The most primitive peoples," said Dermot, "didn't think of God as a person at all. They thought of a *force*, an inscrutable *power*, at the back of everything. They might have agreed with Bernard Shaw in calling it a "life force", only they had a clearer notion of the *force* than Shaw, at any rate a stronger apprehension of it. In short, a man's first notion of a supernatural power had nothing to do with an anthropomorphic God the Father, nor with a God the Old Man of the tribe. How man came in time to picture that power may be interesting conjecturally to psychoanalysts, but it has nothing to do with the original apprehension of a supernatural power in the universe."

"That's right," said Joe. "That's what you feel. It's behind the light."

"And it's behind the dark, too," said the Assessor.

Joe looked at him. "Yes," he said and his chest began to heave. "That's it. You've got it." He stood up and sat down.

"Good God!" said Basil. "Primitive animism."

"You hang up a label," replied Dermot, "and run away from the fact."

"When I run away from any fact, including you, you

can write your friends about it," said Basil. "Meantime that you should equate the simple fears and terrors of primitive animism with the Christian concept of God— sweet Lord Almighty, I had hardly expected such a give-away, such revelation."

"I made no such equation, as you know," replied Dermot. "But I will make an equation, if you like, and it's as near a perfect equation as dammit. You mentioned fears and terrors; what the Assessor called the dark side to Joe's light. Here in this country we might find it difficult to *picture* this fear or terror because the old picture of the Devil has gone out of fashion. But in a totalitarian country, among the ordinary humans who do the work, a new picture has taken shape. If you asked one of them to draw a picture of his fear, of the Devil that pursued him, the chances are he would draw a member of the secret police."

"Lord!" said Sandy Graeme, before his laugh came.

Talk became involved and indiscriminate and political, but Dermot knew that Basil and himself were behind the talk where the real meanings and animosities stalked around.

Joe became restless again, smothered by the verbal cotton wool. "About the sons killing the father—about sin——" he groped, looking at Dermot.

"The sons are on the rampage again," said Dermot. "They're getting ready to kill all the fathers, so that they may wallow in the *total* power. When they've finished they'll be haunted by sin once more. It's a wonderful myth."

"Yes," said Joe, and the tip of his tongue came between his lips as he looked at his private picture. "Yes, I see."

"How you love sin!" declared Basil. "How you wallow in the very notion of it! Must man forever have to crawl before the witch-doctors, the mumbo-jumbo gods of denial and sin set up—here—in this wonderful country —by the murderous capitalist caste system?"

"I should like him to crawl out, certainly," said Dermot. "You are merely making him crawl back."

"One minute," said the Assessor and he looked at Dermot. "What exactly do you mean by 'crawl back'?"

"I mean that totalitarianism is a social regress, it's throwing man back thousands of years, back to that tribal age when man the thinker, the individual questioner, had not yet emerged. Now I mightn't mind that. I rather fancy that was the golden age on earth. I have great sympathy with Basil's ideas, or rather ideals—though he may hate the word. The only trouble is that man cannot go back to an earlier culture pattern. When he tries, he destroys himself."

"Here," said Sandy, "do you mean, by totalitarianism, communism?"

"Particular *isms* are particular labels, and we argue about them, meaning different things, until we're fit to cut each other's throats. I'm referring to the fact of the police state, to total compulsion by the handful over the whole. In such a state, if I were talking freely as I am now, I should be purged, that is, shot. I want to talk freely and I don't want to be shot."

"But your primitive communal tribe wasn't a police state," said the Assessor.

"No," answered Dermot. "That's the point. To try to re-create it by police methods is anthropologically mad. You can't *now* suppress the individual spirit which has learnt to *question* authority. On this questioning of authority, this exploring, all science and art are fundamentally based."

"Are you sure you can't suppress it?" asked the Assessor.

Dermot's expression grew doubtful and stormy. "I don't know," he admitted. "Man's mind may yet be conditioned like one of Pavlov's dogs. At one time I should have said that that was utterly impossible. Now—I don't know. When I see the shadow of the police state darkening this country—I just don't know."

"This country?" said Sandy.

"Yes, this country. We cannot believe that. We think we are different. We think we could never behave like Germans, Russians, Italians, or what have you. Don't you believe it. It will be more difficult in our country to shove us over the border-line, simply because the notion of individual freedom or responsibility has had longer to sink into our marrow; but for that very reason, by God if we are pushed over by a group collaring total power, complete with *secret* police, there will be bloodier ructions here than anywhere. The submerged or instinctual impulses are the same wherever you encounter them, white, black, or yellow." Dermot's eyes had flashed, but as he finished he took out his cigarette-case as if what he had said was so obvious that it wearied the mind.

"You really think so?" persisted Sandy.

"Look, Sandy," said Dermot. "I have heard you tell of the Highland clearances in your own native parish. These bloody barbarities happened no more than a century or so ago in the Highlands of Scotland. Never mind who was to blame. *They happened.*"

"And you imply that—that——"

"The nature of the human beast doesn't change in a century, even in Britain." Dermot lit a cigarette.

Basil was sitting back, with a satiric grin on his face, showing no desire to break into the talk, as though it were beneath serious discussion.

His expression compelled Monson's attention. "You're not saying much."

"No need," replied Basil. "Such talk always drowns in its own swamp of emotional doubt." There was an unusually cool precision in the way he spoke, a relish.

Dermot looked at him. "I suppose doubt cannot arise in the mind that is already conditioned." As he smiled he saw the gleam come into Basil's eyes.

It was the gleam, the flash of teeth, in the dark hinterland behind the verbiage where they had been prowling round each other.

"Doubt ceases to trouble the adult mind that has scientifically worked out a proposition," said Basil, not leaning forward but pushing back into his chair as though to give his answering smile further scope. "Besides, your tribal theory was very enlightening— coming from one who actually *wants* to crawl back into the primitive holes and music of the Gaels."

"But——" began Joe.

Basil laughed abruptly, as though the ineffable Joe had pulled a trigger. He kept on laughing.

But Dermot knew Basil had leapt in and slashed.

Later, at the corner of the street, the Assessor said, "I'm afraid it's not the talk any more. Good night."

"What did he mean by that?" asked Joe as he walked on with Dermot.

"Talk is now a smokescreen," answered Dermot. "Let us go this way. You're not in a hurry home, are you?"

"No," said Joe. "I don't want to go home. I used to like sitting alone."

"Now the thing creeps in like a reptile."

"Yes," said Joe. "That's it."

"Clever of the old boys to have sent a serpent into the Garden of Eden, wasn't it?' '

"Yes," said Joe, and he stopped.

Dermot stopped also and looked back. "Come on, Joe."

The street began to rise and curve and now on their left trees grew beyond the railing.

"You're puffing," said Dermot, coming to a standstill under an overhanging branch.

"I was thinking," said Joe.

"What were you thinking? Let's take our wind."

Joe was still troubled over the discussion about the two kinds of regress, Basil's and Dermot's. He wanted to know wherein the difference lay. When talking to Joe, Dermot found himself using pictures, images, in a novel and even astonishing way. With anyone else the images simply wouldn't have come. The talk grew friendly and deep as the night. It was quite different from the talk in the club. Even around the same points of discussion, what was evoked seemed infinitely different. Presently Dermot's voice trailed away. "Let me think for a minute," he said to Joe.

The footsteps kept coming on, then the slight active figure crossed the thoroughfare and went up a residential street. It was Basil, going home. Dermot had stopped a little beyond the street entrance, and as he lost sight of the figure he began talking again, but hesitantly, as though listening to his own thought. He actually heard the door slam, so quiet was the night where they stood.

Their talk about meaning and purpose grew so intimate, so gentle, that Joe adventured on his profoundest convictions, and Dermot found it strangely fascinating because Joe couldn't explain himself in words. At one point Dermot had the involuntary image of Joe's trying to take some wonderful little wild animal out of a hole or burrow. It was extraordinarily difficult, because the wild animal eluded his probes. At last he seemed to think he had got it out, but for Dermot it was still at the back of the hole.

"Wait a bit, Joe," he said. "That's difficult."

But Joe couldn't wait.

"Wait, now. Give me time to think."

The footsteps came on. As they crossed the street, Dermot saw the figure. It was undoubtedly that of the man who had been with Basil in the art gallery. It went up the residential street. As the beating of his heart interfered with his hearing, Dermot wandered a few thoughtful paces down by the dark railing. "That's profound," he murmured. This time he saw the light from the door where the man entered. The conference with Basil was on. He wandered back, followed by Joe, to the same tree. "I think I have got it, Joe, though it's elusive as a butterfly. Do you know what they called the butterfly in the Gaelic in the old days? 'God's fool'."

"Did they?"

If Mackie has been caught and held, he thought, they'll be in a stew. There would have been a zero hour. Mackie at least knew of Deas and the Mures' house. If he blabbed? . . .

"It's the fool part of it," said Joe at last out of the depth.

"God's fool," said Dermot.

"Yes," breathed Joe. "God's fool."

Dermot looked at him and suddenly realized, in a flash of profound vision, that Joe was exactly God's fool.

Everything became translated a little now, and Dermot saw a paradisal landscape with Joe's strangely earnest face wandering from bush to flowering bush. He changed it to an island, a fabulous island. He began to tell Joe about Cladday; he started strolling back the way they had come, for it was cold standing.

"Heavens, Joe, it's half-past ten! I'm late!" After five more minutes he got rid of Joe.

And in a further ten minutes Basil's visitor came down the main thoroughfare. Dermot saw the tram he boarded,

126

but was too far behind to catch it himself. This did not worry him, because a taxi stance was round the corner. Besides, the man might know him.

When he got out of the taxi he went down a side street and presently saw before him the entrance to St. Patrick's Close. He did not want to draw attention by standing still. There was no one in the close. He walked on, listening, and occasionally glancing back over his shoulder. The taxi wouldn't have beaten the tram by more than a few minutes.

Occasionally a man or woman disappeared as if suddenly sucked from the street by the tall buildings. He crossed the street and disappeared into a cobbled alley, stood there with switching eyes, listening, then returned to the street and began walking back, but with St. Patrick's Close now on the other side. Three noisy youths impeded his way and one asked for a match. "Haven't got such a thing," he said. "Right y'are!" called the youth good-naturedly and they went on dribbling their imaginary football. He saw the man coming down the off side of the street. He knew his shoulders. He turned into St. Patrick's Close and by the time Dermot came abreast of it had disappeared. There was a narrow street on his left. He went into it and, seeing no one, stood with his back to the wall, searching his pockets as if he had lost something. He felt uneasy and realized he was no good at this shadowing game. All at once he knew there was someone in a doorway three yards away. His muscles tensed and his breathing stopped. He tied the top button of his coat and walked back onto the street and up towards the tram lines. No one followed him. He was now reluctant to go home, but there was no sense in giving himself away. Dammit, he would have liked to have given Basil's friend half an hour just to see if he would come out again. His next port of call might have been interesting. He

127

stopped and lit a cigarette. But he couldn't go back. It was too late. He would be too conspicuous. Christina came into his mind again. His conscience had been worrying him about her. Suddenly he decided to go home, to write and post a note to Christina, asking her to meet him to-morrow night. He must warn her.

His thoughts pursued him, and sometime during the night he woke from his vision of the sorrowing woman and fancied a sound had stopped. He wondered if Grear had been on the phone, yet, though he grew intensely wide awake as he waited for the telephone to ring, the vision of Christina did not fade. On the contrary, it developed the sort of preternatural presence that made him move his head and blink his eyes in order to get rid of it. But in a few moments, when he thought he had dismissed it, he found himself concentrating on it. The telephone did not ring, and that did not help to banish his illusions and vague menacing anxieties.

It was with a sense of relief, of gratitude, that he heard Grear's voice over the phone in the forenoon, and as he went along to the quiet hotel where they were to have coffee he was aware of an almost feverish curiosity about what had happened last night to Mackie and then in a moment was shaken by the thought that nothing might have happened at all.

This was so unlike him that he actually slowed his pace and looked around. The sun was shining and people were going about their business. Everything was normal—and yet it wasn't. It was perfectly obvious, of course, that everything was normal. Yet it wasn't. The shop fronts, the walls, the cars and buses, the human figures, were like projections on a screen that at any moment might disappear, be shrivelled up utterly. He nodded to his common sense, saying that, of course, this might very well happen, for the new atom bomb was said to be incredibly more powerful than any yet exploded. Rationalizing the illusion made it interesting. Just as the cinematic screen was a two-dimensional illusion of a three-dimensional world, so our three-dimensional might be a cinematic illusion or projection from a four-dimensional world. He smiled. But he felt wary and intolerant, watchful and antagonistic. He felt in a mysterious way that something had got a grip of him and that he was going the whole hog.

Grear's news produced on him the effect of a blow, a punch that dissipated all sense.

"Someone blundered," said Grear, "but of course I don't know everything. My chief—it was done on that level . . . I know enough for my own job. As you will for yours. But strategy——"

The odd thing was that Grear did not sound bitter or ironic. It was the same bright face. The matter had been taken out of his hands; the blunder was at a higher level. The hierarchical system remained unaffected. Grear was going on with his job. The same smile even, if now to Dermot's eyes with something waxily insipid in it.

"Look," said Dermot forcefully, "I want to understand this clearly. Mackie actually got away with the plans and no one stopped him?"

"Yes."

"Do you mean that the thing was bungled, that those watching for him made a mistake about the time and place?"

"Your information was passed on with complete precision. I saw to that. That was my job."

"But——!"

"I know how you feel. But you and I are not to blame. That's absolutely clear. Someone—and I am not criticizing—may have been——" He paused. "Someone must have miscalculated."

"Stupid?"

"Or too clever," said Grear.

But Dermot refused the insinuation. "It's beyond me," he declared straightening up. "I just can't get it."

Grear took a mouthful of his coffee and then stirred it.

"What have you done with Mackie?" asked Dermot suddenly.

"He's back at work as usual," said Grear.

Dermot stared at him.

"That was a difficult decision," Grear admitted. "There were many factors involved. For example, supposing you were to take Mackie now and put him through—any degree you like. Could you be certain that you'd get the truth and not a carefully prepared story out of him?"

"I think I'd have a shot at it. From his voice—from—the way he talked—frightened——"

"That's just it. Psychologically he seems to be the introverted type that, once the teeth are set, is more difficult to deal with than a mule. Besides, there appears to be no financial motive. At least, his banking account is in good shape. If the thing is therefore either ideological or personal—in the sense of, say, a private hate, though we can trace none—then we know enough to know how a prolonged cross-examination can be with-stood."

"But what do you gain by *not* putting him through it?"

"We may gain much—from now on."

Dermot looked at him.

"Once we tackled him everything would stop," said Grear, "including his contacts." He glanced around the small empty lounge, considered the solid wall near them with its fresco effects.

"I still don't get it. Surely the theft will raise such a rumpus inside the department———"

"Oh dear no. The theft is of the kind that need not be discovered. It is fairly certain that Mackie will try to put the plans back at the very first opportunity."

"Why?"

"Is that a serious question?"

"I see," said Dermot slowly. "If *they* knew that *you* knew———"

"They would also know that we would have to set about making new dispositions. Precisely."

Dermot was feeling netted. "Can you tell me," he asked directly, "what the plans were about?"

"Yes," answered Grear at once. He leaned forward, his lower arms flat on the small table, and spoke quietly. "There are two plans: one gives the location of what is called D.1. It tells you how to get there. Certain map-readings and signs can be deciphered. The other is—let us call it a blueprint of D.1. itself. What is D.1.? Well, now, if you care to think of an elaborate dump in terms of nuclear weapons and buttons you mightn't be far wrong. It's as important as that."

"Heavens! In that case, I just can't understand how you—how they—could let Mackie———"

"Listen," said Grear. "It's not for us to question. I can conceive that a certain contact behind Mackie may be so vitally important to discover that they had arranged to let Mackie *appear* to get away, while all the time following him with the best plainclothes men in the city, and yet through some unthinkable hitch—perhaps treachery on a detective's part—he eluded them long enough to get rid of his portfolio. I'm not *saying* it happened like that. I'm only trying to get you to understand the present actual position."

"I'm sorry to appear pig-headed," said Dermot with an uncertain smile, for Grear's tones had perceptibly hardened.

"That's all right," said Grear in an official voice. "It is also part of my duty—part of the reason why I'm here—to convey to you, from the highest level, a very marked expression of appreciation for what you have done and the assurance that it is not, and will not be, forgotten." It was a neat little speech, delivered with quiet dignity. For a moment Dermot felt that he was on parade, that something invisible was being pinned on his breast. As he grew hot, Grear grew normal.

"We didn't manage it," muttered Dermot.

"Not yet," answered Grear. "But we may. It is hoped that you will pursue your present contacts and find out what you can. I have been *instructed* to give you all this very secret information. It's a considerable compliment—or trust. It is supremely important that time is not wasted."

"But—what can I——"

"Your most fruitful contact has been Christina MacNeil." His voice grew almost amiable. "Things seem to happen when you are with her. And now I'll give you a clearer description of the plans so that you may recognize them at a glance." And Dermot listened.

He did not want to ask any more questions; he needed time to think. He was wondering if he should mention last night, when Grear asked, "I don't suppose you have any new surprise?"

"No," said Dermot, smiling back. He would have to see Christina before there would be a police raid on the Mures. He would see her to-night—if she accepted the invitation in his note.

There was nothing romantic about it: she was simply growing on him. Her face was like something seen in the corner of a wood, or rising behind a heap of grey stones on a still summer day in a deserted strath.

"You prefer that?"

"Yes," answered Christina, setting down her glass of port.

He should have thought of it before, of course. The mustiness in the flavour was like an elusive memory of an olden time; the sweetness was native to the tongue as nectar to the tongues of bees. It was fairly potent, too. It should make her very very slightly drunk.

"Everybody is expecting war and it can easily happen now," he said, for she had asked his opinion. "Would you like to go back to Cladday if it did?"

She was silent, disturbed. "I don't know."

"I could take you there," he volunteered lightly.

Her dark eyes came full on his face. "Would you be going back there?"

"I might," he answered. "Though of course I would have to go where I was told. But it would be the sea. You couldn't think of me fighting on land, could you?"

"No."

"Like your own folk: the sea is in the blood." He smiled. "Think of me, when all the lights have gone out, feeling my way in the dark into Cladday. But perhaps there would be one light."

She did not seem to understand him. "They could always see from well out the light in the house of old Seumas. They used it coming in."

"Did they?"

"Yes. When they got it in line with the light from Anna's lower down it led them between the rock off Eilean Beag and the south skerry."

"Lord! Lord!" he said softly.

She glanced at him.

"Your words are putting spells on me," he explained. "But if war was on, Seumas's light would be out, and Anna's."

Her face stilled.

"And yet," he said, "there might be one light left that they couldn't put out." He rested his arms on the table, leaning forward slightly, and murmured, "Thy lamp of the ocean."

She might be slow, but her reaction was always worth waiting for. He continued in the same voice:

> "Thine own hand at the tiller,
> And Thy love behind the wave."

He thought for a moment that her eyes were filling with tears, but it was only with light, and the strange warm embarrassment on her face reflected the colour of the wine. "Drink up," he said.

He suddenly wondered what Joe would think of her,

and in the same instant he saw her in a small house in a distant strath. That was the quality; she would endure. The shape of the bones in her face had something to do with the structure of rocks. She was self-contained, and the woman in her, grown old as the grey rocks, would still bow to the new moon. *Many a one has crossed over the black river of death . . .*

"Some time I will tell you what happened when we dug up the buried seaman. We were ashamed of doing it; that's why we waited for the dead of night; and by the time we had found out what we had to find out and buried the remains again, the sun came over the rim of the sea. For the sun doesn't stay down long yonder at the height of the summer."

He knew he was enchanting her. But then he was enchanting himself. Enchantment was a sweetness, like the port which he hadn't tasted since his student days. *Between the rock off Eilean Beag and the south skerry.* Pure poetry!

"At the back of it all there was that loyalty of your grandfather, Iain MacNeil. That was the wonderful thing. For after that secret digging-up of the buried Norwegian —when your grandfather found out about it—naturally enough he thought that we suspected him. We should have gone straightforwardly to old Seumas and told him that we must find out who the seaman was, his nationality, ship, and so on. But we didn't want to make any of you *more* suspicious of us. How could we tell you that what had made the skipper and myself appear to spy on you was the sight of old Anna bowing to the new moon and your grandfather taking his hat off to the sun? We couldn't tell you. It was—it was such an unexpected thing. The sheer manners of it was so lost to our day that we couldn't intrude, we daren't mention it. You understand that, don't you?"

In her silence understanding was strangely implicit, but she could not speak of it. Her expression moved him deeply.

"And then," he went on, "when we came back to Cladday a day or two after, there was your grandfather. I had landed the skipper in the dinghy and stood beside him, listening to the usual exchange of courtesies. I thought Iain MacNeil was quieter, more remote. And then it came. He said, 'I think I will not be any more carrying on the coastwatching. There will be no need for me.'" Dermot paused. "The skipper appeared utterly astonished, but I knew he was terribly upset. I must say he behaved very well and praised your grandfather in the right way for the fine discharge of his duties and so on. But it made no impression, I could see that. Then the skipper grew firmer. He said, 'This is a time of war. Each of us must do what he can.' And your grandfather answered, 'I have done that.' There just was no way of making an impression on him. He was stolid as a boulder. It was very annoying in a way, perhaps because we felt guilty. 'I have nothing to report,' were his last words. We had to put to sea at once, for we had our information about a U-boat in that area. The skipper was in a tough mood and said things about West Highlanders in particular. 'So damned stupid,' he would mutter. But he was hurt as well as angry. We had the certain feeling that Iain MacNeil would now retire into his hole and pull the hole in after him." He looked at her. "Did he ever say anything about it?"

"Not much," answered Christina. "He just thought that you couldn't trust him to do his duty."

Dermot felt oddly bewildered. It was as if she had defined the word "suspect". His hand actually shook as he raised his glass and finished it, though exactly why he couldn't have told, and he certainly couldn't ask her just what she implied or if she implied anything.

"It was three days after that, in the afternoon," he continued, looking across the room, "when we came back. There was a long oily swell, and as we came round the island and upon the south skerry we saw a figure out on the point of it. It was Iain MacNeil. He made a signal and we shut off. His hands came up to a funnel. 'Ahoy, there!' he shouted. 'Submarine about six miles—nor'west —four o'clock this morning.' 'How was she heading?' roared our skipper, for we couldn't go too near, as the seas were breaking on the skerry. 'Nor'east!' 'How long did you see her?' 'About one hour—then she went down.' I can't tell you how the whole thing electrified us. As Kenn opened out the engines and we swung away, Captain Laird saluted Iain MacNeil, and Iain, with the waves breaking over his knees, gave him back the salute of an old-timer of the R.N.R. My heart sang. And into Captain Laird's face came an expression I shall not forget as he stared ahead like a viking. 'I have a hunch, lads, that we are going to get her,' he said. And that night we got her. For before she shot us to bits, Jimmy had sent his S O S. We heard the bomber dive just as we copped it."

As they went into the lounge for coffee, Christina gave him a small shy smile. "It's gone to my head a little," she said of the port. It was her first personal confidence. He laughed with pleasure and gave her hand a quick squeeze.

"Yes," he said as they settled in their chairs, "your grandfather was doing his duty by his own land, and Captain Laird and the whole British Admiralty could think of him what they liked!" He laughed again. "And the curious thing is—it's all working round to the same state of affairs once more." He looked at her. "Do you mind if I ask you a question?"

She glanced at him. "No."

"Have they been asking you about me?"

"Well—yes—but——" She was definitely confused.

"Listen, Christina. Don't tell me anything you would rather not. But I'll tell you now what's happening behind the scenes." And he told her what fifth-column activity meant in the world to-day, how it was organized, its aims, and how it differed from the old kind of simple enemy espionage. Now and then he asked her a question to make sure she understood, and was a little surprised to discover how familiar the idea of a "revolution" was to her. Her own sympathies were clearly with what she called "the workers' cause". Obviously a ceilidh at the Mures' consisted of more than singing Gaelic songs.

He became genuinely interested, and when he probed beneath the words he found the place where they both met naturally. At that place "reference back" to Cladday was almost instinctive. In the last resource, this meant that his hold over her could be more powerful than any imposed by words or new ideas. When he said, "I'll tell you what frightens me about it—it's the police, the giving of all power to the police," her reaction was as inevitable as the note from a plucked string. He saw the darkening of fear in her eyes. "And not only in the enemy country, but in our own—particularly our own. I hate it—and am prepared to go a long way to stop it." His own expression darkened. "The workers' cause? Of course! You can take it from me, there is only one question left to us in this country: are we to sell the workers' cause to the police?"

"They all hate the police," she said.

He took a few moments. "Supposing your friend Deas and—and that fellow in the dark-grey suit—what's his name?"

"Do you mean James Stenson?"

"Is that his real name? A well set-up fellow, fair, like an athlete?"

"Yes," she said in a reserved voice.

"He goes up to your place occasionally." As he leaned forward to flick ash into the tray, he turned his face to her with a smile. "You're not particularly interested in him, are you?"

"No," she said at once. "It's Amy Donaldson."

"Ah! I thought Deas had an interest there."

"Yes—but——" She was embarrassed.

"So long as you are not interested in anyone yourself!"

"No," she murmured.

As he slowly crushed his cigarette in the ash-tray, he was aware that she was looking at him. The personal approach was the only one that really meant anything to Christina—as to any other woman. If he made love to her, she might—Cladday being behind them both—eventually tell him everything.

"I know you're wondering about me. Amy—being in with Deas and Stenson—has probably told you to find out all you can about me. Now the only person in all this that I'm concerned about is yourself. If I thought you might get into trouble, then I would *have* to try to protect you, if only for Iain MacNeil's sake. And, frankly, I'm worried a little. I'm worried about the police, Christina. Tell me, what did you say to your friends about me?"

"I just told them about you being in Cladday and——"

"Yes?"

"That we were just talking about it. The chart you had lost, I said, was for Cladday. We were talking of my folk in Cladday, I said, and nothing else."

He nodded. "That's fine."

"You have nothing to do with the police?" she asked suddenly.

He met her eyes and they held his with a sort of faint desperation.

He shook his head. "No." He lit a cigarette. From his

thoughtful expression it was clear that her question was something more than absurd. "Just think," he said quietly. "Amy, afraid of the police, shoved that paper into your bag in the dance-hall. You and I don't know what was on it. But the police *may* know. They said the bag was empty, but——" He shrugged. "What do you and I know? If anything is going on, if the police got a suspicion, then—well—you saw them raid the dance-hall. That's why I gave you my card—so that you would use my name, come to me, if—anything like that happened at your place. I must give you Captain Laird's address, too—in case you might prefer to go to him!"

Half an hour later, he had a fair picture of the top floor of No. 5 St. Patrick's Close. There were the usual two flats—the one opposite the Mures' being James Stenson's. Sometimes Mrs. Mure went in to clean it up. Men like Deas went there; they would be having a meeting and Mr. Mure would go through on his two sticks, for he was crippled now with arthritis, but had been a great Trade Union man in his day. Amy Donaldson was secretly in love with Stenson and sometimes called him Jack, but she went with Deas. It was very handy having the two flats on the same floor when it came to a merry evening. Christina found no difficulty in talking, once she had started, the more so as it was clear she wanted Dermot to have a good impression of her friends. That men should have their "secret" talks was perfectly natural to Mrs. Mure. It was the sort of thing men did, for it was all, as her husband said, "in the cause". That they had to be watchful of the police was, to Christina, quite natural. It was what happened in cities where the poor were oppressed.

"What do you think of this man, Stenson, yourself?"

"He's always quite nice," she answered politely.

"Sometimes he frightens you, just a little?"

"I—don't understand it much." She looked at him. "What makes you think that?"

"I was thinking of Amy."

"I—don't know," she murmured, her lashes drooping, her fingers going up to the edge of the table.

"If I knew more of what he was up to, I should feel happier for your sake—and Mrs. Mure's. But you needn't tell that to Amy! What does he do?"

"I don't rightly know."

He saw she was going to feel uncomfortable again, and said, "Come on, let's have a stroll. As the old bard said, 'My curse on gloom!' "

The talk must have relieved her in some way, for she grew almost carefree, and he was delighted with a new vivacity in her features. The wine had no doubt helped. He took her arm. "In case you run off and kiss Anna's cow."

"It wasn't Anna's cow."

He laughed and squeezed her arm. "Look, Christina, I'm probably taking a trip to Cladday in a month or two. What about coming with me?"

He felt her shrink and almost pause. In consternation, he glanced at her—and followed her eyes. They had just entered a main street where trams were running. Ten yards in front was the figure in the dark-grey suit. She unconsciously clung to his arm. He gripped her hand. "I should like to know where he's going," he said, making her quicken her steps.

"He's going out of town," she replied in a low voice.

"How do you know?"

"Amy told me."

"You don't know where?"

"No. It's somewhere . . . I'm not sure."

"Christina, would you ever forgive me if I left you now?"

"What for?"

"It's nothing to be afraid of. I should just like to know where he goes. Good night." He took her hand. He kissed her.

It was quite a simple matter standing in the same queue, getting onto the same tramcar, strap-hanging inside after Stenson went aloft, and getting off after him at the West Station stop. Dermot was wearing a dark-brown tweed coat and a brown felt hat, and as he tilted down the front rim of the hat he felt as alive as a detective in a new rig-out. He bought an evening paper in his stride and was three places behind Stenson at the ticket-office window, and thought he caught the word "Criach". When his turn came he said, "First return Criach," and, as he presented his ticket at the barrier, saw Stenson board the train about half-way up. Keeping the light from his face, he scrutinized all passengers within the switch of his eyes, got into a compartment, and opened his evening paper as a shield against those still trooping along the platform. From the chalked figures on the notice-board, the train should pull out in about four minutes.

As the train moved, he felt exhilarated. He was satisfied no one had seen him, and the two elderly gentlemen in the compartment were complete strangers. Not even the "cold war" news had any effect. Indeed a faint smile touched his features as he realized the sheer luxury of action, of breaking through the slowly suffocating cloud of human despair, of tearing out of the net that got round the very hands and feet. These fellows, he thought, who go in for fifth-column action, what fun! Give them an ideal, an ideology, and everything in the garden was wonderful. He felt alive and competent. He knew a few body-holds that Stenson just mightn't.

At the second stop the elderly man on his right got up and Dermot followed him to the door. As the train moved on, Dermot stood in the corridor.

When he saw the gleam of the water, it fascinated him. The loch was quiet to-night. A twinkle of riding lights moved him. Deep in his soul he knew that the sea was his element. A moon must be getting up somewhere; and he realized that the night might be too bright. But he was not dismayed, for so far his luck had always been in. Even his brown neutral clothes, meant for the neighbourhood of St. Patrick's Close, might be still more useful in more natural surroundings. And he would be careful. If only he could establish where Stenson was going, the house he would enter, it would be enough.

From its ceaseless underground workings his mind, as the train stopped again and went on, fished up a new and startling idea. Supposing any authoritative group knew when the buttons were to be pressed, they would naturally beat it beforehand to an agreed rendezvous or head-quarters. At such H.Q. all indispensable documents or plans would be kept. They certainly wouldn't be kept in a city tenement where even an old-fashioned bomb might smother the lot, not to mention the commonplace of a police raid. And he had wondered why Grear and his police hadn't raided 5 St. Patrick's Close!

Were Stenson and his group working on a "level", like Grear? My God, was everything a matter of "levels"? Was life getting like that, everywhere, and the word

Enemy or Friend a mere matter of a political point of view? He was annoyed at feeling guilty again for having kept back things from Grear. He had been drilled sufficiently in "Intelligence" over ten years ago to know that what appeared unimportant might be the missing clue in the jigsaw puzzle to those "high up".

He realized that, whatever happened, he would have to be utterly careful not to disclose himself. Better to find out nothing than create the slightest suspicion. . . .

He felt stiff and cramped by the time the train drew up at Criach. Stenson must get out now. . . . And there he was walking straight from his compartment to the exit opposite. Dermot took a moment or two, then opened the door. As he moved up towards the ticket collector, he kept his head down, engaged in breaking his return ticket in halves. As he closed in, he lifted his head—and realized that Basil was approaching from the forward part of the train. He did not look at him. He merely knew, with a sickening dismay, that Basil had recognized him, that Basil was slowing up.

As he got outside, he started walking briskly, like one who knew where he was going. But he knew that he was only a simple child, an idiot. There would be three or four of them on the train, of course, each watching, making sure none was followed. The thing was too elementary. That Basil had already put one of them onto him was as certain as that the moon was shining. And it was shining. And he knew no one in Criach. Any other of the stops, and he could have gone straight to the house of at least an acquaintance.

The procession of passengers was already thinning. Stenson was going steadily ahead. The water-front got shut out by the main street. Dermot had to stop himself from making so obvious a move as going into a pub. By the time he remembered the large Sea-Front Hotel he was walking the other way. Stenson stopped before a news-agent's window which had a display of Penguins. Dermot went on. He kept going on. In passing, another, coming up, could whisper to Stenson. The whole thing was so simple. The open sea-front again. He saw a large house standing back in its own grounds on his right. Without hesitation, at the same brisk pace, he swung in between the stone pillars, followed the curving gravel drive, went up three stone steps and pressed the bell.

An elderly worried-looking domestic opened the door. "Anyone in?" he asked cheerfully, entering as though he were expected, for no doubt the door was already being watched from the road. She closed it behind him.

"What name, please?" She knocked, opened a door on the left, and said, "Mr. Cameron."

A man of his own age, perhaps younger; got out of a deep chair, fair hair ruffled over a rosy face as if he had been having a snooze.

Dermot pulled up short and stared in a bewildered way. "Excuse me," he said, "I have made a mistake." He was deeply embarrassed. "I am so sorry."

"Wrong house?"

"Yes. Forgive me. He said it was the first big house on the front. I promised to look in if ever I happened to pass. Too bad disturbing you."

"Who are you looking for?"

"Robson is the name. But please don't let me———"

"Robson? No, there's no Robson here that I know. There's Angus Robson—at Clua———"

"Well, I'm blowed!" said Dermot. "Of course! Clua it was. Worse and worse!" He laughed, backing towards the door. "I always get mixed up on this front and I happened to be———"

"I know Robson. I rather fancy I know you."

"Cameron is my name."

"That's right. I'm Norman Gavin. Nothing more exciting than a thirty-foot launch, but I have set a spinnaker. Have a drink."

"Well—thanks—but this is really too much."

"On the contrary, it's an honour." He glanced at the clock on the mantel. "Good God, that's not the time?" But it was. "Heavens, I've got to get in to town. I might manage to drop you at Robson's."

"If you took me in to town it would be a sheer gift."

"Splendid! Thank God you came in. I was sound." He poured two whiskies. "Brutal, hurrying you like this. Very best!"

When he brought the car to the door, Dermot was careful to walk in front of the lights. As they passed between the stone pillars, he saw a man moving away along the three-foot wall.

Gavin drove fast. He explained that he had promised to pick up his wife, who was at some sort of highbrow musical show; she couldn't get away often, because the old Nannie was a bit nervous in the house alone with two young nippers, especially at night; no domestic help —hell of a business. He talked away brightly, delighted to have Dermot's company. When Dermot suggested there should be no housing shortage in Criach, Gavin laughed. "Same here as everywhere else—unless, of course, you take Criach House, or old Sam Duncan's mansion, still under care and maintenance; you would get them pretty nearly for the asking."

"Taxation is the devil."

"Money might be managed—for a time, anyway. It's help that's the devil. If you were to say to me here and now that you could lay hands on a reliable maid, I should know that God had sent you."

Dermot laughed, thoughtfully. "If I do hear of one, I'll drop you a note."

146

"Don't. Bring her, and then we'll believe it. You came down by train?"

"Yes. They're doing up my old bus. The last train——"

"But there's no train to-night."

"I thought on Saturday night——"

"I forgot. There is a late one, I believe, on Saturday."

The talk was in full yachting rig when the car drew up to drop Dermot, who had to promise that if ever he were in Criach again he would give Norman Gavin a chance of showing that he was at least half-reasonably hospitable. On his part, Dermot suggested that Gavin might have lunch with him some time. They parted with lively expressions of good will.

Then Dermot went to the West station and waited for the last train from Criach. No one whom he knew came off it.

As Dermot turned away from the station, he was troubled. He should go straight to Grear, but he didn't want to go to Grear. There were upsurgent moments when Grear was the other side of Basil's penny, and which side came down didn't matter a lot. . . . A sudden unprintable phrase could be a sort of vile relief, but a relief. It brought him back to reason. He would have to see Christina.

For they would be bound to pump her, through Amy, of course, when she would fall like the gentle rain. If only he could support his sudden appearance in Criach by planting a story on Christina which she could tell Amy . . . yet to call on Christina now would be exactly as if he had found out from her (as he had) that Stenson was going out of town, left her to go to Criach, and then come back at a late hour for further talk. He just could not show himself at the Mures'. . . .

Joe! The idea came like an inspiration. The only one to send for Christina was Joe. As he strode swiftly along, he saw Joe and Christina, hand in hand, walking away down the field of his imagination. They hadn't been thrown out of the Garden of Eden and they weren't in search of it. He didn't know where they were going. But there they were, their backs to him, slowly growing smaller as they wandered away. He laughed to himself. Joe always did raise images in his mind.

Joe himself was quiet. He stood in his shirt-sleeves on the middle of the studio floor and looked at Dermot. He had every light on.

My God, thought Dermot, Joe is having a private show to himself. For a moment, appalled, he could not speak. When he got control, he said, "Your walls are blazing, Joe." He walked a pace or two through the silence, for clearer angles. "You get it better with the full broadside." He stopped. He grew perfectly still. "They're not blazing," he said in a low astonished voice. "It's not Van Gogh at all. Joe, it's the light, it's the still light." He could not move. He turned slowly and looked at Joe. For a while they stared at each other. Then Dermot began to breathe heavily and Joe broke out of his stance.

"I wondered," Joe muttered. He was trembling. Dermot saw his forearm shake as he brought a palm up over his forehead.

Dermot found a place to sit on and there was silence for some time. Then he got up. "I want you to do something for me, Joe. Put your jacket on." He spoke quietly. After a

148

short search, Joe found his coat and hat and put them on. Dermot turned away from the pictures and Joe followed him.

His plan was simple. Joe would call at the Mures', ask for Christina, tell her confidentially that Dermot wanted to see her for an hour, and then escort her to his studio.

"Yes," said Joe.

"If they ask her—that is, if the people in her house ask her—who is wanting her, she could say——" He paused. "She could say, some friends from the West."

"Some friends from the West," repeated Joe.

Dermot glanced at him. "Wake up, Joe!" he said gently. "I won't join you. I'll follow behind."

"You'll come behind."

"That's it. Now have you got the name?"

"Yes," said Joe. "Christina. It's a wonderful name."

"Christina MacNeil: Miss MacNeil."

"Strange. I wonder who made it up first."

"Made what up?"

"Christina. Williamina you can understand, or even Benjamina, which I have heard. But Christina. It's remarkable."

Dermot himself had a sudden shock. But Joe had a habit of providing him with these unexpected glimpses of another landscape. "It's quite a common name," he said.

"Yes," said Joe. "They made it quite naturally *then*."

Fellowship, the commune of kindness, the infinitely natural acceptance of the good news.

"It's the light that never was on sea or land," said Dermot. "That's what you've got, Joe."

Joe stopped, and his face was strangely worked upon. "Don't you see that that's not the way to put it. The light *was*."

Dermot looked at him, waiting for Joe to say something about Christ.

"That's what Wordsworth *saw*. That's what all his

poetry is *about*," said Joe. "He only said it *never was* when he was bothered with himself too much, bothered with the world, when he was *thinking* about it afterwards, and all the critics seized on it because it was something to think about. That's their awful job: to think. Don't you understand?"

"Yes," said Dermot, beginning to wonder if Joe could be trusted to carry out his simple plan; it was getting late.

"Wordsworth was a poet only when he saw the light. And when you see it, it isn't *was*: it *is*. The light *is*. And when the light is not, then there's darkness. The universe goes out. Surely that's obvious."

"Yes, Joe. Let's go on."

"That's the whole thing," said Joe, his voice quivering. "And—and—it's thrilling." He walked on. "It's the only drama. Darkness is not drama. When the buttons fly off it's not creation we'll get: it's death. The light will go out."

"It won't go out, Joe, if you manage to survive and take a girl like Christina with you. So we must keep moving."

"Christina."

"Very nice girl. But she won't understand a word you're saying, and she certainly won't see the light in your pictures."

"That doesn't matter," said Joe. "That's not what matters at all fundamentally."

"She comes from a little island in the west. And the only painter out there is God."

Joe stopped, but before he could say a word Dermot had him by the elbow, moving him on.

"Basil has it all wrong," said Joe. "I see it now! There cannot be a regress when you're searching for light." He stopped stubbornly. "This is important! This is the whole thing! Even if you're searching only for a song . . ."

And in the instant, Dermot thought of Ellen. He should have got Ellen. Then it would be perfectly natural to ask Christina out at this hour. Joe could not be trusted, because he was drunk with the excitement of one solitary human being's having seen his light. He guided Joe to a telephone kiosk and ordered him to stand there.

But he was told over the phone that Ellen was at the Highland Institute, and expected back fairly soon. He left no message for her, got a taxi, made Joe pull himself together, explained once more, in the taxi, what Joe had got to do, and presently let him loose.

When at last he had decided that Joe must have bungled things or gone missing altogether, he saw the two of them walking up the other side of the street. Joe was talking away to Christina and once Dermot saw her face lift and smile. He let them get a little bit ahead, then went up his own side of the street. There were too many about to know if anyone was following them. His taxi was waiting round a corner and he gave the driver instructions. He knew the route Ellen must take from the Highland Institute and watched as he drove slowly on. Suddenly he saw her in a small gay group. He knocked, the taxi turned round, and came up on the group from behind. He got out, took a few quick strides, and called her by name. He hesitated as she recognized him; she came sauntering towards him. The others drifted on.

"You do drop out of the blue," she said.

"And into the sunlight. Wave them good-bye."

In the taxi she asked, "What's all this about? Kidnapping me?" It was as if she liked things to happen in this way.

"Ah—if only! I can do without you for a while, but then it gets the better of me."

"And where are you taking me now?"

"Does it matter?"

"I still grow warm when I think of that awful night you kept the taxi going round and round. I would rather sing at once and get it over."

"You're *not* going to sing. If you threaten to sing——"

She laughed. "How frightened you look!"

"Of all the women I know——"

"And you know a few. Yes? . . ." They might have parted the other night. There were no obligations in their friendship.

He stopped the taxi.

"Before we go any farther," he said, as they stood on the street, "I want to make it quite clear that I do not expect you to sing. I have to make a perfectly correct call, and happening to see you on the street, I thought your distinction might make it easier for me."

"That's very thoughtful of you." She was looking at him.

"I don't think it should be dull, but one never knows, does one?"

"One hasn't the faintest idea," she agreed.

"That's one thing about such rare encounters as we have had: they have always led to the unexpected."

"Have they? I hadn't noticed."

"Ellen, you're a very wicked woman, but you're very charming."

"Do we stand here a long while? I come from a respectable home, where they're expecting me."

"I know they are. I phoned them."

"You did?"

"Yes. As it happens, my voice was not recognized——" He paused. "Don't!" he said sharply. "Take no notice."

Joe and Christina were now going up the side street.

"It's as simple as this, Ellen," he confessed. "I have fallen for Christina's face."

She considered him thoughtfully. "So I hear," she murmured, without abating her look.

"And I knew you would help me."

"Once in a desperate moment I told you I loved you."

"That's why," he said. "Love has duties."

"Are you never serious?"

"More often than you, as you know. Wait till I tell you how I love you. Now about Christina. It's a curious mix-up. The chap she's with—he's an artist. One day he will be famous if the buttons aren't blown off him. He wants to paint Christina's face. He's a friend of mine and I'd like to help him. I'd also like to help Christina. Her folk were kind to me and she's a nice girl. So to-night he would insist on getting hold of her. He's really a decent fellow, Ellen. Really sincere. And it suddenly occurred to me it might be easier for Christina if I got you along. So off I hived in a taxi. I also thought you might like to see his pictures. Have I done you wrong?"

She smiled. "If only there was another man with a face like yours."

He took her arm. No one had followed Joe and Christina.

When Joe came to the door, he stared at Dermot and Ellen.

Dermot laughed and introduced Ellen. "He has forgotten us already," he explained to Ellen.

Christina was standing by a fairly large canvas near the off end of the studio. Dermot greeted her, but Ellen went right up and took her hands and looked into her face. "My dear, how nice!" Her eyes were lively with meaning. "And how adventurous! I never would have thought it of you."

Christina slowly blushed.

"Has Joe been explaining his pictures to you?" Dermot asked her.

"Yes," answered Christina.

"What lovely colours!" exclaimed Ellen.

"You think so?" Dermot said.

"Yes. I don't know what they mean, but they're—I don't know—they're lovely." Her eyes sparkled. "I'm sorry," she said to Joe, "that I don't understand them. I'm really ignorant."

"You do," he said, "if you like them."

Dermot heard the quiver in his voice. He looked at Ellen, for she could act being sympathetic very beautifully. Then he looked at the pictures. Their idiom was suddenly completely strange, foreign. He thought of Paris studios and girls who came in and out sophisticated and oddly clad, with thin burning faces and sharply cut hair. Then he saw that the pictures in the Paris studios were taken in from the world of earth and sunlight outside; just as Christina was taken in here, not as a sophisticated creature but as an extra picture. And Ellen . . . Ellen had her own art. . . . And Dermot suddenly realized that he did not want to get his disturbing vision of Joe's light again, just as he did not want to hear Ellen sing. The idiom was not strange, not foreign, it was merely too disturbing. And this was delightful and exciting. It made him feel like a drink—or making love to Ellen.

"Haven't anything to drink have you, Joe?"

Joe looked bewildered. "Do you mean water?"

"No, I don't mean water. I mean celebration. I think your show should be celebrated." He paused. "I've got an idea! I'll go home for a bottle. I've got a better idea!

154

Ellen will come with me. That will give you time, Joe, to arrange with Christina for sittings. Feel like a walk, Ellen? It's only a quarter-of-an-hour away."

On the street, he laughed. "Isn't Christina wonderful?"

"She's like something in a pool."

"She's the pool itself. A sea-pool, with strange vivid things under the tangle. You probably think that butter wouldn't melt in her mouth?"

"She's making the butter melt in Joe's mouth." Ellen laughed with wicked delight. "It's lovely to see Joe stealing her from you."

He stopped. "Such a thing would never occur to Joe. I'm certain of it; absolutely certain."

"And it would be quite impossible anyway, wouldn't it, yes?"

He looked back, and around, and ahead, then went silently on. "I don't know," he muttered. "I have seen the butter melt."

"Tell me," she murmured.

He took her arm and told the story of the new moon in Cladday, of the girl who came rushing and threw her arms round the cow's neck and whispered into the cow's ear.

Now Ellen stopped. "Oh, Dermot, what a lovely story!"

Dermot looked at her. "Isn't it?"

"Yes," she murmured. "It's divine. It's like something that doesn't happen any more in the world."

"It doesn't," he said to the glisten in her eyes. He bent forward and kissed her brow and as they went quietly on she pressed his arm and clung to him a little.

Before his door, he paused, searching for his latchkey. "Heavens, I hope I haven't to ring the old dame up!" The man who was standing in the shadows farther up the street on the other side did not move away. At last Dermot produced the key and ushered Ellen in.

"I hope your old dame isn't—peculiar," whispered Ellen.

Dermot shook his head, smiling. "She's used to it." He was feeling savage. It was, of course, the simplest matter in the world for Stenson or Basil Black to phone back to someone in town to keep an eye on Dermot. And although nothing could be more happy, more innocuous, than being first discovered in Ellen's company, still it was an infuriating intrusion into this world of colour and delight, of human relations that gave life a living glow. He waved Ellen to the freedom of his sitting room and went on an unnecessary hunt for glasses. By the time he was pouring two drinks, his anger was choked down, his eyes were bright, his manners dangerously alive. At least Ellen must have thought so, for she told him, with admirable objectivity, that he looked a bit of a devil.

"You're taking risks."

She laughed softly, scoffingly, and talked of Christina and Joe.

"Joe always sets up images in my mind," he told her, after suddenly draining his glass. "They appear to me now like two persons lost in a wood—a painted autumn wood."

"And the robins will put leaves over them."

"Exactly!" He jumped up and kissed her in tribute. "That's it. My God, Ellen, that's it. You're a very fascinating woman." He wandered half round the room and back to the bottle. "Drink up."

She shook her head. "You don't usually drink so quickly yourself."

"Obviously you're too much for me."

"What's upsetting you, Dermot? Is it really very bad?"

He nodded. "I'm trying to pluck up courage to ask you to sing."

She looked at him long and slantingly.

"You're a devil yourself, Ellen."

She shook her head sadly, looked at her glass, and slowly drained it.

He went and sat on the floor beside her. They talked for a little while, then he asked her to sing.

She sang very quietly.

He could do nothing against it. The mooring ropes melted away and were not.

When the telephone rang it was a machine gun ripping right through. It was black, and fixed, and malignant. It had silenced Ellen as it had destroyed the country where they journeyed, that country which he was always a little afraid of, because its beauty, its containing harmony, was sad with the mute cry of the forever lost. He looked at the black hump on his desk with a profound hatred; he felt the fighting blood surge malignantly inside him.

"Aren't you going to answer it?" whispered Ellen as if she might be overheard.

"Let the damn thing ring," he replied in a flat voice, his eyes narrowing upon it.

She glanced at his dark head, felt the ruthless intensity, and, in a faint alarm that touched her spirit with an ultimate intimacy, let her eyes rest on the door. She could not stop her hand going to his shoulder.

The persistence of the black hump had a devilish automatism. It was giving him time to get out of bed. So he knew it was Grear. And he knew that he hated both Grear and Stenson, hated what they stood for, hated them for what they must destroy

Ellen watched him as he got up and went to the instrument, saw him assume his normal character as a man might put on a coat, heard his voice say lazily, "Hallo!" Then, "Oh, is that you?" with a polite quickening of interest. After listening for a little while, he said, "I'm afraid I can't. Not, anyway, for another hour. . . . No, please don't send a car here . . . Wait! Send a taxi, an ordinary taxi, at once . . . I can't promise. You must leave it to me . . . Right."

"People are troublesome, aren't they?" he said casually as he turned to Ellen and offered her a cigarette. "What about a small drink before we go? A taxi will be along in a few minutes." He ignored her refusal and poured her a tiny drop with an expert hand. "By the way, you needn't mention to-night. Anyway, not about Christina and Joe and me. Let them find out."

She looked up at him as he stood with his back to the radiator.

"Sounds mysterious, doesn't it?" he said smiling. "I'll tell you what it's about, if you like. It's very confidential; it's really hush-hush in the high spheres. But I know I can trust you. The fact is I've lost an official chart. As it happens, it's a chart to the sea and land—of the song you were singing. A naval chart. Sounds like a bedtime story?"

"I never know when to believe you."

"The sad thing is that *you* and *me* are not beginning to matter much any more. They're after us."

"Tell me, Dermot."

"I lost it in that fight when I rescued Christina. We don't know if the enemy has got it. I am prepared to risk everything to find out."

"Do you really mean it was a real chart?"

"Yes. But—it's beginning to mean more than that to me. When I hear you singing—I know how much."

"Is its loss—serious?"

"You would like me to be clear. It's really difficult, Ellen. We are like those children in the wood. Christina and Joe, you and me, we're about as helpless as the flowers that bloom in the spring. I cannot even tell you whether its loss is serious. The authorities would never hesitate to use me for purposes I know nothing of."

"Is it war, Dermot?"

"I hope not, Ellen. Though I'm beginning to wonder—if that matters."

"You terrify me."

"There's the taxi." He put the whisky bottle in a pocket and slipped on his overcoat.

"But we're going the wrong way," said Ellen, as the taxi started off. "Have you forgotten Joe and Christina?"

"I believe I have," said Dermot. The man was now walking away and Dermot tried to get a glimpse of him as they overtook him. "Do you mind?"

"I never know——"

"What Joe is really interested in are the bones in Christina's face. Did I ever tell you about the bones in Christina's face? . . ." In a short time the taxi delivered them at Joe's.

As he paid the taxi driver, he spoke to him, and in a few moments he was producing his bottle in the studio. There was a happy hunt before two whole cups and two whole tumblers were set down in a line. Dermot asked Christina if she had ever drunk whisky and Christina answered, "Not since I was a young girl." Dermot's hand so shook with laughter that Ellen took the bottle from him. But he got up from the floor to deliver the toast. Ellen watched him as he said in a quiet easy voice,

"To the light in Joe's pictures, to the country in Ellen's song, and to old Anna's cow that Christina kissed." He exhibited the manners of an ambassador and Ellen would have given the world for words to include Dermot himself in the toast, but not a word would come to her. Christina, who had known the use of whisky only medicinally on Cladday, coughed and spluttered and Joe was concerned. They were very happy for a little while, then Dermot drew Christina apart, so that, as he said, Joe might be free to instruct Ellen.

"I'll tell you," said Dermot to Christina as they sat in a corner, "exactly what happened after I left you." And then he told her, but without mentioning Basil. He suddenly felt, he said, that he was being suspected and followed by one of Stenson's men, so he had simply called on a friend named Gavin, and shortly afterwards had set out in Gavin's car. That was all that happened. "Now," Dermot continued, "I have been wondering just what you might say to Amy about all this."

She brought her dark eyes to his face.

"You are looking very well to-night," he said. "Do you like Joe?"

"Yes. He is very nice."

"I thought you would get on well together. Has he asked you to sit for him—so that he could paint you?"

"He—started drawing me—when you were off."

"Did he indeed! I'll try not to be jealous. You can trust Joe, Christina, as you would Kennie—or even me."

She was embarrassed. He could see the whole thing was a little too much for her, yet in some mysterious way it was as if she had entered a country which she might not understand but which she liked.

"Strange pictures, aren't they?" he said, looking around.

"Yes."

"You like them?"

"I don't know. At first I was—frightened of them. They seemed strange and not like anything. But now I don't mind them."

Dermot went speechless with wonder.

"Did Joe explain them to you?" he asked.

"Yes."

"And did you understand him?"

She hesitated and looked down and caught a frill of cloth between her fingers. "No. I am not good at English. I did not get much education."

"Did you tell Joe that?"

"He said it did not matter. He said it was all the better."

"Did you believe him?"

She hesitated, her brows netting a faint worry. "No. But he meant to be kind."

Dermot could not speak for a moment. "Was there nothing at all you got from him—about—about what he's trying to do?"

"Oh yes," she said at once.

"What?" He stared at her.

She felt his eyes, so he removed them and waited.

She was silent for quite a little time. "He asked me about Cladday and—and what I remembered, and if I saw the light on it when I remembered it. And I said yes. It lay in my mind like a summer day. He asked me about the colours. And he wouldn't let me rest till I told him. But I couldn't tell him because—because the English words, like blue and green, they're too hard for the sea out yonder. Our Gaelic words——"

"They're deep and you dive into them," he murmured.

"Yes," she said. "I wish I could have told him. I said all kind of things. I forgot he was an artist. I'm sure he will think me very ignorant."

He could not reassure her, for he felt himself entangled

too deep. "You said you got something from him about what he's trying to do." He spoke quietly.

"Yes," she answered at once, "he said he would like to paint Cladday as I saw it in my mind, with the light on it, but without seeing any one thing too much. I can't explain, but—I thought I knew when he was speaking."

He nodded, silent.

"Then he said something about—about his own pictures," she volunteered, a faint excitement in her voice. "He wondered if I would remember them, after-wards, with the light on them like—like Cladday."

"What did you say?"

"I didn't know what to say. I didn't think I would. It was so different, so new. But——"

"Yes?"

"I don't know. Perhaps, long after, I will."

"I think you will," he said simply.

It was Christina who broke the silence. "You were going to tell me what to say to Amy."

"Tell her that I had to see a man about a ship and had to leave you early. It was purely a matter of shipping business but urgent. That's all. You don't know any more."

She nodded thoughtfully. "Will I tell about—I didn't catch his name?"

"Duguid. Joe Duguid. My name is Dermot and I should like you to call me that. Tell about Joe, if you have to. Say you met him in my company once and I gave him your address because he wanted to paint you. You can say you expect to get paid for it, but that nothing is fixed yet. Leave that to me. You must get a job anyway." He was worried. He wanted to ask her to find out all she could about Stenson and his doings, but he couldn't, he just couldn't. He got up. "Thank you, Christina, for our very interesting talk."

162

She stood looking at him for a moment, but she said nothing.

Presently all four of them left Joe's studio and found a taxi waiting. They dropped Ellen first, then Dermot got out and paid and instructed the driver. Before he closed the door, he said, "Look after her, Joe." Within twenty minutes, he was in Grear's study.

Grear was friendly and bright. "It's late," he said, "but I thought you wouldn't mind. It's going to be a critical week, this coming one. Have a cigarette."

Dermot thanked him and waited.

"I just wanted to make sure that if you got a sudden call you would be ready."

"As bad as that?"

"Difficult to say. In upper circles there is a certain tension. It's happened frequently, but—it can't go on happening." He made a diversion into Balkan politics. "This time it's a case of an incalculable reaction—to a definite move. The move will be made week after next— zero hour being actually scheduled for the Thursday. The public know nothing of this. I know little myself. So it's a sort of stand-by for us."

"Thanks for telling me."

"I haven't told you anything. You understand that?" He was thoughtful. "There is something else." He smoked his cigarette with the slight awkwardness of the man who did not smoke many. "We shall have to clean up all we can, this coming week. We must find out all we can lest zero hour, the week after next, presses the buttons. That's really what I wanted to see you about. If you have anything at all to tell me, however vague, this is the time."

"Christina had dinner with me to-night. But she knows nothing." He had meant to play down or not mention some of the evening's events, but now he found himself giving a careful description ·of the top floor of 5 St. Patrick's Close. "I don't think you would find much in Stenson's flat—though to-night might be a good night for having a look through it, because he's not there."

"How do you know?"

Quietly, as though the matter were of no particular moment, Dermot described at length what happened from the time he first saw Stenson on the street until he returned in Norman Gavin's car and waited for the last train from Criach, except that he did not mention Basil by name.

Grear kept looking at Dermot after he had finished.

"I was sorry I muffed it," Dermot admitted.

Grear seemed lost in thought. "What did you expect to find."

"I don't know. Pure curiosity. Acted on the spur of the moment. But I think you can take it that Stenson won't be at number 5."

Grear sat as still as the figure of the statuette and his skin looked clean as cold water. The clear eyes, glistening bright, came on Dermot's face. "Why didn't you tell me this at once—when you left the West Station?" The tone seemed one of pure curiosity.

"I felt I had better get in touch with Christina first, which I did. If she is questioned now about my leaving her so quickly after dinner, she will say that I had an urgent call on shipping business with Norman Gavin."

"You went to number 5 for her?"

"Oh no. I sent a friend. I met her in his place. My house was being watched."

"Was it?"

"Yes."

"You were followed?"

"No. I got your taxi to do a circle."

"You were never trained as a secret agent?"

Dermot smiled. "The only thing I couldn't cover was my arrival here." He looked at Grear.

Grear now smiled back. "You may take it that's all right." He sat quite still for a full minute, then excused himself, hospitably indicating the decanter, and withdrew.

Dermot got up and helped himself to a drink. Grear was phoning and wheels would be set turning—well, why not? He breathed more freely, had a sense of relief. Let them get on with it! . . . So there might be a world show-down soon. Cladday and the western sea. . . . He finished his drink. No point in feeling bitter. Two millstones, grinding the human oats to dust. . . . Fancy being tender about a fellow like Basil, because he was a fellow club-man . . . not wanting to mention his name . . . out of human loyalty! He lit a cigarette. Not a question of fighting at all. Hell, he would blow the enemy to bits. . . . What was he annoyed at? Couldn't he trust Grear and his crowd to do their business? . . . Was that it? . . . An island of light swam into his mind: Joe's studio. Ellen's dark eyes looked at him but he refused the song. Christina, utterly fantastic as it might seem, would come to a profound wordless understanding of Joe's pictures. . . . He stood quite still, and the unexplicable anger fell away from him, in an inner twilight where even the inanimate listened . . . to the notes of Ellen's song falling away silently beyond the horizon. . . . He heard Grear's hand on the door and sat down.

Dermot could see he was preoccupied, though he spoke lightly through that waxen rather insipid expression with its social smile, which always, for some mysterious reason, brought the statuette to mind.

"You seem to have collected quite a few faces," he said.

"I wouldn't say that. Just those you know," Dermot answered modestly.

"It's more than that. You mentioned, for example, one of Stenson's men who saw you on the Criach platform. You're sure he was one of Stenson's?"

"No. I just had the sudden feeling he was."

"You never saw him before?"

Dermot knew that Grear was looking at him. "Yes," he answered quite deliberately.

Grear waited.

Dermot's brows gathered. "Frankly, I hate giving any man's name unless I am dead certain."

"You had seen him with Stenson before?"

"I—think so."

"I know your attitude to the police spy. But the time is critical, as I told you. What we are fighting is the police state."

Dermot remained silent. He could not embark on an argument with Grear.

"We can defeat the enemy only on his own level with his own weapons. If you like, we have to descend to that," Grear continued.

"I appreciate that."

"Very good. There is one further thing I really wanted to see you about. But first let us get a picture, a sense of proportion. You realise, of course, that all our lives are involved in this. It's on a vast scale. To talk about saving civilization is beginning to have no meaning."

Dermot nodded, his calm expression covering a mounting irritation.

"You'll remember the old Shakespeare one about the globe itself and all which it inherits."

166

"Vaguely."

"How did it go? . . . 'the great globe itself, Yea, all which it inherits, shall dissolve And, like this insubstantial pageant faded, Leave not a rack behind'."

"I remember."

"Remarkable how Shakespeare could draw an exact chart. On the highest level there is just no dispute about him. Wonderful, I think."

Dermot glanced at him. Grear was smiling, deeply appreciative of the way in which Shakespeare had taped everything. Then Dermot saw that Grear moved in this greatness, that it excited him, that probably as a youth he had spouted the words. He had got them exactly correct, like a scholar.

"Whether Shakespeare's vision is going to be fulfilled, any day now, depends on fellows like you and me, in a thousand places," Grear went on. "I mentioned earlier a certain decisive move. It will be, in the history of the globe, a final gesture, when quite literally to be or not to be will be the question. It's on that scale."

Dermot sucked his cigarette. "You think we can affect it?"

"Yes. Within determinism, there is the free will of the mind. The will is free to determine."

"I was never good at metaphysics," said Dermot. "I would rather you showed me how you think *we* can stop the pageant from becoming insubstantial."

"Simply by doing our duty on the spot with an absolute firmness. Let that happen in the thousand places—and we can abide the question."

"Obviously the same tactic or strategy applies to the enemy. So what?"

"So the enemy will know *how* we stand, and, knowing, he may hesitate. If he hesitates—the globe may roll on. Given time, the argument may then be lifted by all men to Shakespeare's level." Grear looked more animated than Dermot had ever seen him. He looked polished and Dermot wondered if he had ever secretly entertained the ambition of being a lecturer in English.

"You may be right," said Dermot. "It sounds a little heady to me."

"It is," said Grear. "That's what distinguishes it. Now let us bring the head to practice." He sat quite still. "What you have told me to-night is of real interest. I have been thinking over it. It looks as if Stenson and his men—by the way, they are a small group and perhaps not very important except in this, that at any moment they may disclose the very important; in the same way as Mackie may yet give us the clue to the high official we're after. To a tremendous degree we are working in the dark, particularly for this psychological reason and you must get hold of it—it's this: how will any man, holding certain ideological opinions, react to a decisive situation when suddenly confronted with it? For he will have to go one way or the other, he will have to fight with us or against us. How will your friend Basil Black act at the decisive moment—if left free to act?"

Dermot remained silent.

"You may be uncertain. Perhaps Black himself is uncertain. *Many honest men will be uncertain.* That's our problem," said Grear.

Dermot nodded

"However, there are the few who are not uncertain. Stenson is one. He may be looking for a place outside the city, now that things are drawing to a climax. For obvious reasons he wouldn't have a headquarters outside the city. So I do not place much importance on your seeing him going away for a week-end except—perhaps—for this: it's interesting that he should have kept to the sea-coast. Oddly enough we have our eye on a certain fast river

168

launch. I'm now going to tell you something very confidential. On a night next week—probably Thursday—Stenson's real headquarters will be investigated."

"I see," said Dermot slowly.

"Would you like to come in on it?"

Dermot was silent. "Perhaps—not."

"Perhaps you're wise. It was merely a question of identifying faces."

"Perhaps you could tell me—where?"

Grear looked at him. "You prefer a lone hand!" He had just given Dermot details of the proposed raid when the telephone bell stopped him. Dermot had not seen the instrument. "Yes . . . I see . . . uhm . . . no, it's too late now . . . I'll arrange it . . . good night."

"I had asked someone round to meet you," Grear explained. "But it's getting late and he hasn't come back. However, I'll arrange a meeting. And now, it's perhaps time we were in our beds. Pour out one for the road and I'll get you a car." He left the room.

Dermot got up very late next day, Sunday, and apart from a long walk in the afternoon went nowhere and saw no one. He was satisfied, however, that he was being followed, and made it easy for the man. What Grear may have said on the phone he did not know, but it was unlikely that anyone had been sent to Criach. They would not frighten Stenson or make him suspicious before the raid.

Yet the more Dermot thought over things the more he felt that Grear was underestimating the importance of Criach. If it had been a plain week-end, why that cunning way of Basil's getting off the train? And the fellow watching Dermot's moves now? He got out a sea chart of the Criach area, then hunted out a large-scale relief map of the whole district and studied the westerly approaches to the city.

Maps and charts had always fascinated him. Now his eye ran along a widening estuary, wandered around the great firth he knew so intimately, followed deep-penetrating sea-lochs, rounded promontories and large islands, navigated sounds, and finally got lost in the small print of inland places, mountains and streams, hill burns like spidery dark veins. Then in a moment a couple of names had him from the time of Deirdre, Deirdre the beautiful tragic woman of ancient Gaeldom, whose song of farewell to Scotland Ellen sometimes sang.

As he came out of his dream his eye saw the map afresh and slowly he realized that here was a hinterland at no vast distance from the city where anything could happen, with always the intricate seaways of approach or escape over the hill or round the headland. There were whole areas where nothing would be heard but the cry of a curlew or the bleating of a sheep; yet hikers would pass that way occasionally . . . and any two or three strangers could be taken for hikers.

The contour lines began to gather body as his imagination got going. In no time he was deploying small forces of the enemy, postulating ocean-ranging submarines, setting up wireless transmitting stations, issuing subtle confusions to vast bodies of workers, until his fantasies grew ridiculous and he was wearied of them. Extraordinary how fecund the destructive instinct was! The amount of vital force it could deploy had always astonished him. His eye began looking on its own for the Deirdre names. There they were—but how remote now! Poetry, the individual beautiful woman, Joe and his colours—how childish! How infantile—in this adult age! To be moved by a simple tune . . . His hands fell on a map that crinkled harshly, his brow drooped, his expression grew arid.

The following evening he saw the Assessor coming like a tower. The Assessor glanced into the window with its sporting gear and smiled. He was like one who had always turned up.

Basil was in the club and whenever Dermot saw Joe he knew that Joe wanted to speak to him, so he nodded coolly and turned away.

It was a club for discussion, which in practice meant argument. Professor Barclay's description of the recent Neo show as the writing on the wall, was going the rounds, a drop of honey for the buzzing wits at a time when any kind of honey was a godsend.

Basil was supporting the professor, and though it was perfectly understood that Basil was condemning the show because of his political alignments and the professor because of his moral convictions, yet the combination was oddly stimulating, even arresting.

"If you had your way, you would not allow a show like that to happen," a musician said.

"Neither would Professor Barclay," retorted Basil, "and he stands for whatever moral or democratic values our tradition has produced—whether you like it or not."

"But what has art to do with moral or democratic values?"

"When it hasn't—you get that kind of show," replied Basil.

Joe got tied up in his own words, and when after much stumbling and harassment he thought he had made his position clear, everyone laughed.

Dermot was very interested in the combination of Basil and Professor Barclay. It contained a suggestion of repression by the old Church in Scotland that was like bringing history alive again. The new puritanism—from different standpoints?

"Yes, but surely the more civilized course is to allow the show to be seen and then to criticize as we criticize now," suggested the Assessor.

"That's the usual red herring when you want to avoid the issues involved," said Basil. "I could retort by saying that if you allow certain things to go on long enough they'll destroy you. Or would you suggest one should never stop anything, never stop the rot in order to see how the rot rots?"

His intensity was exhilarating. Hang it, the fellow could stand up to things, give him his due. And they were now launched on a beautiful argument.

Dermot remembered Professor Barclay in the Parthenon, two nights after Mr. Douglas had been attacked, having a discussion with his friend Mr. James, a higher Civil Servant, a suave discreet man, on the delinquencies of our age and the historic parallels. It had been learned and, somehow, reassuring. But he found he was not now trying to remember their arguments: he was looking at their faces. Actually he was looking at Basil's face; and Basil suddenly said to him, "You should know about simple tunes."

"But," replied a roused musician before Dermot could speak, "that's all rot. That's going back to primitive folk tunes. That's regression with a vengeance. Do what you like with economics, but when you get a revolutionary dictator ordering a revolutionary composer to knock the guts out of his symphony and stuff it with folk tunes—God Almighty that's—that's murder. That's the end."

"It might suit me," Dermot answered.

As the hubhub grew hot, Dermot came out ever more strongly on Basil's side.

"Perhaps I don't know anything about music," Dermot admitted at last. "And I disagree with Basil in the business of purging, even of purging symphonies. But I am beginning to see how strong the simple tune is. I am beginning to see, quite literally, the force of it."

"You mean music is brute force?" the musician demanded brutally.

Dermot drew on his cigarette slowly. "Music acts on the emotions," he said. "A simple tune may move people to go places when a symphony wouldn't."

"God Almighty, it's the new dark age all right."

"It may be," Dermot answered, looking the musician thoughtfully in the eye. "And if it is, the tune will win. Your revolutionary economist knows that. He is perhaps backing the right horse in the international stakes—if I may shift the metaphor."

"I must object to that," said Basil, "as the reintroduction of the political red herring."

"But you see the force of it," suggested Dermot. "Anyway, I do. Moreover, in the simple tune there is health. If our age is diseased, it needs health. I am a little surprised that you, Basil, should jib before so obvious a hurdle."

There was no end to it, until Joe and the Assessor and Dermot found themselves on the street. Even then the Assessor said, "You were perverse to-night."

"Not altogether," answered Dermot. "It's a terrifying business." He was again seeing Basil, the Professor of Moral Philosophy, and the discreet Mr. James. Let their profound convictions come alive in *action*—and what? It was a very odd and remarkable world. Add atom bombs and bacteriological sprays, radio-active clouds and missiles that searched for their target, and the streets became more flimsy than any of Hollywood's paper boards.

Joe was getting restless. "I must go," he said. Dermot went with him. "Christina is waiting all this time," Joe said.

"In the studio?"

"Yes. She wants to see you."

Dermot's steps quickened. He asked when she had come, if Joe had phoned him, but he was thinking of the fact that she had come. Suddenly he asked, "Have you fixed up anything with Christina?"

"No," said Joe.

"I don't know about your business, Joe. But Christina is out of a job. She's got to live."

"I didn't know," said Joe.

Dermot glanced at him. He knew that Joe had a small quarterly allowance paid through a bank. Joe was completely unworldly but he was also very careful about his money. He never took a drink from anyone, always ordering his own beer. Orgies of treating were not unknown at the club, but the accepted custom was that each one bought his own drink when he felt like it.

"Do you never employ models?"

"Not for a long time," Joe answered, and was obscurely silent again.

"Never mind," said Dermot. "I'll find something for her. We'll talk about it again." He was under the impression that he had told Joe she had been a maidservant who had lost her job. By the time they reached Joe's door, he remembered quite definitely having told him. Could it be conceivably possible that Joe was extra careful about his pennies?

Christina's face looked very pale above her simple black dress. She was as odd a creature as Joe, awkward a

174

little, almost angular, yet with something about her that was difficult to define; something authentic that could not find expression and was a little lost. Joe went into his tiny screened kitchen and left them alone.

All that Christina had to tell him was that someone had gone through Stenson's flat on the Saturday night when they were in bed.

"How do you know?"

"I overheard Mr. Stenson telling Mr. Mure this afternoon when he came back."

"Stenson came back this afternoon?"

"Yes. He said nothing had been taken but he had left things so that he knew."

"I see," said Dermot thoughtfully, but aware that she was looking at him. He met her eyes and smiled. "You think I had something to do with it?"

"I don't know." She glanced away. She did not look upset, but he saw her restless fingers and she was unusually pale.

"I hadn't actually, but I am glad you told me. Was that all they said?"

"They spoke for a little time. Mr. Stenson said something about pulling out on Thursday. They couldn't wait too long or something. I didn't understand." She suddenly swallowed and he saw that she was actually under nervous tension. He realized that the decision to tell him had cost her a lot.

"Thank you, Christina, for telling me."

"I didn't know what to do."

"You did right," he said. She was breathing more quickly and he was afraid her emotion might break through. "Your grandfather waded out on the skerry to shout to us. Sit down and I'll tell you about it." He spoke to her quietly about Iain MacNeil and then about old Seumas. What they stood for, he stood for: that's all he knew, he said; so she was right in coming to him. The only loyalty in the world for them both was to *that*. If it came to war, then the only thing worth saving was *that*. "I have got a very bad memory. Tell me old Seumas's verse about the moon."

She smiled back uncertainly.

"You won't? All right."

"Donald—Mr. Mure—he's a fine man, too. And Mrs. Mure—I'm very fond of her. It's awful."

"You have the *folk* on both sides seeking the best, perhaps wanting the same thing," he said, "and they are driven to war. That's what is called tragedy. We've had it a long time. And there's not a great lot you or I can do about it now. We're in it."

"Joe says he won't fight."

"He told you that?"

"Yes."

"What do you think about it?"

"I don't know," she answered.

"You mentioned the line, *Thy love behind the wave*. With Joe it's *Thy light behind the wave*." He looked up as Joe came in.

"I can't find the teapot," Joe said to Christina.

"It's on the shelf just above." At once she got up and walked away.

"She tidied things up," Joe muttered, "and she likes tea."

Later, when Dermot had dropped out of the taxi, after arranging a supper for Wednesday evening, he phoned Grear. "Remember that affair fixed for Thursday night?"

"Yes," came Grear's voice.

"Make it Wednesday if you can. Can you?"

"It *might* be arranged."

"Good. Just a matter of having all the rations on the spot. Thursday would be too late."

"You can't come round just now?"

"I'd rather not, if you don't mind. Feeling a bit done up. By the way, they know the flat was inspected."

When at last he replaced the receiver, he thought: he can worry over that! He stood quite still for a moment, acutely aware of the world's brand of bitterness.

Dermot carefully timed the departure from Joe's studio on Wednesday night, so that when presently they got off a tram, Joe and Christina were in a mood to enjoy the walk by the river. Not that they could see much of it, only glimpses now and then, but Dermot said that many a night that was enough for him, because he could feel the companionship of the river. He asked them if they could feel it, could feel the quiet deep water flowing away to the sea. Sometimes Joe would stop abruptly as masses and angles, lights and black shadows, made a pattern for him.

"You should see more of this, Joe. It's the dark side," Dermot suggested.

"I have seen a lot of it," said Joe

"It should help you with the light."

"It's the light's dark shadow," said Joe, and when they had gone a few paces he added in the same quiet voice, "and we know the shadow too well."

Christina walked between them.

Some figures crossed the street hurriedly in front and went up a dark entry. They were adults but they looked small, like waifs. Far away a ship's siren boomed mournfully. A low powerful lorry came towards them with a long body bearing an aeroplane like a monstrous dragonfly whose bloodless wings had cracked noisily as they broke. When it had vanished the air was powdered with a dry invisible dust and a sudden extra taint of fumes which vanished also in a swirl out over the river.

"Man has created his own monsters, Joe."

"The dark is dramatic," Joe answered him. "That's all it is."

"How do you mean 'all'?"

"The darkness creates drama ready-made for man; but man has to create his own drama of the light. It's not so easy."

"Man loves the dark."

"Evil is easy," answered Joe. "It's an indulgence."

Dermot glanced past Christina, whom they were seeing home, to Joe who looked wrapped about by the gloom. A street light shone upon him, glittered in his eyes, and fell away. Dermot suddenly decided to send them on alone. He was deliberately taking them into the shadow of evil without their knowledge. This realization pierced him. He remembered Grear's expression when he had told him that he had taken an artist to study the area around St. Patrick's Close in the darkness. Grear had thought it a clever dodge to cover Dermot's spying. And Grear had been right. "Let us cross here," he said.

They crossed and presently were coming near the spot where Dermot, in their company, had meant to stand and observe what happened after the police raid, and in particular what escape, if any, there might be towards the river, when, as he was searching for an excuse to send them on alone, a booming voice arrested them. They were at the corner of a narrow street and the voice came from a lighted window on the first floor a few paces up this street.

"I forgot!" Christina cried. "Ellen is singing tonight." She had stopped and gripped her hands. Dermot asked her when and Christina said it was at half-past ten.

"We're just in time," he answered. "Let us go up a little way and listen." It was a region of warehouses and workshops, narrow streets and lanes, yards and tenement houses. He had been through it twice and now stood at the corner of a transverse lane of broad cobbles. It was odd that Ellen should elect to join them in this way. It cheered his heart. Nothing now could happen anyway as far as he was concerned. It was the thought of an escape by river that had attracted him, an escape to the sea. In some mysterious way he had felt almost jealous of that, had felt he must be in on it. But now he had stopped well short of the house that in a few minutes was to be raided. It was along the lane and up to the left.

"Are you sure?" Christina asked anxiously.

The wireless voice was talking on special perils of the lambing season. March had come in.

"Yes," he answered: "And lord! isn't this lucky for me! It was I who suggested the programme. In fact, Christina, it was you through me. And I clean forgot!" His voice dropped to an amused whisper: "It really was Captain Laird."

The wireless voice ceased, and here was the Scottish Home Service announcing a programme based on— "*Carmina Gadelica*, that wonderful and indeed immortal collection of oral literature written down by Alexander Carmichael from the recital of men and women throughout the Highlands and Islands of Scotland, from Arran to Caithness, from Perth to St. Kilda." Invocations, runes, labour songs; charms; verses to the seasons, to the sun and moon, to the stars. " 'Again and again,' wrote Alexander Carmichael within living memory, 'I laid down my self-imposed task, feeling unable to render the intense power and supreme beauty of the original Gaelic into adequate English . . .' "

"Did you ever read *Carmina Gadelica*?" Dermot asked Christina.

"No," she answered. "I didn't know of it."

A man coming along the lane turned in at a doorway.

"It was a remarkable civilization," the aerial voice proceeded. "But perhaps particularly remarkable in this that it informed even its superstitions, its charms for healing cattle, with that ultimate power which pervades the universe and which they knew, at once profoundly and simply, as the power of God. The mother of our Saviour could be invoked naturally before the beauty of the moon. One can call it paganism if one likes, but if so then it was a paganism informed by Christian thought— no, not by Christian thought, but by Christian love. . . ."

"A good place for listening to it, Joe," whispered Dermot. "And don't they love it full on!"

Joe looked at him and smiled obscurely.

Dermot now felt on his toes, experienced a wild dancing recklessness. Two men looked at them as they passed up the narrow street. "Smells," murmured Dermot, sniffing the air, "thick smells. Did this kind of smell, when you first got it, give you a feeling of evil?"

"Yes," answered Christina.

"Murders up narrow places and behind doors and bloody murders in butchers' shops?"

"It frightened me," said Christina, "till I got used to it."

". . . and it was in that sense that the sun was God's eye. Men uncovered when they first saw the sun in the morning, and again at night when the sun was setting," continued the wireless voice in its Highland rhythm. "But already what they said to the sun was being hidden, and even before Alexander Carmichael the old men were reticent, for the young scoffed at them for thus saluting the sun and at the old women for bowing to the moon. Listen." Whereupon an aged Island voice recited:

> "The eye of the King of the living,
> Pouring upon us
> At each time and season,
> Gently and generously.
>
> Glory to thee,
> Thou glorious sun.
>
> Glory to thee,
> Face of the God of life."

Dermot felt his heart turn over in him. It was like another form of Ellen's singing, and Ellen would be singing any time now.

". . . not only 'the intense power and supreme beauty' which Alexander Carmichael wrote so surely of, but also the shape, the perfect form, perfect in its chiming economy, of that traditional poetry recited, let us always remember, by old people who could neither read nor write. Let us illustrate, first in the Gaelic this time, and then in the English, the blessing of the boat by the skipper and his crew before they face the sea. First you hear the skipper alone and then, at each appropriate place, you hear the response in unison of the crew . . ."

But Dermot heard no more, for into the lane from the direction of the house to be raided a man came, and in a moment he was running swiftly towards them. Out from a doorway leapt a second taller man and in an instant there was collision, the smack of a blow, and the taller man was toppling over backwards; as he hit the street, the runner kicked him twice, paused an instant over the body, then came on. Dermot, throwing his overcoat at Joe, flashed out to meet him, but this time the runner did not hit, he swerved and completely foxed Dermot who had braced himself for the impact and the blow. At sight of Joe and Christina, the runner continued in his swerve and headed up the narrow street with Dermot on his heels.

And he could run. He was a medium-sized man but lithe and manifestly powerful in impact. The way he had booted the fellow whom he had felled was enough to have had Dermot after him at any time. Dermot's running and jumping from school events onwards had been more than useful for his side, and as he set off he felt twenty-two and the wind singing in his ears. To have missed that tackle! Within fifteen yards he had the measure of his man, who, realizing the fact, dodged up a cross lane and gained several paces. But something in the region of the stomach was worrying the fellow now, for his arms had stopped swinging and his shoulders were hunched. Then there appeared a slim portfolio in one hand, and he dodged, arms swinging again, up a narrow entry, round a smoking heap or midden, and as Dermot followed after him, a crouching figure shot upright and Dermot, instinctively ducking away, missed being felled by a couple of inches. Then with the portfolio swinging the fellow was off again for he had seen that Dermot was trained to a rough and tumble.

It had not dawned on Dermot that the man would naturally take him for a plainclothes policeman. He had been able to think of nothing but the chase and downing the quarry. When he had him down they could argue. But now the portfolio was beginning to stir a certain curiosity, a certain wonder. Clearly he had been carrying it fixed to his body under his jacket. Why?

Dermot now knew he was no longer twenty-two. He was thirty-two and hadn't run for five years. The fellow nipped back down the entry and Dermot, slowing warily as he emerged on the lane, merely lost distance. But a growing wrath, partly at his own ineptitude, spurred him on. He would get the blasted fellow, he swore to himself, or drop dead.

It was certainly a fantastic hunt. In one dark entry there were wild screaming moments when a young courting couple were disrupted. A stable yard, with Dermot crouching, listening, knowing his man was waiting for him, beginning to wonder if he might be crawling away, yet reluctant to use the electric torch which he had deliberately brought with him. A stableman entered the yard with a swinging lantern, exactly as he might in the country. Dermot glimpsed a crouched body by a stone waterbutt, and as the stableman set down his lantern to pull back the red doors, Dermot slid forward to close on his man. But his move was anticipated and the man leapt onto the waterbutt, gripped the top of the stone wall, heaved himself up and dropped out of sight. "What the hell!" yelled the stableman as Dermot followed with so magnificent a display that it was graceful, for he had had time to get his athlete's wind. As he landed, he gave way, pulled his head in, rolled over twice, then bounced to his feet. In the process three very foul words clove the air and something more solid missed him.

The hunt ended in a timber yard. It was a slow business after the swift earlier passages, slow enough for Dermot to know that it was very deadly. If he made one slip and the fellow got him down—he just mightn't rise again.

And then the fellow would get clean away.

His own determination narrowed in a deadly way. He took the torch out of his pocket, gripped it carefully in his fist, and crawled three yards to the end of a timber pile. It was a wide yard with stacks of wood here and there: a place where two men could play hide and seek for long enough; where the man with the cooler patience would win. This did not exasperate Dermot, on the contrary it keyed his senses to their highest pitch, and when one board slapped loudly on another, he crouched motionless, knowing his man would, after that false step, either get away rapidly or stop dead. He had stopped dead. He was a cool customer. Dermot stared towards the pile ahead on his right.

Some stars were out for now he could see vague space between the timber piles. Keeping his face down, he went forward on all fours, first a slow hand that felt the ground before it pressed, then a knee, keeping close to the timber and listening acutely. The fellow must have got among some loose planking for again Dermot heard him and knew he was on the move. Either that, Dermot took time to think, or he is attracting me deliberately, ready with a batten to smash me, if I rush in.

As the silence lengthened, anxiety began to get the better of him. Perhaps the fellow was crawling away all the time, crawling out of earshot, round his stack of timber to its other side; then on tiptoe he would be off. But Dermot waited, and at last he saw a vague movement, like the movement of a black dog, going round the top end of the stack to his right. Slowly he got to his feet and walked lightly over a covering of sawdust towards this stack, stood, hearkened, then very slowly, feeling with his feet, turned and came back down the stack to its end. There he waited, braced.

But the fellow didn't come round the pile. Dermot stood motionless. Again anxiety gripped him, but he did not move. Then an extraordinary thing happened right at his feet which might have given him away had he not stiffened against the impulse to throw himself flat before the thrown bomb went off. The rat squealed as the cat killed it. His suddenly pounding heart affected his hearing, but presently he distinguished a scratching as of finger-nails on wood over towards the wall. He moved round the corner, disturbing the cat and the cat growled. He realized, rather than distinctly saw, that the man was trying to open the yard door.

There was a squeak of wood against wood and Dermot on his toes moved quickly. He saw the man's back and was jumping in when the wooden bar that fastened the double door suddenly gave and the man slid. Dermot, thrown off his throat tackle, managed no more than a weak left to the head. The man, still half crouching, hit against the door and rolled off it, coming almost to his knees. Dermot, falling against the door with his shoulder blades, could have kicked him. The man was off and before Dermot could trip him he leapt on a pile of timber against the wall. As Dermot grabbed at a leg he let the torch go. He caught a turn-up of the trousers in his right fist. They were now both lying on a high rounded pile of pit-props, the man trying to heave himself on, Dermot hanging to the cloth and keeping his head clear of a smash from the other foot. For a few seconds, nothing gave. Then the other foot came round with a stinging kick at Dermot's hand that knocked it nerveless. But instantly he reached higher with his left, got his head between both legs and his arms round them. Now he had him. There was a wild clawing scramble in which the props gave, and the man, cursing fiercely, came rolling down. An end of a prop hit Dermot fair in the middle of the forehead, and he fell away, but even as his body squirmed on the ground in a very dim consciousness it yet gathered itself to protect the face, the vital parts, against the stray boot in the maul; gathered itself and rolled over; and now he was on hands and knees, with eyes lifting from the ground. They steadied on a boot a few inches from his mouth. But the boot did not move. Presently he had enough strength to heave the two props off the man's inert body, then he sat for a little while with mouth fallen open, knowing he would not let himself go to sleep.

27

His first impression was that the man was dead, but when he had got him on his back, eased away the clothes at his throat and felt more carefully for the heart, he wasn't sure. His own reactions were none too certain and beyond feeling somewhat stupid he hardly felt anything at all. His torch was not in his pocket, which seemed very strange until his memory cleared. As he turned away on all fours to look for the torch one hand landed on the leather portfolio. After deciding that the torch was buried, he did a final sweep out from the pile and found it. When he pressed the button, the light at once shone on a ground of brown sawdust. He came back to the body. There was still no sign of life. Perhaps, he decided, best plan would be to get out through yard door and find help. But that would mean leaving body—which might come round. Better take body . . . About to drop the portfolio, he became particularly aware of it. Rearing on his knees, he listened.

The metal clip moved under his thumb nail and the catch clicked free. He pulled up the documents and the beam of light circled the large characters D.1. in black against a pale blue background. He stared at them. They were beautifully formed in freehand and might have been magical characters from the way they cleared his head. But his hands shook a little as he withdrew the contents of the portfolio and laid them on top of the leather case. He listened again, looked at the body, and opened out the plans.

There could be no doubt that these were the actual plans, the stolen originals, which Grear had described to him. Beyond any doubt, here they were. He folded them up, and opened out a third sheet, not unlike one of his motoring maps and covering the district which he had so recently studied in his own sitting-room. It was marked . . . here a cross was neatly made in red ink, points were circled in red ink, straight blue lines were drawn with care, and here and there what were presumably woods, bridges, and other physical features, were indicated by appropriate signs. Perhaps some sort of triangulation system, for the red cross was in the middle of the water at the inner end of the sea-loch, Loch Criach. Perhaps a combined air and land. . . . He was startled by a car siren's three quick blasts. He stuffed the plans into the portfolio and listened once more. Then he dragged the body to the yard gates and found one half of the gate swinging loose. How nearly the fellow had escaped!

It was a narrow lane, but some two hundred yards along on the right he could see the relative brightness of a street; even as he looked a car shot past the opening. He got the body over his right shoulder and staggered along towards that street. His luck was so extraordinary that it made his heart thud, weakening him. Stop a car, get the body taken to hospital, phone the police. Grear would think he was a pure miracle worker! This exciting thought made his leg muscles tremble still more and he stopped. It would be a pity if the fellow were dead now. As he eased the body against the wall, the mouth grunted by his ear. The fellow was actually coming round! As the body slewed and fell over, something hard hit the pavement. While supporting the body, Dermot actually groped for it with a feeling of that extraordinary competence which nothing could defeat. He found it. It was an automatic pistol. The fellow hadn't even been given a last-minute opportunity to use it! Dermot paused in sheer wonder, the cold metal against his palm; then he put it in his pocket, slipping to the cobbles as he did so, with the body on top of him. The mouth was now emitting stertorous gasps. "Easy does it," Dermot muttered encouragingly. He was so pleased with himself that he had gone a few yards before he missed the portfolio which the falling body had jerked from his left hand. So back he went and recovered it. There was nothing like being methodical. Am I sure now I have got everything? he asked himself, breathing heavily, inflamed with effort. Yes, he was sure. "It's no distance now," he reassured the body as it slowly writhed and he set off on the last fifty yards.

Here was the street and he was just turning into it when two men, walking past, stopped.

"Hullo," said one of them. "Anything wrong?"

"Man collapsed," Dermot gasped. "Give me a hand."

"Sure," said one of them, easing the body from Dermot's shoulder.

"Collapsed up the lane; must get him to hospital." The sudden need for a story so occupied his congested mind that he could do no more than observe the curious stealthy way in which the second man, who had not spoken, took his eyes from the portfolio and glanced quickly up and down the street. Then Dermot had a moment of such extreme apprehension of danger that he heard in what seemed a drawn-out silence footsteps approaching distantly on the pavement. As this second man stepped towards him, he was actually sucking in wind to let out a yell even while his fist was drawing back, when a knee hit him below the belt so forcefully that he doubled up with a jerk and emitted no more than a grunt.

He felt the crash of a fist below his ear, but the boot in his body was little more than a crushing softness as he passed out.

The crashing of the seas fell away, and the precipices, and he was in a glade of hazel trees with dappled light and leaves slipping coolly up over his forehead as he stooped under a branch, but what it was that happened there, in that golden glade, he never afterwards remembered. It was a dark scramble for his wits before he recognized that the face and voice were Christina's and that the place where his head was being made comfortable was her lap.

They were on the street where he had fallen. He heard the words: "God, he's got a skinful!" in a thick passing male voice, envy in its harsh 'laughter as it receded. Christina's hands restrained him as he struggled to sit up.

"Joe has gone for help," she said.

He lay still and the pains eased. His overcoat was under him. As her hand brought his hair back off his forehead, he felt soothed still more, though now a little tremulous and sick. He had to sit up. She helped him and held him with an arm, but he suddenly needed to be sick and got stretched out on his face, her hand holding his forehead. Nothing came up; the effort roused stinging pains and brought out a cold sweat. He was glad to lie back with his head on her lap. But her lap was too high and as he tilted his head backward he felt her ease it down between her knees. "Did they get off?"

"Yes," she answered. "Rest yourself." Her hand was on his forehead gain. He let go completely with a sinking feeling of drowning ease but suddenly he began to shiver. It was hellish cold. He tried to snuggle to her, but this was so damned silly that he had to sit up. She helped him. He felt weak as a kitten and sick as a very sick dog.

"I'm feeling rotten," he muttered, excusing himself.

"Yes, yes," she whispered, "but just rest yourself. Joe will be any time." Both her arms were round him, supporting him. He felt like a child. His blood began to warm, to warm inside the shivering husk of the body. He had to restrain an urge to turn blindly to her for soft comfort.

"They're coming," she said.

He heard the footsteps and straightened himself. When his tongue had passed over his lips, the ingoing breath left them icy cold. "Damn them," he muttered senselessly of those who were coming.

The policeman. Always the policeman.

"Yes, I'm all right," Dermot answered.

"No bones broken, eh?" The constable was probing him. "Where did he kick you?"

"In the guts," Dermot answered perversely, for it hadn't been quite in the guts and he thought some ribs were cracked because of a sharp pain. The constable had obviously had courses in first-aid for he helped Dermot to his feet with skill and kindliness. Joe was ready with his hands and quiet as a brother.

"I think you should let him lie down," Christina said.

He felt her mind in his body, her own secret ways of knowing. This strengthened him. A car drove up and a man in a dark overcoat spoke to the constable and asked Dermot how he was feeling. Dermot muttered that he was all right. Christina got in beside him in the back seat and when they arrived at the police station, a doctor went over him carefully. There were tender spots as though he had been kicked in more than one place, but the doctor did not think any serious damage had been done, and if there were any fractured ribs they would soon find out. "You got a nasty one there," he said touching the forehead. He wiped and dabbed the swollen spot and it stung but only slightly. Dermot drank some brandy, felt squeamish for a little while, then the prickling coldness receded before a reviving warmth. The doctor watched his face. "We'll get an ambulance for you and have an X-ray: that will make certain," he said cheerfully. "You have had better luck than the other fellow who was kicked." He helped Dermot to tuck his shirt in and get dressed, asked him who his doctor was and said he would phone him. "Don't let them badger you with talk too much," he added.

But the inspector was almost equally considerate and Dermot told him roughly what had happened, without mentioning the portfolio. He did not know any of the police in this station and his story was perfectly simple. The inspector complimented a humanity that could pursue a man because that man had performed a brutal act, then excused himself rather hurriedly.

Joe and Christina went with him in the ambulance and waited until at last he came out of the hospital on his own feet. "Bit of a swindle," he greeted them when they had got into the taxi, but Christina noticed that his face was dead white in the light and gloom from the street lamps and saw again the spot on his forehead. He wanted to brighten the journey by saying he felt he had been through a mangle but he hadn't the energy. There was a private car before his door and at once he thought: Grear. But it was his own doctor, a close personal friend of his own age, and this relieved him. "What on earth are you doing here?" Dermot asked.

"So that's the way you feel?" The doctor had just arrived. "Dragging me out at this time of night." He was looking at Dermot critically. "What you need, my boy——"

"I have something upstairs. Come on up," Dermot interrupted him.

"Good night," said Christina.

"You're not going?" Dermot looked at her.

"What you need is your bed," said the doctor.

"Good night," said Joe, and Dermot let them go.

The stair climb made him dizzy. They had a drink and a talk and the doctor phoned the hospital. Stretched out in his deep chair with his feet up, Dermot experienced a floating ease that he did not wish to lose. The feeling grew that he would like to tell the doctor everything, all about the portfolio and the rival forces in this hellish world.

"That's all right," said the doctor coming away from the phone.

"Good. Help yourself and sit down."

"I'm going to help you into your bed this very minute."

"Don't be an ass, John. If you knew what a blasted fool I made of myself to-night." His hand shook and he set the glass down again. "This fighting gets us nowhere."

"It's got you into a bit of mess—and might have got you into your long box."

"Fun and games," Dermot said. "I mean the awful bloody meaningless slaughter of humanity by itself."

The doctor gave him an acute glance. "Come on, Dermot: into bed. I'll give you something that will make you sleep in ten fathom. You must save your vitality for to-morrow when you'll need it. Up!"

In his bedroom Dermot wanted to argue. He put his hands into his jacket pockets to empty them and brought out the automatic pistol.

"Good God," said the doctor, taking it from him, "you don't carry that around with you?"

"I think it's loaded," said Dermot quietly.

The doctor examined it, removed the magazine and shook out a live bullet, then looked at Dermot.

"He didn't get a chance to use it," Dermot said, regarding his friend with a deliberate enigmatic smile. His mind was achieving an abnormal lucidity at the expense of his doped body, so he sat on the bed as naturally as he could. "Extraordinary, isn't it, that no one can see both sides—as aspects—of a higher unity? Their dialectic, the dialectic of the totalitarians, implies it, even states it. Yet they see their side, their aspect, as the whole shooting match. Damn funny, isn't it?"

"Very," said the doctor.

"I think the expression 'whole shooting match' extraordinarily apt, don't you?"

"I do," agreed the doctor, skinning the jacket off him.

"Wait a bit," said Dermot, pushing the doctor's hands from his tie. "This is important." He smiled benignly. "For the dialectic notion is dead right and hellish simple —old as life. Take Newton, greatest Englishman that ever lived, with possible exception of Shakespeare." He paused. "Very funny how they trot out Shakespeare. When they trot out Shakespeare, feel for your automatic." His vision gathered smiling distance. "Variant of well-known joke." The doctor got his tie and collar off. "What was I saying?"

"Something about Newton," said the doctor, unbuttoning the waistcoat.

"Yes. Newton. Vast mind. He saw time and space as absolutes. You understand? Then along comes Einstein —and he sees they are not absolutes. Not absolutes at all, but aspects of a greater unity behind, of a space-time unity, a continuum. Wonderful. By God, I think it's wonderful. I think the universe is wonderful."

The doctor slipped the braces over his shoulders and began to unbutton his trousers.

"Wait a bit," said Dermot. "I see the whole thing. Stop! Leave haste where it belongs, with the devils who can do nothing but shoot, blow up. Malignant principle. So you have malignant bastards who use malignant principle, and we—we crawl to them, worship them. Dear God, what a—what a come-down."

"Get out of your trousers and I'll fetch your drink."

"Drink!" Dermot smiled with fathomless humour. "What I've had's gone to my head already. This is the cheapest drunk ever. . . ."

The doctor found him talking when he came back with his bag and at once set about getting off shoes, socks and trousers. Soon he was examining the naked body on the bed.

"Science probes me once more," declared Dermot. "I am speaking," he explained, "to the higher unity which science ignores, which science denies——" He yelped.

"Science got you that time," said the doctor.

"Only the flesh," said Dermot.

"As it happens, you're right," the doctor agreed. "Purely muscular. You have been lucky, my boy . . . now swallow these."

When the doctor had tucked him in, Dermot said, "You're not going?"

"Not for a little while," the doctor answered. "I have got one or two cases to write up and two forms which I must post to-night. I'll use your writing-desk. Now—off you go!"

"You're a tyrant. And to-night—for the first time—I could tell you exactly who—what—God is."

"God will keep," said the doctor.

Dermot kept on laughing after the door closed. For he knew John was out there in the sitting-room, so Grear could ring up if he liked. Blast it, he should have told John not to answer. His heart began to thump, so he lay still. He didn't want to be left alone. Waves of exhaustion began to wash his brain. He should have told Grear. Why hadn't he told Grear? What the hell sort of fear was this, lurking somewhere, away back, in shadows? . . . Christina would ask no questions . . . A man's head, his tortured damned head, needed a woman . . . the ultimate rest . . . unity. . . . A moon swam up in his sky and a cool air of serenity and peace blew over him . . . and he drifted away.

29

The doctor found him asleep at eight o'clock the following morning, had a talk with his landlady, a serious elderly woman, and came back before eleven to a patient having breakfast in bed.

"That's better," said the doctor.

"You think, because you're nationalized, that you can order a chap about and fix his affairs."

"I can fix you anyhow anytime. How's the body?"

"Full of creaks and warnings to keep off."

"That's the stuff." The doctor laughed.

"You sound sadistic."

"I am. I hope you get a crick in the spine every time you feel like a knight-errant, not to mention an expositor of Newton."

Dermot's laughing face flushed. "Was I bad?"

"Tight's an owl," said the doctor. The telephone rang

and he went out, pulling the door behind him. He returned to say, "One of your lady loves who didn't quite seem to know her own name and decided on Joe. Didn't know you went in for that sort of thing."

"Christina!"

"The girl outside last night?"

"Yes."

"But she looked quite a sensible girl."

"She is. She went running round the lanes and back-yards looking for me. When they heard her coming they couldn't wait to finish me off. Then she sat down plonk on the pavement and took my head in her lap."

"Instead of fetching help?"

"She sent her mere male companion for help. What did you say to her?"

"Death's door, but you had taken a return ticket."

"Why didn't you tell me it was her?"

"I'm a busy man." He removed the tray. "Unbutton, till I see the colour scheme this morning." He poked and chuckled. "A couple of days' rest and you'll be nice and sore." Then he spoke seriously for a little while and left, after phoning Dermot's office.

Dermot got up after lunch with the intention of ignoring the doctor and going to business, for he had an appointment with the Assessor before a conference, and was surprised to find how groggy he was, quite apart from the aches. This annoyed him; much ado about nothing. But in the end he had to phone the Assessor, who agreed to collect some papers and come round. The very sound of his old friend's voice steadied him.

"I don't want to fade out at a critical moment," he explained to the Assessor, "so you can tell them it's doctor's orders." His description of his adventure had been very sketchy.

"Didn't know you really liked fighting."

"Very fond of it," Dermot replied. "Doctor called me a knight-errant."

The Assessor laughed softly through his nostrils and put his bowler hat on the carpet. "There being more in it all than meets the eye?"

"Perhaps." The Assessor's presence was already making him feel better. "I'll tell you what," he said suddenly. "Joe hasn't a phone. I don't want him to go blabbing. Think you could look in and see him some time?"

"Before he goes to the club?"

"That's about it. The simple story—if it has to be told—is, as I told you, that Joe and myself were seeing a lady home and paused to listen to the Gaelic broadcast, when a bag-snatcher, whom I tried to intercept, knocked me down."

"Where?"

"Let me see." Then Dermot named a suburb far enough away from the actual scene. "You need not be positive about it—if necessary. One hears all sorts of things."

The Assessor sat quite still and upright. "I think I can handle Basil."

"That's fine," said Dermot, dismissing the subject. "Now let's have a look at these documents." The phone rang. Dermot gazed at it for a moment, then got up too quickly and caught his breath. The Assessor watched him. "Yes," Dermot answered. "No, I'm not going out . . . yes, certainly . . . oh, in about an hour . . . very good." He replaced the receiver, and turned to the Assessor. "They like leaving you alone."

"Are you getting in pretty deep?"

"Not particularly," answered Dermot, "but the times are out of joint. Any news to-day?"

"The cold war is being hotted up still more. There was an incident yesterday afternoon in the air."

"Another?" His face grew hard and bleak. "Let's get down to honest business." He did not even want the details of the incident.

When the Assessor was gathering up his papers, he looked at Dermot with his small, kindly, twinkling eyes. But Dermot said he would now phone the office and brief his substitute. That he could not at this moment speak frankly to the Assessor affected him deeply, sent a wearied lethargy from the body to the mind. When the Assessor had gone, he felt shut in, the gangway withdrawn. A smouldering anger beset him.

Twenty minutes later, Grear was shown in—bright and cheerful and smiling, as if straight from a cold bath. "Been in the wars again?" His hand was cold and his voice clear as a tinkling cymbal.

"I'll be all right to-morrow. Got a few bruises, that's all."

"I gathered from your doctor last night that they were pretty hefty bruises." His eyes came over his shoulder with a sly friendly humour as he got out of his overcoat.

"You'll also have the police news?"

"Yes. And the hospital news—even if that wasn't gathered in my own name." He laughed. "But I found a little difficulty in plotting your whole graph."

"Sit down. Sorry I wasn't in a fit state to contact you last night. What happened?"

"You mean about the raid? Not too good. In fact, very bad."

"Really?"

"Yes. Word came in, just before I phoned you, that it may be pretty awkward. The police got nothing, so they're inclined to blame me. They had fixed it for the following night, but when I heard from you, I—pushed them. So I'm rather in the soup." As he pulled up the legs of his trousers he glanced around the walls and at the door with a thoughtful smile.

"No one near. I'll get the old lady to send up some tea."

"Not for me," said Grear, "thank you."

"How is it awkward, may I ask? I don't quite——"

As Dermot hesitated, Grear said, "I'll tell you. Word has just come in that those who were raided may make a noise, an injured noise. When honest Trade Unionists, gathering to discuss their interrelated affairs, are raided by the police, what is true democracy coming to? The point being that two or three there were, in point of fact, honest Union men, and they can afford to talk. A question in the House would be particularly awkward just now. So it's all excellent fifth-column disruptive propaganda. There may be a story in the later editions of the evening press."

Dermot's expression hardened. "May I ask what the police expected to find?"

"They are pretty good, the police, on the whole, though, of course, they have to take a risk. I can't go into detail, even if I knew it all, which I don't. One thing I can say. There was excellent reason to believe that the stolen plans would be there, because the fellow who was contacting Mackie who was going to restore the plans to the strong room——" Grear paused. "We know more about Mackie now," he said, and left it at that, though his smile was bland.

"You didn't want Mackie to put them back?"

"We wanted to find them at that meeting."

"But I thought it was part of the plan that they should be put back so that no one should appear to know——"

"It was. But when more was discovered, it wasn't."

"Sorry," said Dermot. He thought for a moment. "I did not want to mention Christina's name on the phone, but it was from her I got the information about Stenson's flat being searched."

"I gathered as much. Tell me exactly what she said."

When Dermot had told him, Grear nodded. "I was, on

balance, against touching the flat, but they thought they would leave no trace. It's one point in my favour. Actually, of course, last night was *the* night, and I fancy the police know it, though it may suit them, after the event, to appear doubtful. In fact, as I had to point out, it was their action at the flat that precipitated the meeting and so may have been the real reason for the plans not being there."

"They were there."

"What were?"

"The plans. I saw them."

It was the face of the statuette, then the mouth closed firmly and the throat swallowed slowly.

"I'll tell you the whole story," said Dermot, removing his eyes. "It's rather a long one. I was round at Joe's studio, Joe and I were seeing Christina home, so we came along by the river to see the night. These two know nothing, of course, of the real meaning of events. I had watched the time and, to tell the truth, I was concerned to see only if anything developed towards the river and the sea. That would have interested me." And so Dermot went on to tell in detail exactly what happened. Once thoroughly under way, he became animated, didn't miss even the incident of the cat with its rat, and gradually experienced a mounting feeling of relief. His reluctance to see Grear, to talk to him, would now have seemed absurd had he paused to think of it. But it never came into his head. Grear did not speak until the moment came when the plans were hauled out of the portfolio into the beam of the electric torch and then only to ask certain questions, to which Dermot's answers made certain that the plans were in fact the originals which Mackie had stolen.

"I didn't want to leave the body. If the fellow recovered and walked off—then—well, I don't know. Perhaps I was wrong, but I decided to take the body with me. The way the fellow had kicked that—plainclothes man, was it?"

"Yes."

"That made me damned mad. So I wanted to make a job of it. I took the body with me, meaning to stop the first car when I reached the street. I had heard one hooting. Anyway, I started off with it. On the way I had to rest and an automatic fell out of his pocket."

"You've got it?"

"Yes. Then came the anti-climax. Somehow, I never expected that their people would be about. Ordinary civilians or patrolling police, yes." Dermot paused a moment, then went on to a finish.

Grear sat very still. "You didn't tell the police about the plans?"

"No. I thought you were the man for that. I was a bit dazed, later; the doctors doped me."

Grear was silent.

"Perhaps I should have left the fellow in the timber yard——"

"No, you were quite right. Without the man——" Grear stirred and the insipid smile came to his face. He did not look annoyed or put out. "Without the man, it wouldn't have been so good."

Dermot waited with an odd sense of bewilderment.

Grear explained a child's puzzle. "To produce plans and say we found them on a man we hadn't got wouldn't impress even a bailie. The police will sweat over this."

"You'll have to tell them?"

"Very definitely. A thing like that just shouldn't happen. One begins to wonder." He sat still again.

Dermot could not think at all. He did not want to be drawn into police circles, into cross-examinations where nothing would be overlooked, no one omitted, where suspicion . . . He saw Christina being questioned. . . . A dark inward motion of withdrawal beset him, the backing away of the suspicious animal from the trap.

"There's a certain very able special branch inspector. You'll have to meet him," Grear said thoughtfully.

"Frankly, I don't want to be mixed up with the police."

"I know. I've told them that. But now it may be a matter *inside* the police. They'll want more than my word. There will be no difficulty about it and it will be quite secret."

Dermot said nothing.

"We're all going to sweat if they work their publicity racket right. And they will. The monopoly of brains is by no means on our side. But if they do their publicity and *then* we find some of them *with* the plans, that would be a turning of the tables that one dreams about but seldom manages. It is, of course, too good to be true: so it is the aim, the end." He smiled with a curious lack of mirth. It was an extraordinary expression that always stuck in Dermot's mind because he couldn't fathom it. The statuette of the god-devil that one shifted about on the mantelpiece, but that never changed.

It was only after Grear had gone that Dermot, suddenly longing for a remote spot in the Highlands, remembered the map in the portfolio. He had been going to mention it when Grear had questioned him about the D.1. plans, and then had forgotten to do so in front of Grear's concentrated interest and his own consciousness of the disastrous end to the adventure of which he was, in his very bones, ashamed.

Now he would give Grear time to get back to his office and then phone him. He must get everything off his chest, everything. Tell everything, get rid of the stuff. Confession! he thought, pausing in his excitement. His eyes actually strayed to the left-hand corner of the mantelpiece, as if it were the mantelpiece in old Armstrong's house and he, a boy, were looking for the first time, the only time, at the Eastern statuette.

The mind was an odd business. The statuette would be doubtless an archetype of something! He must tell Joe that the new priest of our age was a policeman. Tell Joe to draw a police station and show a fellow being put through it; title: The Confessional. The tip of Joe's tongue would show pink. Dermot laughed and moved around. He was very tired; his temples were beating; he could drag his body through the aches without any sharp pain; couldn't have been his lung at all. He dropped into a chair and lay back; his flesh was trembling. His landlady knocked and brought in tea.

The idea of getting away for a day or two—for the week-end—began to obsess him. He needed the sea, needed the smell of salt water, an anchorage, peace. He got out the chart he had been looking at on Sunday. He studied it for a long time, then sat slumped in his desk chair staring through the wall. Presently he got up, but he did not phone Grear; he went and lay on his bed and stared through the ceiling.

After supper Joe came round. Dermot was glad to see him and ask for Christina.

"She didn't like to come round," Joe answered. "Thought you might be in bed."

"You seem to be seeing a lot of her. Or has she taken up her residence in the studio permanently?"

"No," answered Joe, without a smile.

Dermot smiled. "You like Christina?"

"Yes. I find her very interesting."

"Fascinating, in fact."

"Yes, that's it," said Joe. "She's fascinating, extraordinarily fascinating. I never met anyone like her."

"And you've met a few?"

"Yes, I've met many women. In Paris, mostly. But also in Vienna once. They knew the studio life. Women understand artists abroad. They understand about him

203

doing his work. That's the great thing, no matter what happens."

"Very nice for him."

"Yes, it's good for him. He goes ahead then like a house on fire."

Dermot could see that Joe was holding himself in. His glance narrowed still more.

"You think Christina would make a good artist's woman?"

"Yes," said Joe. "You don't have to tell her."

"I have never seen you do anything else but."

Joe now looked genuinely bewildered. "Me?"

"What do you find particularly fascinating in her?"

Joe looked away. "I don't know," he said. "She's full of rest. I think she's beautiful. She's—she's there. She's just there. That's all. No words required. She's—what you look for. She's—what you come on. Then she's there. No explanation. You can't explain what is."

"So she doesn't need to talk to you."

"Oh, but she does!" said Joe excitedly. "She talks the most beautiful talk. I mean it's wonderful. It's really very interesting stuff."

"That's more than she's ever done to me."

"But—but——" Joe looked at him. "Perhaps you didn't listen."

"I have spent hours trying to get her to say three words. You have stolen her from me, Joe: that's all." Dermot's voice had been growing increasingly precise.

Behind their talk there had been all along a certain personal awareness of this new situation, but with a smile trying to come through; now Joe gaped, and as his lips parted the cheekbones stood out, the blue eyes looked stormily from ambush, and the whole face gathered its suggestion of being unfinished, but in its own puckered way with an underling pertinacity, a continuing strength.

"But—but that's nonsense," he declared. "I would never do such a thing. You know that." He was so moved, spoke with such force, that he could not stand still; he threw his arms apart.

"I'm not accusing you——" began Dermot.

"Besides, she talks about you," Joe continued. "She asks how you are. I think—what you say——"

"I did not really mean it, Joe."

"You said it," said Joe. "You—you destroy something I don't like it."

"But look, Joe——"

"I don't like it." Joe was clearly deeply offended. He was hurt and not prepared to listen. "I never expected— I never thought you——"

"You're always learning," said Dermot coolly, irritated for the first time. "You forget that I have known Christina a very long time."

"What's that got to do with it? That's not the point. Besides—besides that—you said other things."

"What things?"

"About money," said Joe. He was now in a highly agitated state.

"Sit down, Joe," Dermot said quietly. "We'll have a drink. I need it. The doctor told me not to try to throw anyone out of the room."

Joe stared at him, then slowly became confused. "I forgot," he muttered.

Dermot poured out a couple of drinks. "I thought you were a pacifist," he remarked, stretching himself full length in his chair. "And I find you prepared to take me at a disadvantage and knock my head off."

"I wouldn't do that," muttered Joe.

"I wouldn't trust you," said Dermot. "However, about Christina. She's out of a job. That's all I meant when I mentioned money. I don't know anything about your affairs or what artists do, but I thought an artist usually paid for a model. I was merely passing the tip. I happen to know that Christina was in the habit of sending something to her mother occasionally. One or two friends of mine are desperately anxious to get a good maid. Christina must be living on her savings, if any. That's the position. My sole concern is to help Christina and see she is not taken advantage of. Now you have it."

Joe stared at the fire, then hardly knew where to look. "It's this money," he said. "It put me into a state—I didn't know what to do. An artist pays for his model. Of course. But I haven't worked on the life for a long time. That's not my . . . you know my pictures . . . I don't now. I was not good at money. I made great mistakes. It landed me in difficulties. Once or twice—it was very bad. Then I made my final decision. It coincided with my new direction; in painting, what I was searching for. I cannot explain it all. But I reduced myself, my needs. I worked it all out, so that the allowance would spread over, so that I wouldn't have to depend on anyone, so that I would be free to go my way, so that—so that—I wouldn't even have to sell a picture." He looked at Dermot, as though he could not expect understanding, yet hoped for it, all the wild agitation subsiding.

"Do you mean you didn't want to sell pictures?"

A faint distress touched Joe's features. "I don't know," he said. "I'm not sure."

"And then Christina came along?"

"Yes," said Joe, as if everything now were clear. He actually looked relieved and took a deep breath.

"Did you mention to Christina anything about paying for a model?"

"Yes. After—after you spoke to me and I thought about it. I saw I was mean about money."

"Yet you knew you had simply tried to forget about it."

Joe's expression softened. "Yes, I—something like that."

Dermot lifted his glass. "What did Christina say?"

"She asked: 'What's a model?' "

Dermot's fist gripped the tumbler, then he began to shake, and as the laughter came out of him the whisky spilled over. When he had set the glass on the floor, he pressed the sore spots on his body. Then he wiped his eyes.

"Thank God," he said. "Now, look, Joe. All this is very important. The doctor will be in any minute and he'll want to sit when he comes. I'll tell you what I have been thinking over to-day. I got a sudden longing for the sea. I know where I can lay my hands on a small cabin cruiser. What about Christina and yourself joining me on Saturday and going for a week-end cruise? Back on Sunday night or Monday morning at latest. You could take some sketching material with you."

"That," said Joe after a moment, "that would be wonderful."

"Talk it over with Christina, but don't mention it to anyone else. You understand?"

"Yes." Joe's tongue tip appeared.

"Let me see—to-morrow night——" The telephone bell rang. Slowly Dermot got out of his chair and went and lifted the receiver. "Yes?"

"Is that you?" asked Grear's voice.

"Yes. Still alive."

"Remember, I said someone might want to have a talk with you?"

"Yes."

"Could he call round now?"

"Well—not now. I'm expecting the doctor and he'll stay a while."

"Oh. . . . What about in an hour's time? You're not too tired, are you?"

"I am a bit. But—I was thinking perhaps to-morrow—but—all right—in an hour or so."

"That's very good of you. You'll tell him what you told me."

"Certainly no more. Haven't the energy."

"That's excellent. Thank you."

As Dermot turned from the phone, he looked so pale, so drawn, that Joe got up.

"To-morrow night, then, Joe—I'm sick of all this—I'll come round—after supper. They won't find me in your place. And—I would like to hear Ellen sing. I think I would like that very much. Ask Christina to make her come."

"Yes," said Joe, "I'll do that." He was very subdued now.

They heard a car stop outside, the slam of a door.

"There he is. Good night, Joe."

Joe hesitated. But he could not find whatever words he wanted. "Good night," he said and went away.

When Dermot arrived the following night at Joe's studio, Ellen was already there, having, with Christina, partaken of a high tea and much talk in a quiet restaurant. "Bless this house," he said, "in the name of sun and moon." He bowed to the ladies. "I place my offering on the throne." He laid what were obviously two bottles wrapped in brown paper on the model's throne. "It contains a sup of the sun and a sup of the moon." He turned to Joe. "May the light dwell in you and in all you do." He lifted his face. "Amen."

"Oh, Dermot," cried Ellen. "How lovely!" She laughed and went close to him and inspected his face and how he stood. "You're looking not too bad, apart from that sinister spot on your forehead."

"You're looking beautiful and a little dangerous."

"Thank you for the little danger."

"And who gave you that bit of Celtic silver?"

Her hand went up to the large round brooch on the fine green velvet over her left breast. "It's a family heirloom. No one ever gives me anything."

"I give you my heart."

Her eyes flashed at him. "Where will I wear it?"

"On your sleeve."

She sighed.

"Lord, Joe, you have on a new tie!" declared Dermot.

"Yes," said Joe. "I—I found it."

Dermot laughed and turned to Christina. "My lady of the night goes in black."

"It's not black, you sumph," said Ellen, "it's blue."

"The deep night sky," said Dermot. "Behind which, as behind the wave. We may now take the wrappings off the offering. It's my party, Joe, with your permission." He exposed a bottle of whisky and a bottle of port.

Joe couldn't find the two glasses, he said, with the worried expression of one to whom mysterious things happen though he knows he is anything but incompetent.

As Christina went towards him and the kitchen, Dermot, watching her action, said quietly to Ellen, "Have you been doing something to her?"

"No. She's been doing it to herself."

"There's something."

"The string of pearls, perhaps?"

209

"Perhaps it's of that nature."

Ellen laughed softly, then she turned to him. "Christina was telling me what happened. Have you no sense at all?"

"Indeed I have. Didn't I get you to come along?"

"You made me tell an awful lie, which I certainly never would——"

"Isn't that what I'm saying? I've got to do something fantastic like that before you look at me."

"You always leave me speechless."

"You say such lovely things then." He considered her. "You are looking very charming to-night, Ellen." His eyes were bright with tribute.

"You are looking terribly attractive yourself, with that sinister spot on your forehead. Does it hurt?"

"Not there."

They laughed, enjoying the game, which always warmed them and made them happy—and even the more happy if for some half-obscure reason, never analysed in words, they had not met for a while.

"I'll sing to you for that," she promised.

"No, Ellen. Please!"

She laughed. "Gracious, Christina! *Four* glasses!"

"I found them behind some things in a corner," said Christina, smiling.

"I always knew they were somewhere," Joe explained, with the worried air of one who can rely on his memory.

His expression was too much for Ellen and Dermot. Only at the second or third attempt did Dermot command the shaking bottle with sufficient accuracy to pour the drinks.

The talk grew a little more extravagant.

Joe persisted in stating simple truths with an aptness beyond wit. Ellen was now sitting on a cushion on the floor and swayed where she sat. Christina and Dermot sat on the edge of the dais with the bottles between them

Joe was restless, with an eye at unexpected moments for the comfort of his guests. When Ellen saw Joe's features run together in a shy smile, she wanted to say something about it, and felt so balked when she daren't that she could only ask him to sit down beside her. Dermot laughed.

But when Ellen turned wickedly on Dermot, he held up his hand against her words. "No," he said, "I refuse to discuss these bloody and idiotic events in this place."

"But it's not your place."

"No, but it's my body."

"Will you tell me about them?" she asked Joe.

"Yes," he answered, "if you command me."

She looked at him with extra interest. "I suppose most men can flatter when it comes to the bit."

"I don't know," said Joe, giving the matter his earnest thought, "but I should say it depends on the bit."

She stared at him. He was quite solemn. But suddenly he smiled deeply.

"Joe!" she said, in a reproving tone.

But Joe was delighted with himself. From a warm face, he said, "I know what Dermot means."

"Do you? Then I command you to tell me."

"It's—it's all the violence in the world." His look grew troubled. "He wants to get away from it for one night."

"Well, that seems fair enough," Ellen agreed judicially. "Though he might have made it clear himself, don't you think?"

"Yes," muttered Joe.

"That's the worst of these Highland natures: they're so secretive and silent."

"He's not always silent," said Joe.

"Really?" Ellen raised her eyebrows.

Joe glanced at Dermot like one out of his depths, but not altogether disliking it. Not knowing what to say, he said, "He wants you to sing."

"Does he? Would *you* like me to sing?"

"Yes, I would."

"I like singing," murmured Ellen. "I could sing to you all night."

"That would be very agreeable," said Joe.

"I like singing as much as you like painting."

Joe looked at her for a few moments. "Do you?"

With an equally serious expression, she answered, "Yes."

"Yes, of course!" said Joe, growing slightly excited. "Now, listen, and I'll show you how one of our old Gaelic songs paints the landscape in sound."

"But——" Joe stopped.

"Yes?" she inquired.

"Please excuse me," he said. "I was going to argue about one art—one art, you know, in terms of another."

"I don't know," she said simply, waiting.

"Excuse me." He was confused. "Please go on."

"I can't now."

"Oh, but you—but you must." He became distressed. "We talk too much. Theories. Then we're lost." He threw his hands apart.

"I never could understand a theory," said Ellen. "I never got my sums right."

"That's what I mean," cried Joe. "They were all wrong."

"Mine were."

"No, no," said Joe. "I mean them, with the X and the Y and the compound interest. Did you ever understand compound interest?"

"No."

Joe nodded and breathed his relief. "Now, perhaps?"

She flashed him her smile. "With pleasure."

Joe looked happy and bowed angularly. Indeed he so far forgot himself as to murmur a compliment in French.

Ellen accepted it graciously, then composed herself for a few moments. "First," she said to Joe, "I will endeavour to convey to you the shape of the wind." She started humming. Joe heard the wind rise to a crest, fall away to rise higher, a wind rhythm that had a shape, a haunting veiled shape, that firmed into a melodic line as Ellen's mouth opened. She stopped and said, "Now I'll give you the line of the mountains." And Joe this time saw the mountains. Then Ellen began to sing a Gaelic song, quietly, exaggerating the rhythms to start with, showing they were almost exactly the rhythms she had already used, before proceeding to sing the song normally, her voice increasing in volume as she gave herself to the song and drew passion into it as flames draw the bright air, and almost as invisibly, so that the human heart was lifted like the flames and aspired and vanished beyond its own reach as the flames vanish when the wind lifts them . . . until the rhythms begin to fall, and height is lost, and the lines of the mountains come down to where, all flame gone, the heart sits alone with itself.

Joe was deeply moved, but the added experience of revelation so excited him that, to their astonishment, he kissed Ellen's hand. And it was no mere esthetic noiseless gesture.

Dermot smiled, moved by Joe also. It was divine that things like these could happen. He sat on the floor in order to have support for his back, and stuck his legs out.

"You didn't hear much of the 'Carmina Gadelica' programme, did you?" Ellen asked him.

"No," he answered. "Tell us about it."

Their voices now were warm and friendly, as if the song had brought them into simple communion. Joe got up and put a bunch of soft material behind Dermot's shoulders.

"I can't remember it, though I read bits of the script afterwards. But there were some lovely passages," Ellen said. "The way the animals were brought in, simple things like that. For example, the man would take off his cap and bow to the sun . . . and the way the words went had the rhythm too. Let me think. Something like this" (and as she spoke the words her hand followed their rhythm): "He would take off his cap and bow, giving glory to the great God of life for the glory of the sun and for the goodness of its light to the children of men and to the animals of the world."

They smiled.

Joe's eyes shone as he said, "The light. That was it always. The Greeks—they went to the gloomy under-world, where spirits of the dead clustered like bats. Even the Greeks. But with our ancestors, as the earliest stone drawings show, it was the God of Light that guided the spirits to the next world. A ship and the symbol of the sun. And in that next world there was light and fruit."

"That's lovely, Joe," Ellen said. "Tell us more."

Joe talked of megalithic drawings, of ancient Egypt, and of how the Celtic people in their art went in for abstract pattern, and he made it all interesting because he was moved, and they watched his fingers creating spirals in the air and patterns on the floor and confusion among themselves, and when Ellen got lost in his verbal and other arabesques, she just watched him, wondering what it was in him that moved him so, what sort of being he was far in himself. His placing the stuff behind Dermot's shoulders had surprised her.

"You are interested in these old things?" she asked him.

"You must know about them if you want to know what life is, how it goes on. You see that in art: the record of what life wants. All the way from cave-man days. Light, for example. It's nothing new. Yet it's new every day. If only we could see the light. If only I could show it." He was trying to restrain himself, and suddenly shrugged, with that expression which seemed to melt the features.

"What did you sing?" Christina asked Ellen.

"One was very old. I don't think you have heard it."

"Sing it, please," begged Christina.

Ellen considered her idly, smiling. "And what are you going to do?"

"I'll make tea," said Christina.

They all smiled.

"Don't let us move," said Dermot. "What does Christina do?" he asked Ellen.

"She sings, but she's very good, too, at stories."

"Is she?" He looked at Christina.

"No, I'm not," said Christina.

"Yes, you are," said Ellen. "And oh, remember! When I asked you if Dermot was disfigured you said he had no more than a mark on his forehead like the love spot in the fable. I was going to have asked you what fable, but I was so concerned about him I forgot."

Christina's face slowly flushed.

"Come on, Christina," said Dermot. "It's turn about and we'll go round with the sun."

"But it's just one of old Anna's," began Christina.

"That settles it," said Dermot. "Bring your glasses, children, and then we'll listen to old Anna."

Presently Christina laid her hands in her lap and began: "Long long ago, Dermot the warrior came to be known as Dermot of the Love Spot, and this is how it happened. On a day of days he was away hunting with his three comrades, Conan and Oscar and Goll, and as the night came on them they started to look for a shelter and at last saw a hut and to the door of that hut they went. An old man came in answer and asked them what they wanted and they told him they wanted a night's rest and he said they were welcome to that. So in they went and there they saw in the old man's company a young girl, a wether sheep and a cat. After the hard day they had, the four heroes needed food and refreshment, but if they needed it, it was pleased the old man was to give it to them, and at once there was the table all laid

215

and the dinner ready. Sit in, said the old man to them, and they sat in; but in a moment what should the wether sheep do but jump on the table. First Oscar tried to take the wether off the table, but the wether knocked him down. Then Conan tried, and the wether knocked him down. Then Dermot tried, and he was knocked down too. In the end it was Goll who flung the wether off the table, but if he managed it, he fell himself after the terrible fling he gave, and there the four of them were on the floor and the wether walking and stamping on them. It was now the old man spoke to the cat and told the cat to lead the wether away to its place and tie it up. And this the cat did without any bother. So you can imagine how overcome the four champions were with shame when they saw that. Indeed the shame on them was so great that they were for leaving the hut that minute. But the old man smiled and told them that they need feel no shame and no discredit because the wether sheep was the World and the cat was the power that would destroy the world itself, for the cat was Death. Very well. After that they were taken to a room, and it was a large room, and each was given a bed to himself. But there was still another bed in the room and that was the bed the maiden came to sleep on, and her beauty made a light on the walls of the room like a candle. Goll was the first to go over to her but she shook her head and put him away. 'I belonged to you once,' she said, 'but I never will again.' Then Conan went and he met with the same answer. Then Oscar went and he met with the same answer. And last of them all went Dermot and to him she said, 'O Dermot, to you also I belonged once but I never can again, for I am Youth; but come here and I will put a mark on you so that no woman will see you without loving you.' And at that she lifted up her hand and touched his forehead and left the love spot there, and it drew the love of women to him as long as he lived."

No one spoke. They sat idly, smiling. Dermot looked across at Joe. "You're enchanted, Joe."

"Yes," murmured Joe.

Ellen was looking at the spot on Dermot's forehead. "It was always there," she said remotely.

"You cannot resist taking advantage of me," replied Dermot, distantly, his eyes mocking her.

Ellen turned her bewitched face to Christina. "That was a lovely one."

"It is just one of Anna's," said Christina. She had told the story with a curious objectivity, without emphasis on any part, as if it were something she had learned at school. No pausing for effect. Just the story.

"Don't think," said Dermot to Joe.

"I'm not," said Joe, but he got up and stalked about and muttered, and Dermot watched him.

"Will I get the tea?" whispered Christina to Ellen.

"Lord, it's hard," said Dermot, easing himself from the floor to his knees and then to his feet. He looked at Christina. "I'll help you get the tea, seeing it's my party." And they went together into Joe's tiny kitchen.

31

"That was a wonderful party," said Ellen to Dermot much later as he drove her home in his car.

"A taste of the wild honey."

"You're really feeling all right?"

"Fine, Ellen. A night like that renews me. I get a craving for it. It was good of you to come round.

She was silent.

"And didn't Christina do her part!" He laughed.

"She's not so simple as you think."

"No one is."

"I suppose that's true," said Ellen. "You're her hero."

"Am I? How interesting!"

"When you landed in Cladday, with your uniform on, you came like a young god from another world and she saw the spot on your forehead."

"I always liked her eyes."

"Do you think you should?"

"Are you going to preach at me?"

"But I don't think she loves you. Not yet. She's frightened."

"But I thought one couldn't help loving?"

"Can't one?"

He turned his head and looked at her, then he laughed quietly. "You have something on your mind."

"A fat lot of good that does."

"That's better."

"Sometimes I could shake you—so hard."

"But you never do."

"No. That's the sad part of it. But some day——"

"Ah."

She looked out of the side window. He caught her near hand in his. "I'm not asking you to sing, even one stave," he said quietly.

She lifted his hand and looked at it, then she put it back on the wheel. "Christina finds no difficulty with Joe. Odd, isn't it?"

"I suppose it is."

"She told me quite seriously that he needed looking after."

"No!"

"And she's rather excited. You're merely her hero, so you don't really count."

"And what about the spot on my forehead?"

"You haven't used it yet—on her."

"How do you know?"

Ellen did not answer. Presently she said, "Draw up here. It's near enough."

Dermot drew up by the kerb.

Ellen turned to him. "Thank you once more for a lovely evening."

"But you're not going yet?"

Her smile rested on his face, then she began feeling for the door handle.

"But look, Ellen——" As he stretched over to take her hand from the handle, she pushed the door open.

"Good night, Dermot." She gently kissed his cheek, then freed herself from his arm and got out.

At once he got out of the other door and joined her on the pavement. "You're in a hurry, surely."

"It's very late," she said, moving on.

"How is your father?"

"Still looking after us."

"But this is absurd. I had been looking forward——"

"How nice of you. But then you are always so thoughtful." She turned her face to him and smiled. Then she stopped. "Here we are."

He stood looking at her.

"Good night," she whispered.

"Ellen! You can't go. Come on, let's have a run."

She hesitated a moment, looking back at him, then waved her hand. He stood still until she had closed the door.

He drove back to the old mews where he had his lock-up garage, saw a man loitering in the shadows of the lane and had a strong impulse to go up and ask him what the hell he thought he was doing there.

As he left the lane and followed the upward curve of a one-sided street, he became aware of the city and stopped to listen to individual noises in its silence. A light flared up far away as if an electric junction had fused. Darkness lay over the city, and odd lights and a haze of lights packed the darkness down on the invisible roofs, below which were the rooms and the tunnels, the pale faces and the bodies. An immense human warren, wide-spread, defencelessly open. Dark, sharp-nosed missiles, reaching the end of their flight, would tilt over in silence and fall far and wide like rain.

He went on, feeling within himself that Joe's coloured room and what had passed there, the ease and the singing, the silence and the lack of care, the god of light and the afterworld, the warmth on a face, the wonder—all fantastic, an escape. A refuge hole. A nostalgic den.

Only the women were real, because they remained personal. A man could no longer be personal. He was caught up, and as an individual mattered no more. He had no longer a destiny. He was not even an ant—yet.

Even this smouldering anger of his at thought of it all would need destruction for its satisfaction. There was no getting past destruction. It was coming, this bloody ghastly rain, this senseless futility. To prove someone right, to justify a theory! As if every damned one of the theories hadn't been in it since the beginning of time. The world as a wether sheep, a castrated sheep! And death as the beast of the night, the prowling cat! Old Anna's traditional analysis was at least as good as the latest hot gospel from Paris.

The slight dazing pain that still came to his forehead under stress brought his hand up to the bruise.

Just as the pit prop had hit him on the forehead he

had heard the oaths of destruction, had known that the human thing coming tumbling down on him would destroy him if it could. But the inanimate had administered its own love spots.

As he entered his room and switched on the light, he looked across at his desk. Sometimes his landlady left a pencilled message or telephone number for him to call up. There was nothing. He went right over to the desk to make sure, then breathed with relief. Grear had had no new notions, so he needn't even tell him he was going off for the week-end. He had had a busy day fixing everything up and felt tired. In Joe's little kitchen Christina had insisted on going over items like milk and tea, her face solemn and sensible. She was a good lass; said she had her story about going away for Mrs. Mure but didn't even trouble him with it. She had had nothing definite to pass on, except that Amy was excited and very secretive, as if something had happened or was going to. Christina had seen her only for a short time. Bless it! thought Dermot suddenly. I forgot to ask her if she had a pair of trousers and canvas shoes. He stood quite still for a few moments, then went to the telephone.

"Yes?" answered Ellen's voice almost at once.

"Is that yourself? I thought you might have been in bed."

"Just going." Her voice was little more than a clear whisper.

"All alone?"

"Yes. Terribly late to call me."

"Were you expecting me to?"

"You're quite mad."

"That's how I feel. You left me."

"Served you right."

"Ellen! Are you listening?"

"No."

"Listen, then. If I got out the car——"

"Go to your bed, and don't be daft."

"So you wouldn't like to come?"

"Of course not."

"Oh well, I'd better go away."

"Yes, do . . . Dermot?"

"Yes."

"It was lovely of you to call me. I confess I was frightened you would. Now go away and leave me."

"I can't leave you. That's the trouble."

"Does it hurt?"

"It does. More and more."

"When it hurts very much, you can tell me."

"The awful thing about you is that you're quite heartless."

"Are you only finding that out now?"

"Yes."

"Go away, Dermot. I'm frightened."

"I'm going away for the week-end. What about—could you—Monday night?"

Ellen took a little time. "Yes. Good night." The instrument clicked in his ear.

"You must always check over your stores, Joe: that's very important," said Dermot. "Start at the beginning with petrol and oil and never take anything for granted."

"Yes," said Joe.

"Don't say yes. Christina, get inside with this and dress yourself properly."

She took the parcel and looked at him. "Very good, sir."

"Now we're talking!" He cast his eye critically over the thirty-foot square-sterned cabin cruiser. "That's everything. Now, Joe. Have you a good heart?"

Joe looked at him with even more surprise than Christina had shown, but he replied, "Very good, sir."

Dermot restrained himself though he shook a little. "I want you to swing the engine. It's an old engine that goes on for ever—once you've got her going. I have a muscle that still objects. But you'd better do the whole thing from the beginning: you'll be the engineer."

Joe was clearly terrified of the engine, but from the squirting of petrol into the cylinder heads to the fixing of the handle Dermot instructed him. "No, no, put your thumb this way, for if she backfired she might break your thumb. Now, round with it!"

There was an explosive cough and Joe's hand was flung in the air. He was very pale.

"Near it. Put that back—yes, that—a very little—hold! Now, once more. And don't be afraid of it."

This time the engine went off with such a terrific roar that Joe staggered back, pale as death. "Close your throttle!" yelled Dermot. But Joe could not even close his mouth. Dermot closed the throttle too much and the engine stopped. "She's got a grand roar, hasn't she?"

Joe's tongue came between dry lips.

By the time they had got the Kelvin engine turning over nicely, Christina was an interested spectator. Dermot ran his eye over the blue slacks and shoes and nodded. "Shipshape."

Soon they were out in the fairway and Dermot was

looking around. "No sun, but he'll come. The forecast was good weather for the next two days and the glass is slowly rising. How do you feel, Christina?"

"Fine."

"Joe is pretty good at the engine, isn't he?"

She smiled, turning her eyes on Joe.

"Did you see our boat exploding into small bits?" Dermot asked him.

"Yes," answered Joe, "and it wasn't very good."

Soon they were at home in the cockpit, the near shore slipping past, the estuary opening out into the beyond, into a great firth whose sea-lochs penetrated far into mountainous lands. Dark-blue lines ran against the horizon. Already a breadth, an opening of distance and adventure, a mounting exhilaration, and Dermot laughed aloud at his crew's sudden consternation when, well after a tramp steamer had passed them, the *Fulmar* began to rock.

"Can you steer, Christina?"

But Christina knew nothing about handling boats and Dermot realized that in islands like Cladday the sea was exclusively man's affair. The western sea, the terrible waters of the ocean. There was a place for man and a place for woman in that world.

The small wheel was against the house and Christina very quickly learned to keep the bow on a distant mark. Dermot went over the engine, checked the oil flow, cast an eye over the cabin, the small open galley, and shut the lavatory door. The sleeping arrangements were simple. Christina—what was it about Christina that made you take her as you would your sister? He was very fond of Christina.

Out in the cockpit again his spirits rose even higher. He had a chart with him. He didn't need to look at it but he unrolled it and looked. In no time he rolled it up again and the harsh sound was music. He could not stand still. He was smiling, wanted to laugh, and let out a shout. "If I were a poet," he said, "I would make a long poem of lines like: the spring tide sets at five knots through the narrows; bear away to the large stone beacon without a cross; clean shore on east side, but look out for squalls; water at well below fisherman's hut; anchor in three to five fathoms off the brown rock; at a moderate offing, Christina kept a steady course . . ."

He was interrupted by a glimmer on the water ahead. The sun came through, and, as it swept across them, Dermot, who was hatless, stood to attention and saluted:

> "Glory to thee,
> Face of the God of life."

They came in the afternoon to an anchorage in a long narrow sea loch where there was good holding ground, though exposed to squalls from the west. No sign of any habitation.

Dermot held his breath where he stood. "That's it."

"What?" asked Joe.

"The silence." The engine had stopped. "Divine, isn't it?" He turned to Christina. "Let's see where things are and get some grub." Inside he was very much the skipper. The two berths in the cabin were for Joe and himself; but there was quite a comfortable berth for'ard for Christina. "Handy for the galley," he said to her, "and you can look out of the little porthole and hear the water on the shore. The fresh water is in that white tank, with a tap at the foot." Not too many blankets and it would be cold in the night, but they could keep most of their clothes on.

The next half-hour found them busy, with Joe in the way and Christina gradually coming through, taking charge of the domestic arrangements, putting things in place, asking practical questions only, and finally showing that their presence merely congested space. Dermot retreated, taking the potatoes with him to the cockpit where he squatted.

"Peeling potatoes," he said, "is at such a moment life's most satisfying occupation. The king isn't even your cousin."

"It's beautiful here," said Joe, looking around.

"The hills and the water and the place where no one is."

"Yes," said Joe. "It's the spring light, that freshness before—before the colour. What a tremendous amount of quiet colour there is—before the living colour comes. The light is—is——"

"Filtered . . . thin. . . ."

"No, it's——" But Joe couldn't find words. He moved restlessly. He was becoming excited.

"I know what you should do," said Dermot.

"What?"

"Sort of still life of Christina peeling potatoes. When a woman is peeling potatoes what does she think of, do you think?"

"I don't know," answered Joe. "Besides, that's not it. It's not that—it's the thing——"

"But it is. I maintain it is."

"But it isn't. That isn't what is, isn't the real thing, which is behind it. Anyone can think about anything——"

226

"I'm prepared to dispute that. However, proceed with your thesis——"

"Dermot!"

Dermot leapt up and was through to the galley in a flash. The tall yellow flame died down and went out with a plop. Christina was pale.

"Lord," he said, "I thought something had happened to you!"

"I thought," she stammered, "boat would go on fire."

He smiled and patted her on the shoulder. Then he explained that the jet of the primus, which swung on gimbals, probably needed pricking, and that in any case she must never let the pressure go too low. "Come out and get some air."

"Have you the potatoes ready?"

He laughed and took her arm. "Come out and stop Joe arguing. I don't know what on earth he's talking about."

Joe, who had followed Dermot, backed away with a face of frightened bits and pieces, but a smile was already beginning to herd them together. In the cockpit he got down on his knees and hunted scattered potatoes from odd corners.

"Before we do another thing," declared Dermot, "we'll have a drink. And look here, Joe, you'll stop your arguing and do what Christina tells you after this."

"Yes," said Joe, nursing more potatoes than he could hold.

"Ay, ay, sir," said Dermot.

And Christina smiled. "I'm fine, now. I'll get the glasses." And she went away.

"She's a good girl that; I mean, to take with you where conditions are primitive and things have to be done," Dermot said.

Joe's brows gathered in silence.

"Don't you think so?" Dermot persisted.

"It's not just that," said Joe. "That's not what it is——"

Dermot threw his head up and laughed with a soft helplessness. "I can't help it, Joe. It was so good of Christina and you to come. The sea always makes me a little drunk. Overlook it."

Joe took a moment. "Very good, sir."

Some two hours later, Dermot left them. "You're coming into the oars fine," he called to Joe, who was pulling the dinghy back to the boat. Christina was standing in the cockpit. He gave her a wave and turned to the slope.

His excuse that he wanted to get his binoculars on the western seaways from a hill-top had seemed good enough until he mentioned that they were not to be upset however late he was in returning. Then he had produced the prepared story of the man who lived a mile or so beyond the crest, an old sea friend (he was actually thinking of Norman Gavin) on whom he might—or might not—call. "If you hear me coming singing in the small hours, you'll know he has been hospitable." There was no fear of the weather; and if they put the yacht on fire they could take to the dinghy.

He wondered how much Christina believed of all this, and thought of them talking solemnly together. He knew now that Christina could talk away to Joe and keep him right on many practical things; also—and this was more difficult to grasp—she was not shy about his pictures and all his notions. Heaven knows what will happen when she gets to understand about one-man shows and submitting pictures to regular exhibitions! he thought, smiling to himself and looking back. She was helping Joe into the cockpit.

It was wonderful. What in the name of little sour apples was he leaving them for?

He saw that he was leaving them under some deep compulsion. He had to go. He didn't want to go and yet he must. There was nothing he wanted to do less than get mixed up in what his mind spontaneously called the bloody nonsense of police worlds, yet here he was, climbing the hillside, with binoculars, map, and electric torch, and being careful to bear right so that he would not come out on the main road too soon.

There was a very real sense in which the thing was maddening. Human beings got bitten by compulsions as cows by clegs or sheep by the maggot fly. All behaved in a maddened way. But the cow or the sheep with some reason for the cleg and the maggot fly existed outside them. The compulsion neurosis didn't exist outside. Man created that mental insect inside him for the masochistic pleasure of having it bite his bowels.

The dead bracken crackled. Birch scrub along a small ravine had a curious bone-greyness on its purple, a reflecting of the March sunlight that was strangely thoughtful and quiescent, a waiting in its twigs and branches for the birth-act below. The whole hillside was dry and drained; the grass grey and flattened like dead hair; the rocks grey. The earth's body was naked and austere and very beautiful.

He followed the ravine. He knew he was following it because he didn't want to be spotted on a skyline, but he put all cunning from him and watched the gushet of water glisten and tumble, saw a wren as brown and large as a penny disappear into a bank, completely disappear, so that he went down and poked at the bank carefully, but the wren had gone, though where it could have gone he had no idea. His foot slipped but he nimbly prevented the water from entering his shoe and glimpsed the wren higher up.

Before going over the top, he looked back and saw

the *Fulmar* small and still on the water like a toy. He put his glasses on her. Joe was sketching, taking notes. But there was no sign of Christina. She could be inside making the beds up, going over the food, reading the labels on the tins, coming to decisions, excited in her new trousers. For some reason he thought of Mrs. Spicer and laughed. Served that domineering dame just about right. He felt friendly to Mrs. Spicer.

When he had crossed the watershed and come in sight of Loch Criach he selected his spying ground with care, then with map and binoculars beside him got down to what he had thought of as a general reconnaissance, with one possible patrol; in other words, to find if he could make any particular sense of the map he had looked at in the timber yard and to try, if that seemed feasible, by approaching Loch Criach from this its inner end, to hide somewhere until the possible arrival of the Basil–Stenson boys and then stalk them to their lair.

Now though he knew all this was vague and amateurish and about as hopeless as finding the black cat in the black dark, yet there had developed the awful feeling of something a little fatal about his acts. It was as though, not wanting to do something yet being compelled to do it, his mind selected only the significant. Grear and Stenson and the Special Branch (the inspector whom Grear had sent had asked the most unexpected questions) had a thousand details to consider. It really was profoundly difficult and intricate for them; a sort of higher mathematics of possible action, and once they had worked out a solution, they had immediately to take into account that the other side might have worked it out also. In the eyes of Grear and the Special Branch, Dermot had simply a knack of blundering on things, as certain men were lucky in betting, or even, more mysteriously, in always drawing a good horse in the big office sweep. It was a factor, like any other, that could be used. After all, there were water diviners.

But Dermot had not been prepared for a shock. He was not such a blunderer as all that. During lunch with Norman Gavin, who had helped him to fix up the loan of the *Fulmar*, he had traversed many subjects and even raised a note of excitement by remarking that he had heard of an Island girl who might be a possible and very good maid. He had no intention of producing Christina unless her temporary service with the Gavins might be useful in schemes that would keep forming in his head. When Gavin had started on housing—his obsession these days—Dermot had sympathetically prodded him. In short, Dermot's varied inquiries and pondering had led him to the conclusion that Basil and Stenson, and, say, perhaps a couple of men with them, put up either in an occupied dwelling of some kind or in one of the two large empty houses of which Gavin had previously told him. Now to stay in a fully occupied dwelling or hotel would mean a continuous and impossible watchfulness in action and speech, unless all others were involved; but to stay in one of the two empty mansion houses would be perfectly simple—if they had taken the precaution to select its caretaker. So after getting the lie of the land and road through his glasses and picking up the two mansions, whose whereabouts he knew, his patrol would consist in no more than reaching in the dark a spot by the entrance to the first mansion on the way out from Criach. He would conceal himself there and just watch as best he could for those who came along, always keeping in mind that they would not come bunched together. Even if they came by car—which was quite likely—the chances were that at least one of them would drop off and do the last part on foot in order to cover up. They would not want to come by car too often because a car could be seen or heard even around an empty house. In the dark it needed headlights. But it remained the simplest and most tempting way.

Dermot got his shock before he lifted the binoculars to his eyes. Loch Criach ran directly away from him. It was the usual narrow sea loch no more than a mile broad for five or six miles ahead. But here towards its inner end several dead steamers were anchored at respectful distances from one another in the middle of the loch. His own shipping knowledge swept in on him. At their best speed they were sitters for the latest type of submarine, which could make circles round them under water and blow them up without surfacing. Accordingly there had been over the last few years an increasing output, particularly in America, of fast merchant ships. What to do with some of these old tramps, whether to hold them in reserve for a desperate emergency or send them to the breakers' yards, was the kind of problem, highly complicated by considerations of available steel, labour and capital, which had given many of his own conferences a "headache".

But all Dermot could think of as he stared at these mute and very real hulks was the red cross which his torch had picked out on the map drawn from the portfolio in the timber yard; and it came upon him with a feeling of absolute certainty that the cross "plotted" one of these hulks.

So profound indeed was this experience of revelation that he lay over and silently stared at the sky as if in that way he might discover the mathematics of the affair. The cross—the red circles—the blue lines . . . the map. On his elbow again he saw the squat dead steamers and, as his eyes lifted, the white puffs from an invisible train shunting beyond the stone jetty which ran into the water at Criach. Like a cluster of beetles row-boats sheltered inside the jetty and on their outskirts swung one or two decked boats. Beyond, Clua was no more than a dark knot with a drift of smoke. An old coaster with a heavy tail of smoke was rounding a distant point. A fast motor launch swept out in a circle from Criach, drumming the loch as if it were a shield; the sound of it came to his ear fine and high-pitched. A seaway full of coming and going; a place whose residents would know their own social circles and be surprised at nothing outside them.

With his binoculars he went over the whole field of vision carefully, picked out Norman Gavin's house, spent a few concentrated moments on the roofs of the two mansions showing among their trees, then followed the shore line very slowly right round the head of the loch, and finally, and with that touch of mounting excitement which stopped his breath, brought his circle of bright vision on the first, the nearest hulk.

The bridge, the winches, the dark-grey backs of the holds, the silent disuse of what was so familiar, the iron stillness, affected him quite strongly, like a legend of death seen through a miraculous porthole. Then something moved, forward, against the fo'c'sle. It was quite plainly a man, an oldish man, from the droop of his shoulders, but it was impossible to tell what he was doing. Dermot got into a more comfortable position where his binoculars could be absolutely steady and spied for some minutes before deciding that beyond any doubt the man was peeling potatoes. The action of dropping the peeled potato into the bucket beyond his knees and then picking up another was unmistakable. Even the way he tilted his head up, while leaning sideways for the new potato, showed how naturally he was enjoying the good weather. As the minutes passed, it was clear that he had peeled more potatoes than even a hungry man could stow away at one sitting. By the time he rose, slung a bucket overboard and hauled it up, Dermot estimated a consuming force of at least three or four men. But though he watched until the shadows came, he saw no other man on board.

34

He took up his position just over the wall near the entrance to Criach House, the spot he had originally decided upon. Unfortunately the warm March day had brought to the water a slight mist or haar which would probably spread. It was going to remain a pitch black night unless a wind got up. It was also growing very cold. He danced every now and then. When a car came he ducked down behind the wall, then followed its headlights for a long distance. Altogether this was probably as good a spot as any other, though after a couple of hours he began to wonder if it wouldn't have been better for him to have chanced his intuition fully, found a shelter on the shore opposite the hulk, and listened for the sound of oars.

As he ducked yet once more and watched the light on the bare trees, he became aware that the car approaching from Criach was slowing down. It stopped opposite the entrance and someone got out. As the door shut the engine revved up and the car moved on. Stooping, Dermot began to make for the near stone pillar, but paused in doubt when he could hear no footsteps. Then, all at once, there were footsteps passing just beyond the wall, as if they had at last decided not to go up the drive but to follow the car. Dermot cautiously lifted his head but could not make out any definite figure. The car had left the half-mile of straight, but now in a moment he realized that its distant upthrust of light was stationary.

Even as he watched, it began to move, swept slowly downward out of sight, to reappear again as the car took the slope to the crest where the road swung sharply right, before it began to descend to a point on the east shore of Loch Glan, several miles north of the *Fulmar's* lonely anchorage. Dermot slipped noiselessly over the wall and on his rubber-soled shoes began following, listening and following. Twice he flattened in the ditch at the first glimmer of headlights on the telegraph wires, and on neither occasion did he see anyone in front though the lights threw up even the slight hollows on the tarmac. But the fellow was walking on leather, with nails in one heel. Dermot had heard him take the road after each car had passed. Presently he heard a voice call quietly. Then all was silence. Dermot remained dead still.

He remained still so long that his body began to gather itself against invisible attack. Were they surrounding him? . . . were they waiting for someone?—a crush of bushes, an oath, a low laugh . . . Dermot crossed the road swiftly and moved ahead.

There was no difficulty in following them now. One of them had obviously blundered into what Dermot soon discovered to be bramble bushes. They were leaving the road for the shore. Dermot got onto hands and knees and, instead of following directly, kept left a little, drawing back from the brambles and crawling up onto higher ground. Here there were small trees and presently he realized that the harsh whispering voices were on a distinctly lower level; but the direction was to the loch and he kept on.

When he heard their feet on slithering stones below, he knew that he himself was on one of those small wooded headlands common to most western sea-lochs; in a few moments he was flat, feeling over a rocky brink. As he drew back, he saw a circle of light searching among boulders. The voices were still low and harsh but more confident. With the wooded headland at their backs, those below were completely screened from the road. The circle of light was lifted and directed outward to the loch, twice describing the figure eight before vanishing.

Dermot watched for an answering signal from the loch but none came. He could not see the water; nothing but pitch darkness below and ahead—except for a faint far tiny glow-worm of a light that must be the hulk's meagre riding light. Even the voices were silent.

They're confident, Dermot thought; but then the man on the hulk, if on the look-out, should have seen the car stop, and needed only a single definite signal from shore. A well-integrated, a discreet service!

Discreet, too, were the swing of the oars, the dip of the blades, and the guiding circle of light cast down among the boulders. The boat's forefoot grounded with no more than a hiss. Legs and feet passed through the circle. Someone slipped, making a splash, and a voice muttered "Hell's teeth!" It sounded very like Basil's voice, but then that was the voice he was listening for.

"Get aft!" An oar-end splashed lightly and Dermot knew the boatman was feeling for a purchase. He heard the keel grumble as it slid. They were afloat. In a few moments both oars were dipping and the boat receding.

All very neatly done; admirably contrived. It was worth a cheer. But he did not even sit up. You could not take any chances with these fellows. While watching to sea, he listened to near things. For all he knew there might be one left below, one whom a returning car might pick up, the fellow who had walked along the road, the man who always covered the rear, who stuck a knee in your stomach.

In a moment he realized how perfect a stronghold, a headquarters, an anchored ship was. Like an old castle with its fosse, its water-ditch. In this case, some water-ditch! It could be captured, but not before those within had time to get rid of all incriminating evidence. Hauling up their rope ladder would be like lifting the drawbridge.

He was waiting for a glimmer of moving light, for any evidence at all of their arrival at a particular hulk. He waited a long time, longer than was necessary for them to arrive and return. After all there was no reason why a caretaker or watchman, genuinely stopping on board, should not show a light. But no light came, not even the faintest echo of toes against iron as feet climbed a swinging ladder.

At last he turned away, going back through the trees as noiselessly as he had come. On the road edge he stood for a couple of minutes, listening, then set off for the *Fulmar*.

From the high crest he looked back but nothing showed in the region of darkness which he had left. Suddenly he thought that perhaps he had completely misjudged the whole adventure. A night's poaching when he was a boy in the Highlands came vividly before him, the secret gathering at the rendezvous, the boat, the man who came with the bag which held the net, the silence, light forbidden, the setting of the net round the burn's mouth at the other side of the sea-loch no more than two hundred yards from the front door of the Big House. . . .

It could be that, it could be that exactly! And it was Saturday night, with more cars heading for the wilds than on any other night, and with no work to-morrow.

He left the road, flattened as headlights swept round, then began picking his way down towards Loch Glan. It was a rocky shore, with no track for miles, and though he aimed to strike the water somewhere near the anchorage, he failed; at least there was no sight of the *Fulmar*. Surely they would have a light on, be waiting for him! He was using his torch freely; they should have seen him coming.

He stumbled along the shore. They couldn't have landed in the dinghy and forgotten to tie her or draw her up? The tide was flowing when he had left and for long after. But Christina would know about tides and the need for drawing a boat up or watching her. That's the one thing she would know. He came to a barrier of rock and turned in to climb its grassy root. It was very steep but from its top he should get a long view.

And there she was, all four port-holes showing on her starboard side in the ebbing tide. He sat down and wiped his face. A marvellous thing to look at. Quiet, cosy and snug, floating like a dream, real, cunningly made by man's creative hand, a light in the darkness, at anchor.

They had forgotten him, on the borders of what destiny, through what immediate trouble of the mind. For Joe would be troubled over the money business . . . and Christina would not risk lighting the primus on her own—not so long as there was that old paraffin stove with the two wicks. . . . He smiled, in no hurry. It was good to be forgotten. It was good to be in the night. . . . The door into the cockpit opened and Christina came out followed by Joe. They stood staring at the land. He heard their voices, low and concerned. Bringing his open hands to his mouth, he called not very loudly, "Hallo!" Then he clicked on his torch and went down to the beach.

Before taking Christina into the hollow of small birch trees, Dermot stopped. The mist from the cold night was growing radiant; the sun was coming through. It came in warmth on his hand uplifted in salute. It pierced down, licking up the mist, and the white side of the *Fulmar* shone. The water glittered. Joe, who had been sitting above high water mark, sketching material beside him, got to his feet, lifted his face to the sky and then looked up the hillside. Dermot waved to him, and as Joe waved back Christina raised her arm.

"She looks very white in her new paint," said Dermot; then, remembering Christina, glanced at her.

Christina was smiling. "Whiter than the swan of the songs," she said quite clearly.

Dermot's eyes remained on her face. It had a faint flush of health, a new shy ease. "Is there a song about it?" he asked.

Her eyes came to his face, then glanced away. "It's just an old verse about things that are whiter."

"What verse?"

Christina hesitated, then, simply as she had told the story in Joe's studio, she recited slowly, searching for the English word now and then:

"Whiter than the swan of the songs,
   Whiter than the gull of the waves,
   Whiter than the snow of the hills,
   Whiter than the white love of the heroes."

After a moment Dermot asked, "What was it that was so white?"

Christina's brows gathered slightly. "I don't rightly remember," she answered. "It was seeing the *Fulmar*."

He turned into the small ravine. "Watch your feet," he cautioned her. Suddenly there was a burst of song from a wren. He caught her arm and they stood quite still, staring at the tiny brown bird on a birch branch. The sheer volume of ringing sound was tremendous. They saw the vibrant throat, the twin beaks. The song over, it vanished.

"I heard him yesterday, but he hadn't got his spring song then. It must be the sun."

Christina was now inclined to linger, to glance here and there.

"Too early for nesting," he called.

But she obviously had a mind of her own in the matter. She had come alive; her body swayed and moved readily, doing its distracted best to keep up with him. That curious archaic shape of the facial bones lost its sort of remote solemnness, was itself like the invisible something that listened in a place like this. Her eyes gathered a dark beauty as they opened wide and expectant. He left her to climb in her own way.

Going over the top, he was careful to follow the hollows and when he came at last to the spot from which he had spied yesterday, he got her to lie where he wanted. Then he took up his binoculars. When he dropped them and turned his face to Christina, it looked at once congested and pale. "I want you," he said, "to look through these glasses and see if you can spot anyone on the deck of the nearest steamer. See these eyepieces: turn each if the focus isn't absolutely clear." She had hardly lifted the glasses, when he struck them down. "Don't get the sun on the lenses or they'll wink far enough." He lay flat beside her and in a short time she had the deck in clear focus.

"I can see three men," she said.

"Know any of them?"

There was a pause, then she lowered the glasses and their eyes met. "It's like Mr. Stenson," she said.

"You're quite sure? Have another look."

She looked. "He's going away," she murmured.

He snatched the glasses and saw only the oldish man who had been peeling potatoes and another whom he did not know.

"You've been wondering what it's all about, haven't you?" he asked presently, lying over on his side and smiling to her.

"I thought there was something."

"I'll tell you." He nibbled a piece of grass. "You remember the night I followed Stenson?" He told her the main outline of the story of that trip to Criach. "So I failed to find out where he went. I wanted to know. If you're sure it's Stenson you saw through the glasses, then that's the place."

"I'm almost sure," she murmured. But her face had a curious distress.

"Tell me."

"Why are you—doing this?"

"I sometimes wonder," he said. "But it's fun, too, finding out, isn't it?—like you looking for nests."

Her smile was not very successful. "You shouldn't," she muttered.

"Why?"

She watched her fingers pluck at a piece of tough grass. "It's not safe."

"You wouldn't like anything to happen to me, would you?"

She did not look at him.

"I'm teasing you, Christina. But—it's difficult. I won't tell you anything more. I wouldn't even have taken you here, but I thought you might know some of them on board that I don't. I'm using you. But I wouldn't do that —if I wasn't quite sure that somehow what—what I'd like to save is what you, too——" He paused. "And Joe." Then he smiled again. "To save the white swan of the songs."

"I know that."

She had at times a literal way of speaking that confused him as no cleverness of allusion ever could. He began selfconsciously to say that he didn't quite mean all that when her steady questioning look pulled him up. Suddenly, to his own surprise, he said with extraordinary force: "I do mean it. I mean that precisely and nothing else. I mean that these fellows are after the swan, that they'll kill it. And not only them. We have fellows too. But these fellows down there, they're starting it, they're after our own swan, and they don't give a damn should its wings be torn to bits over our land our lochs and hills, so long as they have their way. They may think they're doing it for this reason or that, but what the blazes will that matter when the swan is dead?" He stopped, but not as one who had made an outburst that chokes on its own astonishment. On the contrary, he was like one who had told the simple truth at last and felt the better for it, the more confident. His shoulders moved with restless energy, his eyes were stormy.

"That's why it's not safe," she said.

"Exactly. I know."

More energy came into him, as if, after such precise and factual statements, they both knew now exactly where they stood. "What right has anyone to shove opinions down our throats? Let them have their opinions, but, blast them, they're not going to kick them into us. It annoys me, Christina. It does, honestly. And the bitter thing of it is that we have had—that you and I—out of our own background . . . whatever else our people did, at least they had their moments when they knew what was whiter than the swan."

She saw the seaman in the cut of his eyebrows, the seaman who can take his chance and put his craft about in dirty weather. The exhilaration of it was in his face.

"They could worship their God in their own way and salute the sun and the moon. Why wouldn't they? And to think that fellows like them down there, fellows who

will put the sun and the moon out—it makes me sick."
Then he smiled to Christina as if she were perhaps more
personal than a public meeting, but the smile still kept its
critical distance. "Don't look so worried."

"You should leave them alone."

"You would have me run away—you, whose grandfather was Iain MacNeil; whose father——" He stopped
abruptly.

For she twisted away, hid her eyes, and he knew that
she had loved her father very much. But she did not weep.
There was something dumb about her body, as if, like a
thing that had been hit, it bore the dumb burden, the
pain, of the human condition. From the black hair, his
eyes ran over the crotal brown jumper with its green line,
the navy blue trousers, to the white ankles that made the
canvas shoes a rubbed grey. She stretched herself out and
came over on her face. He picked up the binoculars and
adjusted the focus to a fine precision.

The watchman had gone and a faint blue smoke was
showing. The other figure remained, but still side-on and
humped. Any number could be lying about invisible, up
on the bridge, in sunny corners. But they would be bound
sometime to stretch their legs, take a little exercise. He
would have to give most of the day to watching.

Christina was on her elbows again, looking at the
withered heath her fingers pulled.

"They're boiling the potatoes," he said.

She glanced round at him and sat up. "It's time."

"Could you manage to light the primus alone?"

"Aren't you coming?"

He thought for a moment; looked at his watch. "Say,
half-an-hour."

"Will I wait?"

"Yes."

They took turn about with the binoculars and Christina

glimpsed what she thought were two new figures, but he was too late to pick them up. One, she said, looked small and dark; the other much taller. The deck now seemed definitely deserted. Lunch would be on. Five of them, he reckoned: that would be about right. After he had gone over the loch carefully, he said lightly to Christina, "Like to see it on a map?"

With the map spread out before them, he showed her how they had come, the spot where the *Fulmar* lay, where they lay themselves at that moment, Criach, and with his pencil made a small cross. "That's where I want to anchor to-night. Then home in the morning."

She continued to gaze at the map.

"You think we're fine where we are?"

"Yes," she answered.

He laughed. "Come on, or Joe will be wondering."

On the way down he tried to recall one or two recent shipping deals over such hulks but could not quite get the details into shape. However, searching out ownership in any particular case would present no difficulty. How Grear would enjoy doing it!

"You have to start her up, Joe. Christina will steer. Making all allowances, it will take us two hours to arrive in a dark that will just let us see our anchorage." Dermot rolled up the chart. "Now then, action stations!"

Joe swivelled the priming caps, squirted in the petrol, closed the caps and set the controls. He was pale but determined.

"Your thumb!" called Dermot.

Everything happened as on the first occasion, and by the time the engine was turning over regularly, Joe was pleased but exhausted. "The thing frightens me," he confessed, but with a smile, for there was a dour pertinacious streak in him.

Together Dermot and himself broke the anchor out; then came back to the engine. Christina was at the wheel.

"Now, Joe, open throttle a little. That gives her power to take the load. Forward with it."

Joe pushed the lever forward; there was a slowing of the engine, a growl from the water underneath, and the boat came alive.

She had slewed away but Christina was turning the wheel the right way. "Hard round! Go on—right round!" he ordered. The *Fulmar* came round in a sweep. "Steady!" Christina was late and for some distance the course was a perfect zigzag, but Dermot let her fight it out. In the end they were going straight and Christina was trembling, but her eyes were alight.

"I'll make seamen of you yet," said Dermot. "I'm not having any passengers on my boat." He fixed the dinghy's painter, explaining to them how disastrously a rope can go round a propeller. In fact, he explained a lot to them and they caught some of his enthusiasm, his sheer love of small craft in narrow seaways. "And this is only a noise box. Wait till I have you under sail. You don't know you're born." He laughed. "How's the oil, Joe?"

"It's dripping," said Joe.

"Stand in just a little, Christina. . . . Right! Keep her on that."

"Ay, ay, sir."

"It's in the blood, Joe—though she's terrified of it!"

245

"I suppose," said Joe in a little while, "that thing—the engine—couldn't blow up?"

"No, Joe: it could only go on fire."

Joe looked at him doubtfully.

"I've never seen one go on fire," Dermot confessed. "But I have heard of it. Though insurance questions are very complicated."

In the end they settled down, the land slipped past, a headland was turned, a clustering village appeared, and the wonder of it as the afternoon wore on got hold of Joe, for he had never before helped the wonder to happen.

Dusk came down. The lights of small towns shone across the water. The *Fulmar* was rolling, but soon the roll was behind them and lessening. They all took a turn at the wheel. The hills darkened.

"That's Criach," said Dermot at last as he brought the *Fulmar* round and headed for a distant cluster of lights. Presently he got Joe to slacken speed, to go into neutral, to come ahead again, as he nosed in for his anchorage. "That'll do, Joe." He leapt up on top and, going for'ard, let the anchor away carefully until he got bottom. As she swung to it, he paid out a few fathoms of the light chain, made all fast, and in no time was down beside them. "Shut her off, Joe . . . That was excellently done! Food, Christina. Lashings of tea. And see you pull the dark slips over the port-holes."

It was a pleasant meal. The sun was in their skins, and something of the whole day's weather in their blood, lapping the bones. But Dermot knew that Christina was uneasy, so he kept talking to Joe, drawing Joe's impressions out of him, and giving in return those odd sudden images that Joe somehow contrived to excite.

He laughed when Joe, stirred by the notion of their flitting around on future trips, brought up the old Gaelic image of the butterfly as God's fool.

"It was also," Dermot said, "called God's fire, the little yellow fire that takes the soul to heaven."

"No!" said Joe. "That's extraordinary—because— because the ancient Egyptians, they pictured the soul as a butterfly coming out of the chrysalis, as—as—they show it as a butterfly coming out of the mouth of the dead. I wonder . . ."

"But wait, Joe, wait till you're with me under full sail, every white wing spread. Then you can talk of butterflies."

"The ship!" said Joe, "the ship of the dead!"

Christina dropped something.

Dermot glanced at her. "We're upsetting Christina."

Joe looked at her solemnly. She appeared flushed from stooping, but she said nothing.

"What did you call the butterfly at home?" Joe asked her.

"The grey fool."

Though Joe often appeared obtuse to ordinary human reactions, he was always sensitive to anything Christina did or said, particularly if he did not quite understand. He knew now that she was strangely disturbed behind her calm expression. He glanced at Dermot.

Dermot winked and fetched a chart. Presently he yawned. "I think it's time we turned in. I want to pay a very early morning call. So don't trouble if you hear me going out."

"Where are you going?" Joe asked.

"To see some fellows off. I'll be back before daylight."

"You're going ashore in the dinghy?"

"I'm going in the dinghy, yes." He hesitated. "Look, Joe, I'll tell you what it is. There are some fellows in an old tramp lying at anchor some way from here. I'm not sure of them, what they're up to. I would like to know. They may not leave her at all. In which case I'll come quietly back. I won't let myself be seen, whatever happens. That's all."

Joe glanced at Christina and knew from her lack of surprise that she was aware of something which had been going on behind his back. His brows darkened; he became constrained and awkward.

"I saw the steamer yesterday, when we were up above," said Christina.

"You didn't tell me."

"I didn't know," replied Christina, "that he was going."

Joe looked at Dermot, who said, "I don't want either of you in this." He smiled, keeping his eyes on Joe.

Christina broke the silence. "When are you going?"

"About four o'clock," replied Dermot. "Neither of you need move. Sorry if it appears mysterious—but it's a shipping matter and I'd rather not go into it."

Lying in his bunk in the darkness, he could not help smiling, for Joe was still uneasy, more than a little troubled in some deep place. He had been troubled the whole trip, off and on. Was that money business still biting him? Was an artist such an egoist that he could never forget himself, never forget his own affairs? Probably. In which case there was no harm in letting him stew, though it could become wearing. However, it would be a simple matter to put right on the way home, and Joe had what mattered.

Perhaps vanity or egoism was his own trouble. After all, he had a good enough case already for Grear to investigate. It was pretty certain now that two of those on the hulk were Stenson and Basil Black. In any case, it was up to Grear and his Special Branch to decide what to do. His business was merely to give them the facts and let them get on with it. Yet if they raided the hulk and found nothing—he would feel a bit of an ass. Vanity. Sheer egoism. Worse than Joe. There was no reason why he should make any further move. Indeed there was every reason why he shouldn't. For if they saw him, got the least suspicion that someone was after them, then everything would be lost.

Not only that. He might very easily be lost himself. If by any chance they got hold of him, they could not possibly let him go. Putting himself in their position he saw that. To keep him locked up would be dangerous; but to knock him on the head and sink him with a bit of old iron—anywhere in that vast loch—would be child's play. He would simply have disappeared.

Heavens, he would never get to sleep at this rate! . . .

Yet his plan was so simple, so tempting. Before daybreak they were bound to leave the hulk. Last time, they had been back in town on Monday, as he had learned from Christina. They would naturally get some sleep before going back, so there wouldn't be any point in leaving before five or six o'clock. They would join the first trickle of folk returning from a week-end or going to early work. It was inevitable.

All he had got to do was be near the hulk when they left her in the dark. The watchman would row them ashore, leaving the rope ladder hanging against his own return. To climb that ladder and have a look around the ship would be too easy, and he would have a clear twenty minutes to do it in. A fellow just couldn't run away when it was as simple as that.

He had to turn, to stretch his legs. The old bunk creaked.

Sleep was going further and further away. This was maddening. . . .

Yes, he had his pocket compass, his torch. It would be very dark. For coming back, there would be the riding light. . . . There was another light near . . . He had studied the area before turning in . . . Street lights in Criach. . . .

He would never sleep . . .

A couple of hours later, he decided that it would be

fatal to go to sleep. He turned over on his back and resigned himself to keeping awake . . .

He started out of a dark hole, bewildered, light in his eyes, a figure . . .

"It's four o'clock," whispered Christina.

"Good lord!" he muttered, for his sleep had been deep.

"A cup of tea."

He sat up and took the steaming cup from her.

"Joe is asleep," she whispered, handing him a plate with three buttered oatcakes.

He could not speak. She was calm and practical. The island woman getting her man to sea. She would have seen her mother do this many a time.

"Would you like something more?" she asked.

He shook his head, his mouth full and munching. She went to the little galley and presently came back with the teapot. But he wouldn't have any more. She went away with the teapot.

When she came back he was hunting something.

"What is it?" she asked.

"A couple of old rags."

She found them and he stuffed them in his pockets. "I'll put out the light before I open the door." The cabin was lit by a 12-volt battery. "I'll be back before the daylight."

But she followed him out into the cockpit. He unfastened the dinghy's painter.

"You'll take care of yourself," she said.

"Yes," he answered. "You can be sure I will."

He got into the dinghy quietly and pushed off.

She stood until she lost the dip of his oars, then went in and heard Joe stirring. She switched on the single bulb. Joe was sitting on the edge of his bunk. He stood up.

"He's gone," she said quietly, but she looked tired. "I'll give you a cup of tea."

"Don't bother," he muttered.

"It's on the teapot," she answered. "It's no bother."

"You think it's dangerous?"

"Yes. I don't like it." She had stopped.

"You wakened him?"

"Yes. I had to waken him."

He stood as if there wasn't a word left in him, in shirt and trousers, his hair all ways.

She went for the teapot and cups and laid them on the narrow centre strip of table, then lifted one wing and fixed it. Sugar, milk, a packet of oatcakes, bread.

"Don't go out," she said, "without putting the light out."

He came back. "Can't you tell me about it?" he demanded.

"I have nothing to tell." She looked at him fairly. "Just these men."

"Do you mean they're thieves or what?"

"Maybe worse than that. Like the men who kicked him."

"You don't know?"

"I don't know why he was coming here. But when he said last night he was going in the small boat—I was frightened."

He stood silent, but his eyes happened to be on her hands and he saw them tremble.

"Christina," he said, "it's because I can't—I don't know what——"

"Oh, Joe," she cried and threw her arms round his neck.

"Christina, Christina," muttered Joe, for she clung to him with surprising strength. He staggered a little for now he had lost all his bearings.

She let go of him and went back to the teapot.

"Sit down," she said, "and be good."

Joe sat down. He was lost, bewildered, like one afraid to make a noise. He got up. She put his cup in front of him. He sat down.

"Christina——" he began.

"Don't." Her voice quivered.

"Christina," he said gently, "are you very fond of him?"

She looked at him in a bewildered, almost startled way, her lips parted. Then a sweetness came into her expression. "Yes," she said. "He is like one of my own people."

"I understand." His head bowed over his cup.

He was very gentle and kind to her after that, helping with the dishes, pressing her to lie down, assuring her he would wait and watch. "Remember, I can start up that engine, and if he isn't here——"

"Can't you see that's why he taught you?"

He stared at her.

"And you *would* go on talking about—about butterflies and—and ships of the——" She was weeping and he was holding her. In a few moments she was drying her eyes. "I am foolish," she said.

"You are beautiful," said Joe.

When Dermot had got the rags tied round his row-locks, he went noiselessly ahead.

It was so dark that the blade of an oar hit the anchor chain of the first hulk as its bulk loomed on him. He sat quietly for a time, then felt his way on. No stars were visible in the sky, but as he left the huge vessel behind the darkness seemed less dense.

The tide was flowing, and with care and time he came under the stern of the last but one. There he lay on his oars peering and listening into darkness and silence, a darkness that seemed all the denser when his eye dropped from the high meagre glim of a riding light. He knew he might have an hour to wait, perhaps more.

He felt curiously collected and caught himself smiling at Christina. It must have cost her an effort to waken him. But the man who was going to sea had to be wakened by the woman. Whatever her feelings, it was man's business, fate's business. She could not deliberately fail in that—and face him. Good! he thought. Affection or love—it was beyond that, a different kind of feeling. He understood it perfectly and it made him happy. He laughed silently to himself, feeling strong and confident. It's going to be cold, he thought. He pulled the dinghy round the stern of the vessel out of the small wind, then presently with senses attuned to the night he drew away on his first reconnaissance.

It was on his second trip that he heard noises and knew that someone was stirring. He crept close in, then stood away again. Even by mistake the beam of a torch might sweep too far and pick him up. He decided to lie some way ahead of her bows and hearken for the dropping of the rope-ladder or bumping of their small boat, which would be lying astern.

As time wore on, he decided that there was no need for him to go aboard at all; no good pretending that the map with the red cross was one, or a copy of one, which they had pinched somewhere. The first moment he had seen the hulk he had known it was their map. The affair now was altogether too big for amateur bungling; the evidence too strong.

He heard feet on the iron plates . . . a wooden bump against the vessel's side . . . a splash . . . On the starboard side, away from the Criach road. They were taking no risks, showing no light on the vulnerable side. Low voices . . . They were going down the ladder . . . He tried to count, but it was difficult; certainly not less than four or five. Obviously those who had come were going. As simple and natural as that. Now they were pushing off. Not a flicker of light. Going round her stern, as he knew they would. The lift and dip of the oars—hitting out for the shore. Very quietly Dermot dropped down towards the invisible rope ladder. He put out a hand that in a few moments struck it. Without a suggestion of a bump he drew the dinghy alongside and listened; caught the painter and hitched it to the ladder. In his rubber-soled canvas shoes, he climbed slowly, noiselessly, aloft. As his head came over the rail, he listened once more. Then his leg went over and he moved like a cat towards the looming bulk of the bridge with the notion that he would like to inspect at least two places: the chart room and the captain's cabin.

It was very dark but he knew his way about ships. His fingers ran over a door, turned the handle, and he stepped into a room stale with tobacco smoke. He pushed the door to and took out his torch. It was certain that all window glass would be shrouded in a place so recently occupied, but he shot the beam first on the floor and in its reflected dimness looked around, then moved towards a desk on which were lying a neat little pile of green identity cards, a pair of scissors, a pot of paste, and some narrow paper clippings. He touched nothing. His eyes roved—and rested on a portfolio which looked the double of the one he had recently fought so hard for. He laid the torch on the desk, opened the portfolio, and pulled out the contents until he saw D.1. His expression narrowed in a sort of fierce bewilderment, then he shoved the plans back, shut the portfolio and replaced it. There were typed lists on a nail. There was a chart stuck to a wall with drawing pins, freely marked in red and blue. Good God, leaving all this behind, exposed! It was uncanny. There were half-a-dozen rolled charts in a rack. The beam ran over them—and stopped. He pulled one out. There was no mistaking the cardboard case with its ripped corner and small half-obliterated red stencil mark. This was fantastic. He would have to make sure this time; he would draw the chart out, see Cladday on it. Going to the desk, he put down his torch and had got an inch or two of chart pulled out when he heard the footsteps. He picked up the torch and switched it off. After that he could not move. They were mounting a companion-way, they were coming to the door. He heard the finger-nails, the rattle of the handle. A voice muttered to itself, something about a light, in the open doorway. Dermot went forward to strike with all his force, and the door was shut in his face.

But for the fact that he held the torch in one hand and the chart in the other, he might have grabbed at the handle and made after his man. The instant's hesitation steadied him and he listened to the feet walking between the bridge and the main hold. Slipping the chart under an arm, he found the handle of the door; it turned and he stepped outside. As he noiselessly closed the door, he heard the voice call quietly from the port side: "Forgotten something?"

Now Dermot caught the sound of oars, heard a voice answer even more quietly from the water: "Identity cards."

The boat was coming back! She was quite close. Inside a minute she would be rounding the stern to the rope-ladder—and the dinghy. Dermot moved swiftly but crouched at the rail as the footsteps approached from the port side. The door handle rattled once more. As Dermot went over the rail, the chart slid from his arm. He heard it hit the water with a light smack. He went down swiftly, the wooden slats clattering a little, for the dinghy had pulled the ladder to one side; unhitched the painter, hauled the dinghy up, heard the chart rustle against it, stepped in, groped for the chart on the water and found it as the ship's boat was heard nearing the stern. There was no time to push off and get out both oars. From a purchase on the ladder, he moved ahead and with one light oar as a silent paddle kept the movement going and the dinghy near the black wall of the ship. The approaching boat made noises that covered any of his. Then an oar clacked as it was shipped. They were alongside.

"I'm coming down with them," said the quiet voice above. . . . "Here you are!"

"Don't drop them." It was Basil's intense voice.

"Here!"

"Where?"

A torch shone upward for a moment, and in its small field Dermot saw a face leaning down over an outstretched hand.

"Put that light out!" The low, authoritative voice was new to Dermot.

There was a harsh mutter as the light went out, but Dermot had instantly turned his own face away.

"You're there?" came the same commanding voice.

"Yes," answered the man on the ladder.

"Try for word on Tuesday night."

"O.K. If nothing, then Thursday."

When Dermot heard the boat pull away, he began to breathe. As he slowly turned his head he could see her vague darkness on the water. A puff of wind hit him and the dinghy bumped. He was well forward towards the starboard bow. As he carefully shoved off, the stern touched. But the sound from the ship's boat was now receding and there was no sound from the ladder. His oar clattered as he leaned over to fend off. The puff was a scurry of wind, a first stirring of the morning. It passed and he sat for a minute trying to hear the movement of feet on deck. He heard nothing. The dinghy was drifting in again. But he was very careful now. The wind came a little more strongly. The sooner he was clear away the better. But he found he did not want to look up the wall of the steamer, to lift his pale face. He actually felt that he was being watched. This, of course, was nonsense, because he could not be seen, but all the same he didn't like it. Firmly he pushed off again and this time fingered each oar into its swathed rowlock. Then slowly and noiselessly he dipped and pulled.

But at a short distance ahead he lay on his oars. Either the dawn was not far away or the wind was clearing air and sky. He fancied he could see the upper outline of the vessel. When he thought he saw something like a head move, he decided that fancy was getting the better of him. Yet before he reached the next vessel, he stopped again.

He was worried. Then the real reason came to him: the face he had seen in the light was the face of the man who had got him below the belt with his knee and then booted him. What he would never forget about that face was its expression when it had looked up and down the street, for in that moment he had known he was going to be attacked yet, with the paralysing feeling one gets in a nightmare, knew he could do nothing about it. The short scene had often come back to him. The face, as it had glanced from side to side, had been pale with its intention, with its swift yet careful cunning, and then with pure evil. The thing had power. It had power over him still. It was holding him here. He did not want to leave it. He felt his own body go squat and remorseless in a destructive impulse so concentrated that his teeth ground noisily in his mouth and the oar-blades hit the water. As he dug in, the stems of the rowlocks squealed. The spasm passed, and, leaning over, he cupped up some water and ran it down the rowlock stems.

The one certain way to make sure that the fellow on board had heard nothing, was not suspicious of any prowling craft, was to wait for the ship's boat to return and observe what happened. And actually he was so held by his own obscure feelings that he waited until he could just hear the returning boat, before setting out sensibly for the *Fulmar*.

It was only when he was well on the way that the success of his venture came full upon him. He certainly had something for Grear now! This will keep him going, he thought. But the feeling he experienced was not so much one of pleasure as of relief. He was finished with the whole thing now. He could step out of it, right clean out. His mind began to clear. Extraordinary about the chart! He was laughing quietly to himself. The quest of the chart! If its loss had been a blot on his copy book, their lordships might now generously consider rubbing the blot out. Anyway, it would be nice handing it casually to Grear.

But how nearly it had betrayed him again. For the one thing he had drummed into his mind was that he must not, by anything he did or touched, leave a sign of his presence on board. These two would never miss the chart off the rack, but supposing he had dropped it on the floor, the deck! . . . There had been no time to put it back in the rack.

He looked over his shoulder and pulled his left a little more strongly. The night was perceptibly clearing.

Tuesday, was it? . . . and Thursday. . . . They would come ashore for instructions . . . collaring them would be too easy . . . Thursday? What was it about Thursday? . . . But he looked over his shoulder again and suddenly smiled. He would hitch up so quietly that Joe and Christina wouldn't hear him. Holding water with one oar, he shipped the other. The cockpit door opened and Joe stepped out in its light, stooping and peering. The light went out before he could call. That was Christina!

"Hallo, Joe!"

"Is that you?" Joe whispered back.

Dermot handed him the painter, picked up his chart, and stepped into the cockpit.

"You weren't worrying, were you, Christina?" Dermot asked as he sat down.

"No," she answered, "it was Joe. He was wanting to go for you."

"Surely not, Joe."

"Well——" muttered Joe.

Dermot laughed. "Wait till I show you something." He looked like a pleased, excited boy as he pulled the chart out of its cardboard case. "It's got wet a bit, but never mind." He put up the second wing of the table, spread open the chart and in a moment had his finger on a certain spot. "Where's that?" and he looked at Christina.

Her dark head stooped. "Cladday!" she breathed in wonder.

He smiled into her eyes.

"You've found it?" She stared at him.

He nodded. "Good, isn't it?"

She could not speak. Her chest filled with air that came away in a slight quiver.

He explained the chart to Joe in detail, lifting it once near the bulb to read some small lettering. "You come in this way," and his forefinger moved over the chart. "Old Seumas's house is there; Anna's there. If the darkness has fallen and you get their lights in a line, then you'll miss the skerry, which is here. Now Christina's home is just there. . . ." He finished up by saying, "That's where we're going, Joe, on our next big trip. You'll like Cladday."

"I'll put on the kettle," said Christina.

"No," said Dermot at once. "We must get out of here before it's light, and the morning is coming fast. You'll start her up, Joe."

"I'll do that," said Joe, as if starting her up was a thing he looked forward to.

Dermot spread the chart on his bunk so that the wet streaks might dry, pinning down the edges with the cardboard case and a pillow; then he went and leaned against the galley partition. "When we're properly underway I'll light the primus. Any more of that oatcake?"

"Yes," said Christina. "Would you like some honey on it? They used to say at home that it helps to keep the strength in you."

"Um—yes. But there's only one thing about honey."

"What's that?" Her tongue seemed to have got loose.

"I can't eat it unless it's an inch thick."

"You're as bad as Iain Og," she said, piling the honey on. "Not to mention Kennie."

"What about Kennie?"

"Och, Kennie. He would make faces and say, 'It's too sweet for me,' and then he would eat it solid."

The engine gave a mighty cough. They both laughed, but a touch of concern came into her face. "I hope he doesn't hurt himself."

"Not him. I think you have been flirting with him, Christina."

"Indeed and I have not," she said, poking into a shelf.

The engine went off with a splendid roar and Dermot got honey down his chin and on to his breast.

"We'll make a good seaman of him yet," he said, licking himself like a cat.

"Such a mess!" Christina damped a cloth.

Joe had toned down the engine and now they heard his footsteps overhead.

"I do believe he's going to tackle the anchor."

"Stand still, please," said Christina, rubbing the clotted mess off his chest.

"My chin," he said, sticking it out.

She wiped his chin.

"Och you!" he said, saying it for her.

She smiled and coloured and looked at his chin critically and dried it. "That anchor will be too heavy for him."

"You never thought it was too heavy for me."

"Och you!"

He laughed. "Let him have a go at it; it will do him good. I like Joe . . . Don't you?" He stuffed the last piece of cake and honey into his mouth.

"He's all right," she said putting the cloth away.

"Is that all?"

"Do you want more?" she asked, looking at the food.

"O Christina! That's not like you, and you coming out of your mother's home."

"It's—it's that anchor——"

"Listen! . . . It's almost up. Wait! . . ." There was a heavy thud. "Good for Joe!"

"I did not mean it," she said, flushing as she put her knife in the butter.

"I know you didn't. Hospitality is sacred—unless there's something stronger."

She gave him a glance.

"Och you!" he said.

Suddenly she stopped as if he had gripped her. Above the rumble of the idling engine came the sound of voices. Someone was talking to Joe back in the cockpit. Christina saw Dermot's concentration narrowing ruthlessly. He did not move. Then he turned quietly and went aft.

The light was on in the cabin and therefore behind Dermot's back as he came to the cockpit entrance and saw the face rising above the stern of the *Fulmar*. The light caught the face and the hand on the *Fulmar's* gunnel before the shadow from Dermot's body darkened the scene.

Joe turned. "This man is wanting a lift."

Dermot, who was now just outside the door, could not speak.

"I thought if ye were goin' to Gantry," the man said, "ye might take me in. We were over on the other side last night, an' we're late. My friend is in a hurry to get back. A chum got hurt in an accident."

Usually in a tough corner Dermot could think and act rapidly. Now a tremulous surging beset his body, went to his head and scattered his wits.

"Gantry?" his voice said roughly, giving him time.

"Yes, sir. As ye're goin' there, I thought ye mightn't mind takin' me."

Dermot just stopped his tongue asking How do you know we're going there? He could now make out the

262

other figure in the small boat and knew it was the ship's watchman.

"I thought," said Joe, "seeing it was an accident——"

"An accident," repeated Dermot. "But Gantry—what——"

"I have to get to my work at Gantry. I'm a mechanic there. But my friend must get back across the loch quick. He's phoned for the doctor. It's his wife's brother. He fell and hurt himsel' badly."

"I see," said Dermot, as gruffly as any precise skipper. "All right. Hop in."

"Thank ye, sir." He hopped in nimbly and turned to his friend. "Tell Nellie no' to worry: he'll be a' right. So long just now. We'll be seein' ye." He had been leaning over the gunnel as he spoke and pushing the boat off.

"So long," answered his friend, giving way with the oars.

I mustn't let him see my face was all Dermot could think clearly, for he was still beset by a paralysing feeling of calamity. Yet, equally irrationally, the reference to Nellie helped him. It was so barefaced an item in the trumped-up story that it was impudent, maddening. It strengthened him, but dangerously.

"Watch the painter," came his order to Joe. Normally he would have done this himself, but he did not want to have to turn back from the stern into the light. As Joe got hold of the rope, he ducked in to the engine, opened throttle, engaged the forward gear, waited a moment, then backed out and caught the wheel. The *Fulmar* was underway. The motion cleared his head still more.

As he stared over the house, he saw that the dawn was at hand. The sky was visibly paling. He looked for the ship's boat and suddenly saw her off his port bow. She was actually being pulled across the loch, away from Criach and from the hulks. By God, they're good at the game! he thought. Out of the corner of his eye, he watched and waited.

The man he had shipped gave a wave and called, "Cheerio!"

The small boat answered.

For one wild moment, Dermot wondered if he had made a mistake.

His mental confusion was all the deeper because he could not overcome that first glimpse of the face rising out of the water beyond the *Fulmar's* stern. It was mixed up with the face that had looked up and down the street, that had caught the white cunning intensity of pure evil before it advanced on him. An incalculable force. Almost like something out of another dimension or world. He didn't know how to deal with it. His muscles were actually quivering. What had he come on board for? What had he found out? Dermot could not crush down the feeling that the fellow knew everything.

"It's cold this morning," the fellow said to Joe.

"Yes, it's cold."

"Been havin' a trip?"

"Yes," answered Joe.

"If you're cold," said Dermot, "you can get inside."

"Thank ye, sir. Was up most the night." He rubbed his hands and, ducking his head, went in past the engine to the cabin.

Dermot felt he had given his panic away, had shown he did not want the fellow to get information out of Joe, had weakly needed to be rid of him.

Joe came and stood beside him.

"Going to have a good run, I think," he said to Joe.

Joe glanced at him, for Dermot's loud voice was still the gruff skipper's. He answered, "The dawn is coming."

Dermot brought his mouth to Joe's ear. "Go in and pretend to be looking over the engine but watch what

264

he's doing." Then in his loud voice, "Have a look at the oil."

The very absence of the man from the cockpit helped Dermot's wits. Alone now, he was in command. The awful feeling that the face had come into the cockpit to take control began to subside. For what could the fellow know? Nothing. Must have caught some sounds from the dinghy when his oar had rattled and he was fending off from the ship's side. Would have wondered if someone had been on prowl, and on boat's return had followed up. Would have seen light from cockpit when Joe had come out to meet dinghy. Wanted to know who and what they were. Would get off at Gantry and go back to hulk— or report to Stenson.

To defeat his suspicion, what could be said? What story? The fellow would see the cabin, Christina in galley getting breakfast, nothing suspicious—His whole body constricted.

Joe came out. "The oil is all right," he said aloud, then he brought his mouth to Dermot's ear and whispered, "He's looking at that chart of Cladday."

But Dermot already knew it and could not speak.

"How black the hills look," said Joe.

Dermot's brain wouldn't work. Beyond an idiotic premonition that he might escape some trap if he did not land at Gantry, he could think of nothing. And not to land at Gantry would be the complete give-away, lunacy. If the fellow had ever worked at Gantry, he would know the *Fulmar*. She was always laid up there in Dickson's yard. Put in the water only last week.

A thought began to form in this extraordinary state of mental chaos: he must not let the fellow land at all. He must somehow hold him. . . .

The fellow came out. "I feel warmer now. Ye're cosy in there."

265

"Not too bad," Dermot answered, staring ahead. They were making now for the open firth, well off the shore, which could be seen where the grey water ended.

"I'll give Christina a hand," Joe said.

Dermot had to suppress the command to Joe not to go, and immediately Joe disappeared, he felt wide open and vulnerable. More that once in his life death had seemed certain. In the heavy seas, after their patrol boat had been shot to bits by the U-boat, when Captain Laird in the darkness had faded out, he had struggled on, kicking the water from him weakly, but knowing, with a curious calm that, though he would go on fighting to the last kick, this was the end, knowing it with an increasing acceptance, a resignation that held some peace. Never before in his life had he experienced anything like this. And it was humiliating because he knew that this thin-faced mechanic dominated him, had an inner force that produced this blind panic expectancy in his mind.

"She's a nice turn o' speed," said the mechanic.

"About seven knots."

As he came nearer Dermot he said, "Ye're losin' a knot or so on the dinghy."

"Yes."

He was now standing close. Dermot knew that his face was being studied, but he was ready in every muscle, his front protected by the cabin wall. Suddenly the very fact that he was so strung up maddened him. A snort came from the fellow's nostrils. As Dermot turned, a knee got him below the belt, and his head jerked forward to meet an uppercut. But though the pattern of the simple attack was the same it was not quite so effective as it had been on the street, because this time Dermot's fighting instinct had been forewarned and he had always been formidable with the gloves; but perhaps even more because the self-confessed mechanic had the added design of knocking

266

Dermot overboard. As it was, Dermot swayed back on the gunnel as on the ropes in a ring and when the mechanic followed up with a straight left, he ducked sideways. The missed blow, however, had all the mechanic's weight behind it, and as the body heaved forward Dermot clinched. But the rail was too low for the impact; it caught Dermot in the thighs and at once he lost his balance; they both lost their balance and in a tightening clinch they went over.

Joe was in time to see their legs disappear and nearly went overboard himself. But Christina, who had heard the initial sounds of the conflict and had thrust Joe on and followed him up, was instantly by his side. She grabbed him. "Joe!" she screamed, for already the whirling turmoil of the bodies in the water was falling rapidly astern. "Joe!" She rushed to the wheel and put it round—round, hard round. The *Fulmar* lurched and Joe was thrown off his feet. In a wide sweep she came speeding round. Joe was up and gaping towards the water. He saw a head and dived for the engine, pulling the lever back with such force that he partly engaged reverse. The engine gave a roar, a growl, and died with Joe's hand at the throttle. Like one possessed he was out again. The *Fulmar* was losing speed rapidly; slowing up, stopping. Christina screamed at him and pointed. Then Joe's instinct turned to the dinghy, the thing he could handle and move himself. He fell into it but got the coils of rope from his neck, the oars out, and struck with all his power. He could not understand Christina's wild cries. She looked demented and bereft. But he pulled away to where he had seen the head. Then he saw it. It was the mechanic's head. Joe stopped and stared over the grey water. There was no sign of Dermot. The mechanic was swimming towards him. Christina was silent.

It was a moment of terrible silence for Joe, with no sound in the world, no motion except this slow swimming towards him of a thing that made circles in the calm dawn water like a monstrous water rat.

Then even as Christina cried Joe saw a hand come up out of the sea and fall over in a languid gesture like a gesture of farewell. It endued Joe with such maniacal power that he all but rammed Dermot's body, which now lay on its back, with the head tilted backward, the chin and mouth clear.

It was a light dinghy, a varnished shell of an affair, and Joe's seamanship would have been just enough to drown them both if Dermot, in his very exhausted condition, hadn't had enough energy to caution him. "Wait!" Realizing he had already shipped some of the sea, Joe waited.

Dermot's mouth had fallen open. He was gasping weakly and spewing out water now and then, Joe supporting him, with the sea lapping the gunnel. Dermot opened his eyes and muttered, "Take me in at stern."

Joe was so careful now that he made most of the way to the stern sideways on his knees, bumping Dermot's head only once. It was a square stern and Joe was so strengthened by apprehending on his own the whole point of the manoeuvre that Dermot had again to caution him and ask for a little time. Then the combined effort was made, Joe standing back as Dermot's chest came over. Dermot's head fell forward and he was griped in a vomiting spasm when a scream tore the air.

Christina's whole being had been so concentrated on Joe's rescue effort, towards which the *Fulmar* was now nearly broadside on, that the swimmer had not only dropped out of her sight but out of her mind. With the resurgence of hope her body moved to relieve its tension and in that instant her eyes saw a movement, saw a hand. For the mechanic had managed at last, with the help of the rudder, to get high enough to make a thrust at the gunnel with one hand, to reach it, to hold.

She stared at the hand.

A second hand came clawing up but just missed a hold for the rudder gave to the movement of the mechanic's body and the toe on the rudder-bolt slipped. The body slewed away, hanging from the one hand.

Christina's fear paralysed even her throat. Then she found herself before the hand, beating it with her fist. "Go away!" she croaked. She hit the hand in frenzied little pummels. But the hand held and whitened under the heave which brought the second hand—to a hold. The head at once came rising up and the eyes gleamed on Christina just above the gunnel. "Go away!" Though she hardly knew what she was doing, she knew that this man mustn't get on board. It never occurred to her to look for a weapon, to find something, a footboard, anything, with which even to poke him off. She could see only his head and it was beginning to rise farther. With wildly contorted features she put her open hand on that head and poked it down. His right hand let go and gripped her. It was then she screamed.

The dinghy was about thirty yards away. Dermot's head rose. "Pull!" he cried thickly and wriggled into the dinghy, falling in a heap as Joe gave way.

It would have been difficult, perhaps quite impossible without foot purchase, for the mechanic, in his weakened condition, to have boarded the *Fulmar* there and then. But all unwittingly Christina was assisting him, for as she leaned back to tear herself free from the grip the man had of her clothes, she was drawing him up. His feet were now clambering against the planking. His right shoulder was coming over. His hand suddenly released Christina and she went clean on her back. The right knee was coming up when Joe rammed the *Fulmar* and went over backwards on his head. Dermot made a wild lunge at the mechanic's left leg, which was thrashing the water as it left it, and got a grip, but the mechanic's breast was now gunnel high and he had a firm two-handed purchase on the *Fulmar*. His right foot came down and kicked Dermot's hand so fiercely that it momentarily lost all power and fell away useless. But Joe was up and Dermot cried, "Hit him with an oar!"

For a man of such kindly and pacific intentions in life, it must be admitted that Joe hit that mechanic a hefty, even powerful stroke. It landed somewhere between the right shoulder and the side of the head. The body sagged away and dropped. Meantime Joe, having wildly overbalanced, had caught a leaning purchase with his oar blade on the *Fulmar*; the dinghy was pushed away by his feet and he went overboard in a slow graceful motion. As the blade slid away from the *Fulmar*'s gunnel, Christina grabbed it, shouting on him so wildly that Joe held to his end and as his legs shot down and out they fouled the mechanic's body. With the second oar, Dermot, on his knees, gave a couple of paddle strokes that brought the dinghy back the four yards that separated him from a grip of Joe. When he had the grip, he said to Christina, "The heaving line!" and as she stood, apparently unable to let go her oar, he told her shortly where to find it, and his thick voice was commanding.

"I've got him," said Joe, gasping harshly, for he had swallowed some of the sea. This time his mouth and eyes shut tightly as his hand went down. Watching him, Dermot let his head go under, then pulled him up. He saw the mechanic's body in the swirl. "Grip me," he said to Joe, leaning as far over as he dared. All his actions were slow and deliberate.

He lifted his face. "Keep an end of it," he called to Christina. The thin line fell on him. Joe was trying to cough his chest up but he hung lightly enough to the dinghy's gunnel while Dermot got a bight of the line under the mechanic's body. "Haul away! . . . Stop. Make fast there. Tie it somewhere." Christina tied the rope. The body hung with its head out of the water.

It was a bit of a job getting Joe on board, but once Christina had a real grip with Dermot giving a heave from below, Joe went over the gunnel too fast for his comfort.

When Dermot stood in the cockpit he swayed, grey. Then his teeth showed, his legs gave way and he sat down; his head fell back against the seat; his hands slid off his knees to the bottom boards. He muttered something. In the same instant it seemed to him that Christina had his head cushioned against her and that a glass was hitting his teeth.

But his will would not answer him, not even in the slow, half-blind, deliberate way. Then he made his effort, for he could not afford the divine luxury of passing out altogether, not yet.

A vague smile came to his face. "Is it yourself again?"

"Drink this." She let his head tilt back a little more and poured a few drops of the whisky into his mouth. As he curled up and began to cough and vomit, she was full of concern but far from helpless.

"Put the kettle on," she ordered Joe, who was still rasping away but again full of energy. As he hit his knee a crack on passing the engine, Christina heard him swear.

Dermot came round, shook his head, and shivered violently.

"You'll get out of your clothes at once," said Christina.

"Have you still got him on?" he asked Joe.

Joe went to the side again. "Yes, he's hanging there. Will I haul him up?"

"Ay," said Dermot, getting to his feet with Christina's help.

In the end Joe had to go into the dinghy to help heave the limp sodden body over. It fell heavily, for Christina seemed to have little stomach for handling it.

As Dermot stared down at it, his face quickened slightly. "We'll have to try to squeeze some water out of him."

"Change yourself first," said Christina. "And you, too, Joe. I'll look after him." Her voice was peremptory.

"No," muttered Dermot. He got down on his knees across the body and began squeezing and releasing it in an effort at inducing respiration. "We'll have to put something under him." But he was now trembling almost helplessly.

"Come on, Joe," said Christina and she caught Dermot under one arm. Joe caught him under the other.

Dermot gave in. "If you see him so much as move, call me."

Christina promised. "Rub him hard," she said to Joe. "Hard as you can."

"Yes," said Joe, whose teeth had now started to chitter.

In the cabin, Joe had first to roll up the chart; then he stripped Dermot briskly and got him into his bunk, where he began rubbing the naked body with a blanket till his arms ached and Dermot rebelled.

Joe was stripped and towelling himself when Christina called almost quietly, "Joe, he's moving."

Joe, for whom the nude was natural, started for the cockpit.

Dermot rolled off his bunk in the bedclothes, opened

272

his locker and hauled out his change of underclothes, an old pair of slacks, and a heavy Iceland jersey. Deliberately, fumbling a little, he began to dress, sitting on the floor.

"I think he's passed out again," said Joe coming back with the towel in his hand, prancing a little against the cold.

Dermot lifted his head. "Were you out like that?"

A little bewildered, Joe said, "I had the towel."

Dermot leaned against the locker, his head sagging, his body shaking. Then his head rolled over, "Oh God," he groaned, "I'm sick," and began shaking again with laughter.

Joe hurried into his own dry clothes, his fingers white and dead. He controlled his chitters to say, "Get into your bed."

You're frightened of Christina, Dermot wanted to say, but hadn't the energy.

"How you feeling now?" Joe asked.

"Like death. Go out."

"Just going," said Joe.

Christina screeched. Joe bolted.

The mechanic actually had his hands on the painter, had released its first hitch, when Joe grabbed and heaved him on his back. He showed his teeth as he slowly turned over on all fours. Joe didn't know what to do so he sat on him and pushed away his arms and flattened him.

Dermot appeared. "Hold him there. We'll tie him up." He got the heaving line, sat on the legs and began trussing the ankles carefully, methodically. "Pull his hands round."

The mechanic thickly spat out some oaths and then his whole body writhed in a sick spasm. Dermot looked at Christina. "The kettle. Hot drinks."

"Toddy?"

"Weak."

She went away quickly. "Now, Joe, we'll make a job

of his fists." He had to stop in a quivering nausea. "My stomach," he muttered; "his damn knee."

"I'll do it," said Joe.

But Dermot finished the job to his own satisfaction. "I think we're safe now," he said as he got up. Christina appeared with two steaming cups. Dermot sat down on the seat. "Is it hot?"

"Not too hot. I tried it."

He controlled his hand and took the cup. There was a bleak humour in his eyes as he waited to see how Joe got on. Joe made an extraordinary face as if the cup were going to bite him. Then it did, and he spilt some of the liquor.

Dermot managed to set his cup on the seat and started laughing noiselessly and painfully.

"It's boiling," gasped Joe.

"It is not," said Christina. "It'll do you no good cold whatever." She looked flustered, almost angry.

"Very good," said Joe, and he tried again. "I feel it going down." He blinked. "It's—it's good." He had another go. "It's not hot at all," he said to Christina.

"I told you that," she answered.

Dermot was looking at the mechanic, who was lying on his right side with his back to them. Then he looked at Christina.

"Some for him?" she said with wide eyes.

Dermot nodded and she went away. He tackled his drink, sucking it carefully. It stayed down. He took some more; blew into the cup; then finished the lot. When Christina reappeared, Dermot was afraid to move. Internal whirlings were going on. His arms began to tremble and he wanted to lie flat out. Slowly the whirlings subsided and he wiped his icy forehead. The internal warmth was coming.

"Try him with some, Joe."

Joe got down on his knees. "Here, you, have a drink."

There was no response.

"He's shivering all over," said Joe.

"He's probably shamming again," said Dermot. "He nearly foxed you that time."

"He did." And Joe glanced at the painter.

Dermot followed the glance. "As near as that?"

"Supposing he'd got off?"

"We'd have run him down," said Dermot and he looked away towards the shore. In the clear fine light of the early morning the land was very still.

Two cormorants went up the loch, low and fast; an oyster catcher piped from the beach; a curlew swung high out over the loch, calling; a gull came past on outstretched wings with the silence of snow. Christina said quietly, "I'll see about breakfast."

When she had gone Dermot remarked, "She's a good lass, that."

"Yes," said Joe, and at once his brows wrinkled, his cheek bones stuck out, and he looked more uncertain and harassed than at any time that morning. "Remember," he muttered, "about the money——"

Dermot gaped at him.

"I was always—going to tell you——"

"We have company, Joe," said Dermot gently. "Another time." Then he got up and went to the mechanic.

They lifted him into a sitting posture, and after a few moments, when he seemed to be doing some grim thinking, he drank the whole cupful.

"We'll take him into the cabin," said Dermot. "No more chances."

The mechanic growled and cursed them for bastards as they half-dragged and carried him into the cabin. He wanted his hands free. The bloody rope hurt him. "You're frightened of me, aren't you?"

"We are," said Dermot.

40

The mechanic looked across the small cabin at Dermot as the *Fulmar* went on her inexorable way. He had already been told that the rope wouldn't hurt his wrists if he kept them still, that there was no change of clothes for him, that sea water did little harm, and that the blanket wrapped around him would presently induce a splendid heat.

"What the hell satisfaction does it give you to act the police kite?"

"Not much."

"Why the hell then do it?"

"I confess the question worries me." Dermot lifted his eyes from the pale knife-edged expression and stretched himself full length. There was silence for a few moments.

"You don't need to do it."

"How do you know?" asked Dermot.

"Christ, do you think we haven't got you taped?"

"I half suspected as much."

"Surely a chap like you could let them do their own dirty work. God, haven't you made enough out of the capitalist racket?"

"A capitalist never makes enough. You ought to know that."

"Don't I!"

"Well, why ask silly questions?"

"What a dirty filthy game! How you can act the police

nark, hunt fellows who are trying to bring about a decent state of society, seeing you've got what you *have* got, it beats me. How you can act like that! . . ."

"You act pretty well yourself. You're losing, for example, quite a bit of the local accent in a more intellectual expression."

"Superior, too. Smug. My God."

"What did you expect?"

"That's true. So help me."

"Now we know where we are, that's fine."

"You can crow because you've got me down. But it's coming to you. You'll get it all right."

"You may be right."

"Too bloody true I'm right. You know it in your sucking bones. Nothing can stop what's coming. Nothing on earth. You're too intelligent not to know that. Yet your dirty greed, your greed and your fear, make you act like a bloody pimp."

Dermot remained silent.

"Why keep on doing it? That's what beats me. Why deliberately run into it?"

"Into what?" asked Dermot.

"Into what *you'll* get. God, you're not such a child as to think that if you hand me over to the police you'll get off with it?"

"And who's to know if I hand you over to the police?"

The lips parted and the grey-green eyes grew rounder than Dermot had yet seen them. "You think I haven't contacts in the police?"

"How should I know?"

"God!" The face turned away in a withering astonishment. Then the eyes came back. "You're not as simple as that?"

"Are you referring to what the press has called the witch hunt in high places."

"So you know all right."

"Are you suggesting that if I hand you over to the police, someone in the police will pass the tip to your friends, who will then quietly get me?"

"As certain as you're there."

"I see. Doesn't look too good for me."

The man's eyes did not leave Dermot's face. "It's much worse than it looks—for you. Not for me."

"How not for you?"

"What have you got against me?"

Now Dermot's eyes opened. "A fair amount, I should say."

The withering expression held its humour. "Just what? That you knocked me overboard? That that simpleton who's with you hit me with an oar? Will he deny it?"

"That *I* knocked you overboard?"

"There were only the two of us. A heated political argument—and you lost your head."

"I—see."

"You didn't expect me to hand you your case on a plate?"

"No," said Dermot slowly and thoughtfully. He remained thoughtful.

"They'll side with you, of course. You have the bourgeois concept of justice in your pocket. They may clap me in clink for a month or so. But that will be about all—for me. Don't you agree?"

"You may be right."

"You know damn fine I'm right. And even to get me that, you'll have to prove your case in open court. You'll even have to tell that you tied me up, all wet and sodden, in ropes—*three* of you, for hours. And if you felt so bloody ashamed that you'd want to deny it, do you think that girl would stand up to the cross-examination of the

278

best counsel in the city? Not to mention that naked simpleton! You're not such a fool as all that."

"I admit I'd forgotten that in this country a man could still demand justice in an open court."

"Growing smug again."

"It's true all the same. You get off with a light sentence. Then I get bumped off. That's your idea."

"What court have I to try you in? Be realistic—and give the bloody moralistic a rest. This is you against me. I'm giving you a chance to be reasonable. The only chance I can give. If you don't take it—well, it's your funeral."

"What chance?"

"That you land me quietly at Gantry and we'll say no more about it."

"You give me your word?"

"Don't keep on being a bloody fool. I wouldn't expect you to take my word. At least I credit you with intelligence."

"You'll have to be simpler. You can't expect my mind to come clean of the moralistic all in a moment."

The man who had said he was a mechanic considered Dermot. He did not seem anxious. There was no suggestion of cunning pleading. His brain had been busy, obviously. Dermot, who had watched his initial frustration passing, could now feel the power coming out of him again; he could feel it affecting him.

"Are you trying to be funny?" the mechanic asked, deliberately exerting his power.

"No, not that I noticed," replied Dermot coolly.

"Well, put yourself in my place. You land at Gantry. Why should I do anything after that? If anything happened to you, that might mean questions for me. Do you think I want questions?"

"But if I kept my mouth shut, how could anyone think of questioning you?"

"If you keep your mouth shut, why should I worry?"

"And if I don't?"

"Then you're a bloody fool, because—things would happen to you. I'm not asking you to trust me. If you can show me how, by double-crossing you, I could help myself, then I'll shut up here and now."

Dermot was not often stumped in argument, but for the life of him he could not think of anything pertinent to say. Direction, purpose had come into the fellow's talk. Dermot could feel its remorseless grip.

"Sounds like blackmail to me," he muttered.

"Blackmail!" The mechanic made the word, at this time of day, sound incredible. "You actually mean that your vanity over a fight is more than your life?"

"That's not everything."

"No? What more is there?"

Dermot turned his eyes and met the eyes that were waiting for him. "Why did you want to do me in?"

"Because you are a police spy, and I hate the breed. I admit it. It came over me. I was a bloody fool. I suddenly remembered a time before; I suddenly knew you. I saw red. But rub it in if you like."

"What would you have done with my two friends?"

"Christ, don't I know it! What's happened has happened. It's the next step now. And you know the position—for yourself *and* your two friends. Let me tell you this. Don't think anything can be hidden. We have an organisation——"

Joe came in. "We're opposite the point now."

"Right," said Dermot calmly, getting up. "Wait here." He went out soberly to the cockpit.

There was a smile on Christina's face but her eyes were on him. "How are you feeling now?"

"Fine." He looked around. An old puffer was coming ploughing towards them, deep with coal. Away to the

Firth over the starboard quarter a liner rose high out of the sea. A gull sailed overhead, inspecting them critically. The wide estuary sparkled. He could see Gantry in the distance ahead. "It's a lovely morning."

"It is. It's lovely."

"I have run you into a lot of trouble, Christina."

"But it will be all right now?"

"That's just it. If I hand him over to the police, yourself and Joe will have to appear as witnesses and all that. I don't like it. I should never have mixed you up in it."

She was silent.

He took the wheel from her. "They're a dangerous crowd. Particularly just now. It's all or nothing for them now. Heaven alone knows what they might do. I'm worried about you going back to the Mures."

She said quite simply, "I'll do whatever you want."

"Several of my friends would be glad to have you. Even Mrs. Spicer." His face turned to her with a dry smile.

She looked very troubled.

"You wouldn't care to go to Mrs. Spicer?"

"If you think so."

Christina often seemed to have no sense of humour; she could only look dumb and concerned. He thought of her being questioned about her trip by Mrs. Mure, by Amy, by Stenson . . . She would never give anything away, but her face, her manner . . . Very definitely she couldn't go back to the Mures.

"Is not that Gantry?" she asked, for they were now abreast of it. The morning was wearing on.

"Yes. But we're not going in."

Her eyes were a woman's searching eyes.

"We're going on to the Queen's Bridge. The police launch is usually moored there."

"I hope you're not going to catch a cold," she said, withdrawing her eyes and looking pale and more worried.

He sneezed twice, three times. "If I got double pneumonia, would you nurse me?"

"You shouldn't make a joke of it. I'll make some more hot tea——"

"I'm in a fix, Christina. I have to do something I hate very much; particularly for your sake, and Joe's."

"You have to do your duty. That's what my father always said."

He glanced at her, but now he thought her seriousness, with its shy troubled expression, was very beautiful. He caught her hand and pressed it.

41

As Dermot brought the *Fulmar* alongside the wharf some little way below the police launch he felt naked as though the whole world would now see him and, in particular, observe the ceremony of handing over the prisoner to the police. For one wild instant he thought of swinging her head away, but there above was a seaman strolling along from the police launch to offer a friendly hand with a head-rope.

"Stopping long?" he asked as Dermot came up the steps.

"No," replied Dermot. "Forgotten something. There's a telephone box? . . ." When he had got the direction of the nearest kiosk, he could not help saying, "Thank you. Keep your eye on her, will you?"

"Right, sir. But she'll do there."

The fact is, thought Dermot to himself, I'm afraid of that mechanic, frightened of what he'll do when I'm not there. As he stepped briskly on, the mechanic's face gathered its pale, edged, supernormal power. It was a power that cleaved through . . . In a few seconds it obsessed him, and he actually had to assert a deliberate control on the hand that dialled Grear's number. Grear had never been away when he hadn't wanted him. But now . . .

Grear was there, the cool clear voice was always there. The non-committal, bright, intelligent voice answered before a name was spoken. "Oh, it's you, is it?"

"Yes. Something very important. I want you along to the Queen's Bridge at once. Could you take that inspector with you and a couple of men in plain clothes. I don't want a fuss. No fuss—I mean I don't want the public to think anything is going on. I don't—it's very important, that."

"Certainly. Queen's Bridge—where exactly?"

"Small motor cruiser—moored just below police launch. Don't be long, will you?"

"I'll put phone call through, then come straight away myself."

"Fine." Dermot slapped down the receiver and hurried back.

But there was no fight going on. Everything was calm.

"You weren't long," said the seaman.

"They'll be here soon," Dermot answered, aware that his expression had caught the man's attention, so he wrinkled his brows anxiously. "Think the weather is going to keep up?"

"Oh, I think so. Though it may blow a bit, later." He talked of the weather forecast and looked up at white drawn wisps of cloud.

Dermot looked up also. "There's wind there." He was

283

reluctant to go aboard; didn't want to talk to that mechanic again.

"Going far?" asked the man.

"No, not very far. Just trying her out." He gave the man a friendly nod and, as he went on board, heard voices from the cabin. He could not go in. The *Fulmar* had needed a fair amount of pumping and he now started on the semi-rotary pump, calmly, without haste, until he sucked her dry. Then after he had tidied up the cockpit, he entered.

"He's sweating," said Joe, turning from the mechanic's face with a towel in his hand. "He says he's in a fever. The rope is cutting him."

But the mechanic's eyes and his own were already engaged.

Dermot sat down.

"So you've done your Judas act?" The low-pitched voice came at him like a blade.

Dermot removed his eyes and looked into the galley, where Christina could just stand upright. Her face was dead white, her eyes black, and she seemed to be staring at him through an invisible barrier.

Dermot looked at the mechanic again but did not speak.

"Sold yourself to the police!" The contempt in the voice was beyond all speech.

"I wouldn't say that," replied Dermot. A profound lassitude was getting the better of him. A tremor was suddenly in his muscles. He had to control his calm utterance or it might gulp and break.

"Haven't you phoned for the police?"

"Yes."

The head of the mechanic fell back. "Now you'll get it. Christ, but you will!"

"I don't care for the police any more than you," said Dermot, hanging on to his simple thought.

284

The mechanic's eyes were on him again.

"The trouble is," continued Dermot rather laboriously, "that the sort of thing you stand for will mean more police, more police than ever, *secret* police. That—I hate."

"Now you're talking like a bloody child. You must have order before you can get anywhere. Surely to God you can see that it's the end that matters. What the blazes do you think I personally am getting out of this? You know I am trying to help clean up the bloodiest mess that ever humanity got into—for the good of everyone. And what are you doing about it? Handing me over to the police!" His eyes blinked for the sweat was running into them. Joe went and wiped his face. "Why are you doing it? Ask yourself that, right down in your guts—in your precious soul."

"You think—to save my possessions?"

"You know it is! Damn fine, you know. You haven't even the guts to make this a simple case of violence."

He held Dermot's eyes, as if he would at last force out of him what he wanted to know, but what he daren't himself mention; as if what had really been torturing him all along was the unknown extent of Dermot's knowledge.

All Dermot answered was, "It's your violence that's the trouble. My possessions are neither here nor there, and such as they are I've worked for them, like anyone else. I'm the normal business executive you would need in any state. You know that quite well." He spoke rather slowly. He was feeling devilish tired.

"I do know it. That's why I've spoken so plainly to you. In a decent state you would be a key man. I haven't insulted your intelligence by any bogus argument. Why the blazes then run your head into the noose? For you know that's what you're doing, and you're not normally an automaton."

"You seem to know a lot about me."

"Enough to know that you could have been a better man, that you could have helped."

"Was I as near it as that?"

"You know you are. You know I'm right and you know it will worry you to hell. But you can't get past the old sanctimonious humbug. You talk to me of violence. *You!* Jesus."

In the silence, Dermot heard Grear's voice above. He was talking to the man from the police launch. They all heard the voices. Dermot sat heavily like one who could not get up. Then slowly he pushed himself to his feet.

"Remember!" said the mechanic with an extraordinary intensity.

Dermot paused for a moment to look at him.

"Remember! By how much you tell—you'll be judged."

Dermot continued to look at him. Grear's controlled voice called down, "Hallo, there!" Dermot went out.

"You have a genius for surprises," said Grear, his eyes on Dermot's weary but calm face with its automatic smile of greeting.

"You think so?" Dermot strolled away, rubbing his palms on his haunches. The heavy dark-grey Iceland jersey made him look like an unshaven seaman who had come through some dirty weather and was still under the sea's influence.

In his dark overcoat, collar and tie, and Homburg hat, Grear was the city business man with a fair face so bright and clean it might never need shaving.

Dermot stopped, and Grear waited.

"I have a fellow tied up in the cabin," Dermot said. "I'm handing him over. He's the sort of fellow who might make a fuss when you take him out. I think it would be a pity if any of the public saw him."

"Who is he?"

"I don't know his name. He says he's a mechanic who works at Gantry, but I doubt that."

"What happened?"

"A lot. Do you think when the police come along they could get him shifted quietly. Christina is on board. And Joe—the artist. They've been with me. I don't want them mixed up in anything. That's what's worrying me."

"No need to worry about that. What's been happening?"

"I thought they might bring an ambulance; take him up on a stretcher. Something like that. Looks as if he's catching a dose of 'flu."

Grear had been watching Dermot. "Look, Cameron, he'll be removed without a soul seeing him or any fuss made at all. Take that as absolutely certain. No one will see anything."

"It's not for myself," said Dermot.

Grear saw that for once this common statement was literally true; so much so that he asked with concern, "Would you like to sit down somewhere?"

"No, it's all right. He attacked me again, same way, and I fell for it. A knee below the belt—it's surprising. You would think it couldn't be done—too close—but when your chin goes out he steps back and uppercuts with the right. Leaves a sick feeling."

"The same fellow as attacked you on the street?"

287

"Yes. But this time we went overboard. He held me under, too. But I'm used to sea water. All the same, I nearly passed out."

"Did this happen on your boat?"

"Yes." Dermot looked into distance. "Assault and battery—that means a court case, doesn't it? It'll all be trotted out, I suppose, with Joe and Christina as witnesses. It's worrying me that I brought anyone else into it."

"For heaven's sake stop worrying about that. Leave that to me. We'll investigate the fellow. If you have any security information, you don't think we would have it trotted out in a public court?" Cameron was usually anything but dull. But Grear saw he must have been badly shaken for he was talking now as if, behind the talk, another strange argument was going on inside him over which in some mysterious way he had no control. He looked desperately tired, yet was calm and upright, if inclined to sway a little. He appeared to ponder Grear's last words.

"I have a lot of security information," he said almost absent-mindedly.

"About the same crowd?"

He smiled and looked at Grear. "I have found the lost chart."

"The Cladday chart?"

"Yes. It's in the cabin."

"Here," said Grear, "I think the best thing for us is to get down into the cabin of the police launch. I'll get this deck hand to appear to be showing us over. Won't attract attention like that."

Dermot looked startled.

"Come on. He knows I'm expecting someone." He walked away and Dermot had to follow. They were only a couple of minutes in the cabin when the inspector entered alone.

288

Grear at once gave the news, intelligently arranged, and ended with Dermot's concern about a quiet removal of the roped man from the *Fulmar*.

The inspector hardly smiled. "We are used to recovering bodies. We'll quietly haul you up alongside, put your case on a stretcher, cover it with a blanket, and then take it on board. After that you needn't worry."

But Dermot now became concerned about Christina and Joe and what the mechanic might be up to. These ropes on his wrists. . . .

The inspector stood up. "Do you mind leaving this to my men? Ropes are a bit antiquated." From a locker he produced a flask of brandy and poured Dermot a fair-sized drink. "Suppose it's a bit early in the day for you, Mr. Grear? . . . Take this, Mr. Cameron. It may help to stave off a chill. You look as if you'd been through it. Excuse me for a couple of minutes."

As the inspector went out Grear opened his cigarette-case, but Dermot shook his head and sipped the brandy. He gave a spasmodic shiver that startled Grear.

"You'll have to get home to your bed, my man." Grear's voice was cheerful and friendly.

Dermot considered him with a mild thoughtfulness. "Do you want me to talk freely before the inspector?"

"Why—yes." But his eyes were watchful. "Unless there's something that the police——" He stopped. "You asked for them."

"Yes," murmured Dermot. "It's probably urgent. I'll take a cigarette, please."

"If there's something you'd rather not tell them, let me know now before he comes. Quick."

But Dermot could not be quick. He finished the neat brandy and shook his head as if he'd been hit. "It was cold in that sea."

"I bet it was."

"Yes, damn him," murmured Dermot. "When he'd got rid of me," he continued slowly, "what would he have done with them? He would have had to get rid of them. He could have sailed the *Fulmar* somewhere and sunk her. Who would know what happened?" He looked at Grear and saw the insipid smile on the face of the statuette, observed it in a sort of isolated clarity because of the faint gloom in the cabin. He removed his eyes and automatically saw the dark figure of Christina weeping against the railings.

The inspector came in and found him an ash tray, saying briskly as he sat down, "That's all right."

"Is it?" Dermot looked at him.

"Yes. We know him."

"Do you?"

"Yes, that's all right, Mr. Cameron. You must tell us all about it."

"There's a lot," said Dermot, making to crush out his cigarette. "There's a whole lot." He had difficulty with the cigarette and apologised. "I feel devilish tired."

"Naturally. The shock," said the inspector. "Tell us as shortly as you can and then get on your back."

But once Dermot started to talk he found he wanted to tell them everything methodically. It was the kind of story one mustn't miss bits out of. It moved. It was like one of Christina's legends that had a beginning and went on, taking in the significant things, to an important and logical conclusion. Yet when he had got to the top of the watershed and looked down for the first time on the hulks and mentioned the red cross on the chart, Grear asked "What chart?" so Dermot had to go back to his first glimpse of the chart in the timber yard.

"I think I forgot to mention that because you asked so much about the plans D.1., I remember. Yes, that was it." After he had described the chart, he looked at Grear. "Was it one of yours?"

"Not that I know of."

Dermot nodded. "I wasn't sure." Then he went on to the anchorage at Criach and his early morning adventure. The brandy was now having its effect and though his recital was calm it was detailed and by a sort of understatement remarkably vivid. When he had finished, both Grear and the inspector sat looking at him, their minds so charged with implications that for the moment they could not stir.

"Lord Almighty," said the inspector at last on a breath of wonder, a sort of hushed reverence, as he leaned back and went on staring at his own thought.

"He said to me just now that he hit me on a mad impulse. I can see that's true. He must have heard me about the ship and followed up. Then he saw the Cladday chart. He must have got a hell of a shock. Yet he couldn't be sure how much I had seen, how much I knew—and he daren't give anything away. Yet he had to act. It was when he recognized me———"

"Mad impulse my foot," said the inspector.

"Tuesday," Grear was saying to himself, "and then Thursday . . . Thursday. So they knew that, too."

And now the significance of Thursday came upon Dermot. It was Grear who had spoken of it as zero hour. "War?"

Grear looked at him. "It certainly seems ominous. They must have got their—at least their command to stand by."

There was complete silence in the cabin for some seconds. A voice for'ard called, "Let go there." Dermot started.

"All right, Mr. Cameron. They have transferred your passenger to us and are now taking your boat astern again."

"About this ship, this hulk, we must be dead certain we make no mistake," Grear said.

"You can't make a mistake," Dermot answered. "She's the last going up Loch Criach."

Both Grear and the inspector asked questions, but behind the questions they were preoccupied.

Finally the inspector said firmly, as if his mind were made up, "We'd better get a move on."

"At once." Grear sat quite still. "I must see the chief." He got up. "What about you, Cameron? You'll come?"

"I'd rather not. You can always find me—and there's no hurry—if you do one thing at once."

"What's that?"

"Send a couple of men to watch the hulk. That watchman must be collared before he thinks too much and sends a message."

Grear sat down. "Any more ideas?"

"Yes. Don't—don't force the thing. They must have some way of destroying the stuff on board in emergency. Watchman may have his orders to do that should you threaten to board ship. What he'll likely do when his friend—or boss—doesn't come back to-day—I mean your prisoner——"

"Yes?" said the inspector.

"He'll go ashore—in his boat—to send message, phone. That would be the time to collar him."

"Don't you think they'll have a transmitting set on board?"

"Yes. But I doubt if watchman can or would use it. Simpler to go ashore. For he'll always be expecting his friend to turn up. The transmitter will be for other, code uses."

"I agree."

"Having collared him, you can then go through ship at your leisure. You may be able to find out where he goes to receive messages on shore. You might collect the Tuesday message. Anyway, you can have things all set to receive the men who will turn up on Thursday." He smiled to the inspector. "Is that kindergarten?"

"It's good sense for a start off," said the inspector.

Dermot pushed himself to his feet. "Your brandy has rather gone to my head. Will you see me to my ship, Mr. Grear?"

Grear was in a hurry and Dermot did not tell him he was taking the *Fulmar* back to her base in Gantry. Couldn't be bothered, he thought, smiling at Joe, with Christina in the background. "Think you can start her up?"

Joe got the engine going. Dermot warned them in time of the backwash from a passing steamer and after they got rocked they headed down stream. In a little while Christina brought Dermot a mug of tea.

"Ourselves once more." He breathed deeply.

"You should take a lie down to yourself," she answered, anxiously solemn. "It's not hot."

He handed her the wheel. "Ease up your throttle, Joe. We're flying." He tried the tea. "This is good. My mouth is dry leather." He struggled against the deeper lassitude that was creeping over him. "Christina, you are a very dear girl."

"Is it all over now?"

"I hope so. Keep her out a little. Aim to pass just outside that buoy . . . Steady at that . . . Fine. Good job I made seamen of Joe and yourself."

She did not answer.

When he had Joe keeping an eye ahead, he sat down, finished the mug slowly, and, assured they were doing all right, let his head nod forward and closed his eyes. The inside world went dark and thoughtless, but he knew he was awake—until he felt his hands fall down.

When he became aware that they were glancing at him, he grew vaguely annoyed, got up, and scanned the seaway.

"Go and lie down," said Christina.

"Now, now," he answered, "you attend to your job."

"You go and lie down," she said, her face puckered and dark as she stared ahead.

"We'll call you," said Joe, "if we have to."

"You're frightened of Christina, Joe. A bad beginning."

Neither of them answered.

"All right," he said at last. "Call me." He went into the cabin and stretched out flat on his bunk. God knows what's wrong with me, he thought. He hadn't been through much. Had gone through twice as much and kept on his feet all day. This was—this was weak nonsense—silly sort of way to give in. Just childish. But when his hands fell away he let them fall, let the whole body sink down into its dark grave with a profound uncaring.

But he did not fall asleep. The darkness inside his skull kept going round in a slow swirl, a sort of noiseless buzzing. Occasionally he felt its pressure on the bones above his nose but in a vague way. The beginning of a thought would fall back because it hadn't the energy to be born. Grear's face, the intensity of the mechanic's expression, the watchful inspector, would come up and pass away. Once he saw Ellen's face; she was singing but he could not hear her; he watched her face for quite a time before he fell away from it. Presently the buzzing increased and in a few moments his heart was thumping, his breath quickening. As he sat up, he muttered. Then his head began to nod again and in a few seconds he was on his right side in the position he assumed instinctively when going to sleep, the knees bent, the left foot across the instep of the right. He breathed gustily. He was falling deep down this time, letting go utterly. But the dark swirl started, the noiseless buzzing. He waited until Joe called him.

When he had got the *Fulmar* tied up, with Christina ashore and Joe passing their belongings up to her, he became aware, as he boxed the engine in its polished wooden casing, that a male voice was greeting Christina heartily and laughing.

He listened for a few seconds, then went out. The man was behaving exactly as he had seen him behave outside the concert hall in the company of Christina, Deas, Amy and Mrs. Mure. The whole scene came back to him. It was Alex Macrae of the crew of the yacht *Foamcrest*.

"How did you find her, sir?" called Alex, stepping forward.

"Tight as a drum," answered Dermot. "Didn't know you worked here."

"Not too big and a bit of everything in the sailing line. When I heard you had gone out on an engine, I wouldn't believe it." He laughed.

"I needed a smell of the sea," said Dermot, "to pick me up."

"That's right!" agreed Alex. "It comes over you. Don't touch a thing. I'll put her away."

"Thank you. It's strong air the sea air."

"You'll sleep without rocking now! Had a good trip?"

"Fine."

"You wouldn't know there was a tide in it! An engine has its uses."

"Perhaps," said Dermot.

Alex laughed and helped them to get their belongings into the car which was in a corner of a large shed. Happening to glimpse one of Joe's crayon sketches, he whispered to Christina, "I heard you were going in for high art."

"You hear many a thing," promptly answered Christina.

Dermot missed Alex's next remark, but not Christina's. "Do you think you're a beauty yourself?"

"So that's the way the wind's blowing. Well, well. I never had any luck."

"Wait till I tell Morag MacInnes that."

And if Alex laughed heartily, he also picked up some colour.

Dermot was grateful to Christina, and as they drove away he asked her, "You know him well?"

"Yes. He's all right."

"You think so?"

"Yes. He's a great one to talk but he's good-hearted."

Dermot could not think of anything else to say. The expression "good-hearted" swelled up in his mind so that he couldn't get round or past it. He settled down into the driving seat. Driving the car was easy, effortless. Mechanism could take man into the dream state. It bore him away. He would have to trust Christina about Alex Macrae. There was nothing more he was going to do anyway, just nothing. I have done it, he thought—and wakened slightly as if the words had been spoken in some fatal and dark place. They were in the town. He was careful at crossings but firm, and soon they were in quiet streets. When they drew up before Joe's door, he sat still, waiting for them to get their belongings on the pavement.

"Don't go anywhere, Christina," he said, smiling.

"No." She was looking worried again, concerned.

"Hang on to her, Joe, till I see you—to-night."

"Yes," said Joe, his brows meeting.

"Very good." He saluted and drove off, smiling to himself, wondering if Joe had wanted to start talking about money again. Christina shed a lot of concern and sympathy about. It was good to get away where there was nothing to touch one, where one floated buoyant and alone, and went to sleep alone. He sat and stared at the grey-blue, sliding, heavy door. . . . Now he had the car in her stall . . . He came to with a crick in his neck and arrived dully at the conclusion that he would be more comfortable in the back seat. But when he got out, he felt a bit sick and poked about his groin. There was a dull ache rather than a pain, as if the affected part had swollen . . . Not that it was much. It was nothing . . . His teeth bared in a simple ugly spite. He leaned against the car and cursed . . . The sliding door went home and he turned up the mews. There was a high stone wall . . . and then houses in a street . . . But he refused to think about them, or see them in any strange shape, in any frozen arrestment. . . .

They were waiting all right, he thought with a renewed touch of spite. He had seen walls fall in a film. Only in a film, because he had been at sea. . . . One final thing to do: don't make a fool of yourself. Always get home on your own legs. Never mind about the landlady. Who is she anyway? Who is anyone? Everyone is Judas at the end of the day, he thought, and was strengthened still more.

The stairs went up and he climbed them. There was a landing where all was silent. He closed his door quietly and stood for a moment with his back to it, like one who had escaped and was listening. In his bedroom he took off his shoes and got under the thick light quilt.

44

His rest was fitful; indeed it seemed to him that he was never properly asleep but always coming up out of the darkness, annoyed about this, cursing now and then in sheer spite and vexation, yet for long still spells consciously part of a scene, a group, an argument, the mysterious argument over which he had no control, unformed as the darkness which it pervaded like a strange weather of the soul. It troubled him like an illness, induced bouts of vision of an abnormal clarity.

When it came to arguing in this state, he was no fool. He always won his argument. Nor did he stop at the winning point. He went on with an obliterating clarity to expose the whole shooting match. Then he fell back, unappeased, because it was something more and other that was the real argument.

The Assessor was like a pillar. That was clear enough. He was like a bollard you could tie up to. Life's stormy sea. To think of him when he wasn't there was a help. He was what you turned to when you crossed the bar. He took your rope.

In the world of affairs the Assessor was recognized as an excellent business man, who knew what was what, who could make his point out of a devious and penetrative mind, persuasive with fact, his small eyes steady, silent while the other man floundered, the dotted line coming out of him inevitably for signature. But that was not what he really was. Behind all that, he was something other.

Behind everything, there was something other, the wordless argument that was agony and made you sweat, because . . . because there was nothing could be done or told about it.

The flickers of vision before the argument started came from that mysterious and hidden region. Like the flicker of a dark coat from the figure snatched away . . . the mechanic's nameless body had been snatched away . . . handed over, leaving on the emptiness, in one's very mouth, the taste of betrayal, before the mind could rise up and justify, as it could justify, utterly. But let the mind justify as it liked, when, from the utmost reach of its justification, it fell away exhausted, at once betrayal, which had been individual and particular, became betrayal that pervaded all, as if one man were many men, were all men.

Nor did it matter in the least what opinions or theories or peculiar ideologies the man entertained. Like a babbling one couldn't hear, whimperings that didn't matter, they held no significance at all, and left behind in the silence something inexpressibly pitiful—and left also a cold sweat on the brow.

It was late afternoon before he rang for tea after shaving in the bathroom. The sight of food revolted him, but the tea was not too hot and he drank a cupful straight off.

That his landlady would wonder why he hadn't eaten anything was certain, so he tried the bread and butter. One mouthful was enough and he decided to put the rest of the slice down the drain. He emptied the pot of tea. When he heard the maid's footsteps on the stairs, he went into his bedroom to finish dressing.

What annoyed him, even acutely irritated him, was that he did not feel fit enough to go out. He could not trust his control of the body. Not that he minded its aches or its incipient nausea; it wasn't that, it was its treacherous weakness, which tossing about in bed had aggravated, until sudden thought produced revulsion and a pricking heat.

At last he telephoned the office and asked for his secretary. When he heard her story of affairs, he gave her some instructions, said he was not feeling too fit, but hoped to be in in the morning. She promised to inform Mr. Armstrong, who was out at the moment. He thanked her, leaving her with the impression that he would rather not be disturbed, for he was afraid that Armstrong or some other might call round. She was an intelligent girl.

Now he did not know what to do with himself and could neither lie down nor stand up for any length of time. Suddenly he had an urge to look at the Cladday chart—and remembered that he had left his belongings in the car. But the chart? He had made Joe roll it up in the *Fulmar's* cabin . . . then he himself had thrust it into his sleeping bag—or had been going to thrust it . . . After hearing Alex Macrae's voice, he had not seen it; had forgotten it altogether.

Alex would, quite naturally, go through the cabin to make sure everything was shipshape and nothing left behind.

Dermot stretched full length in his chair; his eyes closed and his head fell to one side. When it seemed he was in a deep sleep, his eyes opened wide, he got to his feet, put on his overcoat unhurriedly and his hat, and went out.

The air refreshed him and he walked carefully, without effort.

When he felt fit enough for thought, he entertained the notion that it was odd that the Cladday chart should have taken him on such strange courses. He made use of the irony to strengthen him. Cladday, of all places. The sun and the moon.

The irony had the bitterness that smiled. He looked about him at houses, at a sudden prospect of distant roofs under a smother of smoke, before turning down the mews. After deciding that he wouldn't have had the luck to put his keys into the fresh suit he was wearing, he found he had them. It was a good omen. Christina was a believer in omens. When Joe had talked of the Egyptians' ship of the dead! . . . He gave the sliding door a powerful shove, turned over the wet clothes in the back of the car, found the sleeping bag, crushed it with both hands. The chart was there.

When he had rested for a little while he even decided to light a cigarette. But it tasted like poison and he crushed it out. Going home was easy. He could feel the chart poking at him under his coat, as if it had a life of its own, like a captured animal or bird. There was a humour in this that was very pleasant. He had collared it, he had got it now, and it could poke and rustle away as it liked. He told it this. He felt very friendly to the chart, even to its waywardness, but tried not to laugh on the street.

Once in his sitting-room, he opened it out on the card table and put weights on its corners. Now it lay quiet and gave up its treasures. He pored over them, going from one seaway to another, one name to another . . .

until his eyes came to a certain spot, facing the west, and remained there; presently they lifted and fixed in a curious stare.

It was a sandy soil and the little gravestones leaned awry. It was a dawn twilight of great serenity—almost the rule out there at high summer, but around the slithering sound of the spades, as they opened up the grave, the calm of the coming morning, just before the sun rose, held something not altogether of the world. No doubt the feeling of guilt, of doing something that they did not wish Iain MacNeil or old Seumas or anyone on the island to see or find out, helped a sort of unearthly apprehension. Yet it wasn't altogether that. It was more than any question of disbelief or betrayal of confidence, because they really were doing nothing wrong, doing no more than their duty. They simply wanted to find out who the seaman was, what nationality, any distinguishing mark or identity disc or clue to his ship and its possible loss in that area. When questioned earlier old Seumas had admitted burying the seaman. The weather was that stormy, he said, they could not send to the Main Island "so we gave the body as best we could a Christian burial among us: he might have been one of ourselves." The skipper, grown sensitive to their veiled mistrust of his "spying", could not ask to have the grave opened so had taken this simple if stealthy way out of the difficulty . . . When they had buried the Norwegian sailor again, they too had felt he was "one of themselves". It was then that the full peace of the place came upon them. The skipper stood, looking away to the west, all haste and stealth shed from him. The sea's impulse ran along the shore in a tiny wave, breaking as it ran. The floor of the ocean rose slowly to meet a sky that grew flatter the farther it went, until the horizon, though infinitely remote, held yet a suggestion of a beyond. And the light, the ineffable light, and the calm . . . Kenn and Jimmy went across the sand towards the dinghy, carrying the two spades which they had borrowed from the Main Island, but the skipper stood in a trance . . . Afterwards, he had written in a letter: "As the sun came up I took off my cap to the drowned Norwegian seaman, and to the sun, the white sun of power, as Seumas called it, and to all it had created of life and to this mystery of death. It was a morning of quiet serenity, and I can remember thinking with a strange calm that I should not mind being buried there. For the first time in my life I *realized* death, and it had no terror. I have sometimes tried to think myself back into that calm condition of acceptance, but have found it difficult."

Dermot stirred. He looked at the chart unseeingly, got up slowly and went over to the fireplace. He faced the window. The afternoon was thickening its shadow. He sat down in his chair, stretched himself out.

For a time he dwelt in that calm land of acceptance, saw figures move in the twilight of the morning and in the twilight before the coming of the night. The sun rose and in its light the flowers were small and innumerable and coloured the green turf beyond the sand—the machair—and the moving air was its scented breath. Delightful it was, and light, like the skipping of small birds going from one near place to another. The rain, the fine rain, that made the green grass vivid and the flowers jewel-bright. The great sombre days with the wind tearing, the seas pounding on the strand, and a leaning figure going round the corner of a house.

That was delectable . . . but it was more and other than that.

The skipper had got it for a little while, and could remember having got it, but found it difficult to get it again.

It had calm and dignity, it was timeless, it was brave and simple, it was without words.

"Beautiful it was," Christina had once said of something she remembered.

But the mechanic's face pushed its way in front of Dermot's inner eye and in the gloom of the cabin the face was white. It was sharp and ruthless. It was the face of the secret police—the one face of the whole secret police—in any land; the secret police that deep in him he hated more than war, than atom bombs. Oh, vile! Dermot shut his eyes and groaned, and shut the face out, and was in the dark hulk of a ship and in the hulk were rats.

He let everything fade away on the ebbing thought that it was a pity.

Presently he got up, a curious smile on his face, for he realized that Grear might phone him any minute, call him to a conference on "a high level" . . . though probably not just yet, because he would not have finished with the mechanic. The face of the statuette and the face of the mechanic.

In their characteristic battle the fate of mankind was being settled. The forces that held man's destiny as surely as the sun was setting. These two were what human society had arrived at. All over, everywhere, the "high level" in the dark hulk. A scurrying of the rumoured wind like a scurrying of rats, and ears listening, ears of the police, force ready in the hands . . . all over, everywhere.

It might be by Thursday . . .

Dermot's eyes hardened and glistened in the window light; the smile grew sardonic and he shrugged. He went to the telephone and gazed at it for a little while; then he dialled a number.

"Hallo."

"So it's yourself," he answered.

"Oh, it's you," said Ellen.

"Both of us. Could anything be better?"

"How wonderful that you remembered at all."

"Have I ever forgotten?" He sat down on the edge of the desk.

"I suppose you jot it down?"

"Of course—but where?"

"In that small diary you always find in the wrong pocket."

"You're too much for me, Ellen. Though I confess your voice does me more good than anything I've heard —since I heard it last. I apologise for not having rung you earlier, but I've been wondering about you all day— about to-night. It's a bit complicated."

"You mean you want to call it off?"

"Not—exactly."

"No?"

"When you say it like that, what can I do? My heart warms and the drowsy numbness——"

"Dermot, tell me, you're all right, aren't you?"

"Not too bad. Only I don't feel much like eating in public places. Haven't been in the office to-day. Do you mind?"

"Don't be stupid. Of course not. I'm so sorry. Is it——"

"It's nothing. But I want to see you. There's some difficulty about another woman. I thought you might help."

"*Another* woman?"

"Yes. I wondered if you could put her up for a night or two, or if you knew of some place. You're the only one I can turn to in a difficulty . . . Are you there?"

"I was thinking. It might be managed. Do I know her?"

"Of course. Christina."

"Christina!"

"I'll tell you about it later. If it would suit you, you'll find me sitting in a taxi near your door around eight o'clock. We could go to Joe's. How's that?"

"Yes, for me, but——"

"Ellen."

"Yes?"

"One line, just one. Please."

"Dermot, don't be——"

"*Please*. I can't argue. Haven't the pith."

In a clear voice, warm and unhurried, she sang him the first verse of *Caol Muile*.

Through the silence she asked, "Are you still there?"

"Barely."

"Dermot——"

"God bless you, Ellen. I love you very much." He put down the receiver.

The singing affected him too much. He shouldn't have chanced it. "Damn it, I'm weak as a fly," he muttered and wiped his eyes. He stood about, went into his bedroom, got on his back. The song would not leave him. He did not want it to leave him. Why should he? Why always give in and be worldly cynical and above what touched the heart?

But it wasn't just that. The song—and the singing— had a whole civilization behind it, an attitude to life and to death over a long time. It was what the skipper had felt. It was the voice of Anna, the face of Anna, when she addressed the young moon, smiling across the black river and making her curtsey. The sea and the flowers on the machair; youth and the morning. Twilight. To you also I belonged once but I never can again for I am Youth. It was all there. It had manners. It was bright and sharp, and it grew mellow in age. It was sad to a depth that no lead sounded. Beautiful it was . . .

The polished and sophisticated, the thin reed with its one arid note, the dry reed dry for want of the living mouth and the human spittle. And we thought it wonderful . . .

The dry note and the arid reason, and we built a hulk for them, and created the rats so that we might listen to their scurrying sounds, the new symphony, real because it was rats . . .

Say it, say it once, say it was a beautiful thing that was murdered; even though they have made you feel a fool when you are saying it, say it. Say it once to your own heart, unashamed, before you grow strong again and ordinary and deny it . . .

He watched her coming along the street, got out and showed her into the taxi. "You always surprise me."

"Not nearly so much as you surprise me," said Ellen.

"Once more we're at it. I often wonder how I manage to get on without you."

But she was scanning him in the dim light. "What's been happening to you? You look——"

"Lots. I have been away for a week-end in a boat—with Joe and Christina."

That silenced her.

He could not help laughing. "You really look surprised now."

"I am." And when he tried to provoke her, she merely added, "And you never told me, none of you."

"Don't blame them. I ordered them not to tell you."

"Really?"

"Yes. It was a very mysterious week-end."

"It must have been."

"It was. Don't tell me you would have liked to come."

"I was invited, wasn't I?"

"No. I couldn't risk you."

"But it was all right for Christina?"

"You have touched—a delicate spot—there."

"So it seems."

"You'll have to listen to me, Ellen. And never mind the taxi if it wanders around." He was silent for a few moments. "The trouble is I can't tell you very much. If war breaks out, I'll have a certain sea job. Well, there was a chart which I lost. It was a mark against me. I have been trying to find it. This has brought me, in a mysterious way, up against them who pinched the chart. When I got knocked out in the street, that, as it happened, had something to do with it. But perhaps you can see it's the sort of secretive stuff I can't tell anyone. Christina and Joe don't know much. Christina comes into it simply because she happens to know certain people who are, or may be, involved. I admit, to that extent, I have made use of her. I trust her absolutely. The only trouble is—I would rather she didn't go back to the Mures for a day or two. The Mures themselves are all right. But certain folk who hang around there—if they heard we were away in a boat, they might try to pump her. Christina would tell them nothing—but an astute eye might conclude that Christina's silence covered a lot, and what then might happen . . . That's the position, Ellen. Some day I'll be able to tell you it all. But meantime you know nothing."

Ellen sat silent for a few moments. "Were you attacked again?"

"I had to slip into the sea. It was bitterly cold and I'm still feeling a bit queer. But it'll pass."

"You should be in your bed." Her voice sounded sombre.

"I'll get there. Odd the things that go on behind the scenes. But there it is. You let me off?"

"I let you off."

"You don't sound too cheerful about it."

She did not answer.

"You can feel my pulse if you like."

But she did not take his hand; she looked out of the window.

He drew his hand back and let his head fall against the upholstery. The taxi went along two quiet streets, turned a corner, and presently, without a word more between them, it pulled up before Joe's. They got out and he paid the garage driver, asking him by name if he was on to-night and saying he would probably give a ring later.

"Enjoy your run?"

"Yes, thank you," answered Ellen quietly. But when they entered Joe's studio her eyes blinked so brightly they might have been newly washed.

Joe was so pleased that he didn't know what to do about it, looked worried and called "Christina!"

Christina appeared, pulling her sleeves down as if she'd been doing a washing.

"I have just picked up Ellen on the street," said Dermot, "and only managed to tell her that we were away for an enjoyable cruise."

"And I have just told him that I think it was very mean of you all. I'm particularly surprised at you, Christina."

Christina smiled uncertainly but said nothing.

309

"Why blame it on Christina?" asked Dermot.

"A fat lot of good it does to blame anything on you," replied Ellen. "Moreover I'm not usually picked up on the street." She looked very attractive as she shed her coat with Joe's silent help. "I'm beginning to be a bit doubtful about you, Christina. I thought you were a quiet nice girl."

"She's quiet sometimes," said Joe helpfully.

Ellen gave way to laughter, revolving once before she sat down. "Joe," she said, "if only some others had your sweet simplicity."

"You think Joe simple?" In his astonishment Dermot sat down beside her. "Joe is the most intricate, devious, double-dyed villain it has ever been my pleasure to meet. In comparison, you are a child, Ellen."

"And you—I suppose you haven't got into long trousers?" Ellen hardly glanced at him.

"Would you like some tea?" Christina asked.

Ellen began to laugh again. "Christina, that *would* be refreshing. Can I help?"

"No," said Christina. "I was just soaking some things that got the salt water in them." Her eyes went to Dermot's face, then she said hurriedly, "I'll get the tea." And away she went.

"Will you take off your coat?" Joe asked Dermot, with that sudden solicitude for another's comfort that was somehow always surprising.

"Just in a minute."

"Joe!" called Christina and off Joe went.

"Babes in the wood," murmured Dermot.

"You were never further out—and that's saying a lot," answered Ellen.

"You think so?"

"I know it. Why don't you take off your coat?"

"Can't be bothered. Presently."

"Have it your own way. You always do. If ever there was a babe in a wood . . ." She shrugged.

"If ever there was anyone who did my heart good . . ."

"Looks like it. What did you do with your wet clothes?"

He laughed softly, weakly. "I wondered if you saw her eyes."

"Were you all in the water?"

"No, no." He could not stop shaking with laughter. "Only Joe and me." He added, "Besides, haven't I a landlady?" But it was no good, for he remembered pawing his wet clothes in the back of the car, where they still lay.

"You've been drinking," said Ellen.

"That's right," he agreed, wiping his eyes. "Whisky is the only thing that keeps a tired heart going. Which reminds me." He brought a full half bottle out of the pocket of his coat. "What about a small one?"

"No, thanks. Tea will do you more good."

"Tea! What tea? They seem to be taking a long time with it."

"With Joe's help, it won't be so long."

"You sound cryptic and anything but kind." Then he tumbled to her meaning. "I'm dense. My density often astonishes me. But surely they see enough of each other. I don't mean that but you know what I mean."

"Have you had any food to-night?"

"Food? I have had so much I don't want any more."

"I thought so." She took the half bottle out of his hand. "You'll have some tea first."

"Ellen, you surprise me. I didn't know you could be so hard."

"Well, you know now."

He regarded her quizzically. "Do you know, I rather like you like that. You look as if you could go places."

"I know one place where you're going very soon."

"Not my bed. It's a lonely place."

She did not answer.

"Did that stump you?"

"I'll fetch the tea."

"You can't do that," he said. "If they want to be alone . . ."

"You're denser even than you think."

"How so?"

"The babes in the wood are leaving *us* alone."

His eyes widened on her face. "No!" It was a breath of superb astonishment.

Her colour heightened very slightly, so that her expression grew stormy.

"Ellen!"

They fell into each other's arms. Then she pushed him away. "Behave yourself," she said.

"But—Ellen——"

"No. I feel angry. You have fever." Her voice was firm, but she was breathing heavily and he thought she was going to cry.

"You are very good to me." His voice was gentle.

"Oh, don't say that!" She turned her back to him. He looked at it, saw it heave as she strangled her sobs, saw the pallor of her neck and the dark hair on the bent head. Something came to him then, as the sea to the sand or the flower to the machair, and it quietened him. He looked down at his hands and all was translated in a strange marvelling.

He glanced sideways and saw she was now drying her eyes with her handkerchief, subduing her emotion as strongly as she could. This suddenly affected him deeply, but with an effort he kept his hands to himself. As she turned she did not look at him; her bright glistening eyes cast a quick glance towards the small kitchen, then she picked up her handbag and went down to the end of the room where, above the mantelpiece, hung one of Joe's pictures which had always attracted her. He watched her wipe her face in long smooth wipes, her head tilting slowly, and something of profound intimacy touched him. When the handbag snapped shut, she looked at the picture for a long moment; then she turned.

Dermot felt suddenly shy of her and saw the half-bottle of whisky. He picked it up. Joe appeared carrying a tray and Christina followed with a couple of plates of bread and butter and cakes.

"Had you to grow the tea, Joe?" Dermot asked.

"No," said Joe, "we had to boil the water."

Dermot laughed. A sudden buzzing in his ears made him dizzy. "What about a dram first?"

"Won't you be having your tea?" asked Christina.

"Yes," said Dermot. "But what about a small one first? Never mind about glasses." He got the top off the bottle and poured some whisky into a cup.

"Not for me, thank you," said Ellen.

"No, please," said Christina.

"Joe, you'll have a drop. We must keep the chill away . . . To the end of a successful cruise!" He took a mouthful of the neat liquor. Then he began talking, explaining how, when one really needed a dram, whisky actually tasted good.

When he had finished his whisky, Christina filled his cup with tea. But he wouldn't eat. So long as he could sit where he was he knew he was all right; a fine heightened happiness came upon him. He had to ignore Ellen but he could not help that, nor did it matter, for she was there.

Ellen had lost her bright talk, but not her wits, and she said to Christina, "You're staying with me to-night."

"Are you sure it will be no trouble?"

"It will be a pleasure. The only thing——" She paused.

"What?" asked Christina.

313

"I don't think we should be late. My people wouldn't mind, but—they would like to see you."

"Yes, surely," said Christina. "When would you like to go?"

"After we've finished. Would you mind?"

"Oh no. I—I———"

"We'll all be delighted to have you."

"Thank you very much," murmured Christina, who was clearly a little shy of the arrangement but prepared to do her best.

Ellen began talking to her of her folk at home, describing them not without humour. There was much charm about Ellen in this quiet sensible mood. She seemed to forget the men in a genuine feminine way and she actually drew a story out of Christina about Mrs. Spicer.

Presently she stood up. "I think it's about time we got this man home to his bed. You could phone for a taxi couldn't you, Joe?"

"Yes."

"I knew there was a catch in it somewhere," said Dermot.

"All right, then, you go," Ellen said to Joe, "and Christina and I will wash up." Ellen turned to Dermot directly for the first time. "When you get home I think you should have a dram and two aspirins."

"Aspirin? Haven't got such a thing," said Dermot.

No one had aspirin. "And we think we're civilized. Dear me," said Ellen. "There's plenty at home," she added thoughtfully. "Off you go, Joe."

Christina and Ellen were busy, for during the dishwashing they had to make up a story about Christina's visit and then to gather such belongings as Christina had in Joe's. Left to himself, Dermot took another drink and reckoned that should see him through.

Ellen thought it would be friendly if all four set off

in the taxi. It was a bit of a crush and they laughed and Ellen said she would like to feel Dermot's pulse.

"Now that it pleases you," he said.

"Your hand is burning. Will you see him into his bed, Joe?"

"Yes," said Joe.

"Who is your doctor?" she asked Dermot.

"You would like to know, wouldn't you?"

"I would."

"If anyone disturbs me to-night, I'll hit him with an oar. What has a doctor ever done to anybody except put him to bed? That's where I'm going—at the end of a perfect day."

Ellen was silent.

"There's something about that place of yours, Joe. Has an extraordinary effect on people. Wonderful," babbled Dermot.

"Thank you," murmured Joe.

"Don't mention it. Made me think of Cladday. You've never been to Cladday? However, you're going. We're all going. Perhaps Ellen would sing to us. Ellen is a siren. Sitting on a rock, combing her hair with a golden comb. Who was the fellow had to stuff his ears when the sirens sang? They knew about it, Joe, long long ago. They did an' all."

"I never thought of it like that," said Joe.

"I know the song they sang."

"I never thought of the song itself," said Joe, stirring in excitement.

"Makes a difference, doesn't it, when you know the song?"

"Yes," said Joe.

"Has Christina ever sung to you, Joe?"

Joe glanced at Christina. "Only just once or twice," he muttered.

The taxi drew up.

"You'll wait till I get the aspirin," said Ellen and went away with Christina.

When she came back with the small bottle, Dermot thanked her for the sweet gift.

As they drove off, he let himself collapse in his corner.

When Joe asked him in his room if he would ring for his doctor, Dermot said, "Look, Joe, I'm sick of myself. It's just my guts and I've got a touch of temperature. Forget it. Now I'll take three aspirins and a bloody good dram and you'll have one with me." He tore off his tie and collar and sat down. "No word about that fellow."

"Were you expecting word?"

"They can't leave you alone. Once you dabble in the police state it goes on—and on. Never mind. We're for it anyhow." He shot out his feet. "You'll find a carafe of water in the bedroom."

When Dermot had swallowed his aspirins, Joe suddenly began to take off his shoes.

Dermot was touched. "And how are things with you, Joe?"

"Good," said Joe.

Dermot made his effort. "That money you wanted to talk of?"

"Oh, never mind. You're tired. I—I haven't much. Just forty pounds, paid each quarter. Three pounds a week. Rent and light takes half of it. I didn't—I couldn't —I didn't know what to do. She can earn four or five pounds a week. I mean——" Joe got very involved, though the situation was very simple.

"Didn't you tell Christina?"

"No, not at first. I offered her three pounds a week if she—if she would sit for me. She said yes. But it's getting on for the end of the quarter—and—and sometimes I get a little short, though I am very careful now.

I divide out. I make little bundles. But it takes time to—to start making money. I got out of the way of it . . ."

Presently Dermot interrupted him: "You told Christina?"

"Yes. This afternoon—I confessed. I told her all. I said I couldn't go on paying. I said I would try to make some money, and then perhaps if she would come back to me . . . I said I was sorry because she had inspired me and—and brought me back. I—I got a little excited and didn't put it very well, but—but she said nothing."

"Nothing?"

"No," said Joe, "she—she just smiled." The tears went running down over the smile on his own face. He didn't seem to be aware of them, and wiped them away with the back of his hand when he felt them as naturally as he would have blown his nose. "She is beautiful. She is beautiful because she is simple. She was quite calm."

Dermot could not take his eyes off that bony face, which was not at all like something unfinished now, but strong and tender as though its creator had been concerned only with essentials. There was also a warm harmony between the colour of the skin and the fair hair. The eyebrows had a way of puckering that gave to the blue eyes an effect of far-seeing vision. He looked like a fellow who would go striding away somewhere.

"You fixed things up?"

"She said she did not want my money just now. She said she would work part of the day at a job; then she would come to me. She said it was easy to get a part-time job. She said—she said she would like to help me." His restlessness so overcame him that he had to get up. "She thought that way would be better."

"Better than what? Pour a drink."

Joe's hand was unsteady but he managed to go on pouring the whisky into the two tumblers until he had emptied the bottle. "I asked her—I told her she could have all my money and run the studio—anything—but of course I knew it was too little and———"

"Did you ask her to marry you?"

Joe stared at him. "No." He looked completely bewildered.

"A little water. Wait—I'll help myself."

Joe sat down. "No," he said again. He looked utterly lost.

Dermot sipped his drink.

"I am not used to getting married," Joe muttered in a breathless way. "I never got married—before." He looked like one who was appalled or was going to burst. He said, "She might not. I don't know. She said she was very fond of you. I thought I understood. But———" He stopped.

"I am very fond of *her*. That has nothing to do with it. If you married everyone you were fond of . . . Did you think you were pouring ginger-ale?"

Joe grew bewildered.

"Do you want to ask her?"

Joe got up abruptly. "I don't know. It is very important. It's a terribly important thing."

"You may know that to your cost."

"Yes," said Joe. His tongue flickered. "There's the cost. But I don't care about that," he cried suddenly, throwing his hands up. "I don't care. Curse the money!" cried Joe. He stopped. In an intense voice he said, "It would be beautiful to marry her." He gulped, discovered himself walking like one who had lost his way, and sat down. "Excuse me." He was trembling.

"Here's success, Joe!"

"Perhaps she won't—thank you." Joe lifted his tumbler and drank it like so much ginger-ale.

"You'll be drunk."

"Yes, thank you, I feel a little drunk." He got up. "I have kept you from bed. I will go now. You must excuse me. Good night." He turned at the door as Dermot called him. "I nearly forgot it," he said, lifting his hat. "I hope you sleep well."

"It's more than you'll do. Good night, Joe."

Dermot let himself collapse in his chair. In a little while his mind held the vague thought of love. The age, the times they lived in, had made personal love, love between a man and a woman, look like some strange and reprehensible passion—old-fashioned, unreal. Better get it over by coupling like brutes in the tribal interest. This had affected him. There was no doubt it had affected him . . . As if Joe's recent presence could still stir up images, he suddenly saw Ellen's bare feet among the flowers on the machair, and he knew that if he had the strength he would kiss her feet in gratitude for their cool solid reality, wandering there.

The following morning Dermot thought he was feeling not too bad at all. His head was light and clear and his body pleasantly immaterial. The toast hadn't a very good taste and seemed unusually tough, but he cooled the tea with plenty of milk and drank three cups. There had been no word from Grear and he didn't want any. He was finished with all that. He reached the office.

Concentration was difficult and after a little time his head began to swim. This irritated him. It was not that he really minded being out of condition: it was the damned fuss. He opened his hand and tried to keep his fingers still, but couldn't. The tremor was very pronounced. He felt pretty certain there was a drug for this condition, but did not know of it. He hung on until lunch time and then suggested to his secretary that he might not come back.

"You shouldn't," she said in a half-strangled voice.

He had an uncomfortable feeling of hungry eyes behind her spectacles, and went out to the cloak room where he proved his theory that he had drunk too much tea by being sick. The loss of the bloated sensation made him feel better.

When he had told his landlady that he had a slight chill and felt like resting for a bit, she discussed hot drinks, but he put her off on the plea that all he needed was a good sleep, and was presently surprised to find himself deliberately going to bed. Bed was a clean cool place.

It was pretty cool of Grear all the same not to have told him what had happened, at least whether or not they had collared the watchman. Though Grear was the last person on earth he wanted to hear from, still it wouldn't have cost him a frightful effort . . .

He awoke feeling very much better. The world, too, was remarkably quiet; in fact the twilight stood in the bedroom window. He was able to listen to very remote distances. He listened and lay, and wondered what folk made all the fuss about, but he refused to think and tried to sleep still more. For he hadn't slept much last night, had burned and thrown some of the bedclothes off, and then hauled every stitch on again, while his thought had gone on diverse journeys and evoked the queerest images, dominated by the vague notion rather than image—the sort of image that was not quite glimpsed—of humanity trying to strangle itself, like an affrighted maniac. He caught a contorted face once or twice, and it wasn't the mechanic's face, which was a face that could be glimpsed, separately, behind it.

The meaning of all this could be understood if one bothered to make the effort. Odd thing was that for moments one *lived* it (before consciously switching on thought) and then it possessed an extraordinary power; which, of course, was also understandable.

The difficult question was: why do it? Why should humanity strangle itself like a maniac? It made the heart burn so that the very skin went on fire. He got an impression of humanity which was appalling. The word "appalling" swelled like a balloon. It had a wonderfully apt sound.

But there had been moments, moments so intense, moments of pure feeling so overwhelming . . .

Now he began to turn in his bed. The accursed business was starting once more. That deadly and damnable sentence—"the first betrayal is the worst"—came into his mind from nowhere again, as if he hadn't whacked at it and knocked it to hell during the night. He sat up. Coffee, he decided: not tea. He would have it in bed. Then, later, he would get up, for someone was bound to come with the dark—Grear, an inspector—and he was damned if they—or anyone else—was going to find him in bed.

But it was the telephone that brought him out of bed, after hesitation, reluctantly. "Yes?"

"I'm glad you're still alive."

"It's not you, Ellen—not really?"

"No. Only what's left. How are you?"

"First rate. Busy at the office to-day and all that. And how's yourself?"

"You must excuse me troubling you," explained Ellen, "but I promised Christina to find out. She hasn't come back yet."

"Hasn't she? Perhaps she won't. But if she does, will you give her my love. It helps to know that someone thought of me."

"I'll do that. Now I must run. Glad to hear you."

"Ellen—don't bully me."

"I like that! You were such a bully last night that I was too terrified even to suggest taking your temperature.

"I thought you had taken it. Don't tell me I dreamt it. All night I could think of nothing else."

He heard voices behind her. "Good-bye," said Ellen coolly and cut him off.

His brows ridged; fingers went out to dial her number; then he slowly replaced the receiver. His expression darkened in anger. Curse them, the whole damned crew of obliterating maniacs. Anger and hatred overwhelmed him. Violence so possessed him that when he got into his chair his flesh trembled and shook. His oaths were black and meaningless as though his brain were poisoned.

It's the sort of thing a fellow has got to watch, he decided presently. He felt sick. But every time, during the night, that he had thought of Ellen, that black poisonous smear had come seeping in and over. It really was hellish bad. It really was making a mess of life. The prolonged, drawn-out waiting for the business did get under the skin, and then it only needed—oh, shut up! God, if it's violence they want, they'll get it!

He got up and wandered into his bedroom, lay on his back, shivered, and drew the quilt over him. Something the matter with me, he thought, something's gone wrong. He was not usually like this. But it was not idiotic war any more—ah, shut up!

The bout passed again. His landlady appeared and he told her that he had a touch of temperature and perhaps had better not eat anything solid. She brought him a glass of warmed milk. At nine o'clock at night he got up, dressed, and went into his sitting-room. Better get properly tired out. He was wondering if he would ring up Grear and clear the whole blessed thing off his mind by finding out what in fact had actually happened, when he heard voices and footsteps. His landlady seemed surprised to see him up. "Two gentlemen to see you. I told them you were in bed."

"Who are they?"

"They said they were friends of yours. I told them . . ."

The Assessor came in, followed by Basil Black.

"What's all this I hear?" asked the Assessor smiling and looking at him.

"Rumours. What did you expect? Glad to see you." As Dermot cheerfully turned to pull a chair forward his eye caught the Cladday chart in its cardboard cylinder lying fully exposed on his desk, indeed it was flood-lit for he had earlier switched on his desk-light in order to write a note of thanks to the owner of the *Fulmar*. When he had his guests seated, he switched off the desk-light and hospitably considered the fire. "I even think I have a drop left."

"How do you manage to get it?" asked Basil.

"What's the good of being in shipping, in export, if you can't pick up a few perquisites?" Dermot looked at him quizzically. "Haven't you got a favourite publican?"

"He seems loath to favour me."

"I wouldn't blame him."

Basil smiled, his dark eyes bright.

"And now tell us what it's all about," said the Assessor. "We heard you had gone cruising. And then this afternoon I gathered you were indisposed."

"Seasickness. Besides, who told you I was cruising?"

The Assessor glanced at Basil and then back at Dermot. "Why, weren't you?"

"As a matter of fact, I did get a hunger for sea air. Thought it would put me right, but I've been so many days off work that I didn't want the thing publicized exactly. And who told you, anyway?" he asked Basil.

"Heard it in the club," replied Basil. "Then the Assessor came in and I asked him. But he said it couldn't be true because he had been to your office in the afternoon and learned about you not being fit yet. So as we left early, it occurred to us that we'd find out from the only one who knows—and perhaps even cadge a drink."

"Very thoughtful of you." Dermot drank to them, having successfully restrained the question that had sprung to his tongue concerning the name of the person who had told Basil in the club. For he was certain it hadn't been anyone in the club. But he realized he must not betray too close an interest.

"Your gills do look a bit pale," the Assessor said.

And Dermot knew in that moment that his friend had been uneasy about him. "As a matter of fact," he replied with a frank air, "it's a touch of chill in the innards. And perhaps I haven't been going the best way to get rid of it."

"There's been a fair amount of gastric 'flu about," said the Assessor. "A bright March sun can be deceptive."

"Perhaps the cruise didn't help," suggested Basil. "Were you at sea long?"

"I don't think that did much harm. One gets out of condition mewed up all winter in an office." He smiled to the Assessor. "Was half-thinking of joining the merchant service."

"What's wrong with lobster-fishing?"

Dermot laughed. "Perhaps you're right. Begod, I believe you are. I was just thinking that we not only go soft but bits of us atrophy. And not only physical bits."

The Assessor nodded. "Was reading a remarkable thing the other night: a bit of Charles Darwin's autobiography. Ever read it?" Neither had read it, and he continued, taking the burden of the talk on himself, "It made me think of you in particular, Basil." His eyes grew merry. "I have often told you that the *means* not only condition the *end*, but that the fellow using the means becomes like what he uses."

"If only you could talk simple sense," said Basil.

"Darwin found it simple enough in all conscience," replied the Assessor. "Up to the age of thirty he was fond of poetry: Wordsworth, Coleridge, Shelley. Even as a schoolboy he took an *intense delight* in Shakespeare. Liked pictures, too; and music was a very great delight. But after his mind had become what he called a machine for grinding general laws out of large collections of facts, he found he could no longer read Shakespeare. The great Shakespeare who used to delight him was now intolerably dull and *nauseated* him. In the same way he found he had no time for pictures and music. This curious and lamentable loss of the higher esthetic tastes, as he puts it, makes him think, and think humbly. He wonders, for example, if those parts of his brain which are now atrophied—and he says atrophied—might have been kept active if he had insisted on reading a little poetry and listening to a spot of music once a week. All this troubles the great revolutionary scientist profoundly. For the loss of these tastes, he says, is a loss of happiness, and may be injurious to the intellect, and even more to the moral character. I thought it about the most remarkable confession I ever read."

"And you thought of me—why?" Basil asked.

The Assessor considered him. "I wonder? Or do you think it's too great a compliment to be partnered with Darwin, even though your fact collections are economic while his were merely biological."

Basil was amused. "Still flogging your theory that violence breeds violence, I suppose. But *you* remain artists, damme."

The Assessor's body shook softly. "Not quite," he said, giving Dermot a glance. "You go on tuning the piano more perfectly than ever, but you don't play it. That's the idea, if I may be so personal as to refer to your profession." Basil had a share in a small music shop.

"You would like me to go on playing the old bourgeois tunes; Bach of the church organ and divine Mozart, not to mention 'Home Sweet Home'. That's the real idea. You would then feel safe."

"You're missing the point. Shakespeare wasn't bourgeois to Darwin. He isn't bourgeois even to present-day revolutionaries of the highest caste and the purest faith. But the point came when he *nauseated* Darwin."

"So I have got to watch out?"

"That's the idea. In Darwin's time, as in Marx's, they didn't know so much about the human mind as we do. Nowadays fellows like Freud and Jung can forecast with considerable accuracy how human masses will behave when subjected to certain influences. And their psychological forecasts are as astonishing to the theoretically pure, to the ideologists, as Darwin's nausea was to him. Your ideologists just don't believe it. And won't—until the horrors happen."

Dermot was sitting with a faint smile on his face, trying desperately to keep the room steady. Now and then he moved his head, as if appreciating an argumentative point, and it helped to stop the room from tilting too far up. Thoughts went through his head: *He has seen*

*the chart . . . How much does he know? . . . What has he come
here for? . . .*

"And you think I don't know all that?" Basil asked.

"Whether you know or not," answered the Assessor
blandly, "you daren't act as if you did. No man can
question his religion and go on living in comfort and
power—or the prospect of power."

"And that doesn't hold for you?"

"It was a generalization," said the Assessor.

"So what?"

"So while we both generalise in this charmingly
rational way, that other part of us, which Freud and his
brethren know so much about, goes about its cruel and
destructive business."

Dermot was a small boy in his chair listening to the
grisly voices of his elders. He had a far memory of
scrambling from his chair and running outside into a
clear evening air. But he smiled, and the Assessor turned
from that smile to the bowler hat on the floor. As he
lifted his bowler he had a final shot at Basil's "scientific"
attitude by coupling recent research in field anthropology
to the recent revolution in psychology—empirical twins
that made "complete nonsense" of Basil's "British
Museum theories" . . . and saw Dermot's whole forearm
shake as he put his glass away.

Basil noticed it too. "All this bloody talk and you
haven't even told us about your cruise yet," he said
brightly. "You had good weather anyhow."

"Yes, very good," said Dermot.

"I see you had your chart."

Dermot turned his head and looked at the chart. "Yes."

"Thought fellows like you didn't need a chart for the
Firth?"

"That's where you're wrong." Dermot smiled.
"Perhaps you don't know much about the sea?"

"He'll have to agree for once," said the Assessor, getting up. "Come along. It's high time he was in his bed."

Basil sat on. "You do order people about."

But Dermot did not ask them to stay, did not offer another drink.

The Assessor watched him get out of his chair. "I had thought the talk might amuse you," he said apologetically.

Dermot flashed him a glance of understanding. The Assessor's unusual loquacity had been a device to relieve him from having to talk and entertain, to let him look on, even look at Basil if he wanted to.

When he had closed the door behind them, he stared across at his desk. He would have to telephone Grear. Basil had heard something . . . They had been seen in the *Fulmar* at the Queen's Bridge . . . perhaps already news had leaked through from the police . . . perhaps the watchman . . . He would have to give Basil's name. He had seen Basil more than once give the chart the sort of look that appeared to be staring at nothing. The suspicion that it was Basil who had found the chart on the street, coming home from the club after he, Dermot, had left with the Assessor, had occurred to him during the night. It was the simplest explanation. From subtle indications of Basil's behaviour in this room, which he had never been in before, Dermot now felt assured of it. He would have to give them Basil's name.

He began to cross the room. His legs were shaky. The physical effort, which suddenly was difficult, sent a blood flush into his head. He hated the whole business. But as he saw he might collapse, his purpose narrowed and increased. He would do it though he had to hang on by his teeth. His teeth bared. He reached the table. But his hand fell short of the receiver and clawed the chart from the desk as he collapsed, his head bumping off the edge of the desk as his body slid heavily to the floor.

When he came to, his friend the doctor was leaning over him.

"You're a fine fellow, aren't you?" said the doctor helpfully.

"Was it Ellen who . . ."

"What Ellen?"

Dermot blinked again and looked about him. He muttered something about having to phone, but the doctor told him flatly he would do a damn sight less, and presently was undressing him on his bed. When he had him tucked in he went on being busy, threatening to stick the thermometer in his mouth if he didn't stop gabbling. But he was watching his patient even while he was listening to his heart.

At last he sat on the bed. "You're past the crisis, I think. Swallow this."

"What crisis?"

"You've been going about with, I should say, a temperature of about a hundred and three. But I'm not going to ask you any questions. You have a capacity for idiocy at times that is quite bottomless. However, we both know that, so it's all right. Only you're not going about any more until I tell you. I'm in charge—and you're on your back. The total responsibility is mine—even to Ellen."

"But look——"

"I won't look. Let everything go. What's the use of you dead—even to Ellen?"

Dermot smiled. "I do feel a bit queer."

The doctor sat with him until he had gone off. Whoever Ellen might be, it was the Assessor who had phoned him. The Assessor had, indeed, been peremptory about his going round at once, saying he feared a sudden collapse. He considered the sleeping face with minute attention. It was a good-looking face, but with that suggestion of something gaunt, hauntingly tragic, that sleep sometimes brought out.

During the next two days, Wednesday and Thursday, Dermot felt that the level of space he lay on had sunk low; at times he had the illusion of imponderable waves curling over and down on him. He did not really care, and the doctor grew a trifle annoyed at the way his temperature shot up at night.

Thursday had become a secret obsession with him and in the half-dream state got mixed up with a picture he had forgotten since he was a boy, a picture of the Crucifixion. And though he could read the psychology of this quite simply, it did not help much, because he could not give away the secret of Thursday even to his old friend the doctor.

Not that any of it mattered much. Plainly humanity was "like that", and particularly himself, so the mind may as well shift on to something else or to nothing. Then an acute touch of unreason, a sort of panic surge, came from absolutely nowhere and pierced him. The wiping of his face helped to wipe it away.

Once when the surge got him, he cried in bitter angry desperation: "Christ! Christ!" and wondered afterwards why it was that Christ's name had become so fierce an oath in the desperate mouths of destroyers. Their favourite cry! He must mention it to Sim, the psychiatrist. Perhaps Christ was an archetype who would forever haunt the mind of man, with no chance of being destroyed; for when you destroyed him outside (as a projection) he merely returned, by an immutable psychological law, inside you. You could destroy him only by destroying yourself. Perhaps that was why his name was cried at the savage moment; for at that moment self-destruction stood near.

To curious and what seemed lucid thoughts like these, he was intermittent prey. When lucidity was achieved, he always felt a bit better, though perhaps only a bit more resigned, as if the level he lay on had sunk, like a raft, a little lower, if comfortably lower.

But all the time his mind was searching for something deeper and more intricate. Christ was simple. You could see him quite clearly standing in the garden of Gethsemane, standing quite straight, with his head down. You need not look before or after. You turned away. You knew.

But this other thing: no single shaft of intuition could light it up. It was too intricate. Humanity in the mass, the congregation of human heads and bodies round the Crucifixion: that was difficult, and when the mind was balked, when intuition was blocked, nothing supervened beyond incipient nausea.

One could babble of economics and systems and ideologies, but these were in truth the merest superstructure, as near to a man, as useful, as his jacket. In the moment of stress, a man took his jacket off. They cast lots for Christ's seamless coat. It really was as obvious as that, the economic aspect. But at the deeper level where life itself was, and the archetype . . . where they crucified the archetype . . . where destruction and self-destruction became a frenzy . . . what was happening there, what destiny . . .

"There's something worrying you," said the doctor. "Come on: out with it."

"It's something I saw in the paper a few days ago," Dermot replied, the smile in his eyes. "It made me laugh at the time, it was so gargantuan."

"Thank God for a joke. Let's have it."

"By an expert in America, who said that the atom bomb now took fourth place in destructiveness. First came bacteriological warfare, second came biological warfare, and, third, climatological warfare. Although they had now got an atom bomb a hundred thousand times more powerful than the first one they exploded, it was, in the destructive race, pretty much of an also-ran."

"Why bother your head with that kind of poison?"

Dermot laughed softly through his nostrils like the Assessor. "You haven't brought a newspaper?" It was Friday morning.

"No."

"And you've cut off my telephone?"

"In a week you could be as fit as a fiddle—if you gave yourself a chance. You can be about the most exasperating devil I know."

"You do brighten me up. Any news?"

"Same old news. What did you expect?"

But when the doctor went away, he rang and made his landlady produce his newspaper. Except for a new child murder sequence of a gruesome kind, it was, as the doctor had said, the same old news, hardly more potent than cased dynamite. No ingeniously new threat of war . . . Not even a paragraph about a police raid on a hulk . . .

Living on hot drinks was a weakening process. Grear was bound to have phoned, of course. He would be one of the two who, according to the landlady, had not given a name.

All at once he became obsessed with a desire to know what had happened, what had really happened. The truth —if only for once—about something, about things that he himself had taken part in. Not the war threats, not the crisis forever new which merely drugged the mind, like Grear's Thursday . . . A blatter of rain hit the window. It was a raw cold day. But he was feeling better, knew he had got the turn, knew how careful he could be when it came to looking after himself. They thought he wasn't careful; they thought he was a fellow who took risks. Nothing was farther from the truth. So careful of himself that he had let Basil off with the real business, had handed it to him on a giddy plate. Now nothing would have happened. And all because he had had a hot feeling, a touch of fever! He burned with shame and impotence. Then his expression hardened and grew quiet. He turned the bed-clothes back and without haste, carefully, got to his feet. Even his trousers had been put in the wardrobe, but patience overcomes all things. Rest if you have to, but don't give in; and if your hands shake, it's only with the cold . . . He was absolutely all right, and yet here he was unable to stand. It was humiliating. He fell back on the bed and all but wept.

A week later he was sitting before a large fire, feeling pleasantly weak and normal, dreaming of the sea, the cool sea, the blue and the green, the shining sun, the sand and the horizon. The sick stag turned to its sanctuary. Not nostalgia but atavism. He smiled. That's where he was going. And this time Ellen would be with them. He had it all made up. Indeed they had already sailed for days. To think of the universal lunacy, the murdering idiocy, which compelled one to take part in it as a duty . . . The thing did not bear thinking about. With health and the horizon in the offing, the sun breaking through, the young moon and birds piping along the shore, the passage between Eilean Beag and the skerry . . .

> *Glory to thee,*
> *Face of the God of life.*

If the gentry of the crises, the power-addicts and the geo-egoists who cracked the deathly whips, wanted big words, then all right let them have 'em; tell them we're going in search of a real civilization, one of our very own, distinguished by a way of life which had as its economic doctrine and its philosophy, its work and its religion, its duality in unity: a sure hand at the tiller and love behind the wave.

If they know of a better, let them produce it. But with hatred at the tiller and cruelty behind the wave, they'll pile the old ship on the skerry as surely as man made the garden of Gethsemane.

That Figure in the garden . . . the skipper in the sandy cemetery . . . Christina weeping against the railings . . .

But his images now had light beyond them, the light that rises beyond the gulf of darkness, and suddenly, light-heartedly, he wondered how Joe had got on with Christina.

He had not meant to phone Ellen until Grear had come and gone, but now he could no longer contain himself. He paused for a little to let the sudden flurry of the heart subside, then even as he was stretching out his hand the phone rang. He had wanted the first talk to be with Ellen, but he did not hesitate. Lifting the receiver, he made a vague sound.

"Ellen MacArthur speaking. How is Mr. Cameron to-night?"

"I'm afraid he's had a slight relapse," replied Dermot in his best imitation of his landlady's voice.

"Oh no . . ." It was despair, but the voice rose valiantly. "What does the doctor . . . it's not serious?"

"The doctor can do nothing about it."

"But surely—but surely there are specialists. What's the doctor doing?"

"It's the heart."

"But—but they can do things to the heart. Mr. Morrison is the best heart specialist in Britain. I know him. When is the doctor——"

"He can do nothing for Mr. Cameron's heart. There's only one person——" But Dermot's high mimicry had suddenly cracked.

Then her voice came low and lovely and exhausted with surprise: "Oh, Dermot, it's not you?"

"You're too much for me, Ellen. You always were."

"Oh, Dermot, you—you fraud."

He could not speak for a few seconds. Then he asked, "Who is this Mr. Morrison who knows about your heart?"

Ellen took a few seconds longer. "I'm trying to forgive you," she said uncertainly. He heard her sniff and his very flesh melted.

"Dermot."

"Yes?"

She waited. "Dermot?"

"Yes?"

"You're all right—aren't you?"

"Yes, fine."

"You—you don't——"

335

"No, I'm feeling grand." He was so shy now that he could not find more words of any kind.

She cried out sharply, but he said truthfully that he had merely yanked the telephone in sitting down. "How's Christina?"

"You haven't heard?"

"What?"

"About her and Joe."

"No! Tell me!" His voice rose in expectation.

"Listen, Dermot—you're really feeling——"

"I was just overcome for a moment, hearing your voice. Sort of weakness. It's the kind of thing you do to me. I forgive you."

"That's more like yourself. Goodness, you frightened me. If you became serious I think I would run away. Christina got an awful fright. It was the morning after the first night she was here. Joe must have been watching for her coming from the top window. He met her on the street quite out of breath. But he couldn't say anything. It was something dreadful, she felt, some sort of terrible calamity. His face was white with excitement and there were all these awful stairs, up to the top. She thought of the police. She could hardly walk into the studio. But there was no policeman. She turned and looked at Joe. And Joe couldn't speak. They stood like that. Then Joe said, 'Will you marry me?' "

But Dermot could not laugh. "What did she say?"

"She couldn't say anything. She got so weak in the legs, she said, that all she could do was hang on to him. But of course it's all right. Joe thought they should go out and get married there and then. Don't you think it's lovely?"

"It's all right. I'm very glad for both their sakes."

"Dermot!"

"Well, *he's* got it over. That's fine. Couldn't be better. Give them my congratulations."

Ellen was silent.

"Tell you what I was thinking when I had nothing better to do. Don't know how it'll appeal to you, but you said you were disappointed you weren't with us on that cruise. If you really meant it, that is?"

"Well?"

"Well, I thought it might be nice to sail them home to Cladday in a few weeks. I've seen the beginning of May wonderful sea weather. I thought if you would care to come that would be pretty good."

"Very nice of you to think of me."

"Not at all. I often do."

There was a pause.

"Dermot, what's gone wrong?"

"Wrong?"

"It's not—Christina?"

"Christina? What on earth do you mean?"

There was a knock on the door. Dermot turned his head. Grear came in, saying, "Don't let me interrupt you."

"Excuse me," Dermot said into the phone. "Someone has come in. I'll ring you later. And please think over my proposal."

"I did phone because, apart from anything else, I wanted to know how you were getting on; but your doctor was very firm. Quite right."

"You were in touch with him?"

"Oh yes." Grear smiled, and Dermot had the illusion that this interview had taken place somewhere before: the way he smoked his cigarette, as if it were an awkwardness rather than a pleasure, the shine on his face like a fine invisible varnish, the youthfulness that was without date of birth.

"I wondered what was happening."

"I suspected that, but I couldn't tell your positive doctor much. However, let me say at once that everything turned out very well. Very well indeed. You'll be thanked from on high—privately, of course."

"As long as it's privately," said Dermot, a faint colour touching his smile.

"We know your weakness." The thin laugh rippled. "We discussed it as a factor." Grear's blue eye was sly and merry. "In connection with that mechanic—as we may continue to call him. In fact, it's the only thing I want from you now: a decision. Then you needn't worry. And if you don't want to know more than you do, you needn't ask."

"Not that you would tell me if I did."

"You have no idea how much I was troubled over the amount I did tell you. But there's always a minimum amount and always a risk. In your case the dividend returned was out of all proportion."

Dermot was beginning to feel slightly uncomfortable. "This decision?"

"We had nothing against the mechanic except your story of the two attacks. In the second attack, you had your two witnesses, so he knew he was for it on that score. But the attack, as an attack, didn't interest us specially. I mean, to prove him guilty of mere violence, attempted murder, that was nothing unless we could use it for something. Our first concern with him was to get him to confess himself a member of his gang—or fifth column, as we carefully designate it. When we had finished operation Hulk, we brought evidence to bear on him—skilfully, of course—to make him feel, not only that we knew all about him and what he had done, but that by his rash enterprise on the *Fulmar* he had given away the whole show and all his friends. And *we* knew that *he* knew that was true. For such a case it's an immense help when you can work up to a major truth."

"It sure is," said Dermot. "Let's have a drink." His mouth was getting dry.

"Now," continued Grear, taking a tiny sip of his very diluted whisky, "we saw our way to make a bargain with him. For he is a very intelligent chap. But where you have intelligence you also often have vanity, much vanity. His obvious initial mistake was in disobeying orders. He should have stuck to his post, the hulk, and communicated instantly any suspicious circumstance to his higher-ups here. The technique of Intelligence is fairly constant, wherever in operation. You should know that," said Grear playfully.

"Yes."

"So we had him rather in a cleft stick. He had disobeyed orders, but with an excellent intention, as so often happens—fortunately for the other side. No doubt he had meant to take a simple passage with you to Gantry, find out what he could, report, and be patted on the back for his initiative. But it didn't work out like that, because he happened to meet more than he bargained for." Grear's glance was bright with compliment. "I think it was the Cladday chart that did it. Odd how that chart has kept turning up."

"Such an innocent spot, too."

Grear laughed. He was fond of intelligent conversation. "Probably something profoundly metaphysical here. The sight of innocence, they say, does rouse certain men to a ravishing fury. Anyway, it roused the mechanic! And as your lives didn't matter compared with his end, he logically set about you."

"Destructively, anyway."

"But destruction has its logic, surely."

"You're right again."

"So you can see it was easy for us. He had gone against orders, failed, and sold everything, including his friends. But his vanity—that made him grovel inwardly. So we approached that. We wanted certain information. I need not go into detail. We comforted him by making him feel we already possessed it and merely wanted confirmation. It's a simple technique, for we spoke of his friends and their confessions. And the old watchman in particular was easy meat. Our bargain was that we would persuade you not to proceed with the attempted murder charge and so hide from his friends and everyone else the whole story of his folly on the *Fulmar*, *if* he gave us what we wanted. We did not fail to make clear, of course, that the attack itself, if brought to court, would mean ten years at least. And we offered to accept any story about his capture by us. It took time, but his vanity turned the scales, and the other night he talked."

"That suits me."

"We thought it would. Actually it suited us very well too. So we may take it then you don't want to proceed against the mechanic?"

"You may," said Dermot smiling also but not looking at Grear.

"One of our minor reasons, by the way, for wishing not to involve you publicly, is that—well, you've got such an excellent intuition in such affairs that on some future occasion——"

"You may take it now," interrupted Dermot, "that as far as I'm concerned you've had it."

Grear laughed with unusual merriment. "That's why you're so good. So we've been thinking of sending you on a cruise—but not for a few weeks. Purely for your health this time. However, we'll come to that. Meantime, I don't think there's anything else you want to know?"

"Look here, Grear——" But Dermot stopped and swallowed his drink and what he was going to say. "How did things go at the hulk?"

"We got the watchman on Monday night, his message from his headquarters on Tuesday night, and five of them on Thursday night, including the so-called James Stenson."

"No one else I know?"

"Basil wasn't there."

Dermot's eyes at once met Grear's.

"You look surprised," said Grear. "You have perhaps a tenderness for a fellow clubman?" His irony was not unpleasant. "But you succeeded in keeping him at home."

Dermot's brows gathered. "I thought he might have spotted the Cladday chart. I was on the way to phone you—when I passed out. That worried me. But if he was suspicious, why didn't he tell the others?" Dermot was roused and direct. "I would never let anyone or anything interfere with what I thought I should do." His expression grew hard.

"Perhaps we misunderstand each other," said Grear mildly.

"I think you said I succeeded in keeping him at home?"

"I understand he called on you—and caught 'flu for his pains. His doctor assured me it was genuine 'flu."

Dermot smiled now.

"You're a genuine Highlander," said Grear. "Prepared to let me have it at a moment's notice."

Dermot merely told him of Basil's visit and the chart

on the desk. But Grear thought it too fantastic for Basil to have suspected that it was the Cladday chart, because, after all, charts *are* carried inside cardboard cylinders, and Dermot had just been on a cruise.

"Perhaps," said Dermot.

"Otherwise, he would certainly have passed on his suspicion. Surely anything else is unthinkable?"

"Right," said Dermot. "Tell me——"

"But wait; are you satisfied?"

"Whether a man passes on a *fantastic* suspicion must at certain times be a matter of touch and go; for example, he might not like to appear windy. Whether a man even contracts 'flu at certain times must be a matter of touch and go; and how far his unconscious helps even he may not know."

Grear was silent. "That penetration may be your secret," he said at last.

"Don't be absurd," said Dermot. "What are you going to do about him?"

"Nothing, for the moment. For the moment, that suits us. He may want to make one or two contacts. This kind of thing takes time to clean up."

"You got stuff on board?"

"Yes. Very interesting. And a short-wave transmitting set, too. Quite a neat little show. We are working out just how effective it might have been, given all the other bits in the wider jig-saw and assuming a lot of bomb havoc of one kind or another and smashing of transport. Very fascinating. But materially not really of such importance as you may have thought. The real importance, what we were really after, were no more than three or four men. We didn't, of course, find their names there; but—we know now where we're going, so to speak."

"You know the high-up in Mackie's department who was behind the betrayal of the D.1. plans?"

Grear smiled. "You're asking, aren't you?"

"Perhaps not," answered Dermot. "Only, these plans caused me some small inconvenience. However, I realize that you have in fact told me nothing. I would not expect you to."

"In that case, I think you're entitled to one fact. Your discovery of the plans on the hulk is our one really big thing in the way of evidence. That clinches them. They can explain away, or try to explain away, their own stuff as they like; for much of it could be made to look innocent enough. But here were official plans, of the very highest secrecy, of vital importance for our survival—*and they know it*. That's what's making them shiver in their shoes."

"Well, I'm glad I did something anyway," said Dermot.

"You did; and you certainly made them know it. That wild chase over the roof-tops and the timber-yards—after the police had bungled the raid—and rather blamed me: it was important all right. And it was vital to them, for their timing of the theft was perfect—*if* it had come to war. But it didn't. There was an anxious night, a week ago. On the surface nothing was happening beyond a certain diplomatic tension in high places. But our side had taken a stand. We were not moving back an inch. And they knew it."

"They climbed down?"

"Oh no. But they found it convenient to accept our interpretation of a clause in an international agreement which they had hitherto tended to overlook."

"As near as that?"

"My dear fellow, chance, a sudden folly, an accident, a pigheaded idiocy by a small power, can bring it even nearer; in fact, in history, has generally brought it off. You can, after all, carefully prepare for a showdown. You cannot prepare for an accident."

"And how are things now?"

343

"Tension eased; positively a friendly atmosphere; everything in the garden lifting its head up."

Dermot looked for irony and found none. "Thank God," he said. He stuck his legs out and was aware of his whole body sinking in a divine ease. For the first time his weakness ran through his flesh like a sweet elixir. He realized the smothering horror of the cloud that had been hanging over the world and over himself. "Perhaps now you won't mind my saying something?"

"Perhaps."

"I confess the carelessness in the loss of these top-secret plans—at such a moment—seemed to me criminal. I thought, after the warning I was able, by pure chance, to pass on——" He paused. "If it was a warning?"

"It was. Heavens, Cameron, that was the greatest service you are ever likely to do your country at a desperate moment. You can take it, I am sincere now."

Dermot was silent for a little. "In that case you will forgive me for wondering—as I did wonder for a time— if the plans were bogus plans which I had given you time to make up and plant on Mackie."

"You wondered for a time?"

"Yes. Only for a time because if they were bogus plans then that fact could have been communicated to the gang through the high-up traitor whom you didn't know."

Grear looked at him. "Don't you think you'll be wasting your time as a mere skipper of a small ship? I mean, when you can see a problem like that."

But Dermot did not take his eyes off him. There was silence for quite a time. Then Dermot breathed, "My God, they *were* bogus."

It was the face of the statuette and the eyes remained on him with their glassy unsearchable smile. The smile slowly spread and Grear lifted his glass. "You really have an excellent imagination. But you're looking tired. Too many questions for one in your condition. About that—and this is why I wanted to see you. Your ship is ready."

But Dermot was suddenly tired. The doctor had ordered a quiet half hour as his full limit for the first time up. "Now that tension has eased and there's to be no war, who wants a ship?"

"No war?" Grear smiled. "We merely make ready for their next move. So we're back where we began and you and I take up again the position we were discussing some little time ago, when you left my office with the Cladday chart under your arm. Notions have developed since then, and you will, as I told you at the time, discuss them technically at a higher level when I have got the matter of personnel right. I have been going on with that, though a little disturbed recently, and I'll submit to you, when you're feeling like business, certain names for a crew. This is a particular kind of job, as I don't need to tell you again, and this trip will be in the nature of a preliminary reconnaissance, during which you will check up on certain facts and possibilities, which Western Strategy will put to you, with regard to defence in that area. You'll get what technical help you require, of course. It should take two or three weeks—and, it has been suggested, might be the very kind of holiday you need, and might even like."

"Look, Mr. Grear, this is all very nice and I am properly impressed and honoured. But I am a civilian, and, frankly, short of mobilisation, which is what we had earlier talked about, I don't understand——"

"Mr. Cameron, you have special knowledge of the area. There have been consultations with——"

"I cannot help that." The bone in Dermot's face was as clearly defined as when the doctor had seen it in sleep.

345

His voice was firm and cool. "I have made arrangements for a trip on my own."

"To Cladday?"

"Yes. I am taking Joe and Christina and—perhaps—another person with me. I don't want any other kind of arrangement—short of being legally ordered."

"I understand. Thank you for being so frank." Grear's nod was like a small bow. "It was thought you might like the trip. There was no question at all of an order. Please don't think that. And as for mobilization—it does not, at the moment, arise. So that's all right."

"Thank you. I don't want to appear tough, but——" Because he now felt awkward, Dermot was annoyed, angry, and therefore looked more expressionless than ever.

"At least I might have waited until you were feeling fitter," Grear apologized. "Simply, the boat is there. As for taking Christina and—the others, I shouldn't imagine there would be any difficulty. They would no doubt want to live on Cladday. Might give the whole affair a real cruising civilian air—all to the good. Needless to say, there will be no depth charges about!" He smiled.

Dermot remained silent.

"However," said Grear, "at least it was meant well." He paused. "Let me put it like this. Think over it, when you feel like thinking over it, and then I'll take your considered answer without more ado. How's that?"

Dermot was thoughtful. "Very good," he said coolly.

Grear got up. "If that doctor of yours came in he would give me tally-ho. But I shan't apologize. You have rather been on my mind. And at least I did try to keep a certain court action out of the picture—even if it suited us!"

Dermot got up, feeling more awkward. Grear had really behaved extraordinarily well. "It's not that I want to be obstructive," he said, as Grear got into his coat. "You have regular naval men, who know the Cladday area, far more competent than I am to advise. Doesn't make sense to me. I should feel——"

"Look, Cameron, it's unlikely that you would be asked to do a job unless you were considered the best man for it. I think we can pay our bosses that compliment. If you're wanting a way out, at least don't take the line of questioning their judgment." He hesitated. "I seem to have been spilling secrets all night. In strictest confidence, I'll suggest one more, but don't let them see you know it. In the first place, there is no question of your first-hand knowledge of that area. In view of the kind of operational craft contemplated, there is therefore no better man than yourself for the job. Your record is known—including some quite recent exploits. All that's taped and settled. There is, however, another consideration; and here you stand alone." Grear paused. "It's a question of understanding the local personnel in the area, of understanding them so well that—may I say, you could hand them the sun and moon on a plate."

But the mild joke brought no smile to Dermot's face. "I know a few people in Cladday," he said.

"That's the key place—because of its westerly situation. Remember I am speaking in strictest confidence, but the question is now being discussed—*of really fortifying Cladday*."

Dermot looked at Grear almost vacantly, his lips apart, as if he had not heard properly. Then his brows gathered sharply as if stemming a physical dizziness. Grear, realizing Dermot's condition after so long a spell of fever, apologized once more and this time went.

Dermot stood with his back to the closed door, staring across the room. Fortifications, he thought; gun

emplacements; on Cladday; blow the place to bits . . .
"Christ," he muttered, "what a mockery—what a mockery
of man's simple dreams!"

51

He got into his chair and his head fell back. Hand them
the sun and moon! . . .

The mockery was so profound that it was terrible and
solemn.

Nothing could be done with the human mind when it
thought like that. Hand them the sun and moon on a
plate . . . hand them the dope on a plate . . . and you can
do what you like with them.

Hand them dynamite on a plate and take the sun and
moon from them . . . call it the new loyalty . . . and they
will go quietly. They trust you, because you understand
them.

Evacuate the sun and moon, for the island is going to
be fortified. We want no fuss and you're the man for the
job. You stand alone. We have you taped.

We will find alternative accommodation.

Clichés multiplied and went through his head like
resounding lines in a new and monstrous poetry. Devils
let loose in his mind hunted them with fabulous energy,
forking them out of the mire with a flawless skill.

It was a remarkable performance, integrated like a

work of art, coming to a conclusion like a philosphy, presenting on its plate the summed-up bonus.

Perceptive of the conflict in the august drama, perceptive of the ultimate duality in human destiny and capable of its expression in definite and ineluctable terms:

> *nationalize the means of production and all is well:*
> *nationalize the means of production and all is hell.*

Then take the large whisky you haven't got unless you know a blender in the export trade.

But Dermot knew one so he helped himself. He was exhausted and his muscles wouldn't lie quiet on the bone, but he was also feeling better.

Thunder had rolled from the landscape and the light was coming through. Grear had at last made a complete job of the business; his logic had reached its conclusion; the argument was resolved and the course set.

It cleared the decks for action. He smiled . . . for beyond Grear's argument uprose that other argument; there were plans to be hunted of a kind Grear hadn't yet taped.

Not escape to a lost pocket of earth, but adventure into the heart and thick of the world's monstrous argument to retrieve—against the odds—the lost chart.

And if in man's madness it did come to utmost violence, to lost pockets of earth with small surviving groups from world catastrophe, then more real than ever would be the need to know how to salute the face of the God of life, bow to the white moon of the seasons, and find again what was behind the wave; to keep for the human heart something at least of that serenity which the skipper felt when he stood in the dawn on the sands of Cladday.

With that as the hand on the tiller he would do a good job for them, thorough and complete. For with him he would have his second crew, the right crew for reconstructing the chart that was lost. Action ahead, and hope. It made one feel better. It cleared the air and let the sun through.

He hadn't forgotten Ellen, but now he was able to remember her. Now he was able to remember her and she came into his mind unattended by cloud, clear against the bright air, the song lying quietly in her smile, in the eyes that always looked at him, assessing his mood, as if mood were all.

He dialled her number and found her voice.

"Have I been long?" he asked.

"Not that anyone else would notice," she answered lightly.

"Ellen."

"Yes?"

"I'm no good on the telephone. Could you come round?"

There was a pause, but her voice answered lightly enough, "Do you really think I should?"

"Yes. Look, I'll tell you. I'll phone the garage and a car will fetch you. Do come, Ellen. I—I'm sick of seeing other faces."

She hesitated still, as if there was something in his voice she couldn't fathom. "All right, then, Dermot," she answered in friendly tones, "you can take it out on me."

"That's right," he said. "Put down the receiver." And she put it down.

It would be like the doctor, he thought, to come after all, though he had said he couldn't come to-night. Dermot grew very restless. The doctor had warned him to go slow for a bit and not take chances with his heart.

When at last he heard the car, he went to the window; then down the flight of stairs to the front door and opened it for Ellen. He was in his dressing-gown and said

"Hsh-sh" mysteriously, for he had to get back up the stairs without making a fool of himself.

In his chair, he relaxed completely. "You put such a strain on my heart," he explained, pale to his smiling lips.

She could not answer him for his drained face hurt her, so she smiled like a capable woman and saw the whisky which he had forgotten to finish. "Ha-ha!" she said, sniffing it. "So this explains it. I must say I thought you had more sense."

"You'll find sherry in the cupboard."

She took her time, her back to him, talked of what she saw in the cupboard, found a sherry glass and nearly filled it, settling the room about them.

"You bring me life," he said, as she sat down.

"Someone has to do something to you."

"So long as it's you. It was kind of you to come, Ellen. Take off your coat."

"No, I'm not taking off my coat and I'm going in five minutes."

"That's fine. An odd thing has happened since I phoned you." His voice was easier now. "Did you think over what I asked you?"

"About the cruise?"

"Yes. But let me tell you. It's very confidential. I'm down for command of a small ship—naval, you know. They want me to test her out, in a trial run, to, of all places, Cladday."

"Really. And are you?"

"Yes. I should like to. My first command and all that."

"How excellent! And just what you need. My congratulations."

"Thank you. So I hope to be able to take Joe and Christina to Cladday in style. Would you like to come?"

"Well—that would be very nice—if——" Ellen appeared to think. "When?"

"In a few weeks. It wouldn't be so nice without you. I mean, you could always give us a song. And Joe would go daft on light, when not on Christina. I should like you to meet old Anna. She'll tell you about the sun and moon. And she's about the last. The four of us might make a good salvage party."

"Salvage?" she repeated, not looking at him.

"I think we have things to do, Ellen, before the sun goes down on us and the moon doesn't rise."

Now she looked at him.

He looked sideways at his hand, at the moving fingers on the chair-arm. She divined that he was shy, deeply moved and shy. "There's no avoiding things. I don't want to. But—there's something we might salvage. Something, rather fine, out of our own past, and when I think of it—I think of you." He got up.

She got up also and looked at the floor as if she had dropped her wits.

"Will you come, Ellen?"

"Yes."

"And marry me?"

She went blind against him.